NO REFUGE
from the
GRAVE

NANCY HERRIMAN

No Refuge from the Grave
Nancy Herriman
Copyright © 2022 by Nancy Herriman

Beyond the Page Books
are published by
Beyond the Page Publishing
www.beyondthepagepub.com

ISBN: 978-1-954717-88-6

To Lisa M.– Thank you for your endless support

Books by Nancy Herriman

Mysteries of Old San Francisco

No Comfort for the Lost
No Pity for the Dead
No Quiet among the Shadows
No Darkness as like Death
No Refuge from the Grave

Bess Ellyott Mysteries

Searcher of the Dead
A Fall of Shadows

Stand-Alone Novels

Josiah's Treasure
The Irish Healer

☙ CHAPTER 1 ❧

November, 1867
San Francisco

"Ah, Celia, dear. I knew you'd come through for me." Patrick Davies hefted the drawstring bag, the coins within it clinking. He smiled, adding a wink for good measure. Celia had once found her husband's smiles charming; she no longer did. "Now to finally pay off that fellow who faked my death certificate for me. He's been wanting the money."

The fellow *would* be wanting the money. His work had been sufficiently realistic to have convinced numerous officials that Celia's husband had perished in Mexico. Clearly, though, Patrick Davies was very much alive—if more wiry and ragged than when he had slipped out of their rented house without a farewell three years ago. He'd been bound for a ship headed far away from San Francisco and from her. His absence, however, had only lasted until he'd discovered a reason to arise from the dead and renew their acquaintance.

"I promised I would get you the money and I have, Patrick." Celia watched as he tucked the bag beneath the bed's pulu fiber mattress, likely purchased used from a better class of hotel than the one Patrick had taken up residence in. "I trust you'll not be requiring more funds."

He rearranged the blanket to conceal the hiding place and dropped onto the bed, which sagged deeply beneath his weight, slight as it was. "Are you worried you'll not be getting rid of me?"

Yes. "I cannot afford to continually finance your debts, Patrick. I had to take money from my clinic funds to pay off what you owe that professional criminal, Mr. Griffin—"

"Ah, your blessed clinic." He pressed his palms into the mattress and leaned forward. "Keepin' you occupied while I've been away?"

Her face heated.

"'Been away'? As though you had merely partaken of a pleasant holiday. You abandoned me, Patrick." She was getting loud, her voice filling the cramped space, echoing off the cracked plaster and water-stained wallpaper. "Fled San Francisco in search of what, exactly? In search of what?"

He smirked. The expression mocked her rush of emotions, which she preferred to keep so carefully under control. "Did you miss me, after all?"

Calm down, Celia. She'd mentally rehearsed this meeting on her way to his lodgings, over and over, and her outburst had not been part of her imaginings. "I cannot cover your debts any longer, Patrick. Stop sending notes and messenger boys asking me to do so. And cease borrowing from Mr. Griffin. He's a dangerous man."

"Well, Celia, you may be a little late in offering me a warning about Caleb Griffin. But I wouldn't mind hearing how—" Patrick patted the mattress above where he'd stashed the coins. "How you managed this sum. What did you hock to find the cash?"

The anger that had warmed her skin retreated, replaced by cold mortification. She'd pawned a gold brooch set with pearls, given to her by a patient in gratitude for a successful treatment, and Celia resented that she'd had to sell any of her few, valuable possessions.

"It does not matter where I obtained the money, Patrick, and suffice it to say there shall be no more. Goodbye to you."

She marched out into the hallway, interrupting a scraggly bearded fellow in the middle of lighting up a cigar.

"Well, hullo, miss," he said, eyeing her through the tendrils of rising smoke.

Bloody . . .

She squeezed past him and hurried down the steps, tightening her gloves around her fingers, even though the knit cotton wasn't loose. *Do not look back. Do not look back.* Because she could feel Patrick's gaze on her as she fled, daring her to glance up at him where he stood on the landing. Her footfalls were a hollow echo in the uncarpeted staircase. A rapid rat-a-tat against the warped and splintered wood, the sound competing with the shouts of an argument in one of the rented rooms she passed, the bawling of a young child in another, a woman's cynical laughter from somewhere else entirely. The air around Celia smelled of mold and sewage and spilled liquor. Stank of wretchedness and misery. Patrick Davies, of the dazzling blue eyes and most winning of laughs, had ended up here. Far from Ireland. Far from the bright promise of life in America he'd once sworn he would provide for her.

"Ah, Celia," he called down, leaning, she was sure, over the balustrade in order to best catch sight of her. "You're bound, you are, to hurt yourself, rushin' like that."

She stumbled on the bottom step and thrust out a hand to catch herself. The oak banister she grabbed was tacky, causing her glove to stick to it. "Why be concerned about me now, Patrick?"

He laughed. "Thank you again."

Heart pounding, she dashed across the short entry hall, reached for the front door, and threw it open.

"You be careful out there, Cecilia," Patrick called out before she slammed shut the door. "There are more dangerous folk than Caleb Griffin in San Francisco."

• • •

The clouds were gray and heavy with rain, all the indication required that the city was going to be treated to another round of downpours. If he were back home in Ohio, thought Nick Greaves as he turned off Montgomery, he'd be able to smell the rain before the first drops arrived. In the heart of San Francisco the aroma was too faint to compete with the various stinks that floated in the air and rose from clogged sewers. Nick hadn't been in Ohio to breathe in the fragrances of rain and cut hay and corn growing in August fields, though, since he was a boy. He'd had no reason to ever return.

A damp breeze chilled his neck and he flipped up the collar of his coat. Ahead, the policeman who worked this beat had managed to cordon off the front of a building, its bricks charred black from a fire.

Wasn't every day that Nick got called to look into a possible arson, but the detective who usually handled such cases had decided to quit the force and move to Portland, Oregon. Nick wondered if the fellow would be able to smell approaching rain in that town.

Nick caught sight of his assistant, J.E. Taylor, at the scene.

"There you are, sir!" Taylor signaled to Nick, his ever-present notebook flapping in his right hand.

"Here I am, Taylor. And stop calling me—"

"Yes, sir. Mr. Greaves, I mean."

Nick pushed through the crowd that had collected to gawk. Even on a Monday afternoon, there were still folks with enough time on their hands to get in the way of police business. He'd inform them that he was a detective, but the announcement never impressed anybody enough to get them to willingly move aside.

"What have you learned so far, Taylor?"

"Looks like the fire started in the rear of the building." He examined the notes he'd made, his even features screwed up in concentration. Good old Taylor. Always reliable. Nick hoped—and not for the first time—that his assistant wouldn't ever get promoted to detective, even though he deserved the position. Nick would never find another assistant as competent. "The owner was just here saying there was work being done on the gas lines. He claims that's what caused the fire."

Nick contemplated the store's banner, blackened by smoke, that drooped over the front window. *Z.A. Everett, Bookseller & Stationer.* "If this was an accident, then what are we doing here?"

"Weren't no accident!" some fellow, eavesdropping, called out. He stuffed his thick hands into the pockets of his denim overalls and puffed out his muscular chest. "Everett done had that fire set! Right? Am I right?" he asked those gathered around him. Heads bobbed in agreement.

"Do you have proof or is this just an opinion?" Nick shouted back.

The fellow shrunk into himself, like a turtle retracting its head, his bluster deflating. "Well, heck, everybody knows it was done on purpose. That ain't news."

"If you stumble across some hard evidence, kindly let me know. That goes for the rest of you, too." Nick scanned the crowd, which quieted. A few took the opportunity to trot off. He turned back to Taylor. "So, what do you think?"

"The cop who works this beat has told me it's not the first suspicious fire in this area, Mr. Greaves," he answered, tucking his notebook beneath his arm so he could hunt around in the pockets of his gray policeman's coat for a cigar. He came up empty and sighed.

"I'll buy you some cigars on the way back to the station," said Nick. "Tell me about this fire."

"Here, sir. Let me show you what I found. There's a side hallway that leads to the rear of the building. The fire didn't spread that far, so it should be safe to take without risk of the ceiling collapsing or anything."

Taylor stepped over the rope tied between two hitching posts and entered the door he'd indicated. Nick followed, entering the dark passageway where a staircase led to upper floors. The acrid aroma of burned wood hung in the air, the smell dragging up one of those memories of the war that still haunted Nick. The Wilderness on fire, and not just trees alight.

"Sir?" Taylor always noticed when Nick had one of these moments.

"Just getting my bearings, Taylor. Seeing what there is to see." Taylor wouldn't believe his excuse but Nick wasn't trying to convince his assistant of any truth. It was a comment made in order to temporarily put the ghosts to rest. They'd return later. They always did.

A door stood open that connected the hall to the interior of Mr. Everett's stationery store. Water dripped to land in puddles, the remnants of the fire department's ambitious efforts to knock down the flames. The glass of a case that once held items for sale had been shattered by the heat. The brass arms of the overhead gasoliers had survived but the shades had not, fracturing into pieces onto the remains of a large table once used, Nick supposed, to display books and maps. Shelves lining both walls had burned and collapsed. The store's cast-iron heating stove sat alone in the corner, whatever chairs or crates had been situated nearby turned into ashy scraps of wood.

"Not much left, is there," said Nick. A fresh burst of wind blew through the broken display window, stirring up ashes.

"If this was arson, his insurance won't do him any good, will it, sir?"

"No, Taylor."

His assistant strode down the hallway and nudged open a door at the end. "The fire might've been caused by a black powder ignition."

"Interesting."

Outside, Nick had been anticipating just a sliver of space between buildings. However, the lot behind Mr. Everett's store was vacant, fresh gouges in the dirt indicating where a building had been jacked up and rolled off the lot. Nick had seen the three-story structure being towed down Sansome last week, interfering with the traffic.

"Convenient access," Nick mused. Especially if you were looking to start a fire and burn down a building without too much trouble.

"Here's why everybody's thinking the fire was suspicious." Taylor pointed out what appeared to be the residue of a black powder spill. "Some of the powder must've been damp, sir, and didn't ignite."

"Hmm." It looked to be the source of the fire, though, which had raced into the tinderbox of a store stacked with books and paper. "Any witnesses spot somebody suspicious hanging around before the fire?"

"Nobody's come forward to claim they did, Mr. Greaves. Not yet, at least."

"Why did Everett come up with some story about a gas leak causing the fire, Taylor? Looks pretty obvious what happened, and that it was likely intentionally set. Plus, I don't expect a stationer to keep a supply of black powder on hand that might've spilled outside his store."

"Maybe he hasn't been out back here yet to see the damage, sir. Mr. Greaves, sir," said Taylor. "I didn't have a chance to talk to him, because a fellow in a nice suit of black clothes showed up the moment I arrived and they went off together. His insurance agent, according to the woman who runs the bakery next door. A Mr. Pierson."

Nick leaned through the opening where a door used to access a rear storage room. The powerful ignition of the powder and the subsequent flames had done more damage to it than to the main room. "Wonder what Everett's insurance agent has to say, and if *he* thinks it was an accident."

"Mr. Everett might make a tidy sum of money if he can convince the fellow it was, sir. Mr. Greaves," he said.

Nick swept ashes off his coat where it had brushed against the wall. "Time to look for Mr. Pierson and find out just how much."

• • •

A fat cold raindrop rolled off Celia's bonnet to land at the nape of her neck, raising gooseflesh, and spatters dotted the broad plank pavement lining both sides of the road. Many of her fellow pedestrians, those who'd been more attentive to the day's worsening weather and carried umbrellas, unfurled them, circles of black to defend against the wet. When Celia had left the house, she had been so preoccupied by her planned meeting with Patrick that she'd rushed off without an umbrella or a proper cloak. As a result, she'd be soaked through by the time she reached home, her half boots and the hem of her skirt thoroughly muddied.

Blast.

"Mrs. Davies!" shouted a woman. "Mrs. Davies, here!"

A buggy wheeled over to the curb. The woman guiding the horse smiled at her from beneath its foldable leather roof. Celia struggled to recall where she knew her from.

Celia tented her face with her hand to protect it from the pelting water. "Yes?" she asked, peering out beneath her gloved fingers.

"Georgie Pierson. Remember me?" the other woman asked, her brows arching above her light eyes. The ribbons of her bonnet matched their hazel. An intentionally striking effect. "We spoke at the Alaska lecture we both attended at the Academy of Natural Sciences. You were there with your cousin, Miss Walford."

"Yes, I do remember you, Mrs. Pierson." It was curious to encounter her in this neighborhood, though. Not far from the wharves and all those who frequented such places. It could be risky for a well-dressed woman such as Georgiana Pierson to travel the streets between the Barbary and the docks. Celia herself had encountered enough rude looks and comments from men in the past few blocks to hurry her along.

Mrs. Pierson scooted over on the buggy's seat. "Would you care for a lift to wherever you are headed?"

"I would definitely appreciate a ride." Celia leaped over the rivulet of filthy water filling the gutter—best not to examine the contents floating past—and grabbed the seat handle. She hoisted her skirts and used the step to scramble up. "Thank you for the rescue."

Mrs. Pierson's smile widened, revealing the slim gap between her two front teeth that most women would be self-conscious of. "You are very welcome. Luckily for us both I happened to be traveling this way. You have a distinctive gait, Mrs. Davies, if you weren't already aware of that fact. I believe I could pick you out of a large crowd simply by the forcefulness of your stride," she said. "Are you bound for home?"

"I do not wish to inconvenience you."

"Not an inconvenience at all. You're on Vallejo and so am I, up Russian Hill."

It was interesting that Mrs. Pierson already knew where Celia lived. "I comprehend my good fortune at having you drive past and notice me, but how are *you* lucky?" she asked and settled against the padded seat.

"Ah, my small concern." Georgiana Pierson leaned out to check the road for other conveyances then snapped the reins. "I've been meaning to stop in at your clinic and speak with you about it, but I haven't so far been able to screw up the courage."

"You can trust me to be discreet in all medical matters, Mrs. Pierson."

"It's not a medical matter. The situation would be much simpler if it were," she replied, steering around a horsecar stopped in the intersection. A flock of passengers disembarked and rapidly fluttered off in all directions in search of cover from the weather.

"Then what is it you require?" Celia asked, fairly certain what the woman's response would be.

"I can tell by the displeased tone of your voice you've already guessed."

"I have guessed that you wish to make use of my supposed investigative skills, Mrs. Pierson," she said. "Despite what was written in the newspapers about my involvement in a recent murder investigation, I can assure you I am not a detective."

The articles had made Celia sound like a novelty circus act. *Come see the female detective. She walks, she talks, she solves crimes.* Those were not the precise words but they may as well have been. She wondered what Nicholas Greaves had thought about the stories, if he'd been amused or displeased. Far more likely the latter sentiment than the former. She'd never learn his opinion, however, now that they had been forced to put aside any friendship, any affection they'd had for each other. Now that Patrick Davies had returned.

"You *have* figured me out, Mrs. Davies," she said. "I hope you're not too angry."

A boy dashing across the street slowed to jump in a puddle, sending dirty water everywhere. He let out a whoop, startling the carriage horse, and rushed off. Georgiana Pierson muttered an unladylike curse under her breath and regained control of the animal.

"I am not angry, but I do not have the time to help you." Celia clutched at the rail as the buggy lurched forward again. "Between the operation of my clinic and my role as my cousin's guardian, my days are filled."

"But you *must* help me, Mrs. Davies," she pleaded. She turned the buggy up Stockton, driving alongside the horsecar rails embedded in the road. "I can't go to a professional investigator and I'm definitely not about to approach the police. My husband would find out and I don't want to distress him. He's already . . . let's just say it's better that he not learn I've been wanting to consult you about this particular issue."

Celia could feel her resolve slipping. Mrs. Pierson was persistent and her mysterious "issue" was beginning to intrigue her. It was likely meant to. "What is the difficulty you're in?"

"So you will help?"

"You need to explain what you want me to do first. Then I will decide." *What are you doing, Celia?* She'd promised Addie and Barbara that she would never get involved in such affairs again. Her housekeeper would be furious and her cousin . . . equally furious and less likely to forgive her.

Georgiana Pierson exhaled. "Thank you. I didn't dare believe you might agree, especially after Jane Hutchinson warned me that you'd turn me down."

"You're acquainted with Jane?" Celia's friend did seem to know everyone who was anyone in San Francisco, though. "You spoke with her about me?" And very recently, because otherwise Jane would have come to the house straightaway to alert Celia about the conversation and she must not have yet had the opportunity.

"I wanted her opinion before approaching you," she replied. "She offered the use of her parlor this very evening for our tête-à-tête. Her husband's away inspecting real estate, I gather, and she insisted that she would welcome the company."

Knowing her friend, Celia imagined Jane was just as intrigued by Georgiana Pierson's issue as she was. "What time are we meeting at Jane's?"

"I thought six, if that's convenient." She brought the carriage to a halt where Stockton crossed Vallejo. The incline leading to Celia's house was too steep for the horse to manage, especially with the surface slicked by rain. "My husband and I are dining very early because Edward is entertaining company tonight."

"Six this evening would be fine," said Celia.

"Good. I will collect you here at a quarter before the hour."

"You haven't explained, though, precisely what it is you require, Mrs. Pierson."

The woman rolled her lips between her teeth; Barbara had the same habit when she was uncomfortable about what she had to say. "I need you to recover, if possible, an item that was taken from me."

She'd never been asked to hunt down a stolen object before. *Admit it, Celia, you are intrigued.*

"Have you put an advertisement in the newspapers offering a reward for its return?" Celia asked despite her curiosity. "Or contacted the police? They would be better equipped to investigate and arrest a thief."

"Although the item means a great deal to me, it's too trivial a piece for the police to be interested in tracking down, Mrs. Davies. And an advertisement in the paper would be too embarrassing," she replied. "I'll explain everything this evening."

Celia gathered her skirts and climbed down from the buggy. She shivered in the wind sweeping up from the bay, cold and damp. It was too early for a fire to be lit in the parlor at home, but the kitchen would be warm. One of her neighbors passed close by, huddled beneath his hat as he hurried along Vallejo, and Celia nodded at him. Otherwise, the streets were empty aside from the grocer on the corner, bringing in the crates of unsold apples stacked outside the shop's front door.

"Here, take my umbrella, Mrs. Davies." Georgiana Pierson reached toward where she'd stashed it.

"The rain has let up. There is no need."

"Until later, then," said the other woman. "You've lifted a weight off me, Mrs. Davies. I can't thank you enough."

"I've not agreed to anything yet."

"I feel you will, though," she said, smiling. "I just know it."

A quick search through the city directory revealed that a Mr. E. Pierson was employed by the Western States Fire and Life Insurance Company. Nick instructed Taylor to gather information on other recent suspicious fires while he headed to the agency.

It was prominently located on Montgomery, a street occupied by a score of other insurance companies along with banks and the better class of stores. Its office also boasted the advantage of west-facing windows, which kept the worst of the gloomy, rainy afternoon at bay. Rent wouldn't be cheap, but if the agency Mr. Pierson worked at wanted to be taken seriously, this street was the place to be.

Nick pushed open the company's door, the bell overhead chiming pleasantly. The narrow but deep room was warmed by a stove, and a handful of well-dressed men sat at polished walnut desks, spaced apart with the sort of distance that afforded privacy to the folks discussing their insurance needs. Cut-glass gas fixtures shed a warm light over cabinets and pigeonholes brimming with papers, glinted off framed placards advertising the insurance that could be purchased for assuredly reasonable premiums. *Dividends declared Annually! No extra rates for Insuring Females!* No doubt females were delighted to learn that.

A fellow at the nearest desk looked up from his paperwork. He affixed a welcoming smile to his face at the prospect of a new client, his exuberant side whiskers shifting in tandem with the grin.

He hopped to his feet. "How might I help you, sir?"

"I'm looking for a Mr. Pierson." Nick flapped open his coat, showing the badge he kept pinned to his vest, which had the usual consequence of wiping the grin off the fellow's face. "Detective Greaves."

The agent glanced over his shoulder. Nick couldn't figure what he was looking for. Help, maybe? The other occupants of the office didn't appear interested in coming to his aid. One moved closer to the middle-aged woman he was assisting, emphasizing his unwillingness to get involved.

"Mr. Pierson?" Nick repeated. "Is he here?"

"Mr. Pierson is no longer with our establishment, Detective . . . what was your name again?"

"Greaves," said Nick. "When did Pierson leave?"

"It's been . . ." The fellow contemplated the air above Nick's head for a few moments as he thought. "It's been a few weeks now."

Far too recent for the city directory entry to have been corrected. "What was his reason for departing the agency?"

The air got another round of contemplation, longer this time. Having decided upon a response, he exhaled. "Mr. Pierson has settled on a new occupation. The insurance business was not for him."

"He visited a customer of yours this morning, I'm told," Nick said. "Strange thing to do if he's not affiliated with this agency any longer."

"I cannot explain Mr. Pierson's actions, Detective. A courtesy call on one of his former clients, I presume," he said. "Might I ask why you wish to speak with him? Is there some concern about a claim that he settled, perhaps? Although I cannot fathom why the police might be interested in the concerns usually attended to by the Board of Underwriters."

"Has the Board of Underwriters had reason to come by here and question Mr. Pierson, or any of the other agents, about suspicious insurance claims?" Suspicious claims arising from arson, for instance.

Nick had been loud enough to draw the attention of the middle-aged woman, who glanced over, a concerned frown creasing her face.

"We are a trustworthy and reputable agency, Detective Greaves." The agent had taken offense and his expression hardened. "Unlike others in San Francisco."

"Ah, of course. Then I don't have to worry about a suspicious fire at one of the buildings Mr. Pierson may have written a policy on. Don't have to wonder if the reason he was chucked out was because he'd been making money on the side when his clients cashed out their questionable claims."

"I . . . I . . ." he spluttered. "What an outrageous idea."

"I'm a detective. I often have outrageous ideas," Nick said. "Can you confirm for me that a Mr. Everett was one of Mr. Pierson's clients?"

"Mr. Aldrich might be able to help you. He heads the board that manages this agency and took over Mr. Pierson's clients upon Mr. Pierson's departure."

"And is Mr. Aldrich here someplace?" Nick scanned the other men in the room, not a one daring to look in his direction. Their paperwork had proven to be mighty interesting.

"No, he is out. At a meeting. I'm sorry."

"Any idea where this meeting is taking place? I need to speak with him, and I'd rather not wait until he finds a free block of time."

"No. He doesn't tell us where he's going. He doesn't have to."

"Of course not." Nick grabbed a blank piece of notepaper and pencil off the man's desk and scrawled his name along with Everett's. "Tell Mr. Aldrich to contact me at the main police station. Unless he'd rather that I return with somebody from the Board of Underwriters to review all your files."

The fellow blanched. "I'll tell him as soon as he returns that you need to speak with him urgently, Detective. You have my word on it."

• • •

Addie was in the parlor reading the newspaper aloud to Barbara when Celia entered the house. "'. . . and everywhere there is dirt, everywhere there are fleas, everywhere there are lean, brokenhearted dogs. Every alley is thronged with people,' is what Mr. Twain writes about Smyrna, Miss Barbara. In yesterday's paper."

"Sounds like parts of San Francisco, Addie," Celia's cousin, listlessly plunking out notes on the piano, replied. "Why go all the way to Asia Minor to see what you can see here?"

The diffuse light from the parlor window fell upon Barbara's thick dark hair, which she'd arranged into a chignon at the nape of her neck. *When had Barbara taken to wearing her hair in that fashion? The effect was* attractive and very mature, but then her cousin no longer was the young teenaged girl Celia had taken on as her ward when Uncle Walford had passed away.

"Hullo," Celia called, removing her dirty half boots.

"You've returned." Addie's perusal of the muddy hem of Celia's skirt was quick and condemnatory. "You got caught by the rain."

"Yes, I did."

Boots removed, Celia grabbed hold of the clean leather slippers stashed by the door and headed for the staircase.

Addie dropped the newspaper onto the parlor tea table and hastened after her. "Is it done then, ma'am?" she asked. "Have you given that devil his money?"

Celia swept into her upstairs bedchamber. "I did give Patrick his money."

"*Och.* You didna."

"I did."

"*Och.*"

Addie, continuing to mutter about devils and Patrick Davies, helped Celia out of her mud-splattered dress and into her plain blue gown. Leather slippers in place over her bare feet, Celia went to her dressing table. From its top drawer she removed a sandalwood box, its scent warm and sweet and spicy, that held memories in need of purging. Specifically, a ribbon-wrapped stack of letters. She could not understand why she had kept them. Had she hoped that the notes from Patrick were proof she'd not been wrong to have wed him? That they had actually loved each other at one time?

"I pawned a piece of jewelry in order to pay him, Addie."

Addie gasped. "Not your mother's pin and earrings."

"Not those." Her housekeeper referred to a pair of lovely and delicate azure enamel drop earrings and their matching pin that Celia's mother had willed to her. Celia possessed her mother's Christian name and so little else—a crimson shawl, some jewelry, a sterling silver hairbrush, the merest recollection of her voice and the smell of her jasmine perfume—that to pawn the earrings and pin would be a desperate act indeed.

"I pawned a gold filigree brooch a patient gave me," she said. "The amount I received was enough money to satisfy Patrick." Barely.

"The devil."

Was Patrick a devil? Or merely a very weak and selfish man? *You were only eighteen when you wed him, Celia, and terribly impulsive.* Young, heartbroken, and naive. Horribly naive. *Hasty marriage seldom proveth well.* She'd reread that fragment of Shakespeare in the weeks after Patrick had left San Francisco and found the truth of the words horridly bitter.

"Not only have you gone and given him money, you held on to his letters." There was no mistaking the disappointment written upon her Scottish housekeeper's face.

"Then you shall not mind burning them." Celia handed the stack of letters to her housekeeper and left her bedchamber. "I'd like dinner served at half past five, Addie. I am expected at Jane's at six."

"I didna know you planned to go to Mrs. Hutchinson's tonight."

"Neither did I until an hour ago, when the woman who gave me a lift home informed me of the gathering," said Celia. "I will explain once I myself understand."

"Aye, ma'am," Addie replied uncertainly.

Downstairs, Barbara looked up from Addie's discarded newspaper. "You should definitely read the whole report from Mr. Twain, Addie. It's rather interesting."

"Thank you, Miss Barbara. When I've the time to finish reading the story, I will." Addie, Patrick's letters held at arm's length as though the papers were toxic, strode through the parlor and into the rear of the house, bound for the Good Samaritan stove in the kitchen.

Celia found a spot on the parlor settee between the carefully arranged embroidered cushions and a pile of neglected mending.

Barbara tossed the newspaper back onto the tea table and took the chair across from Celia. "Where were you this afternoon?"

"Out." Celia did not want to discuss with her cousin where she'd been, whom she'd seen, and what she'd done. "Have you completed your assignments for the day?"

"Yes." She sighed. "I don't care for the new tutor you've hired."

"She is the best we can afford." More importantly, she was the only one of the five women Celia had interviewed for the position who'd not balked at Barbara's half-Chinese ethnicity.

"Well, she won't be as good as—"

"Yes," said Celia, interrupting Barbara's comment. They'd been forced to release the prior tutor when the young woman's connection to a murder suspect—the investigation that had resulted in Celia's name being printed in every newspaper in town—had become known. "By the way, I have told Addie to prepare dinner early. Do you remember that woman we met at the Alaska lecture? Mrs. Pierson?"

"The loud and overconfident one?" she asked. "She wore that teal gown with the scalloped black embroidery all over the skirt and sleeves that everybody kept commenting on. The dress *was* really pretty and so is she, but still, I thought it a bit much for a stuffy evening listening to a lecture about the supposed benefits of America having purchased a bunch of frozen tundra."

"She is the one I mean." Barbara was correct that Georgiana Pierson's elegant attire and bold manner had ruffled the envious women who'd also been in attendance that evening. "She has requested that I go to Jane's house with her tonight."

"Can I come?" Barbara was fond of Jane.

"Normally I would agree, Barbara, but Mrs. Pierson wants to speak with us about a private matter."

"She should come to your clinic if she has a medical problem."

"It is not her health she wishes to consult me about."

Barbara's eyes narrowed. "Oh, I see. Mrs. Pierson wants to hire you to do some investigating for her, is that it? And she wants to rope Mrs. Hutchinson into her scheme, too."

"What's this, ma'am? Investigating?" Addie had returned with the tea things in time to overhear.

"We are getting ahead of ourselves. I did not promise Mrs. Pierson that I would agree to help her in any fashion," Celia answered. "But she pleaded with me to make time this evening to discuss some small item she's lost or had stolen, so I agreed. Reluctantly, I might add."

Addie set down the tea tray. "Her request portends ill, that's all I've got to say. Coming right after that meteor shower the other night. The one written about in all the newspapers."

"Did you consult your astrologer about the meteors, Addie?" Barbara asked. "Did she predict something dreadful was soon to happen? That Cousin Celia was going to get mixed up with another dangerous investigation, maybe?"

"I've nae need for your teasing me about my astrologer, Miss Barbara. And something dreadful is always happening around here." She poured out the tea and stalked off.

Barbara reached for one of the biscuits Addie had brought in along with the tea. "Well, I hope you tell Mrs. Pierson no, Cousin."

Celia elected to not respond, sipping her tea—oolong, which Addie knew Celia favored—instead.

"What happened with Cousin Patrick?" Barbara asked and took a bite of a biscuit, catching crumbs in her palm. "That's where you were this afternoon, wasn't it? Paying him off."

So much for avoiding the topic of Patrick. "Yes, that is where I was, if you must know."

"Where did you get the money from?"

"Not from the funds your father set aside for my use, Barbara," she said, setting down her cup. "I sold a piece of jewelry."

"Hopefully not anything really nice." Barbara finished the biscuit and wiped her fingers together over the napkin in her lap. "But what will you do, Cousin, when he asks for more?"

· · ·

"Home for a late lunch, Mr. Greaves, or an early dinner?" Mrs. Jewett, his landlady, hustled into the entry hall to greet him. "I wasn't expecting you."

"I was nearby. Looking into an arson that might be associated with insurance fraud." Nick removed his hat and inspected its wide brim for ash residue.

"Insurance fraud? Whatever next?"

"Makes for a change from murder, I suppose." *Thank God.* He'd seen enough death to last him a lifetime. In his position, he wasn't going to escape seeing more, however. "I also thought I'd stop in and visit Riley. Maybe get a bite to eat before heading to the station."

"I'd be more than happy to fix you some food, Mr. Greaves."

Her smile dimpled her left cheek. Nothing she liked better than getting to spoil Nick, who lived in a suite of rooms in her house that had once been occupied by her son, lost in the war. The Jewett boy had been a handsome fellow, based on the image captured in the daguerreotype displayed on the parlor mantel, its silver frame regularly and faithfully polished and dusted. He'd had a flop of dark hair and smiling eyes, a jaunty set to his shoulders. The sort of man Nick might like to have known.

He accepted his landlady's offer of food and headed into the house's small dining room.

"Your dog's out in the rear yard, having a snuffle in the grass, Mr. Greaves," she said.

"Hope Riley isn't getting into your flower beds."

"There isn't anything blooming out there any longer, so it doesn't matter." Mrs. Jewett paused in the doorway. Her smile took on a mischievous tilt. "I should tell you that we're to have company this week."

Nick pulled out a chair at the table, scuffing the legs across the figured emerald green carpet, and sat. He reached for the morning newspaper she'd left there for him to read. "A new boarder?" He'd lived in this house ever since he'd returned from the hospital after the war and had been her only lodger in all that time.

"No. She won't be staying that long. Just a visit."

"A friend of yours?"

"My sister's oldest girl. Her name's Violet," she replied, doing all she could to sound nonchalant. Which wasn't easy for a person who'd never been particularly capable of keeping her emotions hidden. Nick liked that about his landlady; her openness and honesty. Both of which were pretty hard to come by in his profession.

"Violet."

"I call her Vi," she said. "She's always been my favorite of my nieces and nephews. A lovely young lady. And she plays the pianoforte so beautifully."

Great. "Are you matchmaking, Mrs. Jewett?" He hadn't given his landlady reason to believe he was engaged in a relationship, though. Celia Davies hadn't come by to annoy him in months. Ever since she'd learned her husband wasn't as dead as some Mexican document had claimed.

"I'm simply having my niece for a visit, Mr. Greaves."

"But is it safe for a lovely young lady to be in the same house as a single man, Mrs. Jewett? Don't want to harm Miss Violet's reputation."

Her eyes widened. "You can be sure I won't be leaving Violet alone in my house with you, Mr. Greaves. My heavens."

"I'm sure you wouldn't."

He snapped open the newspaper, laid it out atop the table, and bent over it. Didn't take long to find an article about a fire at a house near Clark's Point two days ago. As frequently as the city tocsin sounded alarms, he expected he'd locate a story. Back in August, there'd been talk that the fire that had consumed the skating palace on Long Bridge had been intentionally set. Arson was becoming epidemic in San Francisco. As bad as an outbreak of smallpox.

"Besides," his landlady continued, interrupting his thoughts, "Vi isn't counting on you being around much. She's aware of your occupation and that you're always busy with your police work."

Too busy and too uninterested in forming a romantic attachment, when the only woman he'd seriously consider settling down with had turned out to not be a widow after all. "You've been gossiping with your niece about me, Mrs. Jewett?"

"She was curious about you, that's all."

"Ah."

"A handsome man like you, Mr. Greaves." She clucked her tongue against her the roof of her mouth. "It isn't right that you're alone."

"I have you, Mrs. Jewett. I'm not alone."

She blushed; she always did when he said nice things to her. Which didn't happen often enough. "You know what I mean."

"Well, I'm confident that an accomplished young lady like Miss Violet wouldn't be interested in a crusty old policeman like me."

"You are not crusty nor old, Mr. Greaves. You're only thirty years of age!"

"Thirty-one," he corrected.

"Well, whichever it is, she's fine with that." She sucked in a breath, realizing what she'd admitted. "I mean she wouldn't mind, even if she was interested. Which she isn't."

Nick shifted in his chair to better look at her. "What exactly have you told your niece about me?"

"I think I'll be fetching you some lunch now, Mr. Greaves. I'm sure you need to return to the station and I mustn't keep you." Cheeks red, she scurried off to the kitchen.

He chuckled and resumed reading about the fire. Saturday at midnight. A house that was luckily—or intentionally?—uninhabited that night. He wondered if a specific insurance company had sold the owners their policy. There'd be only one way to find out. He was sure Taylor would do a good job of asking.

● ● ●

Owen Cassidy pushed his broom in bursts across the sidewalk in front of Roesler's Confectionery, moving the pooled rainwater around but not succeeding in getting any of the ever-present grime to budge. Why bother? The rain, if it came down near as hard as it had the other day, would do a better job scouring off the muck than he was at the moment.

Shoot, Cassidy. You gotta do this chore right.

Because it was nothing short of a miracle he still had a job at Mr. Roesler's candy store. After he'd been caught a couple of months ago snooping through Mr. Roesler's list of customers to uncover the identity of a killer, and all. Anything to help Mrs. Davies and Mr. Greaves with a case, though. Anything that might convince Mr. Greaves he'd make a perfect cop one day. Mr. Greaves did always say that being a policeman was an awful job, but it had to be better than sweeping sidewalks and trying to keep the candy display cases clean.

The rain started up again, cold as drops off a melting icicle. Not that he could recollect the feel of a melting icicle that easily. It'd been too many years since his parents had moved on from a failed farm back East and dumped him in California. They'd promised to come and fetch him when they struck it rich and could all be together again. Promised it wouldn't be long. But it *had* been long, and no amount of his searching for them had brought them back.

You're just a stinkin' grass orphan. That's what the boys he'd fallen in with used to call him when they wanted to upset him. A grass orphan. Not really without parents but near enough, given that the folks who were his ma and pa had lost interest in their only son and abandoned him.

Owen's eyes took to stinging, and he swiped at them with the back of his hand. Wasn't like getting upset about the situation would help.

The rain started falling harder, and he retreated to the cover of the store awning. The bootblack who favored the corner across the street shot a glance at the sky and folded up his box and stool. No point in waiting for men whose shoes needed shining when the weather had scattered everybody like marbles struck by the taw.

Owen was about to go inside the store when he caught sight of somebody he really didn't want to see. The fellow trotted across the road without checking the traffic, confident that a cart or wagon wouldn't dare run him over. Sure he'd always come right side up in every situation. Despite being a crook, he'd managed to escape the law all these years, so maybe he wasn't wrong to be so unbothered.

"Well, there you are, Cassidy." Caleb Griffin bared his teeth—whiter than those belonging to anybody else Owen knew, but then Caleb was awfully vain—in what passed for a grin.

"How are you doin', Caleb?"

Caleb laughed. "Associating with Mrs. Davies is giving you fine manners now, I see."

Owen jerked his head toward the shop door. "I gotta get back to work."

"Hold on there." Caleb grabbed Owen's apron, giving it a sharp tug that pulled Owen off-balance.

"Um, are you needing something, Caleb?" *Heck, Cassidy, why else would Caleb be here? To inquire after your health?*

"I want you to hold on to this for me." Caleb handed Owen a slip of paper, warm from having been clasped in one of his large, sweaty paws. One edge was ragged where the paper had been torn. There was a word written on it. *Validus.* Along with an amount of money.

Owen's eyes widened so far he felt his skin bunching up against his hairline. "Five hundred dollars?"

"Keep your voice down, Cassidy, will ya?"

Caleb glanced around, wondering who might've overheard. All Owen noticed, though, was a pair of men dashing through the rain to climb aboard a waiting produce wagon, a fellow splashing across the intersection, and a Chinese laundryman scurrying along with a bundle of dirty clothes clutched in his arms.

"Sorry, Caleb. Didn't mean to be so loud." He stuffed the piece of paper into his pants pocket. "Is there anything else you need me to do?"

Shoot, Cassidy! Why do you keep offering to help Caleb? The fellow was nothing but trouble, even if he had saved Owen's life, which was a debt he might never be able to repay.

"Just hold on to that piece of paper, you understand? Keep it as safe as possible and don't show it to anybody," he said. "There'll be five dollars in it for you if you return it when I ask for it."

"All right." Owen took to trembling. He always did right about this point in any conversation with Caleb that had gone past two or three sentences. "I can do that."

"Good," he said. "I'm going to be heading out of town for a while. Just not safe for me to be in San Francisco at the moment."

The note Owen had stuffed into his pocket started to weigh as heavy as an anvil. "But, I didn't think you were afraid of anything or anybody, Caleb."

"I know when to fish or cut bait, Cassidy, and it's high time I cut bait. Once I've collected on a few debts I'm owed, that is." He grinned. "Don't worry, though. I'll be back and pay you your five bucks."

Caleb sauntered off like he didn't mind the rain battering his shoulders or hadn't a worry in the world. Like he wasn't concerned about some mysterious scrap of paper he'd transferred to Owen's care or whatever it was making him have to flee town.

"Shoot," breathed Owen, clasping the broom handle against his chest, almost comforted by the sturdy thickness of the wood.

Shoot.

✂ CHAPTER 3 ✐

"Did Georgie tell you why she was so desperate for this meeting?" whispered Jane, handing Celia's mantle to her servant, who already held Georgiana Pierson's velvet talma wrap bundled in her arms.

Mrs. Pierson had gone ahead of them, striding through the house and into Jane's parlor as though she were a frequent guest. Which, so far as Celia was aware, she wasn't. An intriguing woman, though, comfortable and confident.

"She wants me to retrieve an item that has been taken from her," Celia replied. "But what that item is, she has yet to say."

"Georgie was equally mysterious with me." Jane instructed her housemaid to bring tea to the parlor and ushered Celia through the entry hall.

"How well do you know her?" Celia asked.

"We've been acquainted for some months through charity events we both attend," she said. "She can be very plainspoken, but I don't mind."

"We'd not be friends if you did mind someone plainspoken." *Like me.*

"True." Jane's answering smile lit her eyes. When Celia had first met her, she'd supposed that Jane was simply a genteel woman of wealth, delicate and possibly given to vapors, a description Celia's aunt back in Hertfordshire might have used. But beneath Jane Hutchinson's frilled peach gown and fine-boned frame was a spine of steel. "It has been bothering me all day why Georgie insisted on meeting at my house, though, rather than simply speaking with you at yours."

"She implied you'd made the suggestion to meet here."

"Not precisely," said Jane. "This morning, I was at breakfast with the wife of one of Frank's business associates when Georgie came marching across the hotel dining room, stopping at our table. She said it was urgent that she speak with you in private, but didn't want to alert her husband to the meeting and didn't want it to take place at your house, either. Before I knew what had happened, I'd agreed to hosting her here."

Celia slowed her steps to delay their arrival. "How is she even aware that you and I are friends?"

"Baffles me, Celia." Jane glanced toward the open parlor doors. Inside, Georgiana Pierson was humming a nameless tune. "But I am definitely intrigued."

"Shall we discover, then, what it is Mrs. Pierson wants of me?"

Jane leaned in close. "Maybe she'll offer to pay you for your help."

"Pay me? I doubt she would do that. Furthermore, what might Mr. Greaves think if I started hiring myself out for pay as an investigator?" Although, after having to pawn that brooch, a payment would come in handy.

"Would he have to know?" she asked, winking.

"You are incorrigible, Mrs. Hutchinson."

Jane laughed quietly, and they entered the parlor. Jane extended her arm to point the way. "Here we are, Celia," she said, raising her voice.

A fire crackled in the hearth, shedding warmth over the tasteful furniture—not too garish, not too overstuffed or fringed. No gilded décor, but a restrained display of porcelain statuary and Chinese urns. A fitting quantity of portraits and paintings hanging from the picture rail. Celia had always found the Hutchinsons' parlor to be a haven of tranquility, the thick Brussels carpet dampening the noise of footfalls, hushing voices. The tranquility somewhat disturbed by Mrs. Georgiana Pierson, who'd taken the most prominent spot on the sofa and wore a Cheshire cat grin.

"I've asked Hetty to bring us some tea." Jane settled onto the chair opposite her. Celia had no choice but to take the other matching armchair; Georgiana Pierson's ginger gros de Rhine silk skirts sprawled across the sofa cushions.

"Time enough for me to gather my thoughts, then." Mrs. Pierson's gaze scanned the parlor. "I must tell you, Mrs. Hutchinson, that you have the loveliest home, and an admirable setting up here so near to Clay Street Hill. I expect one day they will build houses upon its very peak, which will be the envy of the entire city."

"Not until horsecars or the like are able to ascend that incline, Mrs. Pierson," Jane said. "But thank you for the compliment."

Hetty entered with the tea and slices of cake, which she set on the marble-topped table between the sofa and the chairs. She gave Mrs. Pierson a mistrustful glance—*even Jane's servant is suspicious of the woman*—before retreating from the parlor, shutting the doors behind her.

Give her a chance, Celia. For once, do not be so hasty in forming an opinion.

Celia thanked Jane for pouring her a cup of tea and considered Georgiana Pierson. "Jane and I are both perplexed, Mrs. Pierson, why you believe I can help recover the item that you have lost."

"I've truly confounded you both, haven't I? I'm sorry to have been such a bother, and I realize I haven't expressed my deep appreciation for you taking the time to meet with me, Mrs. Davies," she said. "Nor how much I appreciate you permitting us to make use of your lovely house, Mrs. Hutchinson."

Gad, just get on with it. "Mrs. Pierson—"

"Georgie," she interrupted. "Please call me Georgie, Mrs. Davies. I insist."

Celia did not offer that the woman call her by her Christian name. "What is it that you have lost and want my help in recovering?" she asked. "And again, before you thank me for helping, I've not yet agreed."

"All right, I'll tell you." She finished the bite of cake she'd taken and set the china plate on her lap. "I would like you to locate a locket. A gold locket set with red garnets that Edward, my husband, gave me as a wedding present. It is approximately an inch high and, in addition to the garnets, its surface is engraved with a looping pattern of vines and flowers both front and back. Inside, it has an inscription. 'From E to G.' An item of significant sentimental—and monetary—value. Furthermore, if you locate the locket, I'm willing to pay you a recovery fee."

Jane hid her smile behind the brim of her teacup.

"That does not sound like a trivial item, Mrs. Pierson, as you described to me in your carriage earlier today," Celia said. "Furthermore, no matter what the newspapers report about me, I am not for hire—"

"A *sizable* fee, Mrs. Davies."

Gad.

"Have you notified the police?" Jane asked Georgiana.

"I already suggested that course of action to Mrs. Pierson, Jane," Celia said. "And she declined."

"Here's the real reason I don't want to go to the police, Mrs. Davies. Because Edward would learn that I had." She briefly pressed her lips into a thin line. "And I don't want him to know, because I believe one of his business associates is the person who's taken the locket."

"Oh, my." Jane glanced over at Celia, her eyebrows lifting subtly.

"I don't want him to know I'm asking you to search for it either, Mrs. Davies, until I'm positive which of his associates is responsible."

"You're certain you did not merely misplace this precious locket, Mrs. Pierson?" Celia asked.

Georgiana Pierson leaned forward as much as a murderously tight corset—the minuscule diameter of her waist was not remotely natural—permitted. "I am confident I didn't misplace it. I only wear the locket on my birthday and at our annual New Year's Eve party. It is secured inside our safe the rest of the year," she said. "It's my habit to have a jeweler clean it around this time of year, since my birthday is next week. But when I searched the safe, it wasn't inside. Only its empty case."

"You may have forgotten to return the piece of jewelry to its case when you removed the locket after your New Year's party," Celia proposed.

"Are you suggesting I might've been tipsy and mislaid it?" she asked. "Well, I do not drink, Mrs. Davies, so I wasn't inebriated."

"My apologies, Mrs. Pierson," she said. "How, though, might one of your husband's acquaintances have accessed the locket? If it is normally inside the safe."

"We held a party for a few select friends last month, which included his business associates," she explained. "Edward wished to speak to a few of them in private about a new undertaking he's been considering pursuing and took the men into his library, where the safe is located. He may have removed papers from the safe to show to one or all of them. It was then that the locket had to have been taken, when Edward wasn't looking."

"Could somebody else have removed the locket from the safe, though?" Jane asked.

"Only Edward and I know the combination, and the safe is completely fire- and burglarproof," Georgiana replied. "It *had* to have been taken during that party."

Celia lowered her cup of tea, which had gone cold in her hands. "And, as the jewelry case was still inside, that person did not want it to be immediately obvious that its contents were missing."

"Precisely, Mrs. Davies."

"Why might any of Edward's associates have taken a locket, though, Georgie?" Jane asked. "Surely they're not the sort of people who steal things."

Georgiana Pierson's expression turned somber. "Debts, Jane. What other reason could there be?"

Celia recalled the lovely gold brooch she'd pawned that very morning—possibly never able to retrieve it—to pay Patrick's debts. He and this unnamed associate of Edward Pierson's were hardly the only men owing money they struggled to repay; San Francisco was filled to the brim with them.

"Unless the fellow is merely vindictive," Georgiana added. "Which is also possible. Especially considering the person I most suspect."

"And who is that?" Celia asked.

"I'd rather not give his name until you've retrieved the locket and my suspicions are confirmed, Mrs. Davies." Georgiana remembered the plate on her lap and abruptly set it on the table. "So this is the problem I'm facing and the reason this situation calls for discretion. I need that locket recovered along with the name of the man who sold it. Then I can tell Edward. But I can only trust a woman with your talents to help me."

Think'st thou I am so shallow to be seduced by thy flattery? As Mr. Shakespeare might ask.

"There are dozens of pawnbrokers in this city, Mrs. Pierson, and I've no legion of assistants to help me question them all."

"I doubt that the fellow pawned it, Mrs. Davies," she replied. "I suspect he made use of—although I can't be positive, obviously—of a secondhand dealer in fine goods. There are a few that Edward himself enjoys purchasing from. I expect the thief also makes use of them." She provided the names of the purveyors.

"Your husband purchases items from a secondhand dealer?" And how could Georgiana be so certain what Edward Pierson's associate would or would not do with a stolen locket?

"Don't you visit secondhand dealers, Mrs. Davies?"

Most of the time, she hadn't the money to purchase anything except for necessities. Barbara was overdue a new dress. Addie required new shoes. "Why not inquire at these shops yourself, Mrs. Pierson?"

"That would be humiliating. Absolutely humiliating."

Celia considered the woman seated across from her. "I am sorry, but I must refuse, Mrs. Pierson. I've not the time—even should I desire—to pursue retrieving your locket. You must simply inform your husband of your suspicions and allow him to resolve the matter."

"Jane did warn me that you might not help." She looked over at Jane, whose expression was sympathetic but not excessively so, then turned back to Celia. "What am I to do, then? Edward will claim that I must be somehow responsible. He certainly won't believe that one of his friends might've taken that locket!" She flushed, her skin coloring with a wash of red.

Celia waited for the woman's composure to return before continuing. "I am going to be frank, Mrs. Pierson. I do not see what good it would do to locate the piece of jewelry, if Mr. Pierson is unwilling to believe you. Perhaps it's best to accept that the item is gone."

"But Edward needs to understand how awful some of these men, these people he calls his friends, are, Mrs. Davies." She leaned forward again. Were they seated any closer to each other, she'd likely grab Celia and shake her. "I need evidence that one of them took my locket."

"Celia, can't you think of some way to help Georgie?" Jane asked. "I'm sure you could."

She might be able to refuse Georgiana Pierson, a woman she barely knew, but she couldn't refuse Jane.

Celia exhaled. "I'll see what I can do, Mrs. Pierson, but I make no promises."

The woman smiled, revealing more than just the gap in her front teeth. "You can't know how much your assistance means to me, Mrs. Davies. You can't know at all."

• • •

"Nothing linking that Clark's Point house fire to Mr. Pierson or the insurance company he used to work for, sir. At least as far as I can tell," said Taylor, shutting the door to the detectives' office behind him.

"It was just a hunch the two fires might've been related. Obviously I was wrong." Nick stared out the office's window, the flame of the gas streetlamp distorted by the rain streaking the glass. At the curb across the way, only one hackney coach waited for a customer, the horse's head bowed, the driver huddled beneath his oilcloth coat. The weather was enforcing a quiet evening outside City Hall and the police station. Almost as quiet as it was inside the detectives' office. As was typical, Nick was the only detective making use of the room at six in the evening. Sometimes he was the only detective in the room at nine in the morning or two in the afternoon. Which suited him just fine. He preferred having the space to himself.

He closed the blinds and turned to face his assistant, who'd taken a seat on the chair against the wall. "Were you able to speak with the owner of the property?"

"Got a chance to talk with the insurance fellow—from Aetna Fire— who happened to be at the house when I got there. Not much left of the place, sir. Burned to the ground," Taylor said. "But he didn't know anything about the fire at Everett's and said he didn't know Mr. Pierson, either."

"So we can't accuse Mr. Pierson or somebody else at Aldrich's agency of being responsible for every fire in this town," said Nick. "The fire at Everett's store was intentionally set, though."

Taylor struck a match against the floorboards and lit the cigar he'd brought into the office. "Why might an arsonist be so obvious, sir? Mr. Greaves, sir?" he asked between puffs, the cigar tip flaring red with each inhalation.

"Maybe he was expecting all the powder would be consumed in the initial flare and leave no trace," Nick said. "Or he was a complete amateur."

His assistant exhaled a thin stream of smoke. "Since there wasn't anything to learn at that house fire, I decided to go back to Mr. Everett's store. He was there, moaning over the damage."

"Genuinely upset, or putting on a show for you?"

Taylor shrugged. "Hard to say. He swore, though, that he's completely innocent of having the fire set and that Mr. Pierson only came by as a friendly acquaintance to see how he was doing. He gave me a statement to that effect."

"He's not exactly going to confess to arson, Taylor," Nick said. "Did Aldrich ever come into the station today?"

"Not that I've heard, sir."

Nick couldn't blame witnesses or victims or suspects for hesitating to make an appearance at the station, but he sure would appreciate folks being a little more responsive.

"Tell Mullahey to get him in here in the morning." The police officer was particularly good at rounding up reluctant suspects and witnesses.

"Will do, sir," said Taylor. "The Aetna Fire insurance agent did make a strange comment."

"Which was?" Nick asked, grabbing his hat off his desk and putting it on, leveling the brim with a sweep of his fingers. May as well head back to Mrs. Jewett's house and get some dinner. Tonight might be the last night in the place without the accomplished Miss Violet underfoot, and he meant to enjoy the peace and quiet while it lasted.

"Well, when I first got there I asked him if he was Mr. Aldrich, and he laughed. Sort of like I'd insulted him, then he muttered something about the crooks at Western States," Taylor replied. "He then went on to say that if I was looking for Mr. Aldrich, I needed to go to the racecourse, because that's where he most likely could be found. Guess the man likes the horses."

"The agent at his office claimed Aldrich was at a meeting today, which is why he wasn't available to talk when I stopped in."

"I suppose he wasn't exactly being honest, sir."

"Seems so," said Nick. "Which means, if he's also not at his agency tomorrow morning, we know where to send Mullahey to collect the fellow."

"You know, sir, I never have found watching some horses running around a track to be all that entertaining." Taylor paused to release a stream of smoke up to the ceiling. The plaster must've been white at one time, but it was dingy now, like pretty much everything else in the basement police station. "I'd rather see a musical show at Maguire's Opera House or magicians at the Metropolitan."

Nick was about to ask which of those entertainments Addie Ferguson preferred, but he halted the question before it transferred from his brain to his tongue. Mentioning Miss Ferguson meant thinking about the woman's employer, and Nick spent enough time lost in thought over Celia Davies as it was.

"Not enjoying the races makes you a smart man, Taylor." Nick locked his desk and pocketed the key. "And I find it interesting that our Mr. Aldrich likes the horses."

"Gambling debts, maybe, sir? Is that what you're thinking?" Taylor asked. "Debts that might encourage him or his agents to profit off of an occasional arson? Take a cut of the insurance money, maybe?"

"Guess that's what we need to find out."

• • •

"I suppose, Mrs. Davies, you'll begin with the secondhand dealers located near where my husband used to be employed." Georgiana Pierson sat sideways on the seat of the hackney carriage she'd hired, her skirts crowding the padded bench, her eyes gleaming whenever they caught the light of a passing gas lamp. It was raining heavily, the drops pummeling the roof of the conveyance, making it difficult to hear what Mrs. Pierson was saying. But Celia was fairly certain she'd not misunderstood the woman.

"'Used to be employed'"? Celia asked, longing for a lap rug to chase off the cold seeping inside the carriage. The wind rattled the window glass, and there was a leak in the roof, which allowed water to drip onto the floor near Celia's feet. At least she'd brought an umbrella with her tonight so she wouldn't get drenched on the short walk up Vallejo to her house, past the point where the hackney would be able to deliver her.

"Didn't I mention that already? Anyway, Edward formerly worked at an insurance company on Montgomery." Mrs. Pierson's voice sounded strained, although the pounding rain made it hard to be certain. "But he discovered his talents are better suited elsewhere. Unfortunately, he wants to invite the person I suspect is a thief to be a partner in his endeavor."

"And what are those talents?"

Mrs. Pierson smiled, her gap a dark line between her two front teeth. "This is how you do it, don't you? Your detective work. Asking questions and probing people's backgrounds. It's quite fascinating."

"I am *not* a detective," Celia retorted. She should make a complaint to the newspapers for casting her in this unwelcome role. "I am a nurse who operates a clinic."

They turned onto Vallejo, the lights of the houses dotting the sides of Russian Hill looming ahead. The local policeman hurried past the carriage, coughing in the damp and cold, his hat drooping and his coat glistening with raindrops. He never guarded the block where Celia lived. Neither she nor any of her immediate neighbors could afford the man's protective services, reserved for those with spare money who didn't trust the city police department to be adequate to the task of keeping their property safe. In weather like this, the fellow must be questioning if the pay he received was sufficient.

"If you insist that you're not a detective, Mrs. Davies, I'll have to stop referring to you as one, I suppose." Mrs. Pierson paused to look outside. She rapped on the carriage roof, alerting the driver. "I'm up here. On the left. The tall brick home."

"Yes, ma'am," he called down.

"Here is the money for the driver, Mrs. Davies." She paid Celia the amount owed for the ride and peered out the carriage window again. "That's strange. Edward usually lights the outside lantern when I am away in the evening."

"Perhaps the wind extinguished the flame," said Celia.

"No. That's not right. It's simply not."

Georgiana Pierson had the door open before the carriage came to a stop. She tumbled out, into the rain and the wind, her talma wrap streaming around her like a banner.

"Mrs. Pierson," Celia called, sliding across the seat and exiting the carriage as well. "Wait, Mrs. Pierson."

The house, which rose above the level of the street, was dark save for the faint glow of a lamp from behind the curtained ground-floor window. It had a front yard, which was unusual for these streets, where most houses butted snug against the pavement, their staircases zigzagging up from the road to the door. The shallow yard was surrounded by a white fence planted with hedges behind it. Its gate swung in the wind, slapping against the post.

Georgiana had run up to the gate, attempting to push it fully open. But something restricted the movement.

"What in heck?" The driver's voice shook. He grabbed the lantern suspended from the side of the carriage and cast its light over the scene.

The glow reflected off the rain splattering the pavement. Off the heap lying alongside the walkway, its bulk interfering with Georgiana's attempts to open the gate. He held the lantern higher to better see Georgiana, who stood over the heap, frozen in place as if she'd been turned to stone.

For a moment, Celia thought the flash of red she saw meant the man on the ground had resumed wearing his crimson waistcoat. That thought, however, lasted only until she observed that the red did not come from the color of an article of clothing but rather the spill of blood that oozed from a spot high on his chest. A spot from which protruded the handle of the weapon used to inflict the damage.

It was then that Georgiana Pierson began to scream. Loud enough to wake the dead.

❧ CHAPTER 4 ❧

The hackney driver jammed the carriage lantern back onto its hook. "Jesus. Jesus," he muttered, over and over.

Across the road, a curtain twitched and a woman's face appeared at the window. Another neighbor came onto his front step, drawn by Georgiana Pierson's screams.

"What's going on out here?" The question was not out of the fellow's mouth a second before he scurried back into his house. He must have reconsidered the wisdom of standing outside in a pouring rain to satisfy his curiosity about some screaming woman. Nobody had answered him, anyway.

"Jesus," the driver repeated, gathering up the horse's reins.

"Where are you going?" Celia called to him, the wind hurling rain into her eyes.

He shot a glance at Mr. Griffin's dead body, the handle of some sort of tool protruding from the base of his throat. A gruesome sight. "Anyplace but here."

"Go to the police station, please," Celia shouted before he pulled away from the curb. "Tell them Detective Greaves must come at once."

"Jesus," he yelled, driving off in the general direction of City Hall.

Bloody . . . Maybe he'd notify them, maybe he'd not. She peered into the darkness of the road, gas lamps few and far between in this area, wishing she would spot the local policeman. He had been on the road not five minutes ago. Where had he gotten to? Perhaps she should head to the nearest fire department call box and pull the alarm. At least then someone official would show up.

Georgiana Pierson had stopped screaming and was now sobbing. She stumbled toward the stairs leading up to her house and collapsed on them in a pile of waterlogged skirts, her velvet wrap ruined. "Oh my God, Mrs. Davies. What are we to do?"

Celia secured the gate and crouched by Mr. Griffin's body, his legs stretched out straight, as though he'd been dragged behind the fence and its protective hedge. She felt his wrist, so very cold beneath her fingers, for a pulse. Nothing. The pool of blood beneath his body suggested he had at least one more wound on his back. Enough stab wounds to have killed a robust man like him.

Ah, Mr. Griffin, what an end for you. The grave claiming you at last.

She straightened. Perhaps the Piersons had a tarp to cover him until the police and the coroner arrived. It felt criminal to leave him alone on the sandy grass, the rain saturating his clothes and carrying away the blood to soak into the earth. She needed to attend to Georgiana Pierson first, however. Caleb Griffin was past requiring Celia's care.

"We should get you inside, Georgiana." Celia grasped the woman's elbow and helped her to her feet. She weighed more than her minuscule waist implied. "Will the door be unlocked?"

"No. I mean, yes, it should be, if Edward is home. Where is Edward? Maybe I need to find the key." She fumbled with her embroidered reticule, trying to undo the strings to pull it open. She glanced past Celia, her attention flicking over Mr. Griffin. "Why is he . . . why did . . . why is that man here? Right here? In my yard?"

"That man's name is Caleb Griffin. But as for what he is doing here and why he's been killed, well, those are questions for the police," Celia replied. "Come, please. Let's get you inside where you can dry off."

They climbed the steps. Just as they reached the top one, the door flung open and a man stood in the opening, his thick gray hair haloed by the light behind him.

"Georgiana, whatever is going on?" he said. "I was out back and heard an awful commotion."

"Edward. Edward!" His wife, her energy suddenly recovered, ran up to him and began pummeling his chest. "This is your fault! All your fault!"

• • •

"Honestly, Mr. Greaves, somebody pounding on my front door at this hour is somebody here for you." Mrs. Jewett tossed her cloth napkin onto the dining room table, pushed back her chair, and stood. "Nobody else would disturb us while we're eating our dessert. And here I was hoping for a restful Monday evening."

Nick finished chewing the piece of apple pudding he'd stuffed into his mouth. "Maybe your niece has arrived a day early."

"Violet would never be so rude as to show up a day early, Mr. Greaves."

She marched from the room to answer the pounding, which had continued while Nick had tried to hastily polish off his dessert. Mrs. Jewett was likely right; it would be somebody come for him. His break from investigating murders was probably over.

Nick was on his feet when she returned, her face twisted with a frown. "Sure enough, it's for you."

The police officer stood at the front door in his muddy thick-soled shoes, his cape dripping water. He was young, like so many of the cops were, and battling his nerves with a head-high show of bravado. "We got a message at the station for you, Detective Greaves."

Nick handed the napkin he'd inadvertently brought with him to Mrs. Jewett, who hovered nearby. "Who's dead now?"

His response momentarily caught the young cop off guard. "How'd you know?" He cleared his throat. "A dead body's been found up near Russian Hill, Detective. In the front yard of a business fellow who's got a nice house there."

Mrs. Jewett scurried off to collect Nick's overcoat.

"And I'll guess that this business fellow doesn't appreciate a corpse on his lawn," said Nick. "Isn't there another detective available who can investigate?"

"The message asked for you in particular."

Mrs. Jewett returned with the coat, and Nick shrugged it on. "Do you have a name for the unlucky business fellow?"

"A Mr. Pierson, Detective," the policeman answered. "He's got a brand-new house on Vallejo."

"Pierson." What a coincidence. Or was it? And given that the fellow lived on Vallejo, he had a pretty good idea who'd sent the request that Nick be called to investigate.

Well, Mrs. Davies, looks like we meet again.

• • •

Georgiana Pierson swooned on the large sofa in her parlor, her shoes and stockings removed, her wet clothes exchanged for a loose robe her husband had retrieved from her bedchamber. A fire burned in the hearth, warming the room but not reducing the chill penetrating Celia's skin. Did the woman believe her husband was responsible for killing Mr. Griffin? Was that what her words had meant?

Edward Pierson had gone to fetch something warm for his wife to drink. Several minutes had passed, causing Celia to wonder if the fellow had fled. But if he *had* murdered Mr. Griffin and intended to run off in guilt, he wouldn't still have been in the house when Celia and Georgiana had arrived. Would he?

Georgiana's eyes fluttered open. "Oh, Mrs. Davies, you haven't left."

She made for a striking image as she reclined against the sofa's cushions, her blue-and-red paisley silk robe coordinating with the fabric. The parlor was blue and red everywhere—the cushions, the thick Aubusson rug with an animal pattern in the middle of the room, the color of the thread embroidered upon the lace window curtains, the cloth covering the piano tucked into the corner. All very harmonious and lovely. Aside from the drying trail of Georgiana's wet feet scuffing across the wood floor, there wasn't a mark or scratch to be seen anywhere, as if the Piersons inhabited a showroom rather than a house.

"Might I fetch you something, Mrs. Pierson?" asked Celia.

"I expect Edward should return with a warm drink soon. Tea or chocolate, maybe." With a sigh, she sat upright and turned to stare into the fire. "Is that man's body gone yet?"

"The coroner has not yet arrived, so, no."

"Of course."

Celia considered Georgiana, the unlined expanse of her throat, the curl of light brown hair come loose from her coiffure. She was much younger than Edward Pierson, whose gray hair belonged to a man who looked to be at least forty, if Celia were to hazard a guess. She'd been struck by the softness of his features, which belied the thick richness of his voice. She had not known what to make of him in the moments after his wife had ceased striking him, other than to think he'd been composure itself. Perhaps he was used to his wife's attacks.

"Mrs. Pierson, why did you claim that Mr. Griffin's death was your husband's fault?" Celia asked.

She looked over her shoulder at Celia. "Oh, so you are a detective after all."

"Is that not what you wish me to be?"

"Not right now."

"It would be best, however, that you answer my question, Mrs. Pierson. Before the police ring the bell at your front door," said Celia. "For you can be certain I shall mention to them what you said."

The other woman narrowed her gaze. "Whose side are you on, Mrs. Davies?"

"I am always on the side of justice," she replied calmly, folding her hands in her lap. They were cold, and her skirt damp. She wondered if the wet fabric was ruining the silk-covered chair cushion beneath her. "So what did you mean to accuse your husband of being at fault for, if not Mr. Griffin's murder?"

Georgiana flushed; she pinked quite readily, Celia decided. "The shock of seeing all that blood momentarily unhinged me, Mrs. Davies. I spoke without thinking."

"Was Mr. Griffin one of the men invited to the party where your locket went missing?"

Her gaze flickered. A subtle movement, but enough for anyone reasonably attentive to notice. Celia had years of experience as a nurse to make her more than reasonably attentive.

"No, he is not one of Edward's business associates and was not invited to that party. He was not one of the men visiting him tonight, either," she said. "I've never heard of the fellow or seen him before. A stranger and no acquaintance of Edward's, I'm sure."

"Yet, for the briefest unhinged moment, you accused your husband of responsibility in Mr. Griffin's death. Why might you think that if you're positive Mr. Pierson could not be acquainted with him?"

The other woman's expression shifted again, as smoothly and rapidly as the color change of a chameleon, becoming sober. She had the most fluid of faces. Perhaps she'd been an actress before she had wed Mr. Edward Pierson.

"I was shocked, as any sensible person would be upon encountering a dead body in her yard, and not thinking clearly. That's all."

"Of course." *Of course.* Celia got to her feet. "Perhaps I should see where your husband has got to."

Much like in Celia's house, she could have accessed the kitchen through the dining room situated between it and the parlor. But she had no immediate interest in locating Edward Pierson and the hot drink he was preparing. She needed to examine the hall, which led to a curving staircase as well as provided a path to the downstairs rooms. It had been raining for hours. If Mr. Pierson had assaulted Mr. Griffin, the shoes he'd worn would have gotten muddy and left prints. Unless he had been extremely careful to eliminate all trace of the marks.

She moved out of Georgiana's view through the open parlor door. The gaslight from a sconce illuminated the hall. There weren't any tracks across the Brussels carpet runner, though, nor any guilty-looking men's shoes waiting by the front entrance to be cleaned. And the stair runner appeared equally unmarked by dirt. The only grime was the fresh clod of mud that had fallen from Celia's half boots onto the door rug before she'd removed them.

She crossed underneath the staircase and opened the door to a large sitting room that appeared to also function as the dining area. The space was dressed in rose-colored wallpaper and decorated with pale oak furniture, soft and delicate compared to the parlor and quite elegant in appearance. A substantial dining table occupied half of the room. The area near a bow window held a pair of comfortable armchairs arranged around a petite walnut table, a perfect spot for drinking tea and reading. No obvious shoe prints covered the figured Turkey carpet in this room, however.

"Oh, there you are." Edward Pierson strode through the doorway that linked the kitchen to the dining area, using his foot to push aside a pantry door at the rear of the room that had swung open and impeded his progress. He held a japanned tray, the flowered china pot and cups on its surface rattling slightly as he walked. "Were you looking for me?"

Celia stepped inside the room. "I was wondering if I might be able to help you with the tea."

"Luckily for us the stove was still hot from dinner and I could get some water to boil. Otherwise we'd be waiting until our maid-of-all returns tomorrow to have something warm to drink. I couldn't find the cocoa, though, so I whipped together some tea."

He continued past Celia and gestured for her to slide open the connecting doors between the dining room and parlor.

"Here we are, Georgiana," he announced.

"Thank you, Edward," his wife replied, not looking him in the face.

He set the tray on the table at Georgiana's knees. He had even features and was not unhandsome, and the dressing gown he'd tied over his shirt and trousers revealed his trim build. Perhaps Celia had been mistaken about his age. Perhaps his business endeavors had led him to turn gray rather than the passage of time. All in all, he had a pleasing appearance. An open face.

But appearances, as she'd long known, could be deceiving.

"I didn't catch your name," he said to Celia.

"I am Mrs. Cecilia Davies."

"Ah," he replied, affixing a smile on his face. "I don't believe that Georgiana has mentioned you before, but then she doesn't have to tell me the names of everyone she knows."

Aside from the unsurprising trembling of his hands, Edward

Pierson was awfully composed for having a dead man outside on his lawn. Perhaps he was in shock along with his wife, his mind turning to everyday pleasantries to paper over his distress. At the Army hospital in Philadelphia, Celia had tended to a soldier freshly delivered from the battlefield, half his left leg sawn off by a field surgeon and racked with fever. In his lucid moments, the soldier had been cheerful and calm, inquiring after the other men inside the ward, ready with a joke or a poem he had memorized. On the mornings she worked at the hospital, she looked forward to their time together. Then had come the day the cot he'd occupied was empty, an unfinished letter he'd been writing to his mother on the chair at its side, breaking Celia's heart.

"Your wife and I met at a lecture a few weeks ago, Mr. Pierson," she said. "We were at a mutual friend's this evening and shared a hackney carriage home. I happen to live not far from here. Up Vallejo on the flank of Telegraph Hill."

"Ah," he repeated and shook his head. "To come home from a pleasant evening to discover a stranger murdered in your friend's front yard. What do I pay the local for if he can't protect us from these sorts of crimes?" He looked over at Georgiana, who'd resumed staring at the fire. "It's hideous. Hideous. For her to have seen that is appalling."

"You do not know the man?" Celia asked.

"The dead fellow? Of course not," he insisted. "Oh, you're asking because of my wife's accusation. Don't worry, Mrs. Davies. Georgiana didn't mean anything by that. She gets hysterical."

Georgiana Pierson, frankly, did not appear to be the sort of woman anyone would describe as "hysterical."

"Her accusation *was* alarming, Mr. Pierson."

"Certainly it would be, but I don't know the man," he said. "He must have been attacked on the street, stumbled through the gate, and fallen in my yard. That's the only explanation that makes sense. With the rain and the wind, I didn't hear the assault, though. I was, um, outside making use of the little house."

Georgiana roused and poured out tea for Celia, realizing her husband wouldn't ever do so. "Edward means he was out in the privy, which is attached to our house by a covered passageway. He suffers from dyspepsia and happens to prefer the privy to our water closet."

"I am a nurse, Mr. Pierson, so if there is anything I can do to help—"

"No, I'm fine. I take Seidlitz powder for the condition," he replied, waving her off. "But as I was about to say, they've been blasting on the other side of Russian Hill, leveling for the planned road. There have been all types of scruffy men in the neighborhood as a result. No doubt that's who the fellow is."

"A worker at this time of night, Mr. Pierson?" Celia asked. "It has been dark outside for nearly two hours. Plus, as you've just said, it has been pouring rain much of the day. Inhospitable weather for blasting."

"He's not one of the workers, Edward. Mrs. Davies knows the fellow."

He recoiled, putting more distance between him and a woman who was acquainted with murder victims. "You could've said so immediately."

"I suppose I could have done." *But I chose not to.* "His name is Caleb Griffin. My husband is acquainted with him."

"Then maybe your husband can explain why Mr. Griffin was killed outside my house, Mrs. Davies. The police must speak with him. Whenever they show up."

The bell at the door gave an off-key jangle, as though Edward Pierson's comment had at last summoned the authorities.

Pulse lifting, Celia glanced at the mantel clock and stood. "That would be them, I imagine."

Mr. Greaves would be the one twisting the doorbell. He was not going to be pleased to see her. And she dare not examine her own feelings, dwell too long on the memories of his soft brown eyes, his warm voice, the way he'd sometimes look at her—part annoyance, part admiration, part affection. If she'd wished to forget him, though, why have him sent for?

Because she was weak and foolish when it came to Detective Nicholas Greaves.

And there was no one else she trusted half as well.

• • •

"Well, Mrs. Davies, here you are again." He scowled at her. "Might I ask how that is?"

She'd joined Nick beneath the shallow porch overhang, where they could speak more privately than in the Piersons' entry hall. She smiled in response to his scowl. "I was at a meeting with Mrs. Pierson this evening, Detective Greaves, and we shared a hired carriage home. We found the body when we arrived. It's Mr. Griffin."

The officer who'd collected Nick from Mrs. Jewett's stood guard over the dead body, even though, amazingly, nobody was squeezed up against the fence to gawp or shoving their way into the yard. Maybe folks were more polite in this neck of the woods. Or maybe the lousy weather had succeeded where police cordons never did in keeping unwanted gawkers away.

"Griffin." Nick studied the man and woman standing in the entry hall, huddled close together against the cold air coming through the open door. A glass-enclosed gas jet turned on full blast bathed them in a warm glow. Pierson had tied a dressing gown over his shirt and pants as if he'd been planning to sit by the fire and read before a dead man had turned up in his front yard. His wife, also dressed in a robe, frowned at Nick. Mr. Pierson said something to his wife and wandered off.

"What's Griffin's connection to the Piersons?" he asked.

"I was attempting to discover that before you arrived, Mr. Greaves. They both claim to have not known him."

He lowered his gaze to her face. Yep, she had her chin up. And not because he was six inches taller than her. "I'm going to have to insist that you not get involved in this case, Mrs. Davies."

"I may be able to help you with Georgiana Pierson. We must talk later."

Great. "It's stopped raining, so I'll have the officer escort you home. And before you protest, I'll have him drag you out of here if necessary."

"What? You'd not dare," she said, her British accent coming on thick. It did that when she was irritated.

"I would." Although he never had before, so she knew as well as he did that he was bluffing. "Besides, I can see that your clothes are muddy and wet. You need to get home where Miss Ferguson can take care of you. I'll come by the house after I'm finished here."

"All right, you win."

"I never, ever thought I'd hear you say that, Mrs. Davies. Getting soft?"

She smiled. He liked the way her smiles illuminated her pale eyes. "It has been a long day, and I am tired." She glanced over her shoulder at the open front door, Mrs. Pierson alone in the hallway beyond. "She accused her husband when she first saw him at the doorway. Blurted out it was his fault. However, she has blamed her outburst upon the shock of seeing Mr. Griffin's body."

Interesting. "I'll take it from here, ma'am."

"Furthermore," she continued, "he claims he was in the privy—stomach troubles—at the possible moment of the attack and heard none of it."

"Haven't heard that alibi before," he said. "Thank you, ma'am. I'll take it from here."

"Of course you will," she replied. "Oh, I should also tell you that Mr. Pierson had company this evening. Whoever they were had departed by the time Georgiana and I arrived."

"Thank you, ma'am," he repeated.

"Yes, yes, I am leaving. Come by the house, Mr. Greaves. Unless you wish me to arrive at the station tomorrow morning at first light."

"You'll likely show up then no matter what I do tonight." The easing of the rain had finally inspired a couple of the neighbors to leave their houses and gather on the sidewalk. Soon there'd be more, swarming like flies over a piece of rotting fruit. The cop had located a tarp to drape over Griffin's body and was trying to block their view of it. "Officer, once Mrs. Davies has collected her things, escort her home."

"But what about the dead fellow?"

"Here's your relief now." A man who appeared to be the local policeman trotted down the street. "You. Stand guard."

"And who are you?" he replied, pushing his way past the assembling crowd and into the yard. He shot a glance at Griffin and swore. "What happened? I just walked past an hour ago. Didn't notice anything funny going on then."

"A death happened." He'd need to collect the fellow's name and have Taylor question him. "And I'm Detective Greaves, if that information makes you more willing to cooperate."

The local paused to cough, a raspy rattle rising from his lungs. "No need to be testy, Detective. I'll stand guard. I'm paid to protect this area."

Not paid enough, apparently.

"I shall speak with you later, Mr. Greaves." Mrs. Davies gave the local a strange look Nick didn't understand. She joined the city policeman, the rabble parting then re-congregating after they'd passed.

"All of you need to keep back," Nick shouted at the crowd, which encouraged them to press forward. Sighing, he turned on his heel and reentered the Piersons' house, slamming the door behind him.

CHAPTER 5

"What do you mean your husband can't speak with me, Mrs. Pierson?" Nick asked.

The strong light from the hall's gas lamp would've been harsh on most women's faces, picking out scars and wrinkles and other marks. But not on Georgiana Pierson's. Her face was as smooth as the surface of a porcelain doll's. She wasn't as blank or lifeless as a porcelain doll, though. Maybe finding a dead body explained why she kept clenching and unclenching her fists. Or maybe it didn't.

"He has retired for the night, Detective Greaves." She noticed he'd been watching her hands and folded her arms across her wrapper, burying her fingers in the silk. "Edward took a dose of Watt's Nervous Antidote and went up to bed. Sleep helps his dyspepsia, and he was feeling very unwell. He didn't realize you'd wish to question him right away. So soon after . . ." She gazed over Nick's shoulder toward the front door. "After the shock of discovering there was a dead stranger in our front yard."

"That's usually when a detective likes to speak with witnesses, Mrs. Pierson."

"Edward isn't a witness, Detective. He didn't see or hear anything."

Out making use of the privy, supposedly. "Well, I can ask you my questions, then."

"I'm exhausted. Can't this wait until tomorrow?"

"No." Nick turned the brim of his hat through his hands and stared at her. She drew in a long breath and stared back. "Mrs. Davies explained that you and she were at a meeting tonight."

"Yes, we were."

"Where was this meeting and when?"

She appeared to be calculating the benefits of not replying. Since there wouldn't be any, she answered. "We were at Mrs. Frank Hutchinson's house. We arrived at six and departed around seven or so. Maybe a trifle earlier than that."

"Jane Hutchinson's?" Frank would be so thrilled to learn his wife had gotten mixed up in one of Celia Davies's exploits again.

"Yes."

"Feel free to elaborate, Mrs. Pierson. If you're interested in having me leave sooner than later."

"We met to discuss a situation I find myself in," she said. "I sought advice from Jane and Mrs. Davies on how to proceed. The situation has nothing to do with Mr. Griffin, Detective, so do not probe about it. It's a personal problem. That's all."

He'd have to get the details from Celia Davies. "What do you know about your husband's insurance dealings, Mrs. Pierson?"

"What has that to do with the murder of that man out there?"

"Maybe nothing," he replied. "It's my understanding he's no longer employed by the company he used to work for. Why'd he leave? Good jobs like that aren't always easy to come by."

"He wishes to pursue other opportunities," she replied stiffly.

"His departure had nothing to do with investigations into property fires that might've actually been arson, then."

She looked genuinely shocked by the comment. "Of course not. What do you mean by that?"

"Just some rumors I've heard," he replied. "Who do *you* believe killed the fellow out there, Mrs. Pierson?"

"One of the local carpenters building homes around here. Had to be one of them, waiting until after dark to strike," she replied. "A common tool was used to murder the man, wasn't it?"

"From what I could see, ma'am."

"Then, there you have it!"

Right. "Your husband had company tonight, is my understanding. What were the names of his visitors?"

"Not Mr. Griffin."

Nick exhaled. "Mrs. Pierson, we can play twenty questions or you can be up-front. Or I can take you to the station, if you'd be more comfortable there."

She stiffened. "He was visited by two associates of his. The hack came for me before they arrived, so if there were others, I wouldn't know. Mr. J. Lyman Aldrich and Mr. Matthew Hollis. They were both gone when Mrs. Davies and I returned here."

"A brief meeting."

"Apparently so."

"Aldrich is your husband's former boss at the insurance company, correct?"

"Yes," she said, the edge to her voice suggesting her opinion of the fellow. "He and Edward remain on cordial terms, for reasons I don't comprehend, but then Edward . . ."

"Yes?"

"He can be rather foolish about his friendships, Detective. That's all," she said. "Anyway, Edward wished to discuss a possible business proposition with the men. Which has nothing to do with that dead man in my yard."

"You sure about that, ma'am?"

"Absolutely positive."

· · ·

"Have you seen Caleb, Cassidy?"

Owen startled, spilling the mutton soup he'd been spooning into his mouth. *Shoot.* Lucky for him, the big greasy splash hadn't landed on the white—formerly white—napkin spread across his knees. "Don't give me a start like that, Doherty."

The fellow who'd asked the question dropped onto the rickety chair next to Owen's. Johnny Doherty was wiry and fidgety, cracking his knuckles or tapping his fingers when he was spooked. Right then, he was drumming the worn surface of the table shoved in the corner of the boardinghouse parlor with his grimy fingernails. *How'd he even get in here?* Owen's landlady usually watched the front door like a mastiff on alert. Never wanted uninvited guests helping themselves to the grub. As if somebody might wander in off the street to eat her food, which could be pretty durned awful. The meat in the soup was mostly gristle and smelled rank.

"What're you doing here?" Owen asked.

"I got my ways of getting places I want to be, Cassidy." Doherty slunk lower in the chair, which didn't do much to make him less visible. Being so tall and everything. "So, about Caleb. You seen him lately?"

"Umm . . . no." Owen rubbed a hand over his pants pocket, the scrap of paper Caleb Griffin had entrusted to his care bulging the fabric. Maybe it would've been safer tucked inside his shoe. "I ain't . . . I haven't seen him lately. Why?"

Doherty's eyes darted around, surveying the contents of the dining room. Most of the other boarders had eaten a while ago, so it was only him and Owen, the domestic clearing away dirty dishes, and a fellow who'd been deafened by cannon fire during the war. "Caleb's got something a friend of mine wants, and he wants it back now."

Owen's mouth went dry. "Must be something valuable."

Doherty's eyes homed in on Owen's face with a singular purpose. Sort of like a carrier pigeon returning to its roost. "What do you know about it?"

"Just guessing it's valuable, if this friend of yours is so desperate to get it back, that's all." *Why am I always getting myself into these messes? Why can't a fellow just eat dinner, do some reading in his room after, then go to sleep?*

"It's only valuable to my friend," said Doherty. "You sure you haven't seen Caleb lately? He's partial to you. Everybody knows that."

They did? That was not good.

"The last time I saw Caleb he said he was heading outta town. That's all I know." Maybe if Owen provided a crumb of truth, Doherty would leave him alone.

Doherty cursed and stood, knocking the chair backward with his calves. The domestic looked over, her sharp features getting even sharper. "If Caleb contacts you, Cassidy, tell him I want to talk to him about my friend's item. He'll know what I mean."

"I will, Doherty. The second I hear from him—if I ever do again, that is—I'll tell him you're looking for him. You got my promise."

"Hope your promises are worth something. And don't tell a soul about this here conversation, if you know what's good for you. You got that, Cassidy?"

Owen swallowed. "Yep, Doherty. I got that."

• • •

"An interesting choice of weapon, Greaves." The coroner squatted next to Griffin's body. Mrs. Pierson had lent Nick two of her lanterns so there was decent light to see by. "A gimlet. Very effective, though."

Dr. Harris held the T-shaped tool aloft, the long shaft of the screw tip coated with gore. Gimlets were used to bore holes in wood during construction. This particular one had bored a very different sort of hole.

"Lots of houses going up around here, Harris," said Nick. "Maybe a carpenter left the gimlet out where the killer was able to easily pick it up."

"Could be the case." Harris stood. From inside a pocket, he retrieved a handkerchief and carefully wrapped it around the gimlet. "Although any workman I've met is usually protective of his tools."

"Good point," Nick said. "Given that the gimlet was jabbed into the upper part of Griffin's chest, I don't get why he didn't manage to fight off his attacker, though."

"He was stabbed twice in the front but there's another, more significant, wound in his back." Harris pointed to a spot between his own shoulder blades. "The combination appears to have done the trick."

"Meaning, with the rain and wind, he didn't hear the person sneaking up behind him until it was too late." That scenario might make sense. "There are some drag marks in the dirt near the gate. He might've been pulled to this spot."

"Also indicated by the position of his legs, straight out. Not how a person normally falls." Harris tucked the wrapped gimlet into the outside pocket of his coat. "The killer must've sought to hide the body behind the hedges."

"But why right here, in the Piersons' yard?" Had Griffin been walking up Vallejo or coming out of the house, despite the Piersons' claims they'd never met Caleb Griffin? "And what was he even doing around here? This wasn't Griffin's usual stomping grounds."

"Wish I had answers to those questions, Greaves."

"Wasn't expecting you to, Coroner."

"I'll look for any evidence of defensive marks when I get the body back to the morgue." Harris meant the basement space he now used at Massey and Yung's Coffin Warerooms. The city hadn't scraped together the money to provide him with a real morgue. "Along with any other wounds or damage in addition to the obvious."

"Any thoughts about Griffin's attacker? Height, for instance?"

"The angle of the thrusts might tell us if the attacker was taller or shorter than him, but I can't promise an answer to your question."

The police officer had returned from escorting Celia Davies home and was searching the yard and sidewalk for any evidence, a lantern swinging in his hand.

"Find anything yet, Officer?" Nick called out to him.

"Just this, Detective." He trotted over and dropped a wrapped peppermint lozenge in Nick's hand. "Was next to the walk path near the gate. Maybe the rain washed everything else away."

"Mr. Griffin's pockets were turned inside out, Greaves." Harris got to his feet. "There's nothing in them. The killer must have taken his coin purse or money clip."

"And not wanted a peppermint lozenge." Nick thanked the officer, who resumed searching. "They probably took any weapon he had on him, too."

"Oddly enough, they didn't." Harris retrieved a Sharps pepperbox from his inside coat pocket. "Small but effective. It was still tucked into Mr. Griffin's waistband. He never had the chance to use it." He put the four-barrel pistol away. "What do the owners of this house have to say?"

"Not much aside from denying they knew Griffin," he said. "The husband was using the privy out back due to a sensitive stomach. And the wife was with Celia Davies at the time of the murder. Found the body when they returned."

Harris's mouth twitched with a grin. "Ah, Mrs. Davies. Finding herself involved in one of your cases again, Greaves?"

"She's got quite a talent for getting in my way."

A wagon had managed to climb the slippery road, and the signs on its sides proclaimed it was from *Massey & Yung, Undertakers*. The driver had come to collect Griffin's body and haul it away.

"I'll let you know what I find after I've completed my autopsy, Greaves." Harris signaled the driver. The crowd pressing against the fence murmured as the wagon came to a stop. "I'll expect you at the inquest. Along with the Piersons."

"And the visitors Mr. Pierson had tonight." Nick gave Harris their names.

"Perhaps one of them can produce the name of a possible suspect."

"Or maybe one of them *is* the suspect," Nick said. "I'll leave you to your job, Harris."

"Good luck with Mrs. Davies, Greaves."

"I'm afraid I'll need it."

• • •

"You did not come by the house last evening, Mr. Greaves."

Celia Davies strode through the open door of the detectives' office and took the chair set in front of Nick's desk. Beneath her blue mantle, she wore her red flannel Garibaldi blouse and brown skirt. Her working clothes, as he'd come to think of the outfit.

"Good morning, Mrs. Davies. Would you care for some coffee?" He waved a hand in the general direction of the main station office, where a pot of coffee was busy burning down to sludge on the heating stove. One of the cops strolling through the room slowed to stare at her. Frowning, Nick jumped up and slammed shut the door.

"I have already had breakfast, Mr. Greaves," she said, offering a hasty smile.

Her gaze tracked his movements through the room. She smelled fresh with the scent of strong soap and lavender—she always smelled of strong soap and lavender—and he inhaled the aroma because he wanted to. Because it was all of her he'd ever possess.

"I would like to know why you did not come by the house last evening, Detective."

Because I wasn't ready to spend more time with you? He chose a different answer. "It was getting late and I didn't want to disturb you."

"Late? If you were at the Piersons' for an additional hour after the policeman escorted me home, I would be amazed."

"I'd had a long day." He retook his chair. "And like I said last night, I expected that you would turn up this morning to quiz me if I didn't go to your house."

"Addie anticipated that you'd not bother to come by last evening."

"Your housekeeper is a smart woman."

"As I am well aware," she replied. "Did the Piersons tell you anything more than they told me?"

"I only talked to Georgiana Pierson. While I was outside speaking with you, Mr. Pierson dosed himself with Watt's Nervous Antidote and rushed off to bed."

"A convenient way to escape your questions," she said. "What did Georgiana have to say?"

He perched his elbows on the arms of his chair and tented his fingers, looking at her over their tips. "That you'd been at Mrs. Hutchinson's last night. Some private situation? And by the way, Frank's not going to be happy that Jane's mixed up in this."

"I cannot help Jane's involvement, which is limited, so far. It was Georgiana's doing, and we met there to discuss the loss of a gold locket she wishes me to recover."

"That's it? A lost locket?"

"I cannot explain Georgiana's reluctance to tell you the details, Mr. Greaves," she answered. "Although she made it clear she didn't want her husband to learn the purpose of our meeting last night. Intriguing, don't you agree?"

"Or suspicious," he said. "Hopefully I'll learn something useful from her husband. I need to also talk to him about an arson at a building his former agency insured. A clearly intentional fire, based on the spill of black powder we found at the scene."

"An arson?"

"I'm not going to share the details on this case, Mrs. Davies." Even though he had shared details in the past. And probably would in this case, once she wore him down.

She smiled at his stubbornness. "What was the weapon plunged into the base of Mr. Griffin's neck? It was too dark for me to see it clearly."

"A common carpenter's gimlet," he said. "The killer had emptied Mr. Griffin's pockets and stolen his money clip. Harris thinks the person took him by surprise. They left his pistol behind, though."

"Perhaps, then, Mr. Griffin was randomly robbed and murdered, Mr. Greaves," she said. "Besides, a carpenter's tool does not seem the weapon of choice for a man like Mr. Pierson. The interior of his house is spotless and very tidy. A gimlet is messy. Spontaneous."

"Maybe Pierson simply didn't want to dirty a kitchen knife."

She didn't balk at his bluntness; he liked that about her. That she wasn't easily upset or nauseated.

"Furthermore, there were no dirty footprints in the entry hall or up the stairs," she said. "I would expect some trail of mud if Mr. Pierson had been outside, stabbing Mr. Griffin to death—and emptying his pockets—in the brief interval between the visit of his acquaintances and my arrival with Georgiana. Surely he'd not had the time to scrub the floors."

"Maybe he's very quick with tidying up."

"He was barely capable of producing a cup of hot tea last night," she said. "Could you explain why you intend to ask Mr. Pierson about an arson, Mr. Greaves? You know I shall persist in my questions until you tell me. Or I could speak with Mr. Taylor, if you'd prefer."

Nick sighed; she'd worn him down faster than he'd anticipated. "He was seen with the store owner yesterday, even though he no longer works for the agency insuring the business. Left under a cloud, apparently."

"Mrs. Pierson mentioned that her husband was pursuing a new undertaking," she said. "What was the shop that burned down?"

"A stationery and book store on Clay."

"Everett's, by any chance?" she asked.

"You're going to tell me that you're a customer of his."

"I am, in fact."

Great. "As often as you know suspects or victims, ma'am, I ought to be questioning *you* every time there's a crime in this city."

She gave another smile. "As of late you have done, Mr. Greaves."

"It's downright uncanny."

The smile became a laugh. He liked her laughter, too. Almost as much as her smiles. Or the pale clearness of her eyes. Or the smell of her hair. The sooner he learned to unlike all those characteristics, the better. Maybe Miss Violet would help him forget; no doubt that was what Mrs. Jewett was hoping.

"So this is where we are at present, if I may summarize, Mr. Greaves," she said, oblivious to his thoughts. Or, knowing her, perfectly aware and wise enough to overlook them. "Mr. Pierson is possibly connected to an arson which has burned down a stationer's late Sunday or early yesterday morning. Insurance fraud, perhaps? Last night, a known criminal is found stabbed to death in Mr. Pierson's front yard. Also yesterday, his wife seeks to hire me to locate a valuable piece of jewelry which has been recently misplaced or stolen from her, and sets up a meeting that curiously takes place around the same hour as a murder."

"Yesterday was a particularly bad day for the Piersons, wasn't it?"

Nick leaned back in his chair. It didn't creak, like usual. Maybe Taylor had gotten tired of the noise and tightened the joints. "All those events happening in the same twenty-four-hour period is far too coincidental for my taste."

"Mine also, Mr. Greaves," she replied. "Although you are fully aware of the sort of man Caleb Griffin was. Any number of people could have wished to kill him. Even my . . ."

"Even your who, Mrs. Davies?"

"Even my husband," she stated, her expression gone flat and guarded. "Although Patrick no longer has a reason to want Mr. Griffin dead, since I've paid off all the debts he owed the man."

Nick curled his fingers into a fist. How had a good woman like her ended up with a worthless scum like Patrick Davies? "Sorry you had to do that, ma'am."

"Not as sorry as I am." The words hung in the air, their meaning deeper than an expression of regret over a husband's serious shortcomings. She resumed discussing the case. "Georgiana mentioned that her husband had visitors last evening. She never explained who they were, though."

"She told me their names. Mr. J. Lyman Aldrich—the man who happens to run the insurance agency that used to employ Pierson—and a Mr. Matthew Hollis."

"How intriguing to have included Mr. Aldrich."

"A former boss wouldn't be my first choice of business partner, which is why the two men were there." Nick rubbed the old wound on his arm. The one that always took to aching in the middle of a murder investigation. "Wish the local who polices the Piersons' neighborhood had noticed anything or anybody strange around."

"That does surprise me, since I saw him only a few minutes prior to the hackney arriving at the Piersons' house."

Nick sat up. "Where?"

"At the corner before we turned onto Vallejo." She peered at him. "Why, Mr. Greaves?"

"Do you remember the local saying he'd gone past the Piersons' house about an hour before I arrived last night?"

"Ah. Indeed, I do. Which would have been around six forty, based on when you rang the Piersons' bell at about seven forty, according to their mantel clock. However, I noticed the policeman around seven." She perked her brows. "A clue, Mr. Greaves?"

"Could be, Mrs. Davies."

• • •

Mr. Everett was a solitary figure, staring at the remains of his shop while pedestrians made a wide berth of both him and the broken glass littering the pavement. The tang of burned wood drifted onto the road. After departing the police station, Celia had rushed over to his stationery shop, wanting to see the damage herself. She'd not expected he might be there as well.

"Mr. Everett, this is so very dreadful. What happened?"

"Mrs. Davies, it's terrible, isn't it?" He peered at her through his wire-rimmed spectacles, his eyes appearing larger than they actually were.

"Indeed so."

She had no need to feign her shock. The shop had been quite thoroughly damaged, the broken windows providing an unhindered view of the blackened interior. The stereopticon he'd recently purchased—*not my usual item to sell but so popular now*, he'd declared when she had remarked on it, eager to show her both it and the photographs of California scenery he'd also procured—scorched by the flames. The maps she had loved to peruse, gone. The beautiful linen stationery which could be embossed with the buyer's initial, piles of ashes mingling with the charred remains of display cases. The napa-leather-bound blank books, which she had acquired with alarming frequency as her patient lists had grown longer, charred as well. How the very smell of the shop had calmed her whenever she stepped inside, waves of nostalgia sweeping over her as she recalled the stationer's in England her aunt used to frequent, taking Celia along because she begged her to. That pleasing aroma replaced by the stink of wet cinders.

"Absolutely terrible," he added.

"However did this happen, Mr. Everett? I was here only the other day."

Not that being inside the store would have provided a hint that a fire was soon to start. An arson, to be precise, if Mr. Greaves was correct. She had no reason to suspect that Mr. Greaves was *not* correct, but she had known Mr. Everett for as long as she'd lived in San Francisco and had always found him a courteous and good-spirited man. Not the sort of fellow to incur animosity and become the victim of arson. Even more unlikely, in her opinion, to have paid someone to commit the arson for personal gain. Unless his business had been struggling and she was merely unaware; not everyone found prosperity in San Francisco in equal measures. Too many only found ruin and poverty.

"I wish I could say how this fire happened, Mrs. Davies."

He gave her a mournful look. He'd once told her it had been his life's dream to own a shop that sold maps, for he had loved them since his youth. Dreaming of faraway places he would love to visit and possibly never would. She'd replied that certainly he could visit those faraway places, if he put his mind to it; she had come from England, had she not? As if her journey to America had been a holiday and not the result of the restless wandering of a husband who never meant to settle.

"I believe a gas jet failed and somehow triggered a fire, Mrs. Davies," he said. "I'd hired workmen to repair one of the jets a few days ago. They must have done a very poor job."

Not a spill of black powder? "What does your insurance man have to say?"

Celia slid him a sideways look to gauge his reaction, hoping he did not notice her keen interest in his response.

His forehead puckered and he used one finger to straighten the spectacles perched on the bridge of his long, thin nose. "My insurance man?"

"He intends to pay the claim, does he not?" she asked. "I am worried for you, Mr. Everett. I know how much you loved this shop, and you know how much I adored it, as well."

"Oh, yes. Certainly. I'll get my money. Thankfully," he stated, bobbing his head. "Very prompt, he is. Very prompt."

Unless, thought Celia, the damage was proven to be arson. "What do you mean to do now, Mr. Everett?"

"My brother wants me to become a partner in his printing business in Sacramento," he said, eyeing a pair of boys who slowed to goggle at the shop. He shook a fist at them and they trotted off, their laughter echoing. "I had been making plans to join him. Sell this store and go there once I had a buyer. I suppose I can leave immediately, since I don't have any reason to stay."

He had lost his young wife to typhoid last year and would likely now have sufficient funds to make a change viable. Rather convenient, if she wanted to be cynical about the situation.

"I wish you the best of luck, Mr. Everett. I am glad to hear that the insurance company has satisfied your claim," she said. "These things can be so tricky, what with there being so many fires in this town and the police frequently suspecting them of being arson."

"The police did come here." He snatched his spectacles off his nose and took to wiping the lenses with a handkerchief. "Yesterday afternoon. I don't know what they were expecting to find."

"They did not explain to you?"

"I didn't speak with the police. Well, not the detective who showed up. I did speak with the policeman who patrols this area and discovered the fire." He replaced his spectacles and sighed over the condition of his shop. "After it was too late for the firemen to save my store."

"I wonder if the police suspect that someone set the fire intentionally," she said. "Not you, of course. And I cannot fathom you having any enemies who'd seek to harm you in this fashion."

His face, as long and thin as his nose, lapsed into a frown. "There are men, Mrs. Davies. Loathsome, evil men." He shook himself free of his thoughts. *Blast, and here I thought he was about to admit an important detail.* "Don't you worry, ma'am. I'll be fine. Perfectly fine."

Chapter 6

Addie met Celia at the door. "What did Mr. Greaves and Mr. Taylor have to say, ma'am?"

"I only spoke with Mr. Greaves." Celia untied her bonnet, patting her hair to search for loose strands to pin back in place. "The coroner believes Mr. Griffin's attacker took him by surprise, perhaps to rob him." But left Mr. Griffin's valuable gun behind?

"It's the sort of end a fellow like Mr. Griffin could have expected." Addie took Celia's bonnet and mantle from her. "A brutal one. God rest him."

God rest him. "I stopped at Patrick's lodgings again this morning, Addie. After leaving Mr. Everett's shop."

"You didna tell me you meant to go there. Either of those places."

"I had to ask Patrick if he knew anything about Mr. Griffin's death. And do not glower so, Addie." She *did* have the most terrible scowl on her face right then. "I had to go. But he wasn't at his lodgings. The fellow who runs the men's hotel told me Patrick left the city yesterday but meant to be back soon."

Yesterday, Patrick had called out a warning to her. *There are more dangerous folk than Caleb Griffin in San Francisco.* Had his comment been tied to the gruesome murder of the fellow not ten hours later? Or was she reading more into it than was warranted, as the statement was simply the truth.

"So the devil might *not* have killed Mr. Griffin." Addie, tutting, hung the bonnet on the hook by the door. "But why did you go to Mr. Everett's? To see the damage to his shop? I saw the story in the newspaper about the fire."

"Mr. Greaves believes it was arson," Celia explained.

"Not Mr. Everett. He'd nae pay someone to burn down his shop to collect insurance money," Addie insisted. "You've done business with him for ages and all. He'd nae do that."

"I tend to agree, but Mr. Greaves has no doubt that the fire was intentionally set," she said. "There is an intriguing connection between Mr. Everett and Mr. Pierson, Addie. Mr. Pierson used to be employed by the agency that insured the stationery store, and he visited Mr. Everett there yesterday."

Addie exhaled a burst of air, the sound of disapproval. "I knew I had no liking for the Piersons."

"You've not met either of them."

"A sudden, strange request from Mrs. Pierson to have you locate that stolen locket, then Mr. Griffin in their yard plus this arson affair? Doesna sound at all like the sort of folk I'd care for." Addie crisply folded Celia's mantle over her arm and patted it, emphasizing the firmness of her opinion with the motion.

"They are either dangerous criminals or terribly unlucky individuals."

"You might guess my opinion, ma'am, on which it is."

"No need for me to guess." Celia strode into the parlor, searching for Barbara and her tutor. The room was empty. "Where is Barbara? Did her tutor not come this morning?"

"Miss Barbara is out in the yard with the woman, even though it's a wee bit cold." Her housekeeper paused in the parlor to brush specks of dust from the back of a chair. "Her tutor believes, as my mother did, that fresh air sets all to rights."

"The air in San Francisco is not likely to be anywhere near as fresh as the country air in Scotland, Addie." Addie had not been from Auld Reekie but from a small village along the border.

"Miss Barbara did protest mightily. She's out there wrapped in lap rugs from chin to toe. Wouldna want her to catch cold."

Celia's cousin would no doubt make them all pay for her misery. "Make sure to prepare some hot tea for her when her lessons are over."

"Aye, ma'am."

"How is my calendar the rest of the day?"

"You've a patient scheduled in . . ." She glanced at the small clock sitting on the mantel. "In about a half hour, ma'am. No more until this afternoon, though. A quiet Tuesday."

"Good. After I finish with my morning patient, I shall have time to visit Jane." Perhaps she would be able to learn more about Mr. Pierson's insurance dealings. Learn more about the two men invited to his house last evening, as well. Jane was acquainted with so many people.

"So, it's as I feared. You mean to poke around about Mr. Griffin's death. And involve Mrs. Hutchinson again."

"Admit it, Addie. You are just as curious as I am how the many events of the past day are bound together," said Celia. "Furthermore, should I not help Georgiana Pierson? Who has become implicated, along with her husband, in the murder of a common criminal."

Addie, Celia's mantle still draped over her arm, fisted her hips. "I am *not* curious. Not if solving this riddle endangers you."

"Do not tell Barbara."

"*Och*, I see you mean to do whatever you want. Well, you'll nae be able to hide your actions from Miss Barbara. You never have done." She shook her head. "My astrologer was right, ma'am, to warn about that meteor. It did bode ill."

• • •

Griffin's lodging house was up in the North Beach area, tucked among a row of recently constructed homes with a halfway decent view of the Golden Gate. Yesterday's clouds had lifted and morning sunlight sparkled off the water like a shimmering of glass chips, or diamonds, on an undulating bed of gray. *Wish I had a place in a spot as nice as this.*

Maybe crime did pay.

The front door hung ajar and Nick went inside. The ground-floor rooms were empty—nicely furnished and flooded with light, brocade curtains at the windows, embroidered cushions on the chairs—but the sound of voices from upstairs gave him an idea of where he'd find Taylor, along with the other residents getting honored by a visit from the police.

Nick climbed to the second floor and showed his badge to the policeman guarding the door at the end of the hallway. He didn't recognize the man; he must be one of the cops who patrolled Griffin's neighborhood.

Taylor was on his hands and knees, rooting around beneath the bed. The empty drawers of a dresser sat atop it along with a large leather valise, which Griffin had left behind. If he'd had plans to leave town, they'd been thwarted by a gimlet.

"Anything, Taylor?" he asked.

His assistant poked his head out from underneath the bed. "Nothing yet, sir. Haven't had a chance to pick the lock on that case, though." Taylor clambered to his feet and bent down to brush dust off his pants. "Mr. Griffin had to have been meaning to leave town, don't you think, sir?"

Nick scanned the room. Sparsely decorated, just a couple of cane-seat chairs, the bed, the oak dresser, a rag rug on the floor. A washstand, missing any personal items, and some hooks on the wall. A faded picture hanging from the gas jet. "Yes, Taylor. I agree."

"So he knew he was in danger." Taylor found his picklocks and got to work on the valise, his forehead scrunching in concentration. "His fellow lodgers haven't been any help, though. Mr. Griffin kept to himself, I gather."

"He mustn't have been too concerned about the danger, Taylor, because he hadn't drawn his Sharps pistol. Harris found it on him last night."

"Hmm." The latch sprang open and Taylor straightened. "That was easy. Mostly clothes, sir. Mr. Greaves."

"I'm not really expecting Griffin to have left us a message explaining what he was up to." Nick joined him. "Is there a money clip or coin purse?"

Taylor rifled around, removing undershirts and socks, a pair of carefully folded black pants. A tan vest. "A roll of dollar bills. No clip, though. And Sozodont?" He held up the bottle of tooth cleaner and breath purifier.

"Griffin was a bit of a dandy, Taylor."

"He liked his cologne, too." He set that bottle aside as well, along with combs and a hairbrush, a couple of spoons and an ebony-handled folding knife. He then ran his hands over the paisley material lining the case. "Wait, there's something here, sir. A hidden pocket with a book or something in it."

Nick used Griffin's knife to slit the case lining and pulled out a slim notebook. He flipped through the pages. "Columns of numbers with initials next to a few of the rows. Some are scratched out. The debts folks owed him, I'd wager."

"Is Mr. Pierson's name in there, sir?"

"Not that I can see right off." Nick handed the book over to his assistant. "But wouldn't that be interesting to find, Taylor?"

• • •

"How are you doing?" Celia, returning from the garden, where she'd gone to check on Barbara's progress with her tutor, smiled at the woman inside her examination room. She did not need to ask why the woman was at her clinic; the filthy bandage secured around her head spoke volumes.

"Not too well, ma'am. And I am sorry to be disturbing you."

"You are not disturbing me in the least," Celia said. "You're Essie Duncan, if my memory serves."

Her daughter had been one of Celia's first patients. She'd been called from supper to tend to the girl, who was suffering from scarlatina, her body covered in a bright red rash and delirious with fever. By the time Celia had examined the girl, she was past saving. She'd been so young. Her story, though, was the story experienced by so many families, their children's lives cut short by disease.

"You remember, Mrs. Davies."

"Most certainly I do." Celia crossed to where the woman sat in front of the lace-curtained window. She carefully unwrapped the dressing, the linen sticking to the wound, and tilted her patient's head. Blood stained the floral-patterned headscarf tied around her hair. Strands had adhered themselves to the cerate, compounded of wax and oil, that she'd used beneath the hastily tied rectangle of linen.

"That is quite an injury, Mrs. Duncan." What she could see of the cut on the woman's forehead was swelling with the first signs of suppuration.

"I thought it'd stop bleeding, and I didn't want to leave my babe alone to have it seen to when it happened yesterday. My husband, you see . . ." Her voice trailed off, unwilling to admit, Celia supposed, that her husband was not at home when he should have been.

Essie Duncan's shoulders bowed beneath the weight of her concerns for her family. How old might she be? Thirty? Forty? The intervening years since Celia had first met her had not improved Celia's ability to tell, since Essie's concerns had also etched lines on her face to age her. More lines than before.

"I completely understand, Mrs. Duncan."

"I don't want you to think I've left my babe alone now, though." The woman studied Celia as she collected supplies to clean the wound along with a tin of sticking plasters from inside her supply cabinet. She had large, wide eyes that gave her the appearance of constant watchfulness. "My neighbor was willing to look after him for a bit."

"I have every faith, Mrs. Duncan, that you would never leave your child unattended."

She frowned. "It can be so hard."

"At least you have a friend to help you."

"She's a blessing, she is."

"I am certain." Celia arranged her supplies alongside where the woman sat upon the bench Celia used as an examination table. She poured water from the pitcher and dunked a fold of linen into it. The residue of the cerate had to be first removed before she could fully assess the condition of the wound. "How did you cut yourself?"

"It was from that blasting that's been going on," she said, wincing as

Celia cleaned the wound. "You probably can't hear it over here. You're far enough away."

"I have heard the blasting when I've been out on patient visits." A patient who lived nearer to the site had told Celia that the most recent detonation had rattled their dishes and cracked the plaster on one of their front room walls. "They are leveling a lot farther along Vallejo to make way for a large house, is my understanding."

"And blowing off half the side of the hill in order to do so." She shook her head, interfering with Celia's ministrations. "Sorry. But anyway, the place we rent—you remember, right?—is just a street up from where they're doing their work. We'd been told they planned to blast, but I had washing that needed to be hung outside yesterday, when there'd been a break in the rain we've been having. And I thought we were far enough away to not care. So I was at the clothesline, with my little one playing at my feet, when I heard the boom and the hill shaking with a terrible rumble and rocks thrown everywhere!"

Celia peeled off the remaining cerate. Essie had not fully cleaned the wound before applying it. She was fortunate the cut was not in a worse condition. "And one hit you."

"It did! Near knocked me out," she said. "I'm just grateful that rock didn't hit my child. One of these days somebody is going to get dreadfully injured. Or killed."

"Thank goodness your child is unhurt." Celia squeezed the dampened linen, attempting to sluice the cut. "Tilt your head so that the water does not drip all over you."

Essie did as asked. "When my husband finally came home last night and saw the state I was in, he was angry. Terribly angry. He's got a temper, he does, especially when he has drink in him," she continued. "But what was he going to do? Get money out of the rich fellow having the lot leveled? That wasn't going to happen and I told him so."

A confrontation that would have likely resulted in Mr. Duncan ending up jailed rather than rewarded with apologetic funds.

"I shall need to stitch your cut, Mrs. Duncan." Celia watched the woman for any sign of fear; she'd had people faint dead away at the sight of her curved needle. "But only two stitches, I think. The sticking plaster should do most of the work in drawing the edges of the cut together."

"If that's what's required, ma'am."

"It should be quick." She returned to her medical cabinet to collect her needle and thread. "I do not recall if you ever explained to me what it is your husband does." A query to take the woman's mind off needles and stitching.

"He's helping build the sea wall near the Vallejo wharf, ma'am."

An ironic occupation, since some of the blasting occurring in Celia's neighborhood was to procure stone for the project. "Not far for him to go to his employment. How fortunate for you."

"He's glad, he is, for the job," she said. "Nothing's been the same since the war ended and they got rid of so many men at Pioneer Woolen Mill, my husband included. They'll be hiring Chinese to do all those jobs, I expect, since they'll work at a wage no regular person can live on."

Celia was grateful Barbara was not in the room to hear the resentment in the woman's voice.

"He's tried just about everything since then," Mrs. Duncan continued. "Unloading cargo at the docks. Rough lot, there. Glad when he got tired of that. Next got work helping build the new bridge across Mission Cove, but when that finished he had to go back to casting about. Tried to get work at the petroleum refinery on North Point, but it hasn't been running lately. A couple of his mates attempted to get hired on at one of the city's racecourses. My husband thought he'd give that a go too, since he helped with the old squire's horses back home before he came to America. They wouldn't take him, though, and good thing. He could've been working at the Ocean House Course when that racehorse was poisoned. He would've been blamed for certain, seeing how he'd have been the new fellow and all."

Celia threaded her curved needle with a waxed-silk ligature. "I attended a few races back in England, before I moved to America. They are run differently in England than here, is my understanding."

"I wouldn't know, ma'am. I've never been to any."

"Ah." Preparations complete, she leaned in close to Mrs. Duncan. "Please turn more toward the window, if you will."

The woman obediently turned her face toward the daylight. "What about your husband, ma'am?" Her gaze drifted to the place on Celia's fourth finger where a thin gold band chafed her skin. "You didn't talk about him when you came to tend to my Annie."

"He pursues money where and how it suits him."

Unexpectedly, the woman sighed. A wistful sound. "There are days, ma'am, I'd be right content to have my husband pursue money elsewhere, especially when he's in one of his moods. But then I ask myself, what would the little one do without a father? How would we manage? Even a husband like my man is better than none. Isn't it, Mrs. Davies?"

No, Celia wanted to shout. But because of Uncle Walford's generosity—which supported her clinic, paid Addie's wages and the fees of Barbara's tutor, kept them fed and warm and clothed—Celia could survive without a husband's income. Essie Duncan, in need of food and shelter for herself and a child, her opportunities severely limited, could not.

"Isn't it, Mrs. Davies?" Essie repeated, all certainty absent from her voice.

"Please hold still, Mrs. Duncan," Celia said, rather than speak aloud her thoughts. Rather than admit that even she, proud of her self-sufficiency, had not completely freed herself from a husband's vagaries. Could still be entrapped by the whims and workings of a man.

• • •

"Mr. Pierson. Thank you for coming in." Nick strode through the detectives' office and took his chair across from the fellow.

Pierson must have had a quick shave with a sharp blade because a cut bloomed red beneath his chin and there was a missed patch of stubble on his throat. But his black suit of clothes was spotless, his graying hair slicked back, his necktie folded in a proper knot.

"Mr. Greaves."

"Sleep well last night, Mr. Pierson?"

He hunched on the chair, seeming smaller up close than he'd appeared standing next to his wife last night. Being out of your element did that sometimes, made you seem smaller.

"Um, yes, sorry about that, Detective Greaves. The shock and all." The space between Pierson's eyebrows developed a furrow. "What did the coroner have to say?"

"Our friend Mr. Griffin was killed with a gimlet," said Nick. "A quick death."

"As I've said, the fellow was no friend of mine. I don't know what he was doing out in my yard. And I didn't hear anything. I was . . . outside, in the back."

"In the privy. Yes, I heard," Nick replied. "Dr. Harris will let me know his conclusions once he's completed the autopsy. Safe to say, though, Griffin didn't die accidentally."

"It's awful."

There was movement out in the main station and Taylor appeared in the doorway. He sat behind Pierson and located his notebook in the pocket where he'd stashed it.

"The individual you wanted to meet with, sir, doesn't want to come into the station." He meant Aldrich but didn't want to mention him in front of Pierson. "He'll meet you for dinner at Valcin's restaurant on Montgomery. At noon."

"Thank you, Taylor." Nick waited until his assistant was ready before continuing. "Now, Mr. Pierson, you didn't happen to owe Mr. Griffin money, did you? That was his business. Lending money to people in desperate need for it and who didn't want to go to the bank to ask."

He'd question Pierson about the book he'd found in Griffin's travel case, but Taylor hadn't yet had time to pore over the columns of numbers and initials and Pierson wasn't likely to be honest about its contents.

"Why would I not be able to get a loan at a bank, Detective Greaves? I don't need to approach fellows like Mr. Griffin for money."

"Just trying to understand why he ended up where he did."

"In my yard."

"Exactly." Nick leaned back in his chair and considered Pierson. "Was he one of the men invited to your house last evening?"

"As Georgiana told you, Mr. Greaves, neither of us knew the man," he said. "Have you spoken to that woman who was with my wife? Apparently she's acquainted with Mr. Griffin. Maybe she can tell you why somebody killed the fellow and left him in my front yard."

"I've already spoken with Mrs. Davies," said Nick. "But you haven't answered my question as to whether you'd invited Griffin to your house last evening."

"I did *not* invite him to my house."

"Your wife informed me that a Mr. Aldrich and a Mr. Hollis were there last evening. One of them is your former boss, isn't he?"

"You know about that?" Pierson looked confused. And unsettled.

Nick shifted in his chair and rubbed the back of his fingers against his jaw, stubble rasping; he could use a better shave, too. "What happened at Western States Fire and Life Insurance Company, Mr. Pierson? You and Aldrich fall out of love with each other or something?"

"What does my former employment at the insurance company have to do with Mr. Griffin's murder?"

Nick shrugged. "Probably nothing, but the situation has come to my attention, so I thought I'd ask. Plus, I find it pretty interesting you had Mr. Aldrich to your house for a friendly evening chat and maybe some drinks—"

"I don't drink," he snapped.

Okay. "Why did you leave Western States?"

"I believed my talents would be better suited to a different business endeavor, Detective Greaves."

"Did Aldrich encourage you to pursue this other endeavor?"

"Not at all. He wished me well. In fact, that was one reason he came by last night. He wanted to see how I was getting on." Pierson smiled, warming to the story.

"Your wife explained that you'd invited him and Mr. Hollis to discuss a business proposition," Nick said. "This Mr. Hollis. Who is he?"

"He provides funds to businesses he is interested in supporting."

Taylor lifted his eyebrows before continuing his note-taking.

"Ah. The fellow sounds rather like Mr. Griffin," said Nick. "But I thought you could easily go to the bank to get funds. Is Mr. Hollis associated with one of the city's fine banking institutions?"

Pierson flushed, a color nearly as pink as the shade Taylor's face could turn. "He is not at all like Mr. Griffin, based on what you've told me. Matthew Hollis is a legitimate investor with significant personal funds at his disposal."

"How lucky for you and your new endeavor." Nick sat back. "When did these two gentlemen arrive at your house and how long did they stay?"

A question that must have sounded safer to Pierson, because he relaxed, his color returning to normal.

"They arrived at six, as we'd arranged. And stayed . . ." He pondered the heavens before pulling his watch—silver, engraved, thick silver chain and dangling fob—from its pocket in his vest and depressing the latch that flipped it open. He examined the watch face. "Yes, I'd say they stayed only around forty-five minutes. No longer."

Which meant, if he was telling the truth, that Griffin had died after six forty-five but before seven, when Celia Davies and Georgiana Pierson had returned from their evening at Jane Hutchinson's. Murdered in the middle of a rainstorm. With no witnesses. "Might Mr. Aldrich or Mr. Hollis have had a motive to kill Mr. Griffin?"

He scoffed. "In my yard after having visited me? Even if they did have a reason—which I can't imagine why they would, nor could I explain what their motives might be—I hardly think either of those gentlemen would be so stupid as to kill him there." Pierson snapped shut the watch lid and returned the watch to its pocket.

"Unless they sought to incriminate you."

Pierson pressed his lips into a thin, flat line; he hadn't considered that possibility, perhaps. "Neither of those gentlemen nor I am to blame for this Mr. Griffin's death, Detective. I assure you."

Taylor flipped a page in his notebook and readied to write some more. Out in the station, a cop was dragging a newly apprehended crook across the room toward the booking sergeant, his loud protests of innocence causing Taylor to get up and shut the door.

"Which one of the men left first, Mr. Pierson?"

"Matthew. Mr. Hollis, that is. Then Lyman a few minutes later."

Which might provide Hollis an alibi, if Aldrich confirmed Pierson's statement when Nick met him for lunch. "Did Mr. Hollis agree to finance your endeavor? What is this venture, by the way?"

"I wish to open a house brokerage, but I require experienced associates to help establish the business," he replied.

"Ah." From writing up insurance policies on buildings that might conveniently burn down to selling them. Seemed the perfect leap. "And did the two gentlemen agree?"

"Mr. Hollis said he would get back to me, but he seemed enthusiastic."

"What about Mr. Aldrich?"

Pierson paused. "If he can serve on the board, he might."

"I see." Nick stared at the fellow long enough to get Pierson to clear his throat and blink a few more times. "Can you explain your relationship with Mr. Zacharias Everett, Mr. Pierson?"

"He is a close acquaintance of mine."

"Didn't you used to be his insurance agent?"

Pierson shook his head. "No."

"Funny, I was told you were."

"He made use of Western States's services," he said, a nicely evasive response.

"Ah," said Nick. "You were seen at his store yesterday morning. Pretty sad about it having burned down, don't you think? A clear case of arson."

"Arson?" he asked, sending his eyebrows up his short forehead. "Are you sure?"

"Oh, it's obvious, Mr. Pierson. And it got me to thinking about the fact that the newspapers have been reporting a large number of suspiciously swift fire insurance payouts these past few months." Nick raised a hand to stop Pierson from reminding him that Everett hadn't been a client. "During your time at Western States Fire and Life Insurance, Mr. Pierson, did you happen to learn that any of the agents were taking a cut of hastily paid-out claims?"

He frowned. "No."

"Here I was hoping you had, and that was why you'd left the company. Because of your high moral standards." Nick folded his arms and considered the fellow for a few moments. Staring at a suspect sometimes encouraged them to loosen their tongue. So far, Pierson hadn't followed suit. "What can you tell me about Aldrich? It's my understanding he likes to play the ponies."

Pierson twitched, unnerved by Nick's unexpected—what appeared to be unexpected—question. "He owns a couple of racehorses. He's often at the Ocean House Course, even if his animals aren't running."

"Has horse racing been profitable for Mr. Aldrich?"

"I have no idea, Detective. You'd need to ask him."

Nick smiled, which made Pierson twitch again. "I mean to, Mr. Pierson. About that and more. Much more."

Chapter 7

Nick left Pierson to sputter about how rude the police were and headed straight for Hollis's office. He wanted to interview him before he and Pierson and Aldrich had a chance to massage their stories, if they were inclined to hide the truth.

The man's office was compact and rather plain with only a handful of furnishings. The dominant pieces were a pair of desks, the smaller one occupied by a fellow who looked up when Nick strode through the door. Walnut cabinets, lockable of course, and a row of glass-fronted bookcases, also lockable. A portrait of the current president, Andrew Johnson, alongside that of the former, President Lincoln. *How patriotic, Mr. Hollis, and smart to cover both political parties.* There were touches of luxury here and there, though. The silver inkwell atop his desk. The expensive silk brocade seat covers. An excess of gas lamps that guaranteed light no matter how dark the day. They were helpful, at the moment, since the clouds had decided to collect again. Lastly, a few pieces of artwork hung on the walls, including a painting of a horse.

Interesting.

The fellow at the desk—a clerk or secretary, by the look of him—had gotten to his feet.

"Are you here to see Mr. Hollis, sir?" His voice was as smooth and polished as the surface of his desk. An Englishman, based on the accent.

"I am. Is he in?"

"He has just returned from his morning activities." He retrieved what looked to be a large calendar. Notes were scribbled across it. "Do you have an appointment?" he asked, sounding doubtful.

"No, but I think he'll make time for me." Nick showed his badge. "Detective Greaves."

The secretary blanched. "Mr. Hollis has no information about the murder that occurred last night."

Were you told to say that, should a policeman come asking? And rather quick to have heard about Griffin's murder and prepared a reply, since the morning papers had gone to press before they could write up a story. Maybe Mr. Hollis had friends in one of the newspaper offices who'd already alerted him about Mr. Pierson's misfortune with a dead body. Or maybe Pierson had contacted him directly.

"That's for me to decide. Can you fetch him? Now," Nick added when the fellow hesitated.

He retreated through a half-open door at the rear of the office, which he didn't close behind him, allowing Nick to hear the frantic, whispered conversation he had with his boss. After a minute or so, Hollis made an appearance.

The fellow was close to Nick's height and robust beneath his tailor-made black suit of clothes. He had neatly trimmed hair and a close-cut, chin-strap beard that framed his jaw. Handsome.

Hollis didn't bother to offer a handshake. "I presume you've come about last evening, Detective. And yes, I have heard about the death of that man at Edward Pierson's home. Shocking."

Straight to the point. Nick rather appreciated that. "What can you tell me about what happened, Mr. Hollis?"

"Not much. The fellow wasn't outside when I left Edward's house, so he must have been killed after I departed. Because of the rain, I had a carriage waiting and did not dawdle to scan my surroundings or observe anybody lurking about." He shrugged. "That's all I know, Detective. Not much, as I said."

This was going to be easy. So simple Nick had to wonder if the fellow had rehearsed his lines. "Have you ever heard of the dead man, Mr. Griffin, before?"

"No, not ever."

"You don't happen to owe him money?" Nick asked. "Mr. Griffin was in a similar business to yours, Mr. Hollis. Except he didn't go about it as lawfully."

"A criminal, then," he replied. "I've never heard of him, Detective, and I didn't owe him money. Why would I need to borrow from someone like that? But to end up dead in the Piersons' yard is a definite scandal."

"Putting it mildly." Nick retrieved a slim notebook and pencil from his inner pocket. He should've brought Taylor, instead of sending him off to question Pierson's neighbors. "Did you leave Pierson's house before or after Mr. Aldrich?"

"Before. Around six thirty, I think," he said. "I didn't note the precise time."

"What was the purpose of the meeting?"

"I'm sure Edward has already told you. And Lyman—Mr. Aldrich, that is—as well, if you've spoken to him."

Nick held the pencil tip above the notebook. "I always like to hear everybody's version of events, Mr. Hollis."

"The purpose was to discuss a business proposition Edward had. He was seeking funding. In return, those who committed money would be given a seat on the board of his new corporation."

"Will you be serving?"

"Only if Edward is able to secure money from at least three other gentlemen. That was my requirement," he replied.

"Where do you get the funds, Mr. Hollis?" Nick looked around the office as if the answer was in the room. "The money you lend to folks like Mr. Pierson."

"I have been fortunate in my investments, Detective." A cagey response. "All of them legal, I should add."

"How long have you known Edward Pierson?" Nick asked. "Must be quite a while if he trusted you enough to ask you to serve on the board of his hoped-for venture."

"Several months. Close to a year, actually." He glanced at the paintings decorating the walls. Which one was he looking at? The picture of the dogs? The one of the thoroughbred? "Edward strikes me as a reasonable person, but I wasn't initially interested in participating in his business. Not until he told me that Lyman would possibly be part of the enterprise."

Was that all that was required for Hollis to be willing to part with his money? The mention of J. Lyman Aldrich's name? "Mr. Aldrich's potential involvement convinced you."

"Lyman is no fool. I'll say that much about him."

"How are you two acquainted?"

"Through the Dashaway Association. He is a highly respected businessman in this city, Detective Greaves, and is a member of several of the premier benevolent societies."

The Dashaway Association was the largest temperance organization in San Francisco. Their work with men who couldn't resist the lure of strong drink was regularly held up as a shining example of commendable charity. Nick was as leery of shining examples as he could be of commendable charity.

"I thought maybe you knew him through a shared love of racehorses." Nick nodded toward the painting. "Is that one of yours?"

Hollis located the object of Nick's attention. "No, but I wouldn't mind if it were. It's a nice painting, though, isn't it?"

Nick folded his notebook and tucked it away along with his pencil. "You've stated that Mr. Aldrich is no fool. What about Edward Pierson? What is your opinion of him?"

"Do I think he could murder someone? Is that what you're asking?"

Obviously. Nick nodded, encouraging the man to talk.

"He's a difficult fellow to read, Detective, but I don't think he's a violent man," Hollis answered. "I was surprised, though, that he'd included Lyman in his invitation, given their recent falling-out."

"You were aware Pierson had left the insurance agency?"

"Of course, although I'm not sure if the disagreement with Lyman was what led to his departure."

"What was that disagreement about, Mr. Hollis? Do you know?"

Hollis shook his head. "I wasn't provided the details, Detective."

"How did Pierson seem to you last night?" Nick asked.

"He was anxious and high-strung all evening, but I put that down to expecting we'd refuse to support him," he said.

"Did Aldrich agree?"

"No, which upset Edward. That's when I left. When it became clear that the meeting wasn't going to be productive." Hollis's gaze drifted back to the painting of the horse. "Given last night's calamity, I suppose Edward won't be going ahead with his enterprise at all. That will be hard on him. Truly hard."

• • •

"I hope I am not intruding, Jane." Celia handed off her deep-brimmed bonnet and wrap to Hetty.

"Of course you aren't." Jane thanked her servant, who departed with Celia's things. She ushered Celia into the parlor and slid the doors closed with a firm click. "You're here because of Mr. Griffin's murder."

"Has the news already been in the papers?" Celia asked, taking the same chair she'd occupied when Georgiana Pierson had been in this room yesterday, her voluminous skirt spilling waves of ginger silk across the sofa.

"No, I heard the news from Lena." Jane named the woman who ran the Ladies' Society of Christian Aid.

"I see."

Jane's expression was full of sympathy. "I know that you and Lena—"

"Are not friends," Celia said, completing Jane's sentence. "But our relationship does not matter, since I have no interest in being a member of her organization any longer." Not after the way the women had treated Barbara, making her feel inferior and unwelcome because she was half Chinese.

"Anyway, this morning, as I was dropping off some items to be auctioned for their upcoming fundraiser, I got to speaking with her. Somehow she'd heard about Mr. Griffin's death and where he'd been found." Jane took a seat directly across from Celia. "Did you and Georgiana . . . what happened?"

"We found his body just inside the fence surrounding the Piersons' front yard."

"How absolutely dreadful, Celia. Another murder."

Jane had commented before on the alarming frequency with which cold-blooded killings shadowed Celia. "I could use your help, Jane. I need to learn all I can about the men who were at the Piersons' house last evening."

"Then thank goodness that Frank is still away," she replied. "After the last time I helped with one of your cases he forbad me to ever help again. 'Only polite luncheons and women's charity events, Jane,' he scolded."

"Not one of *my* cases, Jane. They are Mr. Greaves's cases."

"Ah, yes." Jane winked. "I keep forgetting."

For good reason. "And I do not mean for you to get in trouble with your husband."

"It's all right. Frank simply wants to protect me from harm. He doesn't understand that I'm bored, especially with Grace away at college now. This house . . ." She flung out her arms as if to embrace the building over their heads, her left hand just missing a potted dieffenbachia sitting atop a stand behind her. "Sometimes it closes around me."

"Jane, I had no idea." She'd always believed her friend to be utterly content.

"I'm fully aware that I'm lucky, so I shouldn't complain." Jane smiled. "Enough about me. What is it you need?"

"Firstly, whatever you might learn about Edward Pierson."

Jane's brows rose. "You think he might have murdered Mr. Griffin?"

"I have no idea, but Georgiana blurted out that Mr. Griffin's death was his fault. And the request to meet here at your house right when the crime occurred . . . Frankly, Jane, I find her entire story suspicious," Celia replied. "I mean to visit those secondhand shops as soon as possible, though."

"At least we can clear *her* of suspicion," Jane said. "Once Lena recovered from her glee over learning that the Piersons have found themselves embroiled in scandal, she wanted to gossip about Edward

Pierson's reason for leaving Mr. Aldrich's insurance company. The gossip is that he'd had a dispute with Mr. Aldrich over a racehorse."

For the second time in less than an hour, Celia found herself discussing horse racing. "A racehorse?" Not suspicious fires at properties he had insured?

"I couldn't get any more details out of Lena, except that she'd heard that Georgie now despises Mr. Aldrich. The disagreement resulted in the Piersons not being invited to as many social events as they used to, for fear they'll encounter the Aldriches and cause a scene. Everybody prefers the Aldriches, as rich and influential as they are, so the Piersons—"

"Are cut, as my aunt in England might say. How did Mrs. Douglass even become aware of this story, though?"

"Her husband is great friends with Mr. Aldrich through the Dashaway Association, apparently."

"And Mr. Douglass is in the man's confidence?"

"Apparently so."

Perhaps, though, they were all connected one to the other. Nests of vipers. Men in their meeting rooms, privileged and secure, away from probing ears and eyes, full of grievances and secrets and desperate for fraternity. Tell all and gain trust. Tell all and risk those secrets oozing away, seeping through cracks in their fraternal armor. Cracks they did not even realize existed.

"Maybe this quarrel is the reason Georgiana wished to be away from her house last evening, rather than encounter Mr. Aldrich. Not because she meant to provide herself an alibi during the commission of a murder," Celia said. "Mr. Aldrich happened to be one of the two men visiting Edward Pierson last night, at Mr. Pierson's invitation. Intriguing he was there, don't you agree? The other fellow was a man named Matthew Hollis."

"I don't know him. I'll ask around."

"I thought you knew everyone in this town," Celia teased.

Her friend laughed. "Not everyone, Celia. Just the ones Frank thinks are worth knowing."

"Which is still a large number of people and more than I am acquainted with." Not that Celia had sought the company of San Francisco society. "Thank you for helping, Jane."

"My pleasure. I do agree that it's odd that Edward Pierson invited Mr. Aldrich to his house," she said. "If they've become enemies, why do that?"

"More critically, why did he accept?"

• • •

Aldrich's chosen restaurant occupied a prominent corner spot, its tall windows sparkling in what sunshine there was, the day once again becoming overcast and gloomy. Fringed curtains and partly closed blinds shielded the diners inside from the scrutiny of passersby, although enough of the interior was visible to make a person salivate at the prospect of sitting at tables draped with white linen and set with fancy china plates. The place was not at all like the saloons and oyster houses Nick frequented, where tablecloths and china plates were unheard of, and the floors crunched with debris brought in from the street on folks' shoes.

"I'm meeting a Mr. Aldrich," he said to the heavily whiskered fellow preventing Nick from proceeding more than three steps inside the establishment.

"Mr. Greaves?" he asked, which meant Aldrich had already arrived.

"That's me."

Nothing crunched beneath Nick's boots as he followed the man. The restaurant smelled good, too. A mix of cigar smoke and cooking meat and expensive colognes. A wall, its double doors standing open, divided the restaurant into two rooms. The main one was a space of dark wood tables, a polished oak floor, cut glass reflecting gaslight everywhere, a massive framed mirror on one wall, and diners' conversation as hushed as fresh leaves whispering in a spring wind. Polite and relaxing inside, away from the constant rattle of wagons and carts on Montgomery, the chatter of pedestrians out on the road, the cry of hawkers trying to sell products Nick was certain weren't worth the asking price.

Aldrich sat at a table a good twenty feet from the nearest other diner, ensuring privacy. He looked up from the newspaper he'd been reading. He had a distinguished appearance, sweeps of gray at his temples lending him a certain loftiness, and held his shoulders back as if he'd never dare slouch and show weakness.

He slowly and carefully refolded his newspaper, making Nick wait. "Mr. Greaves." His deep voice was as well-heeled as his dark clothing. "Good day."

Nick skipped the pleasantries and took the chair opposite. "Nice place," he said, removing his hat and setting it on the table.

"I conduct much of my business here, Mr. Greaves. The staff knows not to bother me and everyone will think that you are simply another one of my clients," he replied. "Furthermore, I don't want the agency employees gossiping again about a police detective visiting our office."

The waiter, a crisp white apron tied around his skinny waist, bustled over with menus. "Here you are, Mr. Aldrich." His close-set eyes surveyed Nick. He expected he didn't look like Aldrich's usual lunchtime companions. "Sir," he finally said before handing Nick a menu, then gliding off as rapidly as he'd come.

From a coat pocket, Aldrich withdrew a pair of spectacles, set them on his nose, and scanned the menu. He wasn't actually reading it, though. His attention was on Nick, no mistaking. "The police officer you sent to encourage me to meet with you explained that this is about some fellow found dead last night. In Edward Pierson's yard, of all places."

"You were at Pierson's house to discuss a business proposition, is my understanding."

Aldrich inclined his head. "Yes."

"Just you, Mr. Hollis, and Mr. Pierson. That right?"

"That is correct."

"And Pierson never mentioned a Mr. Griffin last night. He's the dead man, by the way." The afternoon papers would be out soon and Nick wouldn't have to keep explaining who'd been killed.

"No. Not then or ever," he said. "However, if the fellow had been in the house, hiding in a room other than the Piersons' parlor, I wouldn't have known. Furthermore, Hollis and I weren't there for long."

"Hollis told me you left after he did."

Aldrich's eyelids flickered. Surprised, maybe, that Nick had already spoken to the fellow. "I did. A few minutes later, no more." He considered Nick for a moment. "I suppose that means I can provide Matthew Hollis with an alibi, as he wasn't outside murdering some stranger when I departed."

"You're positive Mr. Griffin was a stranger to him?" Nick asked.

Aldrich exhaled. "Neither of them were outside when I left Pierson's house."

The waiter returned. "Are you gentlemen ready to order?"

"My usual," said Aldrich.

Nick, who hadn't looked at the menu, selected the first thing he noticed. Just because it happened to be about the most expensive item as well didn't hurt. Unless Aldrich stuck him with the bill.

"Tenderloin with mushrooms," Nick said. "And a side of fried potatoes."

The waiter collected the menus. Nick waited until he was out of earshot to continue. "What's your opinion of Pierson's business plans?"

"He wants to set up a real estate brokerage. I told him there are plenty of such firms in San Francisco and it would be difficult to compete with the others, which are more established."

"So you told him no."

Aldrich frowned. He removed his spectacles, wiped them clean with a handkerchief, and tucked them in his pocket. "I did."

"What about Hollis?"

"He was more willing to consider Pierson's request. He doesn't know Pierson as well as I do." Aldrich's poor opinion of Pierson didn't show on his face; he let the tone of his voice do all the work.

"Sounds like you don't much care for Edward Pierson, Mr. Aldrich."

"We don't always see eye to eye on matters, Detective."

"A hotheaded sort of fellow, maybe?" Nick asked.

More eyelid flickering. "Unpredictable but not a murderer."

"Was it his unpredictability that led to him getting fired from your insurance agency?"

"It's not *my* insurance company, Mr. Greaves. I am merely the president," he corrected. "But yes, he did used to work there."

"Did you fire him when you discovered that he'd been taking a cut from the insurance claims he was approving?" asked Nick. "Ones that he maybe shouldn't have been approving? Such as the claim that Mr. Everett will be making on his recently damaged store?"

Aldrich sat back, thinking. Damned if you do, damned if you don't. Tell Nick that Pierson had been okaying shoddy claims without reporting the man to the underwriters association and get in trouble. Deny that Pierson had been engaged in fraud only to have the truth later revealed and get in trouble. Unless, of course, he wasn't engaged in fraud.

"I did not fire Mr. Pierson, Detective. It was our mutual understanding that it was best he depart," Aldrich replied. "And Mr. Everett will soon no longer be my client. He informed me he intended to move his policy to another agency, although now I hear he means to leave the city entirely. I am also aware that the police suspect the fire at his store was intentional."

"Do you mean to pay?"

"Not if the police prove it was arson, Detective. Do I look like a fool?"

Not in the least. "Did you learn that Pierson was profiting off fraudulent claim payouts?"

"I had heard rumors but I didn't have any concrete proof," he said. "Pierson became irate when I confronted him, collected his personal belongings, and stormed out of the office. In front of customers. An inexcusable scene."

"Hotheaded, then."

Rather than answer, Aldrich glanced in the direction of the kitchen, likely hoping food would arrive to save him from the conversation. The door didn't swing open, though.

"Nasty little bruise you have there, Mr. Aldrich." Nick hadn't noticed it until Aldrich turned his head.

Aldrich reflexively reached up to the spot on his right jaw. "Clumsy."

Nick would have to ask Harris if he thought Griffin was left-handed. "Given your poor opinion of Edward Pierson, why did you agree to go to his house last night?"

"In his note, Pierson claimed he wished to apologize for his behavior. That he'd been offended I didn't trust him, which was why he'd gotten so angry that afternoon and had stomped out of the office. And that he had a business proposition which might make amends for his conduct. An opportunity for me to get in on the ground floor, so to speak," he explained. "I had no other plans last night, and I was curious, I admit. I am willing to take a gamble if the profits are worth the risk."

The site of Nick's old wound took to aching, and he reached up to massage the spot on his arm. He'd come to view the pain as an omen of sorts.

"Do you enjoy gambling, Mr. Aldrich? I ask because I heard you were at one of the racetracks yesterday when I came to ask about the fire at Everett's store."

"I'm often at one of the tracks in town." Aldrich gave a genuine smile for the first time that day. A smug grin. "I own racehorses. Two fantastic animals. Bay thoroughbreds the both. My three-year-old is descended from Leviathan. The other, Validus, is out of Sir Archy. The Godolphin of America, they call him. I expect great things from them. They've both won twice already this year. Fantastic animals," he repeated, sounding as proud of his horses as if they were children. "Do you know horses, Detective Greaves?"

"Can't say that I do, Mr. Aldrich. Other than a passing familiarity with the mare my father used to own when we had our farm in Ohio."

His little sister had loved that animal, a brown the color of fresh-tilled soil and with soft eyes. Meg would beg to ride it whenever she could. And their father would let her, because who could ever refuse Meg? A burning spasm shot through his arm, and Nick winced. The pain from his wound wasn't only an omen; sometimes it was guilt.

"Mr. Greaves, is everything all right?"

"A war wound, Mr. Aldrich. Bayoneted in the Wilderness." Nick dropped his hand and clenched it in his lap. "It occasionally likes to remind me of the war." *And how much I'd failed Meg when she'd needed me most.*

"Ah, I see." Aldrich paused as the waiter returned with the food and arranged the plates on the table. Up close, the food—Aldrich's usual was fricassee of chicken—smelled even better than when Nick had entered the restaurant. "You should come to the Ocean House Course, Mr. Greaves. As my guest."

"I'm too busy to spend the day watching horses race." He should send Taylor and his ladylove, Addie Ferguson.

"Of course. You have a murder to solve," he said. "I can't fathom, though, why the police would be concerned about the abrupt death of a man I'm told was a criminal."

Between Aldrich and Hollis, Nick didn't know who was better informed. He'd like to know the person who was giving them their inside information. Could be useful. "I can't speak for all the police department, but as for me, I can be strange like that, Mr. Aldrich. Caring about all sorts of folks."

Aldrich didn't appreciate Nick's comment and briefly scowled at his chicken.

Nick sliced through the tenderloin and took a bite. The meat was so delicious it made him momentarily forget what he wanted to ask Aldrich. He didn't forget, though. "When you were finished rejecting Mr. Pierson's proposition and left his house, did you see anybody suspicious in the area?"

"It was still raining, so there wasn't anybody on the street that I can recollect." Aldrich sawed off a piece of his chicken and rapidly chewed. "Oh, except a fellow in a plaid coat trudging up the street. Absolutely miserable, slogging along the muddy road because the plank sidewalks aren't finished. I'd paid for a hackney to wait for me, and I didn't waste time perusing my surroundings in that weather. Hopped aboard and had the fellow drive away as fast as he could."

"This man in the plaid coat was the only person you saw."

"I noticed the local policeman when I arrived at Pierson's, but when I departed, I only saw the man wearing the plaid coat, yes."

So when *had* Fulton been making his rounds? "You arrived around six, correct?"

"Six ten or so." Aldrich hurriedly ate through his chicken fricassee. He set down his knife and fork with a clink against the plate and peered at his watch. "You'll have to forgive me, Detective. I am late for an appointment. If you have any more questions, you know where to find me."

With that, Aldrich tossed aside his napkin, got to his feet, and departed.

Leaving Nick stuck with the bill.

• • •

"Is it true, ma'am?"

Celia glanced over at the doorway to her examination room. Owen stood just outside, his hands jammed into his pockets, his shoulders tensed.

"You've heard about Mr. Griffin." She set down the notebook she'd been writing in. A notebook ironically purchased at Mr. Everett's shop, its cover a lovely mahogany leather that was far more extravagant than her patient logbooks required. But she loved the feel of the leather in her hand, and she'd been in need of a boost to her spirits the day she had purchased the book.

"So it's true." He dragged his wool cap from his head and crushed it in his hands. "It's true that he's dead."

"It is true, Owen," she said. "I'm sorry."

His face dropped. "He saved me, ma'am, when I was first living on the streets. When I first came to San Francisco and I had nowhere else to go."

"You owed Mr. Griffin a debt yet he was a difficult man to owe debts to, wasn't he?" Both literal and figurative debts.

"He had a way of calling them in that scared you into not refusing."

Perhaps Mr. Griffin had finally encountered a person who'd decided to refuse in a most permanent fashion.

"Let's go into the dining room, Owen. Addie can bring us some tea and some of her biscuits."

He trailed behind her. "It's downright awful. I saw him just yesterday."

"Mr. Griffin?"

"Yep. Miss Barbara has a new tutor?"

His attention had shifted to the garden beyond the dining room window. "You're not here to remark on Barbara's new tutor, Owen. Tell me why you saw Mr. Griffin yesterday."

"He wanted to let me know he was leaving town. He looked sorta anxious, which made me sorta anxious, too," he answered. "When Caleb Griffin is worried, something terrible's sure to happen soon. And sure enough, it did."

"Did he explain what he was nervous about?"

He hooked his cap over the back of one of the dining room chairs. "Not really. Something about having to collect on a few debts and then needing to hightail it out of the city for a while."

Could Caleb Griffin have been at the Piersons' house last evening because he had been collecting on one—or all—of those debts?

"Mr. Griffin was murdered, Owen. Just down the street from here. Multiple stab wounds from a gimlet." She needn't have been so blunt, but Owen had heard and experienced worse.

"Shoot, that's awful."

Addie swept into the dining room, a tray of biscuits in her hand.

"Thought I heard your voice, laddie, so I brought what you'd be wanting."

Grinning, Owen thanked her and dropped onto the chair. Celia took a seat across from him, waiting until Addie returned to the kitchen before continuing on the subject of Mr. Griffin.

"Did Mr. Griffin say anything else?"

Owen grabbed a biscuit from the tray and stuffed it into his mouth, chewing as fast as he could. "Caleb . . . 'Scuse me, ma'am." He swiped crumbs off his mouth and continued. "Not much, other than he also gave me a note to keep. Said I had to guard it, but he would be back for it once the coast was clear."

"Do you have the note with you?"

"No. I stashed it in my room at the boardinghouse." His eyebrows tucked together. "Might not be safe there, though."

"Do you remember what that note said?"

"It had some word on it I didn't recognize at all and the amount of five hundred dollars."

What was the word? she wondered. "Mr. Griffin did not explain?"

"No, ma'am. And it's just plain not smart to ask Caleb questions."

"We must inform Mr. Greaves, Owen. You realize that. The information contained in that note, scant as it is, must be very important and possibly dangerous," she said. "It could be the clue that explains who murdered him."

"A fellow came to my boardinghouse last night looking for Caleb. Johnny said Caleb had something a friend of his wanted, and wanted awfully bad," he said. "I think he meant that note, ma'am. Johnny said I wasn't to tell anybody about it, though. Caleb didn't want me to tell anybody either, but he's dead now, so I figured he's not gonna be mad with me for telling you. Maybe I shouldn't have, though."

"Well, you have—which was very brave—and we now must inform Mr. Greaves. We have no other choice."

Owen's eyes went wide. "What if I'm next though, Mrs. Davies? Because I got that note. What if I'm next?"

CHAPTER 8

Nick leaned against the lamppost, crossing one ankle over the other and folding his arms. Gas lighting was scarce in this part of town, especially along the stretch of Vallejo that climbed Telegraph Hill, and he appreciated something to rest against that wasn't a storefront. Shopkeepers didn't always like having folks lounging outside their front doors. He gazed up the road. He could just make out the house Celia Davies occupied with her cousin and Addie Ferguson. Or maybe he was imagining he could see her house because he wished he could. However, if he stood here long enough, she'd eventually come marching past. Never one to sit still long. Always out tending to her patients.

Or getting mixed up in murders.

Nick readjusted his stance and sighed. He wasn't standing here in hopes of encountering Celia, though, as much as he might enjoy seeing her someplace other than the police station. He was waiting for the local policeman to make his rounds. Taylor had learned that the fellow's name was Fulton, and that he patrolled the block of Vallejo from Powell to Leavenworth and down to Jackson, making the circuit between the hours of four and midnight, when another fellow took over. The bells on the nearby church had rung four times about fifteen minutes ago. The local should come strolling along at any moment.

The owner of the grocer's across the street came out onto the sidewalk and motioned at Nick. "You there. What are you doing?" he shouted, his accent thick with the sounds of his German homeland.

Nick scanned the road—traffic was about as scarce as gaslights on these hilly streets—before heading over. "I'm hoping to run into a particular fellow. The local policeman. His name is Fulton. Do you know him?"

"*Ja*, I know him. I do not pay him, so he does not protect my business."

No surprise there. "I need to talk to him about a crime that took place last night."

The grocer chuckled.

"What's so amusing?" asked Nick.

"I hear stories the man is not to be trusted," he said. "Did he see a crime or commit a crime?"

That's what I'd like to know. "Who tells these stories?"

"The people who also do not pay him. And some of the people who do. It is said he is . . ." The grocer cast about for the word. "It is said he is a deserter."

Damn. Did being a deserter automatically make Fulton a suspect in Griffin's killing, though? Some veterans of the recent war, still stinging from the fight, might think so. Lots of them had no stomach for men they viewed to be yellow-bellied cowards. The law didn't look kindly on deserters, either, even though the war had ended over two years ago.

"But he's on the city supervisors' list?" They approved the men working as local police. Maybe they were slipping up these days.

"Who knows?" he asked. "But if Mr. Fulton saw a crime and did not stop it, then I do not think, sir, he will tell you the truth."

An accurate observation, undoubtedly. "I'll take my chances."

"There he is now." The grocer jerked his chin, indicating the fellow striding along the sidewalk, a long overcoat flapping about his stout legs.

Two raven-haired women wrapped in bright shawls and carrying baskets darted out into the street to avoid crossing paths with the man. They nodded to the grocer and hurried inside his store. The younger of the two shot a look at Fulton before disappearing into the store's shadows, her companion shouting in what sounded like Italian to hasten her along.

"*Viel Glück,* sir," said the grocer to Nick, chuckling, and followed his customers inside.

"Hey, Fulton." Nick dashed across the street to intercept the local, evading a fellow hauling coal up the road, who shouted at Nick to watch where he was going. "I need to speak with you."

It was downright unnerving that Fulton's immediate reaction was to grab his hip. Or, rather, the gun he likely had holstered there. He stopped and waited, though.

Thankfully. Because I sure in hell don't feel like chasing him.

"I remember you, Detective," he said, the words ending in a cough that shook his body.

"Don't think you're going to want to shoot me, in that case." Nick nodded at Fulton's hip.

He lowered his hand. "I told you last night all I know about that fellow's murder."

It wasn't only Fulton's legs that were stout; the whole of him was thickset. Even his neck and head. A man perfect for the job, aside from his rattling cough. Why not work for the official police force, though? Because he really was a deserter and the chief would find out? Or because the money he made as a local was better.

Maybe I should look into it.

"I think you might know more," Nick said.

"Not likely."

A pair of workers from the nearby street leveling project paused their end-of-day stroll to lounge in the entrance to a saloon across the road. They might not recognize Nick, but they likely recognized Fulton and had become overwhelmed with curiosity. Eyes everywhere, it seemed, except when Nick needed those eyes to notice something useful. None of the eyes had seen anything last night, according to what they'd told Taylor. For once, though, the weather made Nick believe it was possible they were being honest rather than simply reluctant to share what they knew with a cop.

"Let me explain why I think you haven't told me everything, Fulton. A witness saw you near the scene of the crime not long before it happened." Nick indicated the general direction of the Piersons' house. The loungers at the saloon noticed the gesture and leaned out of the doorway to take a gander up Vallejo. A dog had come along at some point to lay at their feet, and even its head turned. "Yet you told me you'd last been by the Piersons' house a good twenty, thirty minutes before then."

Fulton stuck his tongue into his left cheek and considered Nick. "Where did this witness claim to have seen me? Around the corner or somethin'?"

"I'm going to give you a chance to fix what you told me, Fulton," he said. "When did you go past the Piersons'?"

"Maybe I was wrong about the exact time. But I didn't see anything."

"Or maybe you killed the fellow yourself."

Fulton's eyes widened enough to see the white around his irises. "I didn't!"

"Okay, okay," Nick said, trying to calm him before he started hacking again. "Help me out then, because I need to find whoever killed that man before somebody else gets hurt." Nick threw in the last bit in hopes it might encourage Fulton to talk.

"Somebody else is gonna get hurt no matter what I got to say, Detective," he declared. "Even if I do my job well. Even if you do your job well."

"Tell me about last night anyway," said Nick. "Just to make me feel better about how well I'm doing my job."

Fulton gave an appreciative snort, which sent him into a fit of coughing. Once he'd recovered, he answered.

"I was makin' my rounds. It was rainin'. Pretty hard at times. There weren't hardly nobody out. Just a carriage or cart now and again. Some drunk fool stumblin' out of a tavern down the street and falling into a mud puddle." He flashed a grin at the recollection. "Way quieter than it is most nights. Got soaked by the weather, which ruined my coat. Saw a couple of hacks waitin' on the corner up there." He indicated the Piersons' house, the loungers' heads swiveling again. "You know, Detective, I might've seen a fellow actin' strange last night. Maybe a block or so from the Piersons'. Lurking behind a building under construction. I didn't investigate because that particular spot is not within my territory."

Figures. "Can you describe him?"

Fulton shook his head. "It was rainin' way too hard for that."

"Have you ever heard of Caleb Griffin?"

Fulton flashed another grin that showed his mouthful of tobacco-stained teeth. "Might surprise you to learn I read the papers, Detective. I know he's the fellow killed. Saw the news in today's afternoon paper."

"Did you know him? Ever see him around here?"

Fulton scanned the area like he owned the streets, the houses of wood or brick, the flat-fronted businesses that edged the sidewalks.

"I've heard of Griffin, but only saw him once or twice. Wore that bright red vest like he was glad to be spotted," he said. "But this area wasn't his usual neck of timber, is my understandin'. Preferred the alleys east of the Barbary."

"What's the word, Fulton? Who is it who killed Griffin?"

The man shrugged.

Nick stepped closer to him. Across the street, somebody in the saloon crowd—which had grown to five or six men and a couple of kids—let out a yell. "Punch him for me, will ya?"

"Folks around here don't like you, Fulton."

"They wouldn't like you, either, if they was to learn you're a cop," he answered. He smelled stale of tobacco, which had done more than stain his teeth. "And back off. I don't like to be crowded."

Nick didn't budge. "Maybe it *was* you who knocked off Griffin. Did somebody pay you to get rid of him? Maybe, oh, make it look like Pierson could be blamed?" he asked. "Like you said, it was a quiet night. A perfect time to commit murder with maybe nobody to notice, so you struck while the iron was hot."

Fulton's expression didn't change. Not a tic betrayed him. "I don't have any reason to want to kill Griffin."

"You sure?" suggested Nick. "Maybe you owed him money and that's why you bumped him off. Because you couldn't pay. Because you're a deserter and nobody will give you a better job than this one."

That. That made the muscles around his eyes tic.

"I don't need to listen to this." Fulton shoved his shoulder into Nick's, pushing him aside, and stormed up the road.

• • •

"The coroner has requested that Edward and I appear at his inquest Wednesday morning, Mrs. Davies. Tomorrow. Yes, tomorrow." Georgiana Pierson stood in the center of Celia's parlor, nervously clutching the strings of her beaded purse. The hem of her checked skirt was flecked with dirt, suggesting she had walked from her house to Celia's and in enough haste to be careless about the consequences to her apparel. "But I don't understand. I gave that police officer a statement last night. Why would the coroner need me to say anything in front of his jury?"

"Dr. Harris is very thorough, Mrs. Pierson," Celia replied. "He will not call an inquest closed until he has collected all of the information he needs, which includes the results of his autopsy."

"But Edward didn't find the body, we did. My husband knows nothing about the fellow."

"Then that is all he shall have to say to the jury."

"Did the coroner summon you? You're the one who used to know the dead man." The statement was accusatory.

"He has done, Mrs. Pierson."

"Then why does he need my testimony? It's not as if I'd observed something you hadn't. It's ridiculous." The more Georgiana spoke, the more agitated she became.

"The coroner's request is simply a matter of procedure, Mrs. Pierson. Try not to worry."

Georgiana began to pace across the parlor. As it was not very large, she traversed the width in only a few steps before having to turn again. "Edward was with his business associates. They can attest that he had nothing to do with the crime."

"Mr. Griffin was not murdered when those gentlemen were at your house, or else they would have witnessed the murder or found the body themselves," Celia pointed out.

"Unless one of *them* killed that man. Don't you think that's possible?"

"The police will not rule anyone out until they are certain they can, Mrs. Pierson." *And neither will I.* "Dr. Harris will be brief, but neither you nor your husband can refuse to attend the inquest. The coroner has the right to fine you."

"I'm aware of the penalties, Mrs. Davies," she replied tersely. "I can't believe Edward bothers to pay that security person."

"You mean the local policeman."

"Yes. Him." At the neck of Georgiana's white blouse, she'd pinned an onyx brooch. She shifted from toying with the strings of her reticule to rubbing the brooch. "Nowhere near our property when he was supposed to be."

Although he *had* been nearby. Just moments before their arrival at the house. Hopefully Mr. Greaves had been able to question the fellow. "He cannot be everywhere at once, Mrs. Pierson."

"That's my point. Utterly unreliable."

"Detective Greaves will interview the man and get answers out of him." Georgiana's fidgetiness was contagious, and Celia took to restlessly tapping her foot. "The local will undoubtedly also be called to the inquest tomorrow morning."

A strange expression crossed Georgiana Pierson's face, but it passed before Celia could decide what it meant. "The fellow won't have anything useful to say, I predict. Any testimony he gives shouldn't be trusted. From what little I've seen of him, he looks like he's a drunk."

"Dr. Harris and Detective Greaves will make the determination about the worth of his and everyone's testimony."

"Of course." Georgiana halted her pacing to gaze out the parlor window. "I shouldn't have left the house last night, Mrs. Davies. None of this would've happened."

"You should not blame yourself," she said. "If your husband did not hear the altercation that led to Mr. Griffin's death, you may not have either."

"Nonetheless, I should have stayed, but I wanted so desperately to speak with you about my missing locket, and whenever Edward has business associates to the house he prefers me to not be around." Said with a palpable quantity of resentment. Too many husbands felt similarly about their wives. Unless their presence was to demonstrate marital bliss or to serve a decorative purpose.

My goodness, Celia, how bitter you've become.

"How well are you acquainted with Mr. Aldrich and Mr. Hollis?" Celia asked. Well enough with Mr. Aldrich to despise him, according to what Jane had learned from Lena Douglass.

Georgiana Pierson stiffened, the hand that had been fussing with her brooch dropping to her side. She turned to face Celia again. "Did the detective tell you their names?"

Best not to answer. She wouldn't want Nicholas to get into trouble. "Your husband used to work for Mr. Aldrich."

"Yes, he did," she replied flatly.

"There are rumors that he'd had a falling-out with Mr. Aldrich. Over a racehorse."

"You heard about that, as well, Mrs. Davies? You have been conducting an investigation. I'm impressed."

At least she'd not denied the rumor. *And I would prefer the truth over admiration any day.* "What is your opinion of Mr. Aldrich?"

"He can be stern, ruthless even. A very successful businessman. But can I be honest with you?"

Please, Celia wanted to shout. "Of course."

"Good. Edward has always, always warned me to be cautious whom I share confidences with. Not every person with a supposedly stellar reputation turns out to be trustworthy, Mrs. Davies," she said. "But I expect, given your involvement in police matters, that you know more about human nature than I do."

"Being involved in police matters has not provided me with any greater insight, I'm afraid." Merely exposed her to the depressingly dark side of humankind.

"To be blunt, I don't trust J. Lyman Aldrich. I've long suspected that not all of his business dealings are aboveboard."

"You suspect he does business with criminals? Did your husband suspect as well?"

"One was murdered outside our house the same evening Lyman had been visiting," she stated, as though the comment offered all the proof required.

Perhaps it did.

"I'm curious about something, Mrs. Pierson. Was Mr. Aldrich one of your husband's business acquaintances who attended the party the night your locket went missing?"

Georgiana Pierson met Celia's gaze. "Oh, yes, he *was* in attendance, Mrs. Davies. And now you understand why I'm beginning to suspect the worst about him."

• • •

Nick climbed the short flight of stairs leading to Mrs. Jewett's house. He'd stopped in at the station before heading home for the night and found two messages. The first, from Taylor, vented his frustration with Griffin's notebook and that he hadn't been able to puzzle out the fellow's code. The other was from Harris, a brief summary of Griffin's autopsy. The gimlet's angle of thrust in Griffin's back suggested the assailant hadn't been significantly shorter or taller. The killer had punctured the carotid artery on the third strike, a fatal gash that would've gushed blood everywhere if the gimlet hadn't been left in Griffin's neck. Furthermore, as far as Harris could tell, Griffin hadn't been inebriated and there was only a single defensive bruise on his forearm. He'd been taken by surprise, the coroner guessed, and hadn't had much of a chance to fight back. Nick had dashed off a note asking if Harris thought Griffin might be left-handed and had one of the station officers take it to the coroner's office. The fellow had grumbled about being a delivery boy but took the message anyway.

Nick unlocked the door to Mrs. Jewett's and stepped inside. He was met by an aroma he wasn't used to—the smell of roasting beef. His landlady was an excellent baker, but when it came to supper she went in more for stews and pan-fried chicken. He'd thought he wasn't hungry after the meal at the restaurant with Aldrich, but his stomach rumbled. He strode down the hallway toward the dining room.

"Mrs. Jewett, it smells like you've outdone—" Nick stopped like he'd run into a wall. If he'd been paying more attention—*blast, Nick, why weren't you paying more attention?*—he would have heard the voices. Female voices. Two.

"There you are, Mr. Greaves." Mrs. Jewett, a smile plumping her cheeks, got to her feet. "This is my niece, Violet. Vi, this is Nicholas Greaves. His friends call him Nick."

The young woman seated at the table made to stand up.

"No, miss . . ." He fetched around for her last name. He didn't want to be on a first-name basis with her when he wasn't even on a first-name basis with Celia Davies. But he couldn't remember her last name because Mrs. Jewett had never told him what it was.

"Violet Westerfield," she supplied. "I am pleased to make your acquaintance, Mr. Greaves."

Her voice was soft, might even be described as lyrical. She wore a simple outfit, a skirt and bodice of dark blue without any fancy embellishments. Her chestnut-colored hair was equally simple, swept back from her heart-shaped face. She was prettier than he'd wanted her to be. Across the table from Miss Westerfield, Mrs. Jewett was grinning, proud as a mother hen, in recognition of the sentiment. She knew Nick well.

"Miss Westerfield, there's no need for you to stand. It wouldn't be polite of me if I made you stand."

She inclined her head and retook her chair.

"Please join us." Mrs. Jewett's direct gaze dared him to say no. "And don't be using Riley as an excuse to bolt from the room. I've already fed the creature."

"I have met Riley, Mr. Greaves," said Miss Westerfield. "He's a sweet dog."

Sweet? Riley? Nick had never thought to describe him or any animal like that. "I'm lucky that your aunt puts up with him."

"Are you going to stand in that doorway all night, Mr. Greaves?" asked his landlady. "Or are you going to come in and sit down?"

He may as well sit. As long as Violet Westerfield was living in the same house, it would be almost impossible to steer clear of her. And he couldn't afford to skip meals just to avoid the young woman. Although there was a new oyster saloon not too far away—

"Mr. Greaves, honestly." Mrs. Jewett was sounding exasperated.

Miss Westerfield hid a smile behind her hand.

Nick sighed, removed his hat, and took the chair at the end of the table. The one farthest from Mrs. Jewett's niece.

"My aunt tells me that you are a police detective, Mr. Greaves. A dangerous occupation."

He accepted a plate of roast beef and mashed turnips from Mrs. Jewett. "Glad to say it hasn't killed me yet." His landlady glowered at him and shook her head. Yes, he was being difficult. "It is a dangerous occupation, Miss Westerfield, but it's one I like to pretend that I'm good at."

"Don't let him fool you, Vi. He is excellent at his job." Mrs. Jewett's pride extended beyond the members of her family.

"I have never met a policeman before," Miss Westerfield said. "I suppose that's a good thing. How rewarding, though, to be on the side of justice, Mr. Greaves. To remove that which is criminal from this sad world."

"It's not always easy, miss, to figure out who's a criminal and who isn't, and removing one too often just makes room for another." Like bailing out a leaky boat. Dump buckets of water over the side only to find there was more liquid sloshing around your feet. "Sometimes the criminals are simply caught up by this sad world, making choices they never meant to make."

Did becoming caught up explain the actions of an arsonist? Or Griffin's life of crime? And how much longer might it be before

Aldrich's passion for his ponies, his love of a gamble, veered into the corrupt and the unlawful? Maybe it already had.

Worst of all, had getting mired in the heat of battle explain why Nick was alive and Jack Hutchinson was dead?

Violet Westerfield was watching Nick with wide brown eyes. They were pretty if you looked into them long enough, which he hadn't meant to do. Not as lovely as Celia Davies's, though. In his estimation, no woman would ever compare to Celia. Not even his sister Ellie.

"Let me get those plates out of your way." Mrs. Jewett scrambled to her feet and snatched the dishes. Nick hadn't finished and he tried to grab his back, but his landlady was too quick. "I've made a nice baked apple pudding for dessert," she said before scurrying out of the dining room, leaving Nick and Miss Westerfield alone together.

"Do you have family in San Francisco, Mr. Greaves?" she asked, folding her napkin and laying it atop the linen tablecloth Mrs. Jewett had dug out from a chest somewhere. An item of finery that had never graced the table for as long as Nick had been a resident. "No, you mustn't have family here, since you're boarding with my aunt."

"I have a sister in Sacramento, Miss Westerfield." The usual pain started to creep over his arm. A tingle that would become a burning ache if he let it. "My younger sister passed away a few years back. While I was off fighting."

"Aunt Martha told me you'd served with the Union forces."

Nick briefly wondered where her Aunt Martha had disappeared to; undoubtedly eavesdropping on them from her kitchen. "I did."

"My aunt lost her son, you know." Violet Westerfield's eyes went soft. "His death has been difficult for her, especially since he was the only one of her children to survive to adulthood."

"Yes, miss, I'm aware of his death." Nick witnessed Mrs. Jewett's grief all the time. Nearly as frequently as he experienced his own sharp, fierce grief.

"Isn't it strange how life changes, Mr. Greaves?" she asked. "One moment, you're sure where you're going, forging ahead with conviction.

The next, you're totally confused and lost, all of your world upended, forced to begin anew."

"Has your world been upended, Miss Westerfield?"

He hadn't meant to ask so personal a question any more than he'd meant to notice her pretty eyes. But he was missing Celia, and having been in her company always made him melancholy and sentimental.

"More like destroyed, Mr. Greaves, due to recklessness on my father's part. He enjoys gambling, however he is not always as lucky as he thinks he is." Her tone was devoid of emotion, as if she'd had to explain her family's situation so often that it had become as rote as repeating a line of prose from a McGuffey Reader.

"He's lost your family's fortune."

"Not quite a fortune by most folks' reckoning," she replied with a tight smile. "But we have bills and it's hard to see how they will all get paid. My brother won't be going to college, as he'd hoped."

"I am sure it will all come right, Miss Westerfield." Nick wasn't at all sure of that. He was wondering, however, if her arrival at Mrs. Jewett's was part of the plan to get those bills paid.

"My mother is determined that we have a positive outcome." She had been folding and refolding her napkin. Suddenly, she stopped, her slim fingers pausing their nervous movements. "Sometimes I'm afraid of what my mother might do in order to achieve that result."

"You think she might want to get revenge against her husband?"

"My mother is a small, fragile thing. She hasn't got the strength to hurt my father herself." Miss Westerfield flushed and pressed her hands to her cheeks. "My goodness, Mr. Greaves. You must be thinking the most horrible things about my family."

He wasn't. Because he was thinking about somebody else entirely.

• • •

He had to find someplace to hide. He just had to.

Owen slunk down beneath the window to his room at the

boardinghouse, risking a peek or two outside when he thought it might be safe. *Who in tarnation are you looking for, though, Cassidy?* It wasn't like Caleb's murderer was going to be announcing his identity like some street barker, a store's name painted on the placard hung over his neck, hoping to entice you inside the establishment.

Owen unwound himself and peered over the window ledge. Usual folks about, crowding the sidewalks, passing in and out of the pools of gaslight on their way home or in search of a meal someplace. Running—or strolling, like Caleb used to do—across the filthy cobbles, sloppy from all the recent rain. Shouts and laughter and saloon music and horses whinnying and cart wheels clattering and doors slamming and . . . *Shoot!* Was that fellow wearing a battered old slouch hat staring at his lodging house?

Owen lurched away from the window, losing his balance and falling onto his backside. He had to get out of town until things calmed down. Until folks forgot about Caleb Griffin and that note he'd given Owen. *Dang!* He had to get rid of that note. If anybody found it on him, he'd be . . . well, it probably wouldn't be good.

He scooted back to his spot under the window and pulled in a few deep breaths, waiting for his heart to stop pounding like it wanted to jump through his rib cage. If he tried to find someplace to hide, where would he go? There were only two folks in San Francisco who'd ever been willing to help him—Mrs. Davies and Caleb Griffin. He didn't really want to endanger Mrs. Davies and Miss Barbara and Addie by hiding out in their place, and Caleb was dead.

"Wait!" Mr. Greaves would help him. Of course he would. He should've thought of him straightaway. Should've given him that note straightaway, too, like Mrs. Davies had recommended.

Owen exhaled and sat up. All he had to do was wait until most folks were off the streets and go to Mr. Greaves's lodgings. He had a fair idea which house he lived in. Mr. Greaves would find somebody to take Owen in. Maybe he could even bunk with Mr. Taylor for a while.

Owen leaped to his feet and squinted at the street. The greasy fellow was gone. Owen threw open the sash and leaned through, but he didn't see the man anywhere. Although it was getting awful dark outside. He dragged out his carpetbag from beneath the cot shoved against the wall. If he packed quick—not like he owned much—he might be able to get away before that fellow noticed. Owen eyed the open window. Maybe he could go out that way. Wasn't too far a drop to the sidewalk.

The floorboards out in the hallway creaked, a slow rhythmic pace like somebody was creeping down it. Owen's heart took to racing as fast as that of a rabbit caught in a snare. The creaking stopped right outside his door. Was somebody rattling the handle? That's what it sounded like. *Shoot. Shoot!* He'd locked the door, hadn't he?

Dang it, Cassidy, are you really that stupid? he thought, his gaze fixed on the doorknob like he could will it to not turn. But he couldn't will the knob to not turn, because it did.

Dang it!

"And that is all, Mrs. Davies?" Dr. Harris asked. He had a devilish twinkle in his eyes, as if he found Celia's involvement in Mr. Griffin's murder an unsurprising—and rather amusing—situation.

The jurors had been keen to hear gory details, which Celia did not provide. Georgiana Pierson's gaze had been fixed on Celia during her entire deposition. Why? Did she fear that Celia would mention the accusation she'd leveled at Edward Pierson when they'd arrived to find the body? Celia had informed Mr. Greaves, whom she presumed had told Dr. Harris. Georgiana had certainly avoided mentioning the outburst during her brief testimony. She had managed, however, to sob about how horrifying it had been to discover Mr. Griffin in her yard and complain that she and her husband would be ruined.

"You returned from an outing with Mrs. Pierson here to discover Mr. Griffin's body in the Piersons' yard," the coroner continued. "The only person you noticed on the road was Mr. Fulton making his rounds."

The local policeman frowned at Celia.

"Yes, I observed him approximately a block from the Piersons' home," she replied. "I should, however, let you know about a piece of information I learned, Dr. Harris. Mr. Griffin told a close acquaintance of mine that he intended to leave town, rather in a hurry, right after he collected on a few debts that evening. Monday evening, that is. He was a man known to lend money."

The jurors, seated against the wall of the stuffy room Dr. Harris had chosen for the inquest, murmured and stared as one at Mr. Griffin's draped dead body, which lay on a table in the middle of the space. Mr. Greaves, leaning against the opposite wall, raised his eyebrows.

"Did your acquaintance tell you who it was who owed Mr. Griffin money?" Dr. Harris asked.

"Regrettably, no."

"Thank you, ma'am. Mr. Pierson. Your turn."

Georgiana's husband took the chair Celia vacated. Prompted by Dr. Harris, he repeated what he had told Mr. Greaves—that he had been indisposed during the time of the crime and had heard nothing because he was making use of the facilities in the rear of his house. An unfortunate choice of words that raised chuckles among the jury and gave the coroner cause to chastise them.

"Did you owe the dead man money, Mr. Pierson?" Dr. Harris asked once the sniggering had died down.

"No. Most certainly not." He glared at Celia. "I have no idea what Mrs. Davies is talking about. I did not know the fellow."

"What about this tool?" Dr. Harris produced the gimlet which had been plunged into Mr. Griffin's body. The jury twittered with excitement at being shown the murder weapon. "Does this belong to you?"

Mr. Pierson shook his head. With considerable vigor. "No. Definitely not. Why would I own a carpenter's tool?"

Dr. Harris set aside the gimlet, dismissed Mr. Pierson, and called up Mr. Fulton. *Did* he look like a drunkard? wondered Celia. Thick-bodied and scrappy-looking, perhaps, but not necessarily an inebriate. He reiterated that, prior to catching sight of the commotion at the scene of the crime, he'd not observed anyone in the vicinity of the Piersons' home. He'd not been on Vallejo when the murder was taking place, no matter what Celia said. Maybe a block or so over, but not near the Piersons' house. He did spot two hackney carriages waiting nearby—the ones that Mr. Hollis and Mr. Aldrich had hired—which was unusual for that neighborhood, but did not see the passengers.

"You attest that you did not observe either of the two gentlemen arriving or departing, then," Dr. Harris said.

Mr. Hollis, putting in a late appearance, entered the room on soft feet at that very moment. Mr. Fulton watched him locate a chair, squinting for the briefest amount of time, before turning to consider Mr. Aldrich. "Nope. I didn't."

"And you do not carry a gimlet with you on your rounds."

"Why would I, when I've got a gun?"

A reasonable comment, Celia decided.

Mr. Aldrich, a severely handsome man, graying around the temples and possessing an upright posture and shrewd gaze, was summoned next. He explained what had brought him to the Piersons' that night and that he'd not happened upon the crime being committed as he'd dashed out of the house in a downpour.

"Did you know the dead man, Mr. Aldrich?" Dr. Harris asked.

Mr. Aldrich asked a question of his own. "Was I one of the people who owed Mr. Griffin money, perhaps? To which I answer that I did not," he said. "I am also not in the habit of carrying a gimlet about. But as I informed Detective Greaves yesterday, I did observe a fellow in a plaid coat on the road after I had left Mr. Pierson's house. I can't answer why Mr. Fulton did not also observe the fellow."

Celia wondered if the man who'd approached Owen about Mr. Griffin's mysterious note wore a plaid coat.

"Wait!" Fulton, who'd returned to a chair near the Piersons, got to his feet. "I saw that fellow, too, Mr. Aldrich. Creeping about. I've never noticed a fellow in a plaid coat in the area before. He's got to be the killer. Remember me telling you I saw somebody suspicious, Detective Greaves?"

Heads turned to stare at Mr. Greaves. "You didn't mention a plaid coat, Fulton," he said.

"Well, I now recollect that he was wearing one, Detective."

"Thank you, Mr. Fulton. Please retake your seat," the coroner said. "Any description beyond what this man was wearing, Mr. Aldrich?"

"The rain was falling too heavily. I saw nothing else of interest besides that man and the wretched state of the roads in that area."

"You might wish to take your concerns about the roads to the city planning commission, Mr. Aldrich," Dr. Harris responded drily. "I see that you have a fresh bruise on your jawline, sir. How did you come by it?"

Mr. Aldrich shot a glance at Mr. Greaves before answering. "A clumsy stumble. I tripped over my dog and hit my chin on the edge of a table."

"Ah."

Dr. Harris dismissed him and called up Matthew Hollis, whose responses were much the same as Mr. Aldrich's. That he had been at Mr. Pierson's house, heard his plea to invest in his real estate brokerage, and departed about a half hour after arriving. Before Mr. Aldrich had done.

"Did you happen to observe a man dressed in plaid in the vicinity, Mr. Hollis?" the coroner asked.

"No, I didn't. Sorry."

The coroner cast Mr. Aldrich a look. "What about the condition of the roads, Mr. Hollis?"

Mr. Hollis smirked. "No comment."

Several people in the room snickered in response.

"Thank you," said the coroner. "Detective Greaves, you're next."

Nicholas Greaves had little to add, other than to provide information on Mr. Griffin's criminal background. The jurors tsk-tsked, expressing their opinion that such folks deserved their fates. Mr. Greaves concluded by stating that the drivers hired by Mr. Hollis and Mr. Aldrich that evening had testified that they did not witness the murder and had taken their passengers directly to their homes after they'd left Mr. Pierson's. He added that, after speaking with Mr. Aldrich yesterday, he'd requested that a notice be put in the newspapers requesting information on the suspicious man wearing a plaid coat.

Dr. Harris spoke last and relayed the findings of his autopsy. The contents of Mr. Griffin's stomach suggested he hadn't been drunk, so he should have been alert to any danger. Based on the wounds delivered, his assailant may have been around the same height as Mr. Griffin—who was not particularly tall, from what Celia remembered of him—but he could not be positive. There was only one defensive mark on his right forearm, which, in addition to the wound in his back, implied he'd been taken by surprise. Celia surveyed those in attendance at the inquest. Who among them was a similar height? And who among them might have been able to sneak up on a cautious man like Caleb Griffin?

After everything was concluded, the inquest returned the only verdict expected—that Caleb Griffin had "come to his death by the act of an unknown person by criminal means." Georgiana Pierson and her husband rushed off before Celia could speak with them. Mr. Pierson's hoped-for business partners did likewise. Nicholas Greaves stopped to speak with Dr. Harris before jogging after Celia.

He tapped his fingertips to the brim of his hat. "Morning, ma'am."

She acknowledged his greeting with a nod. "I presume, Mr. Greaves, that we are left to discover the identity of the mysterious man in the plaid coat."

"Unless Mr. Aldrich has invented the fellow."

"But Mr. Fulton also claimed to have seen him."

"Once he'd heard what Aldrich had to say," he replied.

"Ah." Perhaps Mr. Greaves was correct that the plaid-coated man was an invention. Did that then suggest that Mr. Aldrich might be guilty? Or Mr. Fulton, perhaps.

"I can see you pondering the few clues we have, ma'am." He inclined his head in the direction of the up-sloping road. "Shall we go for a stroll? Talk over what we know so far?"

He was inviting her to discuss a case? "I would happily, Mr. Greaves, except I would like to check on Owen. He was the person who informed me that Caleb Griffin had plans to collect on debts Monday evening. I need to be certain he is all right."

"You could've come to me with that information earlier, Mrs. Davies."

"I did note your unhappy surprise during my testimony, Mr. Greaves, but I only learned the particulars myself yesterday afternoon."

"Well, if you happen to run across any other particulars I might like to know, do feel free to share them."

"There is no need for sarcasm, Mr. Greaves." As she'd said to him numerous times before.

"When it comes to you, Mrs. Davies, I find I can't resist."

• • •

Celia stepped inside Roesler's Confectionery, the overhead bell jingling. Mr. Roesler, his torso swathed in a large white apron, beamed a welcoming smile.

"Good morning, madam." He swept an outstretched hand through the air above the massive glass display case he stood behind. "How might I assist you?"

The space exhaled the most heavenly aromas. That of chocolate and sugar-coated candies. Cinnamon and vanilla and a sweet like ripe berries.

"Is Owen Cassidy in today?" A hasty scan of the interior did not locate him, however. The room, long and narrow and filled with countertops displaying candy jars, held few niches to hide in.

Her question obliterated the smile from Mr. Roesler's face, and he squinted at her. "You're some relative of his, aren't you? I remember you now."

"Is Owen here or not?"

"Mr. Cassidy did not come in to work this morning, and if you know how to reach him, tell him he has been sacked. I'm not putting up with his nonsense any longer." He punctuated his statement with a fierce bob of his head.

"Owen did not come in," she repeated, unease gnawing.

"That is what I said, ma'am. And since you're here, you can take this, too. Since Mr. Cassidy has decided to not show up and collect it himself." He leaned down to retrieve an item from behind the counter. It was a square of hastily folded and sealed paper with Owen's name scrawled on its surface. Mr. Roesler handed it over. "Found it slipped under my door this morning when I opened up. Do I look like the U.S. Mail now?"

"I'll see that he gets it."

Mr. Roesler scowled. "Do you mean to purchase anything?"

"No. Thank you." Celia spun on her heel and rushed back outside, out into the busy streets. Perhaps Owen was ill. Perhaps that was why he'd not come to work today.

Or his absence was due to that note. That blasted note from Caleb Griffin. *He has put Owen in danger and I shall never forgive him.* His death, however, had put Mr. Griffin well beyond any need for her forgiveness.

Celia skittered sideways, like a crab upon a beach, out of the way of a gaggle of pedestrians striding along the pavement. She mumbled apologies. One fellow doffed his hat; the others ignored her. She moved to where she'd not be bowled down like a wicket and contemplated the envelope.

Forgive me, Owen, for prying.

She slid a finger beneath the seal. The outer wrapping enclosed a torn and crumpled piece of paper with a word and a sum of money written in a hand different than that on the outermost paper. *Validus* and five hundred dollars. The note Caleb Griffin had given Owen. It had to be. But why had it ended up at the confectionery? Unless Owen had been attempting to stash it someplace other than his lodgings. Although he could have brought the note to Roesler's himself when he arrived for work. Which he'd not done.

She tucked the note into her reticule, securing it tightly. She was familiar with where Owen lived, a boardinghouse not too far from Roesler's. Hopefully someone there knew more.

Hiking her skirts, she hopped over a pile of manure moldering in the gutter and dashed across the road. Down streets that led to the district of warehouses and docks. Men eyed her. One called out a crude remark. If she'd been carrying her medical bag, people would have offered more respect. Since she was not, she squared her shoulders and hurried on.

Owen's boardinghouse was as she remembered—wood-framed, the cream paint in need of retouching, a few shutters missing. Noxious odors rose from the sewer that passed beneath the street. It was the best Owen could afford, though, and not the worst accommodation. Those were in the dark alleyways near the Barbary, rooms shared with transient men as likely to knife you in your sleep for the few coins in your pocket as help divide the rent.

A ring of the bell at the building's front door summoned a weary-looking woman. She gave Celia a hasty look-over. "We don't rent rooms to ladies."

"I am not in need of housing."

Her answer raised the woman's eyebrows. "You'd better not be ringing the doorbell for any other reason."

Celia's cheeks heated. She'd been mistaken for a prostitute before and arrested.

"I am Owen Cassidy's cousin." The false claim had previously come in handy. "Might I speak with him? In your parlor, of course."

"Cassidy? He ain't here. I ain't seen him since yesterday."

Bloody . . . "Might anyone here know where he could be? He did not arrive at his workplace this morning, and his employer is concerned about him. As am I."

"Didn't show up at work?" she asked. "Sounds like trouble for sure. Wonder if he's cleaned out his things without telling me."

Cursing, she left the door open and stormed up the stairs. Celia followed. The landlady turned down a dark and musty hallway and opened an unlocked door to her left. "He ain't in here. And neither are his things, far as I can tell. Looks like he's cleared out."

Celia stepped inside the room, which was hardly larger than the pantry at her home. It contained only a cot, a chair with flaking paint, a washstand, and rows of empty hooks. A faded gingham curtain flapped in the wind blowing through the open window. "You did not see him with anyone yesterday, did you? A man in a plaid coat, for instance."

"Nope."

Dread knotted her stomach. *Blast it, Owen. What has happened? And where are you?*

• • •

"Well, what did you observe, Taylor?" Nick asked. He'd instructed Taylor to wait outside the undertaker's, watch the folks who'd been at Griffin's inquest as they left the building, and meet him outside the station when he'd finished. "Anything interesting?"

"Not much, sir. The Piersons dashed out of the place as fast as they could and climbed into a hack waiting on the curb for them." Taylor walked alongside Nick, his hands busy hunting his pockets for a cigar. "Although it did look like Mr. Pierson wanted to talk to Mr. Aldrich. Mrs. Pierson wasn't going to have any of it though, sir. Mr. Greaves, sir. She dragged Mr. Pierson away before he could say more than a word or two. Wonder what that was all about."

Nick related what Aldrich had told him about his disagreement with Pierson. "Sore feelings between those two. And not getting any better with Griffin getting killed in front of Pierson's house and Aldrich having to talk to the police about the crime."

"Mr. Aldrich suspected Mr. Pierson of profiting off arson, sir?"

"That's what he implied."

Nick's stomach took to rumbling. He'd been in such a rush to get out of Mrs. Jewett's house that morning that he'd missed breakfast and now it was almost lunch. He'd heard her humming in the kitchen as he'd slipped through the front door. Cheered by her success in bringing Nick and her niece together, he supposed. She wouldn't be happy when she figured out he intended to be away from the house for the rest of the day.

"I asked Harris if he thought Griffin was left-handed," Nick said.

"Sir?"

"The bruise on Aldrich's jaw. Maybe caused by a punch from a left-handed man. But it's the coroner's opinion that Griffin was right-handed. And there's no corresponding bruise on either of his hands suggesting he was the person who'd punched Aldrich." Who wanted everybody to believe he'd tripped over his dog.

"So who did punch him then, sir?" Taylor asked. "And does that bruise have anything to do with Mr. Griffin's murder?"

Nick shrugged. "What about Hollis? What did he do when he left the inquest?"

"He spoke to Mr. Aldrich for a couple of minutes before they went their separate ways. From what I could see it looked like a normal conversation. Not whispering together or anything like that," he replied. "And Mullahey trailed Mr. Fulton like you requested. He went back to his boardinghouse and stayed put. Mullahey wants to know if he should keep an eye on him."

"Yes. Fulton's the most likely suspect. He couldn't explain why Mrs. Davies saw him close to the Piersons' house around seven when he'd previously told me he hadn't been anywhere near there at that time," Nick said. "Plus, Aldrich repeated his story about a fellow dressed in a plaid coat near Pierson's. Fulton conveniently remembered him, too. Hollis didn't, though."

"The request for information about that plaid-coat fellow should be in the papers later today or tomorrow, sir." Taylor found a cigar—partly smoked—and paused to light it. "Should we maybe search Mr. Hollis's house for the coat? In case he returned to Mr. Pierson's house in some sort of disguise?"

"Yes, and while you're at it, have the fellows search Pierson's and Aldrich's too. Just to be thorough."

"But Mr. Pierson wouldn't have been walking along the street, would he, sir?" his assistant replied. "And Mr. Aldrich was the fellow who told you about the man to begin with."

"I'm not saying the request makes sense, I just want you to do it," Nick said. "And maybe Aldrich is counting on us thinking he's above suspicion, Taylor. Although, to be honest, I can't decide if this man in the plaid coat even exists."

"Will do." Taylor clenched his cigar in his teeth, located his notebook and pencil, and jotted a reminder.

"I also have to wonder about the timing of Georgiana Pierson's request that Mrs. Davies meet with her to discuss a missing locket," Nick said when his assistant had finished. "A meeting set up at the last minute for the very night Griffin was murdered in Mrs. Pierson's front yard."

"How could she have known that Mr. Griffin was going to get killed that night, though, Mr. Greaves?"

"Exactly, Taylor. How could she have known?"

Taylor frowned. "You mean *she* was behind Mr. Griffin's murder, sir? But, what reason would she have?"

"Mrs. Davies learned that Griffin was meaning to collect debts the day he died. Maybe Pierson was one of the folks who owed him money, and Mrs. Pierson didn't like that," he said. "Maybe she'd paid Fulton to get rid of the problem, since she didn't stab Griffin herself."

"But why leave Griffin dead in the Piersons' front yard?"

"Maybe it wasn't supposed to happen that way."

They halted at an intersection to let the traffic clear. Nick took advantage of the pause to scan their surroundings. One thing to like about morning—the lack of obvious crooks out on the streets. Just folks going about their legitimate business. Or at least looking like that's what they were doing.

"You know, Taylor, up until Mrs. Davies's testimony today, I was considering that Griffin had come to the Piersons' house because Georgiana Pierson had hired *him* to murder Edward Pierson. Or one of the other men, like Aldrich."

"Except Mr. Griffin got killed in the process?"

The idea had sounded far more sensible when Nick had entertained the thought last night. "Just a notion, Taylor."

"But why would she want her husband dead?" His assistant sounded as confused as Nick felt. "Or the other fellows?"

"As for her husband, maybe getting dismissed from the insurance agency for profiting off of fraud was simply the last straw in a whole host of straws," he answered. The traffic cleared and they crossed the street. "She doesn't seem to have much respect for Edward Pierson. She doesn't care for Aldrich, either."

Taylor's frown took to occupying his entire face. "Has Mr. Griffin ever been accused of murder, sir? I can't recollect any cases where he'd been a serious suspect."

"You're suggesting he wasn't that sort of a criminal."

"I'm just wondering why he'd start now if he'd never dabbled in killings before."

Nick reached up to massage the ache, the damned persistent ache, in his arm. "So maybe we're back to focusing on Fulton as the killer."

"Paid by Mrs. Pierson. And while on his rounds, he snuck up on Griffin and stabbed him." Taylor stepped out of the way of an aproned clerk hauling a crate into a lamp-and-oil store. "Wish I was able to make any sense out of those entries in Mr. Griffin's book, sir. Might help us."

"Keep trying."

Taylor squinted down the road. "Hey, sir, I think that's Mrs. Davies heading this way."

The woman strode up the sidewalk, her skirts kicking wide with every step. Her blue mantle was wrapped tight against the chilly breeze, the ribbons of her bonnet fluttering like streamers. "Looks like you're right, Taylor."

"Mr. Greaves, thank goodness. I am so glad to find you," she said, breathless. "It's Owen. He's gone missing and I am afraid he is in terrible danger."

"Are you sure he's missing?"

"I am positive, Mr. Greaves," she insisted. "He did not come to work this morning at the confectionery, nor has he been seen at his boardinghouse since late yesterday."

"But why be worried, ma'am?" Taylor asked around the stub of his cigar clenched in his teeth. "I mean, maybe he's just sick and holing up someplace."

A gust of wind snagged a tendril of her blond hair, and she impatiently swiped it away from her face. "Because Mr. Griffin gave Owen a note he was to keep safe, Mr. Taylor. At first glance, it does not appear to be particularly significant, but may have been dangerously significant."

Cassidy, when are you ever going to learn to avoid trouble? He was about as reckless as the woman standing in front of Nick. No wonder she'd taken to the kid; peas in a pod. "Why didn't you inform me right away when you learned about this note? Concealing more information, ma'am?"

She didn't answer straightaway, blinking for a few seconds instead.

"Is there something else you're not telling me, Mrs. Davies?"

She lifted her chin. "I am sorry that I did not immediately inform you about the note, Mr. Greaves."

The woman was damned frustrating. "Do you have it with you?"

"I do. It contains one word and a dollar amount. *Validus* and five hundred." She unknotted the strings of her purse and pulled out a crumpled piece of paper, handing it to him. "What do they mean, do you think?"

Well, well. "Validus is a thoroughbred racing horse that Aldrich owns."

"A racehorse again."

"Oh?"

"Jane told me that the falling-out between Mr. Aldrich and Mr. Pierson had to do with a racehorse," she said.

"Aldrich led me to believe Pierson had been tossed because he'd started to suspect Pierson of profiting off of false insurance claims."

"The cause could be both reasons, Mr. Greaves. Or neither," she replied. "All this aside, when Owen came to the house yesterday to ask about Mr. Griffin's death, he mentioned this very piece of paper and that some fellow had approached him at his boardinghouse Monday evening in search of it. A fellow named Johnny."

"There are probably dozens if not hundreds of men named Johnny in San Francisco, ma'am."

"I am aware, Mr. Greaves," she said. "Owen must be on the run and decided to stash the note at Mr. Roesler's for safekeeping. Fortunately for us, when I went there, Mr. Roesler gave it to me."

Nick inspected the piece of paper. Not much in the way of clues, aside from the strange way the bottom was ripped. "The rest of it has been torn off."

"Perhaps the portion with the signature? The message, whatever it means, is of less use without a signature."

"Taylor, go to Owen's boardinghouse and see if anybody remembers the man who visited him on Monday. Try to get a description."

Celia Davies gave him the address and Taylor hurried off. She looked up at Nick, her eyes filled with worry. If only he could assure her everything would be all right as nonchalantly as he'd told Miss Westerfield that her family's fortunes would turn out well. But he would never make an equally casual comment to Celia. He'd only ever been direct with her, honest. And he wasn't about to start making optimistic claims to reassure her now.

He folded the piece of paper and tucked it away. "We'll do what we can, ma'am, but I can't make any promises. His old friends, the folks who know Owen best, who know where he might be hiding, aren't the sort of people who like to talk to cops," he said. "I'll have the beat cops keep an eye out for him, though."

What would he tell them to look out for, though? A scrappy Irish kid with a worn wool cap and a battered jacket? A description that matched any number of Irish kids in town.

"Thank you, Mr. Greaves. I cannot ask you to do more." Her expression hardened with resolve.

"What are you planning, Mrs. Davies?"

She feigned an innocent expression. Celia Davies wasn't much of an actress, so her attempts to look harmless never fooled him. "Nothing more than asking the boys in my neighborhood if they know where Owen might be. That is all."

"I hate to tell you that I never believe you when you make statements like that, Mrs. Davies." She'd set her jaw, which made him even more concerned. *Blasted woman.* "Don't go looking for him on your own. If Owen, who's as wily a person as I know, has gotten in trouble, you are not going to avoid the same fate."

"I shall do what I must, Mr. Greaves, and *I* hate to tell you that you cannot stop me."

"Ma'am, what e'er is the matter? What happened at the inquest?" Addie rushed up the stairs behind Celia, scrambling as fast as she could and tripping over her skirts in the process. "Ma'am?"

"Owen has not been seen since yesterday evening, Addie."

"What?"

"Mr. Griffin gave Owen a note that is possibly linked to his murder." Celia threw open the door to her bedchamber. "Owen did not turn up at Roesler's this morning, and when I went to his boarding-house it was clear that he has fled."

Addie shrieked. "He's dead. The lad is dead. You're to tell me next he's been found in the bay." Her face, reflected in the looking glass set on Celia's dressing table, had gone as white as the linens on Celia's bed.

Through the downstairs rooms echoed Barbara's footsteps, drawn by Addie's cry.

"He is not dead, Addie," Celia replied, firmly enough to convince the both of them. "I believe he has gone into hiding from whomever it is who wants that note Mr. Griffin gave him."

"The lad should have come here if someone had threatened him. We would have protected him."

Barbara burst into the room. "What is it? Why did Addie scream?"

"It's Owen, Miss Barbara. He's gone missing."

"What are we going to do?"

"The police are searching for him, Barbara."

"And you expect them to find him?" she asked. "Just some Irish boy?"

Celia's own actions would answer her cousin's question soon enough. She sat at her dressing table and brought out her inlaid-wood jewelry box, retrieved its key from where it was stored, and released the lock.

"There *is* one person who might be able to help me find Owen," she said, ill over her plans. But what else was there for her to do? "Someone who has many friends among the Irish community." Not all of those friends respectable.

"Mr. Griffin is dead, ma'am," said Addie.

"Not him." Alongside the items made of paste, inexpensive pendants and brooches she wore to the few social occasions she attended, rested her mother's gold cobalt-enamel earrings, flowers picked out with diamonds, and a matching pin. She lifted them out with great care. *Only for Owen, Mama. I'd not ever do this if it were not the last resort.*

"Master Patrick," Addie fairly spat. "You canna be serious."

"But I am, Addie. Most serious."

• • •

Nick strode up the road to where a house not far from the Piersons' was under construction. He'd brought the gimlet with him. Maybe the tool belonged to one of the workers and Georgiana Pierson was right to have accused them. Its long thin shaft did make it an excellent murder weapon. Why use a gimlet, though? A knife was so much more common and versatile. Everybody carried a knife. Even Taylor.

It was early afternoon, and the building site buzzed with activity, the thwack of hammers echoing off a nearby brick building. Stacks of lumber and whatever was hiding in them had attracted a short-legged dog, which nosed around the piles. The carpenters would occasionally yell at it, driving it off, only for the dog to slink back.

One of the men working on the house noticed Nick standing at the edge of the lot. He set down his saw and walked over with a bowlegged stride. "You want something?"

Nick flapped aside his coat to reveal his badge.

The fellow balked. "We got a permit to be doin' this here work. I'll fetch the boss if you don't believe me."

"I'm not here to check your permits." He showed the fellow the gimlet without handing it over. "Might this be one of yours? Or one of your fellow workers'?"

"We ain't got a need for a gimlet. We're not building furniture."

"I thought they were also used to construct staircases."

"We're not putting up staircases yet, Officer." The frame of the building had just been erected.

"I see."

"And that's not one of ours. The boss has us mark the tools with the company sign, to keep them from walking off. Whatever is scratched on the handle isn't our sign."

Nick had noticed the two letters—A L—when Harris had returned the tool to him. "Someone's initials?"

"Probably," the fellow agreed.

Not ones belonging to any of the suspects, though.

Nick tucked the gimlet into his coat pocket, careful to arrange the pointed end so it wouldn't jab his hip. "Were you at work here on Monday?"

"The day that fellow was killed up the road?" he asked. "I was, even though it was rainin' pitchforks. Boss ain't got no sympathy for shirkers, but he let us knock off early."

"The local who does his rounds in this area stated at the coroner's inquest that he saw a man lurking hereabouts that day." A handful of nearby spots might make good hiding places. "Ever spot anybody hanging around who shouldn't be? A man in a plaid coat, for instance."

"Can't say that I did, Officer. Certainly not any fellow in a plaid coat," he replied. "But the local turning up for his rounds earlier than usual and acting jumpy? I did see that, Officer. Mighty strange."

• • •

"Was not expectin' to see you so soon, Celia." Patrick said, smiling.

This time, she'd not found him at his lodgings but at the other place he could reliably be located. Namely, the nearest saloon, one that featured billiards as an added incentive to step inside. No one was at the tables, so the space only hummed with the sound of voices and not ivory balls clacking against each other.

"I was not expecting to have to do so, Patrick."

"Well, 'tis lucky for you that you found me today. I was . . . away for a wee bit."

"I had heard."

The man who'd been standing alongside Patrick at the long bar tipped his dirty bowler hat—a polite reaction to the presence of a respectably dressed female who'd somehow found her way inside a tavern with sawdust-covered floors and a choking blue haze of cigar and cigarillo smoke—and shifted to make room for her, dragging his glass of lager with him.

"What is it you could be wantin' from me?" Patrick asked. "I do wonder. Caleb, perhaps?"

He was not prescient, but rather cannily good at comprehending other people's motivations.

She stepped as close to him as her wide skirts and her nerve would allow. Patrick slid his gaze up and down her length, noting her proximity, and smiled. Humiliation washed hot over her face. The sensation would pass.

"Do you know a lad named Owen Cassidy?"

"There would be plenty of Cassidys in this city, Celia." He waved off the barkeep, who'd wandered over—the fellow's protuberant eyes bulging even more with curiosity over the recently arrived well-attired female—to inquire if she would care for a drink. Or perhaps to demand that she ply her trade elsewhere. "You may have noticed we're fair crawlin' with Irishmen."

"Owen is a boy of around fifteen, with dark curling hair and green eyes. Of average size and wears a tattered wool cap."

Patrick shifted to face the other occupants of the saloon, which only numbered a handful. "Any of you lads heard of an Owen Cassidy?"

Every eye turned to stare, setting Celia's heart to racing. "Patrick, what are you doing?"

"You want me to help you find him. I would just be followin' through."

"I hardly want everyone in San Francisco to become aware that I am looking for him," she whispered. "Owen fell in with Caleb Griffin and I am afraid he is in serious trouble."

Patrick lazily ran his fingertip around the rim of his whiskey glass. "If he fell in with Caleb and his lot, he *is* in serious trouble."

"Have you heard anything in particular?"

"Not a word, Celia, because I haven't the time to care."

"You warned me about other dangerous men and now Mr. Griffin is dead," she said. "What is it you know?"

Patrick's gaze skimmed over the man standing at the bar beyond Celia. She could hear the fellow slurping his lager, so he must have crept nearer. "You there, what is it you're doin' now?"

"Nothin'." The man scuttled backward.

Satisfied he'd moved out of hearing, Patrick answered her question. "Griffin got on the wrong side of a handful of prominent fellows. He was meanin' to leave town. Lay low for a time. 'Tis all I know."

"Any names?"

"I know where my nose belongs, Celia, and it's not pokin' in other folks' business."

A respectful reticence he must have recently acquired. "You have to help, Patrick. I do not know who else to turn to."

"'Tis touching that you need me." He tossed back his whiskey, eyeing her over the rim of the glass before setting it down. "I thought you were cozy with the coppers. That's what me brother told me. Have them help."

"I could have let your brother rot in jail and then hang for my friend's murder, Patrick. He was the only suspect in her death." The painful memories, the emotions had not faded in the intervening months. "But I did not. Instead, I did all that I could to make sure the real killer was found. If that required becoming 'cozy' with the police, then that was what was necessary."

She'd met Nicholas because of her friend's death, discovered that he was a just and good man. Unlike the one she'd wed, who was grinning because he had succeeded in riling her.

"And I am thankin' you over and over, my dear."

"You owe me a favor, then, do you not agree?"

"Me *brother* owes you a favor, but I am listenin' to what you have to say."

She scanned the room for watchful eyes. Satisfied the other customers had lost interest in her, Celia retrieved the coins she'd stashed deep inside her pocket. She held them out for only a few seconds, long enough for Patrick to assess the amount she held, before returning them to the safety of her skirts.

"There will be an equal amount if you locate Owen Cassidy."

"That's not much, Celia. I might be riskin' my life." Those were his words, but even the offer of a scant few dollars would appeal to Patrick Davies. He could never refuse money; he was always so desperately in need of it.

"It is all I have, and I suspect you will not do anything that might risk your life." She considered him. "Tell me you are not responsible, Patrick."

He signaled for more whiskey. The saloonkeeper happily obliged the request and topped up his glass. "For Caleb's death?"

"Are you, Patrick? Are you?"

"I was away from the city, Celia, and I'd paid him his money," he said, his voice hard. "I'd no reason to kill Caleb Griffin."

Could she believe him? She had to. "I need your help, Patrick."

His expression was serious as his eyes held hers. It had been a long time since she had seen him this way. "The lad could be dead, Celia."

"Don't you think I realize that, Patrick? Don't you understand that is what I am afraid of?" she asked. "The police will do what they can, but *you* are acquainted with the people he may be in trouble with. Or who may be hiding him."

"Those men he might be in trouble with will be after you next."

"Then help me find Owen and who might be after him before they come for me."

He held her gaze and then moved nearer. She had a frightening thought that he meant to kiss her. But he sat back and the moment passed.

"Now, look. You've made me act all serious, and you know I don't like to be like that." He tossed back his second whiskey, wiping his sleeve across his mouth when he'd finished. "I'll do what I can."

"Thank you."

"Maybe I'll take the money you've promised me and buy a ticket out of here. You'd be happy if I left again, wouldn't you?" His voice took on a tinge of regret. He was regretful even more infrequently than he was serious.

"I am sorry, Patrick. I am sorry our marriage did not work."

"Celia, my dear, so am I. Very sorry."

Hastily, she retrieved the coins she'd brought and handed them to him. Her hands were shaking. She had no use for the emotions, old and worn-out, that he'd excavated with his words, though. "Be careful."

He winked. "I am always careful. They couldn't kill me in Mexico. Nothing will happen now."

Without another word, Celia hurried from the saloon and out into the afternoon. She rushed up the road, her haste drawing a reproving look from a matron stepping down from a carriage, merchants bustling along the pavement.

Slow down. Calm down.

She drew in a breath and crossed the road, hurrying around wagons and carts clogging the always busy street. She'd likely thrown good money after bad by asking Patrick to hunt for Owen, but she was desperate. And possibly an idiot.

She glanced back at the saloon. A fellow in an ill-fitting, faded army overcoat darted behind a stack of barrels on the curb. Celia reached the other side of the road and increased her pace, risking a quick look over her shoulder. There he was again, following her but not wanting her to realize it. Had he been one of the men inside the saloon? The place had been too dark to be certain and she'd not paid close-enough attention to the other occupants. There was, however, no doubt he was trailing her.

Her heart began to race. She searched the road for the comforting gray of a policeman's uniform, not spotting any. *Blast.* She certainly could not take off running in her dragging skirts and crushingly tight corset and hope to elude the fellow. *Maybe Georgiana Pierson will fortuitously happen along and offer me a ride again.* He was closing in, slipping between the pedestrians occupying the pavement with the ease of a river lamprey.

Just then, a hackney pulled over to let out a pair of gentlemen.

"Driver!" she shouted, running to catch him up before he steered the cab away. He waited and she scrambled aboard. "Broadway and Kearny, please."

Only after she'd settled against the seat and the hackney driver slapped the reins over the horse's flanks did she dare look out the window. The fellow in the old army overcoat stood on the opposite corner, watching as the carriage drove away.

• • •

"We didn't get too many questions answered at the inquest this morning, did we, Greaves?" Harris took the detectives' office chair Nick typically reserved for folks he was interviewing. The coroner removed his hat and stretched out his legs, looking far more relaxed than the usual occupants. "Aside from Mrs. Davies's unexpected statement. Did you know?"

"I didn't. And the kid who told her about Griffin intending to collect debts has gone into hiding." *At least I hope that's what Owen has done.* "So we won't be getting more information out of him any time soon."

"A pity," Harris said. "You know, Greaves, I've been thinking about where exactly Griffin had been killed. Yes, there was evidence his body had been moved, but from how far away? Hauling a man's corpse—

especially that of a man as robust as Mr. Griffin—from the scene of the murder to some other location is not easy to pull off, as you're aware. Also, the job requires the good luck to not be spotted. Pierson doesn't have a lot of neighbors but his house isn't isolated."

"The foul weather worked in the killer's favor, that's for certain," Nick said, momentarily distracted by a fly that had flown into the room through the open window. It buzzed around in uncertain circles. *My sympathy, fly. I'm just as confused.* "What about the weapon used? Odd choice, don't you think?"

"Worked like a charm, though." Harris swatted a hand in the air, shooing away the insect.

"Mrs. Pierson wants us to believe that a carpenter was hanging around after he was finished for the day, waiting to plunge a gimlet into Griffin," Nick said. "A worker I spoke with didn't recognize the markings on the handle, though. Didn't belong to any of the men on his building team."

"The gimlet could have come from another group of men building nearby."

"I'm still favoring Fulton, Harris." Nick leaned back and stared at the edge where the ceiling met the wall. For some reason, the fly had chosen to settle there. "That same fellow remarked on how odd the local was acting on Monday. Jumpy."

"Plotting a murder?"

"Maybe," he said. "There's this, too. Owen Cassidy—do you know who I mean?—is the kid who told Mrs. Davies about Griffin's debt. I think he may have gone into hiding because of a note Griffin gave him the day he was killed and that Cassidy was supposed to keep safe. Mrs. Davies got ahold of the note. It might be an IOU for a bet placed on a racehorse. The name on the piece of paper was Validus, a horse Aldrich owns."

"Validus is a promising thoroughbred. He won big at Bay View Park earlier this year."

"I didn't know you were interested in horse racing, Harris."

"A weakness of mine that my wife tolerates only because I don't lose much money. I'd never want to be in her bad graces, so I watch myself." He smiled. Nick had never met Mrs. Harris and the coroner rarely mentioned her, but when he did it was always with love. *Lucky man.* "You know, Greaves, I recall that Mr. Aldrich was involved in a scandal a month or so ago at the Ocean House Course. A horse set to race against one of his animals unexpectedly died. Mr. Aldrich's trainer was accused of poisoning the creature, but there was insufficient proof to bring charges."

"Aldrich's trainer wasn't Caleb Griffin, by any chance, was he?"

"I don't recall the man's name, but wouldn't it be fascinating to discover that Mr. Griffin was once employed at the Ocean House Course?"

"You know what I think," said Nick. "I went to speak with Hollis at his office. There's a painting on the wall of a thoroughbred, although he said it wasn't his. But three people in this case—Aldrich, Griffin, Hollis— are all connected to horse racing? *Has* to be important. Plus, Mrs. Davies has heard a rumor that Aldrich and Pierson had a quarrel over a racehorse."

"Sounds like you're due a visit to the Ocean House Course, Greaves," Harris said. "Validus is set to race on Friday. Day after tomorrow."

The fly descended from the ceiling and landed on Nick's desk. Nick smacked it with his open palm, the retort as startling as a gunshot. "Guess I am."

• • •

"You pawned you mother's jewelry?" Barbara's dark eyes were wide with shock. She and Addie had been in the parlor, waiting for Celia to return.

Celia carefully peeled off her gloves, an exhibition of calm that belied having just returned from a nerve-racking meeting with Patrick. A meeting that had been followed by an unidentified man trailing her.

"Perhaps a patient will come along who is so generous that I will be able to afford to retrieve it."

"That will ne'er happen, ma'am," Addie stated flatly. "Not to speak unkindly about the women you serve."

"Or perhaps I shall find Georgiana Pierson's missing locket and accept the fee she offered." Discovering its whereabouts might be as far-fetched a scenario as having a wealthy patient parade into her clinic. "I do mean to look for the item, though. Whether she pays me or not."

"Did Cousin Patrick agree to help find Owen?" Barbara asked.

"The money I offered persuaded him. At this point, I have no choice but to have faith he will follow through." Having faith Patrick Davies would do as she'd asked and simply not run off with the money could probably be added to the list of far-fetched scenarios. "As you recommended, Addie, I did not give Patrick the full amount up front. I promised him the rest if he successfully locates Owen."

Although will the lad be alive or dead? Patrick had expressed what he'd believed.

She folded her gloves with as much deliberation as when she'd removed them from her hands and set them on the entry hall table. Her fingers were not as steady, however, when they undid her bonnet ribbons.

Addie's watchful gaze took note. "Come into the parlor and sit, ma'am. You've had a terrible shock. We've all had a terrible shock."

Celia dropped onto the chair by the window. She would tell Addie about the man in the army overcoat later, once Barbara was out of the room. Once she'd had a chance to think through what had happened. Perhaps her conversation with Patrick had caused her to imagine danger where it had not truly existed. Perhaps.

• • •

The rain hadn't materialized, leaving the night strangely peaceful. Stars blinked between the breaks in the low-hanging clouds that streamed in the sky like wisps of pale white hair. It would be a good night for smoking, if he'd ever taken up the habit. Nick stretched out his legs and leaned a shoulder against the back-porch post. Out in the yard, Riley bounded around like he was crazy or like he never had a chance to explore the yard after dark, even though the dog went out every night before Nick turned in.

Behind him, the rear door swung open, squeaking on its hinges. He should probably fix that for his landlady, but he never seemed to get around to anything except police work and moping after Celia Davies.

"You don't have to worry about me, Mrs. Jewett," he said without turning to look. "I'm okay. Just enjoying the fine night."

"It's Violet." She eased the door shut so that it did not creak. "Am I interrupting you?"

Nick dragged his feet underneath him so he could stand.

"There's no need for you to get up, Mr. Greaves."

"It wouldn't be right for me to stay seated, miss."

"All right." She hugged a shawl around her torso and went to stand near the other porch post. "It's nice out here without all the rain."

"It is, and I don't usually have a chance to enjoy it." The lot the house sat on was elevated above the one behind it, which provided a bit of privacy for anybody seated on the rear porch.

"You must be very busy in a city this large."

"There's plenty of police and detectives to handle the load, miss." Even if Briggs couldn't be relied on all the time.

"Have you resolved your case? Have you found a perpetrator?"

"Not yet. So I won't have much time to hang around Mrs. Jewett's, Miss Westerfield. Socialize with you."

She was looking at him, the light coming through the kitchen window reflecting in the whites of her eyes. "Who is she, Mr. Greaves?"

He turned away as if he hadn't heard her question, watching his dog snuffle in the weeds against the fence.

She wasn't about to be ignored, though. "My aunt has mentioned a woman."

"I'm not going to court you, Miss Westerfield, or anybody, if that's what you're after. I'm sorry."

He glanced over. His bluntness had caused her to flinch but she recovered quickly. He did like her. From what he'd observed, she was tough and smart. A good woman. But he doubted he'd ever love her, and he would never marry a woman he didn't love.

"It's me who should be apologizing, Mr. Greaves."

"There's been more than one woman, Miss Westerfield, to answer your question. I was once in love with a good friend's wife." Frank's first wife, who'd been as perfect as an angel. But she'd preferred Frank Hutchinson, a man with ambition who was going places, over a rough cop like Nick, who wasn't. With time, he'd discovered that his feelings for her had been nothing more than infatuation.

"Is she still alive?"

"No, Miss Westerfield, she isn't." His voice didn't even shake when he spoke those words. Maybe he really had gotten over his feelings for her. Riley trotted over and climbed the porch steps to sit at Nick's feet. He reached down to ruffle the dog's ears. "She left behind a baby girl, though, who's become a fine young woman and is very like her, in some ways." Lucky Frank, to have both Grace and Jane.

"Aunt Martha gave me the impression there was someone recent," Miss Westerfield said quietly, almost to herself.

They *had* been spending a lot of time discussing Nick. "Your aunt is no doubt referring to Mrs. Celia Davies." Her name making it sound as though he only pursued married women. "A friend of hers was murdered and I was the detective on the case. That's how we met."

Miss Westerfield gathered herself, rearranging her shawl around her chest and hugging it even more tightly. Turning it into a protective shield, either against the cool night air or against him. Or maybe even against her feelings. "I'm prying, aren't I?"

"I don't mind," he said, not wanting to hurt her. Maybe it was good to sort through his emotions, take them out and examine them like old letters. Hunting for truth among the memories that could prove to be so false, colored as they were by intervening years. "I also presume your aunt has mentioned that Mrs. Davies—who was believed to be a widow at the time we first met, until her husband managed to rise from the dead—doesn't come around anymore."

And, until Monday, they hadn't had any cause to have dealings with each other.

"She has, Mr. Greaves. And since you don't mind my prying," she said, a smile in her voice, "I've got to ask why you aren't interested in courting anyone, Mr. Greaves. Since the woman you are currently in love with is out of reach."

Nick shifted to face her directly. "I honestly wish I could say. Stubbornness? Stupidity?"

"Might I suggest 'hopefulness,' Mr. Greaves?"

"Seems pretty stupid to hope Mrs. Davies's status as a married woman changes, Miss Westerfield."

"You wouldn't be the first person unable to persuade their heart to cease caring, Mr. Greaves," she said, her words as soft as the air and those wispy clouds. "And who knows? Maybe fortune will smile on you and you can one day be with her."

"Dame Fortune hasn't ever been on my side, miss." And he wouldn't hold his breath waiting for a change in her benevolence. "And wishing for a man's death isn't something I usually do."

"I didn't mean to suggest you would." She held out her hand, and he took it in his. Her skin was as warm and soft as her voice, but he preferred the hands and voice of another woman. "I am taking a brief excursion to Cliff House tomorrow and will be heading home on Friday morning, Mr. Greaves. If we do not see each other before I leave, please keep in touch and let me know what happens with you and Mrs. Davies, will you?"

"You'll probably see me again before you leave, Miss Westerfield." He squeezed her fingers before releasing them. "Good luck to you. Find somebody who deserves you."

"You too, Mr. Greaves."

"Me? There isn't anybody who deserves to get stuck with me."

"Oh, the right woman will not find life with you to be a hardship," she replied. "Because she will be someone special."

CHAPTER 11

Thursday morning had dawned without any news about Owen. Disappointing, but Celia knew it was unreasonable to expect an update already. Mr. Greaves and Mr. Taylor were occupied with uncovering Mr. Griffin's killer and Patrick . . . *Patrick will do what he wants.* Which might not coincide with her wishes.

She dashed across the street, bound for the secondhand fancy goods shop on the corner. The third one she'd visited from the list Georgiana Pierson had made. With each unsuccessful visit, Celia was growing more convinced that Georgiana had sent her on a wild-goose chase. An escapade as dubious as the woman's insinuation that the wealthy and distinguished Mr. Aldrich had taken her missing locket.

Or was her insinuation dubious? How above suspicion was the man? After all, Mr. Aldrich was the fellow whose horse, Validus, was named on a note that Mr. Griffin had been desperate to secrete away on the day of his death. The same fellow whose client, Mr. Everett, had lost his stationery store to a case of arson.

"Less than twenty-four hours before Mr. Griffin was murdered," Celia murmured aloud, catching the eye of a passing businessman, who frowned at her. Women muttering to themselves on busy city streets could be questionable individuals.

She halted outside the fancy goods shop and stared up at its sign. A tastefully discreet placard for a business that catered to gentlemen—and gentlewomen—who did not wish to reveal that they were in desperate need of funds and were willing to part with their precious belongings for less than their worth. A shop as different as chalk and cheese from the numerous rough-and-tumble pawn offices in the city. Places where protecting one's reputation mattered little when one needed money to pay for food or rent.

Celia inhaled deeply, her breath, restricted by her corset, catching at the end. Armed with the description of Georgiana Pierson's missing locket, she went inside. The door opened noiselessly, not even a shop bell to announce her arrival. The half-closed window shades permitted very little light into the space, a lantern set upon the display case all that chased away the gloom. It was a shallow, compact room, the walls covered in blue flock-paper, mirrors and paintings and photographs suspended from a picture rail. A set of shelves held examples of parian ware, figurines and bowls and pitchers in creamy white.

She crossed to the case. There were no cast-off inexpensive items in this shop. No one's dull-edged Bowie knife. No one's belt clasps or iron buttons or brass spurs. Gold and silver watches, earrings, engraved money clips . . . those were plentiful and elegantly arrayed on purple velvet.

The curtain covering a door beyond the case swished open, and a woman stepped through. Celia was surprised; few women operated businesses such as this one. She was dressed even more soberly than Celia, and everything about her was neat and tidy, from her clean lace collar down to the white cuffs trimming her sleeves.

"Can I help you, ma'am?"

"Are you the proprietor?" Celia asked.

A frown crossed the woman's face; she must, though, be used to the question. "Along with my husband, who is away at the moment. Would you prefer to come back later, when he has returned?"

"No, no. I was simply surprised—pleasantly so—to find myself dealing with a woman."

"How can I help?"

Celia settled into the story she'd contrived. "I have a soiree to attend next week and was looking for a piece of jewelry to match my attire. A locket or pendant in gold, I think. With a bit of filigree work to match the embroidery on my gown. Might you have any items like that?"

"Indeed we do. There is a locket right here that might suit." With a manicured finger, she indicated the item inside the case.

"Ah, yes. That may be precisely right. Might I examine it?"

The woman withdrew the locket from the case and handed it to Celia. It was not as heavy as it should have been if it was solid gold. She held the locket up to the lantern. Its surface was embedded with small gemstones, but they were not the garnets Georgiana had described. Nor was a dedication engraved inside. Perhaps this was not the correct secondhand shop. Or perhaps Georgiana Pierson's story about a stolen locket *was* a complete fabrication.

"This one will not work for me." Celia handed it back. "Is this all you have? I was hoping for one with garnets or rubies to complement the crimson of my gown."

The shopkeeper paused while she assessed Celia, possibly questioning if she actually had the funds necessary for the purchase. "I do have another locket, which I received only the other day."

So recently? "I would like to see it, thank you."

"Of course." Crouching down, the woman rummaged in the area beneath the display cabinet. She produced a small plain box and removed the piece of jewelry. "We haven't had the opportunity to put it on display yet."

Carefully, as if the locket had been fashioned from glass and not metal, the shopkeeper handed it over.

"Oh, it is quite lovely." Celia was not exaggerating. The filigree work upon its surface was profuse, elaborate, and stunning. The garnets had been cut to sparkle a lush, deep red in the lamplight. She released the latch to reveal an inscription on the inside of the lid. *To G from E.*

"The gentleman who sold it was distressed to have to part with such a fine article of craftsmanship," the shopkeeper commented.

A gentleman. "How remarkable. This locket appears to have belonged to a dear friend of mine. In fact, I am quite positive it is hers." Celia looked up from the locket, straight into the woman's eyes. "Mrs. Aldrich did tell me that her husband had been forced to part with some of their family jewelry. So tragic to find it here, do you not agree?"

"Many people do unexpectedly find themselves in difficult situations, madam," she said, her face not revealing if Mr. Aldrich had been the gentleman seller.

"As I am sadly aware."

The woman narrowed her eyes. "Do you mean to purchase the locket, madam?"

"How much?"

The woman named a sum Celia could not remotely afford.

"Not at the moment, but thank you." Celia handed it back and departed, the shopkeeper staring after her.

She crossed to where she could catch the Mission Railroad car headed north, rather than walk all the way home. What was she to make of finding that locket? Which was, curiously, brought in only a few days ago, long after the Piersons' party. Without the name of the seller, however, Celia had learned nothing of use. She stepped onto the curb where a crowd, peering down the road for sight of the horsecar, waited. She joined them in watching for its arrival. A fellow wove in and out of the pedestrians farther along the sidewalk, his pace brisk as he headed in Celia's direction. A man in an oversized gray Army coat.

Bloody . . . where is that car?

It swung around the corner, the horse clopping smartly up the cobbles. She rushed to grab the railing and haul herself aboard before it came to full stop. Before the man could reach her.

• • •

Taylor poked his head around the half-open door to the detectives' office. "The fellows have searched Mr. Aldrich's and Mr. Hollis's house for that plaid coat, Mr. Greaves, sir. No luck."

Nick set down the pencil he'd been using to jot his thoughts about Griffin's murder. He hadn't exactly had a flood of ideas, so he'd only written a handful of words—*gimlet, Aldrich, Hollis, Pierson, torn note, Validus, five hundred dollars. Arson at Everett's. Dispute at insurance agency. A man wearing a plaid coat. Taken by surprise. Poisoned racehorse? Fulton's exact location at time of murder.*

"Has the notice about the fellow in plaid shown up yet in the papers, Taylor?"

His assistant took a chair. "It's in the *Morning Call* and the *Alta California* already."

"Good."

"One of the officers is at Mr. Pierson's right now. Should be finished, actually," he said, glancing at the clock on the wall.

And likely not finding a plaid coat.

"I had a chance to speak with Mrs. Aldrich about Monday evening, sir. Didn't appreciate me interrupting her tea, though," Taylor said. "Never seen a woman with a stiffer back. Well, other than Mrs. Davies sometimes."

That would be a sight. "Did she say when her husband arrived back at their house after his trip to Pierson's?"

Taylor retrieved his notebook to consult. "Before seven thirty, she thinks, sir."

"Enough time to murder Griffin?"

"Maybe, sir," his assistant replied. "She told me his clothing was damp from the rain. Got awful mad when I asked if there was any blood on it."

Wives could be touchy like that. "And Hollis?"

"He's not married, but his live-in maid said he got home around quarter 'til seven. He doesn't live too far from the Piersons," he said. "She wasn't near as bothered by the blood question. None noticed."

"Which puts Hollis at his house around or before when Griffin was killed."

"Sounds like, Mr. Greaves. But not Mr. Aldrich."

"I don't care for the fellow, you know." Nick was still stinging from having to pay for lunch the other day.

Mullahey rapped on the doorframe. "Mr. Greaves. Taylor."

Nick waved him inside. "Any update on Fulton?"

"He didn't meet with anybody yesterday after the inquest. Huddled in his room at the boardinghouse all day. Didn't even go out for his rounds."

"Maybe he doesn't work on Wednesdays," Taylor suggested.

"Wish I had a day off now and again," Mullahey said, winking.

"You're too good a cop to want a day off, Mullahey," Nick replied.

He grinned. "One of the beat officers who works Fulton's neighborhood is keeping an eye on him today," he added. "Oh, and I got information on a kid who might know where Cassidy is hiding."

Nick jumped up from his chair. "Taylor, check on how the cop is doing at the Piersons'. Mullahey, let's go."

• • •

"Oh, it's you, Mrs. Davies and not the police again." Georgiana had answered Celia's ring of the doorbell herself. "Mercifully."

"The police were here?" Celia asked.

"They searched our house. It's ridiculous."

Georgiana Pierson was dressed in an indigo-blue walking dress, the pelisse and skirt matching and both heavily braided in black. A costume for going out.

"Is this a bad time, Mrs. Pierson?"

"No. No, not at all. My husband is away," she replied. "Have you found my locket?"

"Yes. At one of the shops you suggested I visit."

"Ah, good!" Georgiana gestured for Celia to step inside. A maid, outfitted in a drab olive-colored dress originally tailored for a woman both stouter and taller, peered at them from the top of the staircase. Georgiana glanced up at her and she scurried away. "I do not know why I employ that girl when it's always me having to answer the door." She sighed dramatically. "We can talk in the family sitting room, Mrs. Davies."

Georgiana glided down the entry passage, past the curved staircase. Celia's aunt had attempted to teach her how to stroll gracefully like a "proper lady," but Celia had never mastered the art. Much to her aunt's dismay.

Beyond the parlor, Georgiana Pierson turned into the room. Its proportions and fixtures did make it an elegant space, as elegant as Celia had first thought it to be when she'd been searching for muddy footprints on the Turkey carpet. Perhaps Mr. Pierson *had* borrowed money from Mr. Griffin, his wife's uncurbed expenditures on household furnishings taking a toll on his finances.

"There have been gawkers every hour of the day. Even out here, where hardly anybody lives," said Georgiana, gesturing at the bay window's closed draperies. "I caught two boys peeking over the side fence this morning."

"There are not any gawkers outside at the moment."

"Thank goodness." She shut the door behind Celia, a veil of secrecy protecting them from the maid, she supposed. Perhaps the young woman could creep into the adjacent kitchen, however, and listen at the door that presently hung ajar. "Do you have it, Mrs. Davies? Do you have my locket?"

"I did not have the necessary funds."

"Oh, yes. Of course," she said. "But at least we have proof that it was taken from this house and sold. By J. Lyman Aldrich, I should add."

"My finding it merely proves that the locket had been sold, Mrs. Pierson. Not that Mr. Aldrich was the one who'd done the selling," Celia pointed out.

"You may say that, but I know what I believe."

Clearly. "The shopkeeper mentioned that they've had the locket for only a couple of days. I thought your party was held several weeks ago, Mrs. Pierson."

Georgiana hesitated. "He held on to my locket to reduce suspicion, Mrs. Davies. That must be the explanation. If he'd sold it immediately, it would've been obvious that he was the person who took it from the safe."

"Ah."

"Let me get the money I promised you," she said before Celia could ask more, uncomfortable questions. "I will take matters from here."

Georgiana collected a lacquered box that sat upon the fireplace mantel and retrieved some coins from inside, giving them to Celia. Five dollars. Not quite enough to redeem her ticket at the pawnbroker for her mother's jewelry. She informed Georgiana where she could find the locket and tucked the coins inside her reticule.

Georgiana stuck out her hand. "Thank you, Mrs. Davies. Should we never meet again, I must tell you it has been a pleasure to make your acquaintance."

Celia took the woman's fingers, which returned Celia's grasp with a limp handshake. "We will likely meet again, Mrs. Pierson. The matter of who murdered Mr. Griffin has yet to be resolved."

"I thought you told me that you're not an investigator, Mrs. Davies. Your part is done, isn't it?"

"I sincerely doubt that I am finished, Mrs. Pierson."

She bid the woman goodbye and headed outside and down the stairs to the walkway. She paused near the spot where Caleb Griffin had lain. It looked innocent enough, no visible indication that a man had been killed there, any blood having washed away. Celia glanced at the house. Was it actually possible that Edward Pierson hadn't heard the assault? Mr. Griffin might not have cried out, though. The thrust of the gimlet to his neck may have effectively cut off his ability to do so. Although the thrust to his neck was not the first blow delivered.

Gruesome, Celia.

She turned toward home, the first sprinkles of rain, which the lowering clouds had threatened all day, beginning to fall. She'd gone only a dozen feet down the road when she heard Georgiana's voice, lecturing her maid on the front porch. Her walking dress *had* indicated she meant to go out. But to where? Someplace nearby, since there was not a carriage waiting for her. And why was she acting as though she did not want to be noticed, nervously scanning her surroundings as she hurried down her front walk and out the gate?

Celia hastily slipped behind a half-built fence and peered around its edge. Georgiana strode up the road then dashed across it. There were few houses along the increasingly steep side of Russian Hill and very few neighbors to visit as a result. She abruptly stopped, as if someone had called to her. She glanced down the road and Celia ducked out of sight. *This is quite ludicrous, Celia.* After a few seconds, she risked a look around the fence. Was that Georgiana with a man? It was, indeed. And if memory served, the fellow was Mr. Fulton, the local policeman.

"Mrs. Davies?"

Heart jumping, she spun to face the man who'd addressed her. "Good heavens, Mr. Taylor. You startled me."

"What are you doing, ma'am?"

"I was spying on Mrs. Pierson." She got to her feet with Mr. Taylor's assistance and swiped a hand across her dress where it had collected dirt. "She was up the road speaking with Mr. Fulton. I do not see her any longer, however." Her or the local.

Mr. Taylor ran up Vallejo, in search of Georgiana Pierson. Celia retraced her steps, straight up to the front door of the Piersons' house, and rang the bell.

The maid, startled, answered. "Ma'am? Mrs. Pierson isn't at home anymore."

"Did she tell you where she was going? Who she was meeting?"

"She'd *never* tell me where she was going, ma'am."

"No. I suppose she'd not." Celia considered the girl. "Were you employed here when Mrs. Pierson's locket was stolen?"

She looked offended. "Did she blame me for taking her jewelry?"

Curiously not, even though a maid would be the most logical first person to blame. *Unless you were determined to blame someone else.* "You were employed here at the time of the party, then."

"I was, although the first I heard about some stolen locket was a few days ago."

Mr. Taylor jogged back, halting outside the Piersons' gate. "Didn't spot her or Mr. Fulton anyplace, ma'am."

"Blast, Mr. Taylor."

• • •

Nick halted across the street from the bowling alley—and liquor saloon, although the sign for the tavern was a lot less obvious than the sign for the alley—Mullahey stopping alongside him.

"Not sure I want to know how you got this kid's name, Mullahey." A good friend of Cassidy's, according to what the officer had learned. A friend who was possibly also acquainted with Caleb Griffin.

Mullahey grinned. The expression twisted his misshapen nose, broken in a brawl when he'd been a younger cop. "Called in some favors, Mr. Greaves."

From one of his fellow Irishmen, no doubt. "Wait out here, but don't go too far. Just in case. And make it look like you're not with me."

"Will do."

Nick took the steps leading down to the bowling alley's entrance, guarded by a fellow in shirtsleeves whose suspenders struggled to stretch across his girth.

"We're all full, mister." His voice was almost drowned out by the crack of *lignum vitae* balls striking pins and the shouts of exuberant bowlers. "But there's space in the saloon, if you'd care to wait there."

"I'm not here to bowl. I've got business with one of your pin setters. Thomas O'Brien is his name."

Nick surveyed the alley, gas lanterns battling the blue pall of smoke that hung in the air. Men crowded around two chest-high tables, arguing over scoring or just simply arguing. There were two lanes, constructed of what looked to be pine planking, with an elevated rail in between them that held the balls. At the far end of the lanes, two tall chairs were occupied by boys waiting to reset any fallen pins. A bowler stepped up and released a ball, which arced through the air and landed with a thud halfway down the lane's length.

The man at the door winced at the sound. "Durn it. I hate when they do that."

"So, is Thomas here?"

"Can I ask what your business is with Tommy? Cuz he's sorta busy right now."

"A mutual friend of ours is very ill and wants him to come. Right now."

The doorman gave Nick a once-over. "You and Tommy have a mutual friend?"

When he'd first become a detective, nobody had warned Nick about the amount of patience required to do the job. Not even Uncle Asa, who'd convinced him to pursue the occupation in the first place. "Is he here or not?"

"All right, all right. Don't get testy. Tommy's here, but he can't come with you to see this friend. I need him." The man frowned and tugged on his suspenders. "He can talk for a bit. Only a couple of minutes, you understand? He'll have to wait until he's finished for the day to visit your mutual friend who's poorly."

Wincing as another ball thudded onto a lane, he signaled for the boy on the leftmost chair.

The lad looked around, confused, before hopping down from his seat and running over to them. "Is somebody complainin' again?"

"No, Tommy. This here fellow wants to talk to you about a terribly ill friend of yours."

He looked young, younger than Cassidy. Maybe it was the freckles covering his face that made Nick think so, because Tommy O'Brien's gaze was as shrewd as that of any man who'd seen too much of the world.

He eyed Nick the same way the doorman had. "Oh, yeah? Didn't know any of my friends were sick."

"I've come about Owen."

That got Tommy's attention. Mullahey's source had proven their worth.

"I'll be right back," the boy said to the doorman before pushing past Nick and skittering up the stairs that led outside, the loose sole of his left brogan flapping. He dashed around the corner and stopped in front of an empty storefront, a *For Rent* sign propped in the window, the store's awning offering cover from the rain. "What about Owen?"

"Where is he?"

"How would I know?"

Nick waited for a pack of laborers in stained homespun trousers, their shirtsleeves rolled to their elbows, to pass them. "You didn't ask what was ailing him, Tommy, so my guess is you know he's not sick because you also know where he is. And have seen him recently."

The kid thrust out his chin. "Well, I haven't."

"Okay, fine. Just tell me if you happen to believe he's alive."

"Ain't gonna say." He made a locking motion against his lips.

"I'm hoping you will say something, because I've got another question for you. It's my understanding that you're acquainted with Caleb Griffin."

The statement warranted a hasty examination of their surroundings. Mullahey, rain dripping off his hat, hadn't stayed completely out of sight and Tommy O'Brien spotted him.

He pulled an old copper penny from his pants pocket, of the type Nick hadn't seen since before the war, and flashed it. A signal that a policeman was in the area.

"Let's go for a walk, Tommy." Nick grabbed the kid's bony elbow and hauled him farther down the street.

Tommy shook him off. "No need to manhandle me, mister. Hey, you ain't told me your name."

And I'm not going to. "Owen's in hiding and Griffin has been murdered," Nick stated, keeping his voice low. "Can't be a coincidence."

"Never imagined Caleb would get his," Tommy admitted.

"He was in a rush to get out of town. Who'd he get tangled up with?"

"Some fellows he shouldn't have crossed. Said one of 'em was crazy."

"Were these fellows involved in horse racing, by any chance?"

Tommy squinted at him. "Why you askin' so many questions like this? You a copper, too?"

"I want to find whoever it was who killed Griffin before Owen also ends up dead."

"Uh-uh. I'm headin' back to the bowling alley. Where it's dry and I don't have to answer stupid questions." The boy turned on his heel.

"I need a name, Tommy." Nick grabbed him before he could get too far. "You're both in danger."

"All right. All right. Fulton," he hissed. "Rumor is he was paid to kill some fellah and lo and behold . . ." Tommy made a stabbing motion. "That's all I'm gonna say. And don't come lookin' for me at the alley ever again, got it?"

. . .

Addie cleared the dinner dishes and brought out tea for Celia and Barbara. Rain clattered against the dining room windows, a din like handfuls of pebbles tossed at the glass.

"*Och*," Addie muttered, the china cups clinking as she set down the lacquered tray. "It's not fit for man nor beast out there. Another terrible night."

The wind rattled the shutters.

"The street is going to be a mud bog again in the morning," Barbara said. "Maybe I won't have lessons tomorrow," she added, sounding hopeful.

"I would not count on that, Barbara." Celia accepted a cup of tea from Addie. "You still need to do the work your tutor assigned."

Her cousin pulled a face. "I know. I just can't concentrate. Owen's out there in this weather. When will the police locate him? When will Cousin Patrick actually help?"

"We have to be patient, Barbara. Owen is very clever, and if he has gone into hiding, then he will be difficult to find." Including, she hoped, by those who wished to harm him.

Addie poured out tea for Barbara. "We just need to pray for the laddie, Miss Barbara. He'll be home safe and sound, sure enough. Mr. Taylor promised they're working on a lead."

"I am glad you had a chance to speak with him this afternoon."

After he'd finished at the Piersons' house—following up on the search that had upset Georgiana—he'd come by to visit Addie.

Addie was blushing. "Aye, ma'am." She hastened out of the dining room to evade any more questions.

Barbara was frowning at the cup in her hand. "You went to Mrs. Pierson's this afternoon, didn't you?"

"I located the locket she hired me to find, although she did not give me the means to recover it for her." Celia sipped at her tea, her gaze on her cousin's face. "She paid me five dollars, however."

"Well, if you have to investigate, it's good that you're getting paid," she said. "Will that be enough to claim your mother's jewelry at the pawnbroker?"

"No, unfortunately," she said. "It was curious that, after I departed Mrs. Pierson's house, she ran up the road to meet with a man. Mr. Fulton, the local policeman. However, they both eluded Mr. Taylor's efforts to track them down."

"Why would she meet with him?"

"That, Barbara, is a most critical question." *That I would love to know the answer to.*

Outside, a rumble sounded, deep and heavy. Thunder perhaps, although it was rare to hear.

Barbara set down her tea. "Maybe I should just go to bed. If this storm lets me sleep." She got to her feet and wished Celia a good night.

Celia finished her tea and rose as well. "Addie, I am going to retire early."

Addie reappeared at the doorway between the kitchen and the dining room, her face creased with worry. "Will he be all right, ma'am? Wee Owen?"

Celia had intended to finally mention the man who'd trailed her out of the saloon yesterday, whom she'd also observed outside the secondhand shop today, but she didn't wish to increase Addie's concerns. Instead, she smiled as reassuringly as her own fears permitted. "Detective Greaves and Officer Taylor will find him, Addie. I have faith in their abilities. Mr. Taylor promised, after all."

"Thank you, ma'am."

Celia headed for the stairs, rounding the newel post just as a fist pounded on the front door. A voice she recognized shouted her name.

Addie sprinted into the entry area. "Is it Owen?"

Celia unbolted the door and threw it open. "Joaquin, what is it?"

The son of the Chilean family who lived across the street, his wet black hair plastered to his head, gestured wildly. "The hill. It . . ." He swept his hands in a downward motion. "Mud and rocks."

"The hill has collapsed?" asked Addie. "That must have been the noise we heard. Not thunder, but a mudslide again, from all the rain."

Joaquin nodded. "*Sí*. Come, Señora Davies. There is a *cuerpo*."

A body. All the blood seemed to drain from Celia's face. "I shall fetch my bag."

⚕ CHAPTER 12 ⚕

The news of the landslide, and the discovery of a man's buried body, had saved Nick from an awkward dinner with Miss Westerfield and his landlady. Luckily for the two of them, however, they were both back at the house enjoying the warmth of a fire, while he couldn't feel his feet because of the cold and the damp.

When Nick arrived at the scene, he spotted Celia Davies hunched beneath the umbrella she held, her skirts muddied from having dragged in the mire. She stared at the pile of debris that had landed at the base of Russian Hill. They'd been leveling this area in preparation for road work, and this collapse made the second one in two weeks.

"How is it, Mrs. Davies . . . I'm not even going to ask."

She glanced at him from beneath the edge of the umbrella. "Oh, Mr. Greaves, I did not hear your approach," she said. "To answer the question you did not ask, one of my neighbors received word that the landslip had buried someone. I came running with my medical supplies." She hoisted her black leather medical bag. "It was quickly apparent there was nothing I could do for the fellow. He had no pulse when I arrived. He must have been crushed by the weight of the rubble and rapidly expired. Although he was not immediately beneath the hill, but rather nearer to the road."

"Why send for me if it looks like the fellow was killed in an accident?"

"Because, although he is somewhat mangled, I believe it is Mr. Fulton."

Damn. "You sure, ma'am?"

"Fairly certain, Mr. Greaves. I thought it best that you were alerted."

A clutch of men, their clothes soaked through, had cleared away the mud and rocks and pulled free the unfortunate victim. An adult male, based on what Nick could see in the sputtering light of a couple of lanterns, tendrils of smoke snaking into the misty air. Nick went to look, the men who'd helped recover the body crowding in behind him. Their voices rose and fell as they whispered together.

Celia Davies joined him. "Oh, my. It *is* Mr. Fulton."

"Appears so." A man who was suspected of being paid to kill another man, likely Griffin.

The nearest onlooker must have heard them. "I'll be!" he exclaimed. "It's the local. Done in by a pile of rocks."

Mrs. Davies was staring down at the body. "I do wonder . . ."

"Wonder what, Mrs. Davies?"

"Why Georgiana Pierson met with him this afternoon. Didn't Mr. Taylor tell you that I'd seen them together?"

"He'd said you weren't positive."

"More positive than not, actually," she said.

Nick moved a few paces away from the crowd, bringing her with him. "There are rumors swirling that Fulton had been paid to kill a man. The rumors have settled on the man being Griffin."

"And Georgiana Pierson met with Mr. Fulton because *she* is the one who hired him to kill Mr. Griffin?" she asked. "Perhaps I witnessed her paying him for the execution of the crime. Or meeting with Mr. Fulton because she sought assurance that he was not about to . . . what is the phrase . . . peach on her? What if she was not assured and sought to silence him? And voilà, here he is, quite thoroughly dead."

"Their little meeting might also explain why the cop assigned to keep an eye on Fulton didn't find him at his rooming house this afternoon." Nick crouched next to the man's corpse. Rivulets of rainwater carved crooked streaks in the mud plastering his battered face. A rather grisly sight. "Mighty unfortunate that Fulton happened to be standing too close to a hillside that was soon to give way, though."

"Coincidence?" the woman at his side asked. "Might we conclude, however, that he is not the man in the plaid coat? As he does not have one on now and he was not wearing one the night of Mr. Griffin's death."

"Maybe." He stood. "We've searched at Hollis's and Aldrich's for the coat. And Pierson's. Didn't find it." He'd really been hoping they could pin Griffin's murder on one of them.

"Ah, that is why the officer was searching the Piersons' house today. Upsetting Georgiana, I might add."

He wasn't going to apologize about upsetting either of the Piersons.

"I suppose it is possible that the coat has been discarded or burned," Mrs. Davies continued when he didn't respond. "I certainly would not hold on to a bloodied item of clothing that might link me to a killing."

"Or, as I've said before, the man in the plaid coat doesn't actually exist." One of the fellows who'd pulled Fulton's body free of the rocks lugged over a construction site tarp and covered Fulton with it. "The kid who told me about Fulton being hired to kill Griffin also knows Cassidy, Mrs. Davies."

"Mr. Taylor mentioned to Addie that you had a 'lead.'"

"The kid was cagey, but I got the impression from the way he answered that Cassidy's still alive and he knows where he's hiding."

She grabbed Nick's arm, her hasty movement streaming water off the top of her umbrella. "He is? That is fabulous news!"

"I can't be definite, Mrs. Davies. It's just an impression I got."

She released his arm. "We need more than an impression, Mr. Greaves."

"We're doing all we can to find Owen, Mrs. Davies."

She exhaled, her breath clouding the air. "I know."

What else could he say? He was just as worried.

A pony cart rattled to a halt on the corner, and Taylor hopped down from the passenger side of the seat. Harris tied off the reins and clambered down as well. The curiosity seekers who'd stuck around parted to let them pass.

"What have we got, sir?" Taylor asked, fumbling for his notebook.

"The local policeman has had an unfortunate encounter with a landslide." Nick nodded at the coroner. "Thanks for coming so quickly, Harris."

"Pretty awful weather, Greaves. Not surprised another hillside let go." He tapped fingertips to the brim of his hat, acknowledging Mrs. Davies. "Any reason to suspect the fellow's death wasn't a simple accident?"

"Could be, but I did get information today that named him as Griffin's possible killer. A paid killer," Nick answered. "Don't know if the landslide killed him, though, or if he was already dead and dumped next to the hill."

Harris squatted next to Fulton and folded the tarp back from the upper half of the man's body.

"Any idea how long he's been laying here?" Nick asked him.

"Hard to say, what with the cold rain that's been falling for the past few hours. Chills a body very quickly." Harris tested one of Fulton's bare, pale hands. "At least an hour?"

"Anybody see anything?" Nick asked the few gawkers standing around. "Hear anything?"

They darted looks at each other, wondering who'd have the nerve to speak up about a murder.

"As hard as it was raining?" one fellow scoffed.

That excuse again.

"There's a gunshot wound, Greaves. To the gut." Harris had flapped aside Fulton's coat. The hole in the man's stomach had leaked blood onto his vest.

"Gad," Celia Davies exclaimed. She'd moved close to Nick, the edge of her umbrella dripping water onto his shoulder. He enjoyed having her near, so he didn't mind. "I should have noticed."

"He was buried under a pile of rocks, ma'am," Nick said.

"Nonetheless."

"Not the usual location for a self-inflicted wound." Harris grabbed a lantern from the nearest onlooker and held it over Fulton's torso. "Looks like powder burns. Shot at close range. Small-caliber weapon, possibly. Given the size of the hole."

Taylor whistled and scribbled notes, the rain hampering his attempts. The sightseers whispered excitedly. It wasn't every day that a local policeman—any policeman—was shot. *Thankfully.*

Harris replaced the tarp and handed the lantern back to its owner. Wiping his hands together, he returned to where Nick and the others stood waiting. "I'll be able to say more when I conduct my autopsy, of course."

"Getting shot at close range implies that he knew the person, Harris," Nick said. "Well enough to let them stand close to him."

Somebody like Georgiana Pierson, maybe.

* * *

"Are you making one of your lists again, ma'am?" Addie stood in the doorway to the dining room, a shawl tossed over her linen nightgown, the long braid of her thick brown hair hanging past her shoulder. "You should let Mr. Taylor and Mr. Greaves take care of matters."

"Another man has been murdered, Addie." Celia had spread blank pieces of paper atop the table, where the gas mantle gave off a harsh, bright light to see by. To focus her thoughts by. "I do not know that I will find any answers by drawing up my lists, Addie, but I must at least sort my thoughts."

"It can wait until the morning, ma'am. Do be sensible and take yourself to bed."

"I'll not be able to sleep, so you can scold me all you like." Addie was merely voicing her concerns, however. *And I had promised to never, ever get involved in another police investigation, hadn't I?* So much for promises.

Addie sighed. "Do you want me to put on the kettle?"

Celia smiled her thanks. "If you would."

Addie bustled off to the kitchen, and Celia pondered the blank sheets. She'd gotten into the habit of making lists, reviewing the crime and who she considered to be possible suspects. Perhaps she truly was an investigator after all. But where to begin? There was little to know about Mr. Fulton's murder as yet. So she would start with the few facts of Mr. Griffin's death and other recent events.

Firstly, Mr. Griffin had been in some sort of trouble and had intended to leave San Francisco. Secondly, he'd been in possession of a note that referenced five hundred dollars and the name of one of Mr. Aldrich's racehorses, Validus. A note that he had entrusted to Owen, who'd disappeared after informing Celia of the message and that another fellow was desperate to obtain it. Which meant other individuals were aware Mr. Griffin had given it to him.

Thinking of Owen, Celia said a brief prayer for his safety before resuming.

Mr. Griffin had been stabbed in the back—taken unawares?—and twice in the front, only one defensive wound, his gun still tucked away. His pockets had been searched. There was evidence that he had been dragged behind the Piersons' shrubbery. No doubt to hide his body from being easily seen from the road. A suspicious man in a plaid coat had been observed in the vicinity close to the time of the murder.

On to other events. Mr. Everett's stationery store had burned down in an act of arson. Mr. Pierson, formerly employed at the agency that had insured the structure, had visited him on Monday morning not too many hours after the fire. That same day, Georgiana Pierson developed an urgent need to meet with Celia to request she locate a missing locket, which had not been particularly missing, after all. The hour she'd chosen for the meeting coincided with Edward Pierson entertaining Mr. Aldrich and Mr. Hollis. Some few minutes after those two gentlemen departed, Mr. Griffin was murdered. Celia and Georgiana returned from Jane's to discover his dead body in the Piersons' front yard.

Celia sat back and considered what she'd transcribed so far. One more detail . . . A fellow in a faded army overcoat had followed Celia after her meeting with Patrick and then again this morning. If the man's actions had anything to do with Mr. Griffin's death or that blasted note, she hadn't the foggiest idea.

She turned next to the suspects in the murder of Mr. Griffin. Dr. Harris had proposed that Mr. Griffin's killer was around the same height, which did not exclude any of them. So, the most obvious person to list first was Mr. Fulton, who'd been implicated as his killer by one of Owen's friends. He'd either possessed a personal motive for murdering Mr. Griffin or had been paid, as was rumored, to commit the crime by an unnamed individual.

Mr. Fulton. Personal Motive—Unclear. Prior history with Mr. Griffin? Perhaps he owed the man money, since everyone appeared to. Although, if he *had* murdered Mr. Griffin, he could have easily claimed he'd done so because he'd caught him in the act of committing a crime. Except he had made no such claim. And to use a gimlet instead of whatever gun or knife Mr. Fulton carried on his person? Unless he chose to make use of an unlikely weapon in order to deflect suspicion. It was also possible the gossip Owen's friend had heard was incorrect.

Mr. Fulton. Motive—paid killer. Who may have paid him and why? Georgiana, perhaps. Or one of the other suspects.

Edward Pierson. Motive—Many recent expenses plus the loss of his position at the insurance agency. Also seeking funds to start a new enterprise. Mr. Griffin was in the business of lending money to people who chose to not make use of the usual channels. He'd informed Owen that he planned to collect on debts Monday evening. From Edward Pierson or one of the other men? Perhaps the time to repay had come due and Mr. Pierson had been unable to secure the necessary funds. Also, Georgiana had blurted out an accusation of blame upon discovering Mr. Griffin's body in their yard.

"Even though you'd claimed that you were in shock when you'd said it was your husband's fault," Celia muttered aloud.

"What's that, ma'am?" called Addie from the kitchen.

"I am mumbling to myself, Addie, that is all."

She returned to her jottings, and a key question—why murder the man to whom you owed money in front of your own house and leave him there? Most people, she imagined, would attempt to hide the body elsewhere. If one of the Piersons had paid Mr. Fulton to kill Mr. Griffin, had the fellow simply been terribly slapdash in the execution of his task? *Execution of his task? What, like a badly turned table leg or some such thing?*

Honestly, Celia. Unless Mr. Fulton had been interrupted before he could remove the corpse, which would not have been easy to do on his own, given Mr. Griffin's robust frame. He would have required help. From the person who had murdered him in turn tonight, perhaps. Dr. Harris did think it unlikely he'd shot himself at the base of Russian Hill.

Two people? Celia tapped the unsharpened end of the pencil against her chin. A very complicated scenario. Certainly not impossible.

"Here you are, ma'am." Addie set down the tea things and peered at what Celia had so far written. "Is it making any sense yet?"

"Not much. I have become rather stuck on Mr. Pierson as a suspect."

"Weel, at least Mrs. Pierson couldna have murdered Mr. Griffin. She was with you."

"She may have hired the local to kill him. Mr. Fulton is rumored to have been paid to murder Mr. Griffin." Celia wrote down Georgiana's name. "Furthermore, I spied her speaking with him today."

Addie's brow furrowed. "But to leave Mr. Griffin—God save him—right next to her front gate?"

The same issue faced by suspecting Edward Pierson as the murderer. "Perhaps Mr. Fulton had been interrupted before he could remove the body."

"And if she'd had a hand in Mr. Griffin's murder, arranging to be away from the house with you—"

"Recently in the newspapers for my supposed skills as a sleuth."

"Arranging to be away with you, a friend of the police, while the crime occurred would be canny. And she then murdered Mr. Fulton to conceal her crime." Addie wagged her head. "Dreadful woman."

"Mr. Fulton had been shot before the hill collapsed. I expect Mr. Greaves is presently questioning the Piersons about weapons," she said. "Of course, it is possible that Mr. Fulton's death is completely unrelated to the murder of Mr. Griffin. In his position, he likely has enemies."

She hated coincidence as much as Mr. Greaves, however, and would tie the two events together until she could prove they were not meant to be connected.

"I canna make heads or tails of this, ma'am." She stifled a yawn. "Verra confusing."

"Addie, you should take yourself to bed. I'll clean up when I am finished."

Addie lit a candle off the gas mantle and shuffled off. Celia took a bracing sip of the hot tea before resuming her task.

"Let us move on to the others." The other actors in this play, as Mr. Shakespeare might say.

Mr. Hollis. A man who'd acquired his wealth through lucrative investments. He was at the Piersons' house Monday evening at Mr. Pierson's invitation. He had departed prior to Mr. Aldrich. Therefore, he could not be suspected of killing Mr. Griffin without Mr. Aldrich discovering the body. Unless he'd been hiding nearby with a gimlet at the ready. His motive for murdering Mr. Griffin or hiring Mr. Fulton to commit the crime unknown. Unless his investments had recently fallen in value and he'd tapped Mr. Griffin for money. Arranged to meet him near Mr. Pierson's house, where he could kill the fellow and cast suspicion upon another. *Very cruel, if true.* His alibi for Mr. Fulton's murder to be determined.

Mr. Aldrich. He claimed to have seen a man in a plaid coat after departing the Piersons'. Mr. Griffin in possession of a note with a sum of money and the name of Mr. Aldrich's prized racehorse. A note torn in a most distinctive pattern, if Celia recalled, implying that the absent portion was meant to be rejoined at some point.

"So who has the other half?"

Mr. Aldrich had also been at the Piersons' house Monday evening. Perhaps he'd encountered Mr. Griffin outside, fought with him, produced a gimlet, which he had obtained somewhere. There was the problem with the use of that tool, again. Possible motive similar to Mr. Hollis's. His alibi for this evening presently unknown.

"No doubt it will be sterling, if he is the killer."

Mr. Aldrich and Mr. Pierson had recently fallen out over a racehorse. The argument's relevance to Mr. Griffin's murder was unclear. Mr. Everett made use of the insurance company Mr. Aldrich presided over. Again, did that matter? Georgiana blamed Mr. Aldrich for taking her locket and selling it. Clear animosity between the Piersons and Mr. Aldrich. But why was Mr. Aldrich not the initial victim? Unless Mr. Fulton had erred in the commission of the killing and murdered the wrong fellow. *A fascinating idea, Celia.*

One thing was certain, she needed more information on the relationship between the three men.

Who else?

Mysterious man in a plaid coat. His identity and motive unknown. Whether he should even be considered a suspect was questionable. Likewise, whether he even existed. The coat not discovered in the possession of Mr. Hollis, Mr. Aldrich, or Mr. Pierson.

Mysterious man following her. Ditto, although his actions may be utterly unrelated to Mr. Griffin's—and now Mr. Fulton's—murders and she had merely gained the man's unwanted attention.

The fellow who'd wanted the note from Owen. Owen had neglected to describe the man named Johnny. He was obviously connected to Mr. Griffin and the information contained on the note, but how was also unknown.

She could add Patrick's name, as she'd done before on other lists. Heaven only knew he had reasons to wish Caleb Griffin dead. But the location of the murder was not a logical place for Patrick to choose, and he reportedly had been away from San Francisco that night.

For once, Patrick, I shall leave you off my list of suspects.

She set down the pencil and surveyed her notes, brushing her fingertips across the paper. She'd purchased it at Mr. Everett's shop. Poor man, to have lost the business he loved. Or *was* he a poor man deserving of condolences? The fire had been intentional, and who else stood to gain from a paid-off insurance policy than Mr. Everett himself? He might have set the fire—Mr. Greaves had mentioned the rather obvious presence of black powder at the source of the blaze, a bit of sloppiness that implied an amateur—or he may have paid someone.

Someone like Mr. Fulton? Or someone like Mr. Griffin?

"I do hate to include you, Mr. Everett, but I feel I must."

For him to graduate from arson to murder made for quite the leap, although she had encountered, in her recent months as a purported investigator, other individuals who'd compounded a less serious crime with homicide. Rather reluctantly, she added his name to her list. His motive being that he sought to conceal the arson by disposing of the person who'd started the fire for him. Then tonight, he murdered a witness.

She reread what she'd written. She'd gained far more questions than insights, but that had been the point of the exercise. Tomorrow, she'd begin to determine if she could find some answers.

• • •

"Why are you questioning us about Mr. Fulton's death, Mr. Greaves?" Edward Pierson, wrapped in his dressing gown again, hadn't dosed himself with Watt's Nervous Antidote tonight in order to evade the police, which Nick appreciated. His wife occupied the parlor's settee with a sour expression fixed on her face. Footsteps stomped overhead—Taylor had arrived and was upstairs searching the bedrooms along with the cop who walked a nearby beat—and Pierson shot an angry glance at the ceiling. "We have no idea what happened. We were both here, in the parlor, since after dinner when our maid left."

"Here all night." Neither of them looked damp and muddy, so maybe he was telling the truth.

"All night."

Nick ran the brim of his hat through his fingers. "Mrs. Pierson, who was the man you were observed speaking with this afternoon? Up the street from here."

"I don't know what you're talking about, Detective."

"It wasn't Mr. Fulton?" Nick asked. "My witness tells me it looked like him."

She turned a sickly color. "Absolutely not. Why might I want to speak with the local?"

"That's what I'd like to know. Since he's dead, now." He turned back to her husband. "Do you own any guns, Mr. Pierson?"

"Umm . . . Yes."

"You might presume from my question, Mr. Pierson, that I'd like to see them."

"It. Just one gun, Detective." He looked over at Georgiana Pierson. "Will you be all right?"

Nick rolled his eyes. "She'll be perfectly fine with me, Mr. Pierson. I don't bite."

Pierson scurried off.

"It's just the two of us now, ma'am," Nick said, "so feel free to tell me who the fellow was this afternoon. My witness is reliable."

She lowered her gaze, striking a demure and innocent pose. "A neighbor whom I've been . . . seeing."

"You want me to believe you're cheating on your husband." And not meeting a murder victim just hours before his death.

"It's not like that, Mr. Greaves. I just . . . the relationship I have with my husband is complicated."

Sure.

Pierson came back with a gun. A Colt revolver, similar to the one Nick carried and not a small-caliber weapon.

"This the only gun you own?" he asked.

"Yes. I purchased it when we moved out here. This location is more remote than where we had been living," he replied. "I thought we'd be safer with a gun in the house."

"Wish I could reassure you, Mr. Pierson, that you would be." He handed back the weapon. "But if Griffin's and Fulton's guns didn't keep them safe, yours might not do you much good, either."

Taylor thundered down the stairs and into the parlor. "Found this, sir, but no other weapons." He showed Nick a thin-bladed knife with a delicate ivory handle. It looked more like a paper knife than a weapon.

"Not yet, at least. The neighborhood officer is still searching."

"For what?" Mrs. Pierson demanded. "You've already searched the house once today. What else do you hope to find?"

"Just a quick look-through to satisfy ourselves that neither of you were out this evening shooting Mr. Fulton," Nick said.

"I told you we were both here all night, Mr. Greaves," Pierson insisted.

"Have to be sure." He turned back to Taylor. "Any muddy shoes or clothes?"

His assistant shook his head.

Damn. "Oh, Mr. Pierson, before I go, can I get you to explain a story I've recently heard about you and Mr. Aldrich and a racehorse. A quarrel you two had?"

Pierson turned about as pale as his wife. Maybe it was the lighting in the room that made them both look so ill.

"Just a misunderstanding, Detective, that's all. Nothing significant. It's all patched up now."

"Ah," Nick replied. "What do you know about the accusation that his trainer had poisoned an opponent's horse a few weeks back? Sounds like another terrible tragedy for Mr. Aldrich to have been involved in."

For some reason, Pierson shot a look at his wife, who didn't return the glance. "I didn't believe the allegation," he said. "Lyman? Ridiculous. And it has nothing to do with Mr. Griffin's murder or the local's death."

"I think I'll decide that for myself, Mr. Pierson." Nick jammed his hat onto his head. More to learn during his trip to the Ocean House Course tomorrow. "Guess I'm finished here, then. I'd strongly recommend that the both of you not even think of leaving town."

He stormed out of the parlor, Taylor jogging after him.

"Sir, for once there's a witness," he said once they were back outside. "The fellow came forward when Dr. Harris finished up examining Mr. Fulton's body and was asking folks questions."

"And?"

"This person lives a few lots up from where Mr. Fulton died. He heard the hill give way and ran down to investigate. Says he was just turning the corner when he noticed a fellow running the other direction." Taylor waggled his eyebrows. "A fellow in a plaid coat."

"He *does* exist."

"Guess so, sir. But I don't get why he wore that plaid coat again, Mr. Greaves, after we put that notice in the paper looking for him."

"Maybe he doesn't read and didn't know, Taylor."

Taylor screwed up his face. "You think so?"

"That, or he's awfully bold." And dangerous.

CHAPTER 13

"Concluded your latest case, Greaves?" Detective Briggs asked, swiping crumbs off his chest. For once, he'd put in an appearance at the office before Nick and on a Friday. Early enough to have finished eating whatever he'd brought with him. Eating was about all Briggs did in the detectives' office, on the days he actually showed up.

"We're making progress," Nick said, tossing his hat onto his desk. "Thanks for asking."

Briggs finished picking crumbs off his coat. "Glad to hear. Glad to hear."

What, no insults? What had gotten into him?

"Well, I've got a theft to look into, Greaves. Good luck." Briggs collected his things and strolled out.

Mullahey stepped inside the room. "What's Detective Briggs looking so cheery about?"

"I don't know and it's making me nervous." Nick dragged his chair back from his desk and sat.

Mullahey chuckled. "A Mr. Burkhardt is here, asking for you. Mr. Fulton's boss." He ushered in a pinched-faced fellow who inspected the detectives' office with professional curiosity. "This here is Detective Greaves, Mr. Burkhardt."

The fellow took the offered chair and grabbed his straw leghorn hat off his head, exposing thinning hair and a prominent bald spot. "A terrible business about Mr. Fulton, Detective."

Mullahey slipped out and was replaced by Taylor, who crossed the room to take his usual seat against the wall.

"You mean that he's dead, Mr. Burkhardt," said Nick.

"Crushed by a fall of rocks." He clucked his tongue against his teeth. "What a way to die. Mr. Fulton gave the impression he was far more careful than to have something like that happen. A resourceful and cautious man."

"Oh, he was shot before that hillside landed on him. Didn't you hear? He was murdered."

Burkhardt blanched. "That's why I received a message at my office this morning to attend the coroner's inquest. Murdered. Oh, my."

"Did he have a lot of enemies? Given the sort of work he did."

"He must have caught someone in the act of burglarizing one of the properties he was paid to protect." He sounded impressed. Or astounded. "Losing his life in the pursuit of his duty."

"Not bad for a fellow accused of being a deserter." Nick folded his arms. "It's a crime punishable by time in jail. Yet you still hired the man."

Burkhardt ran a finger around his collar, loosening his necktie that had suddenly taken to choking him. "Such a rumor did not reach our ears."

Was there more than one person responsible for hiring local police, or did Burkhardt just like using the royal *we?* "It reached *our* ears."

"It's not easy, Detective Greaves, finding men willing to do the job, you know. Police work is dangerous."

"That's not news to me, Mr. Burkhardt." Look how Fulton had ended up. "I spend most days wondering why *I* do it."

Taylor chuckled and flipped a page in his notebook.

"How well did you know Mr. Fulton?" Nick asked.

"We were not friends, Detective. Such a relationship isn't advisable between employer and employee."

"So you can't say who might've wished to kill the fellow."

Burkhardt bounced on the edge of his chair. The interior of the office might have initially intrigued him, but now he didn't look eager to stay. "He'd been acting strangely ever since that fellow was killed on Monday. The one who was murdered at the house within his territory alongside Russian Hill."

The carpenter who'd spoken with Nick had also noticed Fulton's odd behavior. "Mr. Fulton testified at the inquest that he'd seen somebody that night. Somebody suspicious. Did he say anything to you about that person?"

"No, he was simply acting strangely," he said. "Although he did ask me if anyone had come into the office and asked for him. He seemed anxious about this person, which was very uncharacteristic. Mr. Fulton did not give me a name, however."

Taylor scribbled as fast as he could push his pencil across his notebook paper.

"When was this exactly?" asked Nick.

"The first time might've been last week. No, the week prior," he said. "He asked again about this person on Tuesday. I was astonished by Mr. Fulton's level of concern. He was not a fellow who was afraid of anybody."

"Did this unnamed person ever come around?"

"No, Detective Greaves," he replied.

"Did Fulton ever mention a note with the name of a racehorse on it?"

Burkhardt shook his head. "I wish he'd confided more in me."

"So do I." Nick got to his feet. "Thank you, Mr. Burkhardt. We'll be in touch if we need anything else."

The fellow sprang off his chair like a jack-in-the-box freed from its container. "Yes. Of course. And if I recall anything else that might be important I'll be sure to let you know."

"We do appreciate that, Mr. Burkhardt."

He slapped on his hat and dashed out of the office.

"Doesn't leave us with much, does it, sir?" Taylor stashed away his notebook. "It would've been awfully helpful if Mr. Fulton had told Mr. Burkhardt the name of the fellow—"

"Or woman, Taylor. Fulton could've meant Georgiana Pierson." Nick collected his hat. "Get Aldrich's alibi for last night. I'll go speak with Hollis. After that, I'm heading to the Ocean House Course with Mrs. Davies. Validus is running this afternoon, and I've got a few questions to ask."

Taylor lifted his eyebrows. "You asked Mrs. Davies to go along?"

"Here's hoping I haven't made a mistake."

• • •

"Celia, this is early. Even for you." Jane looked over from where she sat at a gate-legged table, situated in front of a window that had a fine view of her garden. It was only a half hour past sunrise and Jane had yet to change out of her gold-and-blue paisley robe. "Barbara sent me a note about Owen's disappearance. Is there news?"

"No. Sadly," Celia replied. "I do apologize for the early hour, but Mr. Greaves had one of the police officers bring me a message while I was still dressing, a request that I join him in a visit to the Ocean House Course later this morning. And do not get that look in your eye, Jane. This excursion is for business, not pleasure."

"Of course," her friend said. "You don't have to apologize for being early, Celia. I've been up for over an hour. One of the privileges of Frank being away from home is the freedom to lounge about it my wrapper, which he hates. He claims Hetty will think less of me, but that's poppycock." She smiled over her daringness. "Would you care for some breakfast?"

Celia stripped off her gloves and pulled out a chair across from Jane. "I've eaten, so there is no need to bother Hetty."

"Well, I will have her bring more coffee. Would you like a cup? Our tea isn't as good as what Addie purchases for you. Or perhaps some chocolate? It's from France."

"I would love some coffee. Thank you."

A petite brass bell waited at the edge of the table and Jane gave it a hearty ring. "Hetty dislikes this thing. I can hardly blame her but it does the trick." She set it down, dampening the reverberation. "I haven't learned much about Matthew Hollis, by the way. He rarely socializes—he's unmarried—so my acquaintances didn't have much to say. And the people I've spoken with so far have nothing but admiration for J. Lyman Aldrich. Jealous admiration, I might add."

"Georgiana has blamed him for stealing her locket at that party. Can you imagine?" Celia asked. "I finally located it at one of the secondhand shops she directed me to. Only recently sold, however."

Hetty hurried into the room and Jane requested coffee and another cup, sending the young woman hastening off again. "I have lunch scheduled with a friend today—her name is Alice—who hears all sorts of gossip. Maybe she knows about that party and Georgiana's supposedly stolen locket."

"I'll be interested to hear what your friend has to say." Celia drew in a long breath. "There has been another murder, Jane. The local policeman who patrols the neighborhood not far from the Piersons' house. Last night."

"The reason for this early visit," she said.

Jane knew her well. "I am certain I saw Georgiana speaking with him a few hours before he was shot. It is rumored he was paid to murder Mr. Griffin."

Jane's eyes widened. "Well, that's a turn. But Georgie . . . I can't fathom her paying the local policeman to kill somebody."

Hetty returned with a fresh pot of coffee and a cup, which she placed in front of Celia, then retreated. Jane poured some out for the both of them.

Celia accepted the coffee, which steamed an aroma both warm and acidic. "I feel she's told us a fable as fanciful as some concoction in *A Thousand and One Nights*. Beginning with a locket supposedly stolen by Mr. Aldrich."

"Maybe, by making that allegation, Georgie is retaliating against him for dismissing her husband, Celia," said Jane, scooping sugar into her coffee and stirring, the spoon clinking against the china cup.

"How far did she mean to go, though?"

"But J. Lyman Aldrich is not dead, Celia. Mr. Griffin is."

Celia sipped at the hot coffee, peering over the rim of the cup at Jane. "A mistake?"

"My goodness, Celia. What a grim thought."

"I remain rather curious about Matthew Hollis. The mysterious, unsociable bachelor," she said. "Perhaps it would be worth my while to speak with him in person. I hadn't much time at the inquest to form an impression of him."

"Celia . . ." Her friend's tone was both scolding and warning. "Frank is right. You are reckless."

"You can come with me to Mr. Hollis's office and assess if he is the sort of person who might attack ladies," Celia suggested. "What do you say? You saved me from serious injury the last time I recruited you to assist."

"Which is the very reason Frank forbad me from having anything more to do with your schemes. The risks involved."

"I thought you were bored, Mrs. Hutchinson."

Jane stared at her long enough that Celia began to note the ticking of the walnut clock hanging on the wall. She processed a variety of ways to retract her request. When Jane finally burst out laughing, Celia allowed herself to breathe.

Jane's eyes sparkled. "All right, Celia. When do we go?"

Celia smiled at her. *Do forgive me, Frank.* "How about as soon as you are ready to depart?"

• • •

It must be nice, thought Nick, studying the entrance to the San Francisco Olympic Club, to be a man of leisure and have the time to enjoy the benefits that might be gained from a place like this. He supposed Hollis, who spent his days sitting at a desk speculating on the stock market or getting approached to become a founding member of companies like Edward Pierson's, needed the exercise. If he spent half the time Nick did walking the inclines of the city streets, though, he wouldn't.

A well-dressed young man, his face flushed and his hair damp from a bath he must've taken after his exertions, stepped through the door and trotted down the short flight of steps to the sidewalk. He gave Nick a quizzical look, assessing whether Nick belonged in the hallowed rooms beyond the door, before brushing past him.

Nick went inside, a stuffy dampness hanging in the air. From all the men sweating over their gymnastics and boxing in the main hall, he supposed.

A fellow rushed out from a side room and stopped Nick before he'd walked five feet. "Excuse me, sir, are you a member here?" He drew himself up to his full height, quivering with the self-importance acquired from being authorized to ask that question. It didn't sound like he wasn't aware of the answer, though.

Nick sighed and flashed his badge. He'd take to wearing it on the outside of his coat, like the police officers did, but being recognized as a detective everywhere he went would be more of a bother than having to flap open his coat.

"I need to speak with Mr. Hollis. I was told at his office that I could find him here." At the early hour of half past seven.

The fellow didn't budge to fetch him. "I believe he's training with our boxing instructor at the moment."

"I wouldn't mind watching him spar for a bit." Nick nodded toward the set of double doors across the entryway from where he stood. Through the gap between them leaked the sounds of men grunting, the occasional thud of a weight hitting the floor. "I'm sure he'll be fine. We're already acquainted."

He strode over and yanked open one of the doors. The acrid stench of sweating men was stronger on this side. The exercise area stretched from the street front to the back of the building and was broken into two smaller spaces. The one he'd walked into, the self-important fellow on his heels, was not the boxing area. For a club that boasted several hundred members, the room was sparsely occupied. Maybe most of the members enjoyed claiming to belong, looking forward to the social events more than participating in grunting and stinking.

"Officer, I insist—"

Nick scowled at the man. He towered over the fellow, which Nick had always found helped when he wanted to intimidate somebody into backing off. "How about you pretend I'm a prospective member come to have a gander at what's on offer, rather than have me announce who I'm searching for and why?"

"Why *are* you searching for Mr. Hollis?"

Could've figured he'd ask. "You don't want to know."

Part of the space had been dedicated to an arrangement of rack and parallel bars, presently unused. Men in undershirts and loose pants—or stripped down to their drawers, if they weren't as modest—swung clubs or lifted dumbbells. One fellow had obtained a pair of short pants to wear that made him look like a kid. In one corner, mats had been set on the floor. A tall man wearing a sweat-stained white union suit was leaping and tumbling with the frenzy of a circus performer.

"We have many famous members. When Mr. Twain lived in the city, he briefly enjoyed gymnastics in our facility. Mr. Low and Mr. Babcock are also here," said the fellow at his side, naming prominent merchants.

"Is that so."

A man in his shirtsleeves, muscles straining the linen, was putting a red-faced, rotund man through his paces. He shouted out what was supposed to be encouragement but sounded more like threats. "You can bathe your arms in arnica later to deal with the soreness, sir. But for now you have to keep going. Full circles, sir. Full circles. Twenty-five, twenty-six, twenty-seven . . . "

"As you can see, Officer, Mr. Hollis is not in here."

"I expect he's in the next room, then. The one I can make out through that opening." He strode by the man with the sore arms, nodding in sympathy, and into the adjacent room.

A pair of opponents, both wearing a uniform of padded vests with masks covering their faces and white pants, fenced. A boxing ring had been set up at the far end, but Hollis and his trainer stood on the floor next to it, both shirtless as they threw punches. Hollis was quick with his reflexes and far more muscular than a good shirt, vest, and frock coat had permitted Nick to observe at the man's office the other day.

Hollis spotted Nick heading in his direction and cursed. He stepped back from his sparring partner, lowering his hands. "We need to stop for a few minutes. I have to talk to this . . . gentleman."

The other fellow nodded, slanting Nick a questioning glance.

"You can return to your post by the door," Hollis said to the fellow who'd intercepted Nick and was still trailing after him. The man obediently scampered off. Hollis grabbed a towel on his way out through a side door and threw it over his shoulders. "I can't believe you've come here, Mr. Greaves. What do you want now? Haven't I answered enough questions already?"

The side door led onto a cramped space, lit by an inadequate rectangle of a window. Spare and broken pieces of equipment littered the floor along with baskets full of dirty towels. Waiting for the laundryman to come and fetch them. A row of lockers covered one wall.

"I have a whole host of new questions for you today, Mr. Hollis," said Nick. "Starting with where were you last night and if you have somebody who can prove you were there?"

"What am I accused of being involved in now?"

"Is there a private room where we can go talk?"

"I don't want to go up to the reading rooms looking like this so you're going to have to ask your questions here, Mr. Greaves."

Wedged in tight with Hollis between a rusting pole and some mismatched dumbbells. "So tell me about last night and I'll tell you why I want to know."

"I was at a Dashaway Association committee meeting," Hollis said, wiping the towel over his face and neck. "As was Mr. Aldrich, by the way."

"And what time was this?"

"It didn't last long, so I was back at home around seven. Not any later. The weather was terrible so I didn't dawdle on the way. I hired a cab to drive me home. My live-in maid can tell you when I arrived. Just like she did the last time the police questioned her." Hollis grabbed the two ends of the towel draped over his shoulders. "It's your turn now, Mr. Greaves. You haven't explained why you're questioning me and I believe I deserve to know."

"The local policeman who patrols the neighborhood near Pierson's house was found dead last evening. Buried under the rubble of a mudslide."

"Sounds like a terrible accident."

"Do you happen to own a gun?"

Hollis turned wary. "I don't have a need for one. What happened to the local?"

"He was shot to death before the hillside collapsed."

Hollis muttered a curse word under his breath. "I did *not* murder the man, Detective."

"Good to hear." Nick fished out the note Owen had been given. "You know anything about this?"

"Someone made a bet on Aldrich's horse?" he speculated, squinting at the words written on the paper. "For a hefty sum, I might add."

"That's all?"

"Yes. What does this torn bit of an IOU have to do with anything?"

Nick tucked the note back into his vest pocket. "Probably nothing."

Hollis's fists tightened around the towel then relaxed again. "Listen, Detective, I wasn't planning on telling you this, because I reasoned that the police would learn about it without having to hear the information from me."

He'd be one of the only folks Nick had ever interviewed who held such a high opinion of the police department's abilities. "It's always best to tell the police all that you know, Mr. Hollis."

"I should have, I know. But what you should know is, before Aldrich showed up on Monday night, Pierson got to muttering about some fellow he owed money to. He made it sound as though the man had threatened him and that he was scared."

"Why didn't you mention this at the inquest?"

"I admit I didn't want Edward to look bad," he said. "After what Mrs. Davies testified about Mr. Griffin intending to collect on debts Monday night, if I'd told the jury what Edward said to me—"

"He would've looked like a killer," Nick said. "So why tell me now?

The passing of a couple of days hasn't made the information less bad, Mr. Hollis."

"It was a mistake. I'm sorry."

He almost sounded genuinely contrite. "Did Pierson mention this man's name to you?"

"No, but I didn't ask."

Nick scanned the tall, narrow wood cabinets ranged along the wall. "Do you make use of one of the lockers here, Mr. Hollis?"

"Yes."

"I'd appreciate it if you'd open it for me."

Hollis exhaled. He produced a key from a concealed pants pocket and unlocked the last of the compartments. He stepped aside. "Mr. Greaves."

There wasn't much. A pair of polished shoes. Clothes to change into. A coin purse and a stack of clean towels. A hair comb. No plaid coat. No small-caliber gun. No jacket or shirt with bloodstains on it.

The other man cocked an eyebrow. "Satisfied, Mr. Greaves?"

"Not really, Mr. Hollis, but I'll have to make do for now."

• • •

"Mr. Hollis is not in yet." The man, an officious-looking clerk, gestured at the interior of the office, empty save for him and Celia and Jane. "As you can see, madam." His crisp British accent made his officiousness all the more complete.

"Such a pity, but I must tell you how pleased I am to hear the tones of a fellow countryman," she exclaimed with an excess of enthusiasm. "I have so missed England."

His manner did not soften. "Might I ask what your business is with Mr. Hollis? Are you ladies looking to invest?"

"It is a private matter, sir, so I shall wait until I can speak with him directly." She dropped onto the nearest silk-covered chair and rested her hands in her lap. "I trust he shall not be long."

"Madam!"

"You do not mind if we wait, do you?"

"Is Mr. Hollis delayed because he'd been at Platt's Hall last evening and stayed out late?" asked Jane, who'd been occupied with conducting a perusal of their surroundings. "I've heard that the vocalist who sang is exceptional."

"I expect you are right, Jane," Celia said. "Is that why your employer has not yet arrived this morning?"

"Mr. Hollis was not at Platt's Hall last evening. I am informed of everything that he does, even his social outings." He tapped a calendar spread open on his desk. "I am his secretary and keep track of his schedule. It is my understanding that he attended a meeting of the Dashaway Association."

"A most excellent organization," Celia declared. "Does he belong to any other temperance societies?"

"Not any longer."

An intriguing response. "I expect then, given that such a meeting likely did not extend long into the evening, that he should arrive at any moment."

"He was in the office first thing this morning, as is typical for Mr. Hollis." The secretary swelled with pride over his employer's dedication to hard work. The early bird catching the worm, after all. "He reviewed correspondence he'd received and went out again, as is also typical. He has gone, as he does most mornings, to his training exercises at the Olympic Club. He is an avid boxer. As I also told that . . . that fellow who also came asking for him and did not have an appointment. He looked like a policeman but that can't be possible."

The amount of disdain in his voice suggested that Mr. Greaves had beaten her to an interview with Mr. Hollis. "Your employer sounds like a most admirable man."

"He most certainly is, ma'am."

"Excuse me for interrupting, but is that a painting of Validus?" Jane gestured toward one of the paintings, that of a horse. "I recognize the animal. I saw him at a race I attended at the Santa Clara County Fair last month. He has a very distinctive irregular blaze on his face, along with that stocking on his right rear leg."

"You are correct, madam."

Bravo, Jane.

"That's interesting," her friend continued. "Don't you find that interesting, Celia? He is one of Mr. Aldrich's prize racehorses, isn't he?"

"He is now."

"Did Mr. Hollis once own the animal?" asked Celia. That would explain why a portrait of the horse was hanging in his office.

"He paid the stud fees for Validus's sire. Carefully chose the broodmare. Raised the colt. He has since purchased another horse, but—" The secretary glanced out the window at Celia's back. "Ah, here is Mr. Hollis's eight o'clock, come to review paperwork."

The bell above the door tinkled gently and a rotund man with fabulously thick side whiskers lumbered inside.

The secretary greeted the fellow then turned back to Celia and Jane. "I am afraid I must bid you two ladies a good day." He added an insincere smile to the statement, which was a clear and terse request for them to leave. Immediately.

Celia stood. "Thank you. We shall return at another time. Come, Jane." The secretary did not appear confused as to why she did not leave her card. *Probably because he is so keen to see us gone.*

The rotund fellow politely doffed his hat, the motion wafting the smell of cigar smoke off his clothes, as she and Jane swept outside and onto the pavement.

The door closed behind them and Celia squeezed Jane's arm. "How excellent of you, Jane, to recognize Mr. Aldrich's racehorse, which Mr. Hollis once owned. An interesting fact."

"I have a confession, Celia. I didn't know it was a painting of Validus. I made a guess." She winked and hurried around to the driver's side of the Hutchinsons' waiting tilbury and climbed aboard.

"Very clever, Jane." Celia clambered onto the seat and straightened her skirts. "Perhaps it is *you* who should be assisting Mr. Greaves with his murder cases."

Jane collected the reins and snapped them over the carriage horse's back. "I believe he prefers working with you, Celia, even if he doesn't like to admit how he feels."

Celia's cheeks warmed with an absolutely unnecessary blush.

⌘ Chapter 14 ⌘

"I am astonished you invited me to accompany you to the Ocean House Course today, Mr. Greaves," Celia said. "Pleasantly so, of course."

She and Nicholas Greaves had boarded the Omnibus Railway car to Mission Dolores. From there they would either hop aboard one of the scheduled coaches, which would drive the rest of the way along Ocean House Road, or hire a conveyance of their own. At least the weather promised to be calm as they rattled along Market Street. A fine day for the races. The course had opened only two years ago to great fanfare and a heavily publicized race between Lodi and Norfolk. She recalled the advertisements in the newspapers, there had been so many. Interest in the Ocean House Course had waned since then, though. Although, based on the quantities of deep-brimmed bonnets, long outer coats, and a general air of expectancy, there were several individuals occupying their horsecar who were bound for the races.

Celia glanced over at Mr. Greaves, seated alongside her, his thigh brushing against her blue skirt. He stared out the window at the passing landscape, the number of buildings lessening, thinning out to reveal patchy lots of scrub and sand, the surrounding hills rising and falling to the sea. No matter how often she traveled west from the city, she continued to marvel at how the sprawl of the town reached into the scrub and the sand, consuming it.

"Did you hear me, Mr. Greaves?" Was he lost in similar thoughts as hers? Pondering the speed at which the world changed?

He shifted to look at her. "If I didn't invite you and you'd heard that I'd gone—which you eventually would—I'd have ended up on the receiving end of a tongue-lashing and I wanted to avoid that."

Clearly, he'd heard her. "I do not give tongue-lashings, Mr. Greaves."

"Okay."

Honestly. "This is a good time, I believe, to inform you that Jane and I had an opportunity to visit Mr. Hollis's office early this morning."

"He wasn't there, was he?" he asked.

"No, he was not."

"So you and Mrs. Hutchinson did not need to be gallivanting about so early in the morning."

"Jane and I were not gallivanting. We were collecting clues relevant to your case." At least she'd not slipped and said "our" case, as she too often did.

He frowned, although the expression did not sit long on his face. "I just stopped myself from reminding you to not interfere in police matters, Mrs. Davies, because I've learned there's no point."

"Furthermore, I can be useful, don't you agree?" she asked. "Which is why you invited me to accompany you."

"No comment." He sighed. "So what was it that you and Mrs. Hutchinson were up to so early this morning, if you weren't gallivanting?"

"We went to Mr. Hollis's office to question him about his relationship with Mr. Pierson and Mr. Aldrich," she answered, gripping the seat in front of her as the car bumped over a rough patch of ground. "Under the guise of enquiring about the sort of services Mr. Hollis might be able to provide to two women of moderate means."

He laughed. "Gallivanting, Mrs. Davies. Frank must still be away from town if Jane is able to go along with your schemes."

"Do you wish to hear what we discovered or not?" she asked. "And I gather you were aware of the fellow's absence from his office because you had located him at the Olympic Club."

"Can I keep anything from you, Mrs. Davies?" he asked. "That is where I found him, sparring with his boxing instructor."

"How intriguing." A fellow as fine as a fiddle, as the cook her aunt had once employed, a woman from the area of Leeds, used to say. "A pursuit that should make Mr. Hollis quite strong, I presume. A fearsome opponent in a fight."

"Maybe so, but his domestic has provided him an alibi for last evening, Mrs. Davies. After he left a meeting of the Dashaway Association, he returned home at around seven. I had a chance to ask her after I left the Olympic Club. He didn't murder Fulton," he said. "She also gave him an alibi for Monday night."

"Dr. Harris was uncertain how long Mr. Fulton had been dead by the time he examined the body, Mr. Greaves," she reminded him. "And can a woman dependent upon her employer's good graces for her position be fully trusted?"

"The San Francisco police don't make use of the rack, so we'll have to go with it," he said flatly. "Fulton's boss came into the station this morning. He told us that Fulton had been jumpy since Griffin's murder."

"Perhaps he *did* observe the crime."

"We've also learned that a witness saw the fellow with the plaid coat last night, near where Fulton was shot."

"Ah! But who is he?" she asked. "Has anyone come forward with information on him?"

"No, unfortunately."

It was disheartening, how difficult it could be to collect information. They'd both encountered resistance before. "Most frustrating, Mr. Greaves."

"I showed Hollis that fragment of a note. Didn't have anything useful to say. Although he has helpfully remembered a comment Pierson made to him about owing some fellow money and looking nervous on Monday."

"Which Mr. Hollis neglected to mention at the inquest." Perhaps Jane's friend would have relevant information that might substantiate his comment about Mr. Pierson's monetary situation.

"Hollis was reluctant to cast suspicion on Edward Pierson, which is why he didn't say anything."

"But, now that a second man is dead, he no longer is reluctant?"

He flashed a wry smile. "I also searched the locker he uses at the Olympic Club. Nothing worth noting inside it."

"No plaid coat?"

"Or small-caliber gun," he replied.

The car turned south toward Mission Dolores. If she were sitting on the other side, she might be able to lean through the window and see its crumbling pale stucco exterior and red tile roof, a cross at its peak, the trees and headstones of its churchyard. Catch a glimpse of the more recently constructed house, attached like an unwanted extremity that jutted at a right angle to the squat main building.

"So your trip to Hollis's office didn't uncover anything useful," Mr. Greaves said.

"Oh, no, that is not at all the case. He has a most fascinating painting of a horse on the wall."

"I know. I've seen it." He shrugged. "Hollis likes racehorses."

"That is not just any racehorse, Mr. Greaves."

His eyes moved to her mouth. She must be grinning though she fought against it. "I can see that you're burning to tell me. Why not just go ahead."

"It's a portrait of Validus. His secretary told us, after a very clever query by Jane, who pretended to recognize the animal."

"Well, how about that," he said. "How do you do it, Mrs. Davies?"

Had she astonished him? She rather hoped she had. Even if his open admiration of a woman who was not a widow was inappropriate.

"It seems that Mr. Hollis once owned Validus before relinquishing the animal to Mr. Aldrich," she said.

"Did his secretary say anything else?"

"No, that was all," she said. "I am curious, though, how Mr. Hollis felt about losing Validus. Perhaps he was angry and had plotted revenge. Might he have hired Mr. Griffin to kill Mr. Aldrich that evening, aware that Mr. Aldrich would be at the Piersons', but Mr. Aldrich overcame Mr. Griffin?"

"Hiring Griffin to kill Aldrich is a pretty extreme reaction to losing a horse, ma'am," he said. "And Harris doesn't think Griffin caused that bruise on Aldrich's jaw."

"Perhaps he did trip over his dog." As he'd attested at the inquest.

"And I'll believe that excuse when pigs fly, Mrs. Davies."

The mission came into full view, and the driver brought the horsecar to a halt. Across the way, a real estate developer had erected a large sign advertising house lots for sale. Further proof of the ever-encroaching tide of the city, impossible to hold back.

"I questioned Pierson about his reported disagreement with Aldrich over a racehorse. Made the squabble sound insignificant," Mr. Greaves said. "Harris told me something interesting about Aldrich's trainer being accused of having poisoned an opponent's horse not long ago. I questioned Pierson about that, too, just to see his reaction to his former boss's bout of misfortune."

"A patient of mine mentioned that event also, Mr. Greaves, but not that Mr. Aldrich's trainer had been implicated," she said. "How did Mr. Pierson respond?"

"He got pretty flustered by my attempt to link the poisoning to our recent murders, and insisted he'd never believed the allegation."

"Nonetheless, it might be interesting to learn more about the death of that horse, do you not agree?"

"Well, we're not headed for the racetrack to gamble, ma'am," he replied, reseating his hat as he readied to stand.

"Perhaps we *should* gamble, Mr. Greaves." The other passengers rose and shuffled off the horsecar. Celia stood as well. "We might look less suspicious if we do, and perhaps the fellows taking the bets will have interesting things to tell us. About, oh, prior problems at the racecourse involving a man who is now a suspect in a murder investigation."

He gave a smile of surrender. "Have I ever mentioned that you would make a good detective, Mrs. Davies?"

"You have, and we both concluded that women will never be permitted to serve on the police force, Mr. Greaves. So my skills, limited as they are, shall have to be restricted to what I can do to help you."

"Sorry that they've been needed."

I am not.

• • •

They transferred to a stagecoach that would take them the rest of the way to the Ocean House Course, a good four miles from the Mission Dolores. Nick found himself crushed against Celia Davies even more tightly than he'd been in the horsecar, an uncomfortable situation in more ways than one. She was a married woman with a husband who'd decided to reappear in her life, a man she'd tasked to help find Owen Cassidy. Paid him even though she'd spoken so poorly of Patrick Davies that Nick had presumed she'd be happy to never, ever see the man again. Guess that only applied to when she couldn't find a use for the fellow. *Now you're just sounding jealous, Greaves.* He should have gone to the track with Mullahey and not have brought her. It might even be dangerous. Fights broke out regularly at racetracks. Some fellow had been shot a few weeks back in an argument over a bet. Bringing her along to nose around . . . it was stupid to give into his urge to spend more time with her. If he needed the companionship of a woman, someone like Violet Westerfield would be more than willing. But he didn't want anybody else's company, and he'd rushed out of the house again that morning before Miss Westerfield had arisen in order to avoid telling her goodbye.

"You are awfully quiet, Mr. Greaves." Celia Davies looked up at him with her pale, clear eyes. He could fall into them and happily drown, if such a thing were possible.

"Just mulling over what we should do when we arrive at the track, ma'am."

"Ah. And here I thought you were still pondering why you'd decided to bring me along."

"How about I don't respond to that, ma'am."

To which she laughed.

• • •

The coach bumped and rattled over the last mile of the journey. Celia and Mr. Greaves had been crowded among other travelers like pickles in the bottom of a barrel, ascending into the hills that hugged the sea, only sand and scrub to observe. But then they'd crested a ridge and been greeted by a view of the ocean, gray-blue beneath low clouds. Celia had leaned her head through the window so far that Mr. Greaves had enquired if she meant to jump out. Plentiful vegetable gardens, their produce intended for the city markets, and rolling pastures dotted with cattle surrounded them. At last they arrived at the Ocean House and their destination.

"Well, thank goodness that's over," said Mr. Greaves, taking her hand to help her down the steps of the coach.

"You did not enjoy our journey here?"

"Not that fond of having my teeth shaken out of my skull, ma'am."

They moved away from their fellow passengers. The breeze from the ocean skimmed her cheeks, and the air was salty crisp with a quality she could never adequately describe. The smell and the feel would forever remind her of San Francisco, though, should she ever leave the city and manage to conjure the sensations.

"There is where we're headed, ma'am."

He referred to a collection of low buildings across from a grove of trees and the Ocean House, for which the course had been named. The hotel was a two-story white building of pleasing proportions, the balcony that wrapped around the structure providing shade for the ground floor, and overtopped by a square cupola. The oval track itself was circumscribed by a three-rail fence, around which groups of people had begun to collect in anticipation of the day's races. Some individuals watched from horseback while a handful had driven conveyances to locations where they could observe the proceedings while sheltered from the wind. Quite a few women, enveloped in brightly patterned shawls and cloaks to protect them against the brisk ocean air, were in attendance, meaning Celia's presence would not draw attention.

"Looks like the horses are getting readied for the first race," Mr. Greaves said, strolling in the direction of the track.

Near the low outbuildings, men gathered around saddled horses, steadying them with soothing words as a last-minute inspection took place. A man collecting the price of admission—one dollar each—stopped Celia and Mr. Greaves before they could continue on.

"This is rather exciting," she said, clasping her bonnet as a gust of wind tugged at the brim. With Owen missing and two murders to contend with, she should not feel so lighthearted. But out in the clean ocean air, gulls whirling and calling, animated conversation and laughter surrounding her, she could not help but feel invigorated.

"We're not here for the racing, ma'am."

"You do not need to remind me, Mr. Greaves. And I believe I have spotted Mr. Aldrich. Over there." He was taller than the other men clustered around him. Or perhaps it was simply the towering top hat he wore that made him appear so.

"Anybody else?"

She studied the crowd. "No, but I expect Mr. Hollis is too busy practicing his boxing to attend a horse race, Mr. Greaves."

"He'd have finished his exercises by now, ma'am. He's an early riser, apparently."

"As Jane and I also learned," she replied. "I suppose we could not expect Mr. or Mrs. Pierson to be here."

"Ma'am, I don't know what to expect from Pierson or any of these fellows anymore."

She had to agree. "While you were mulling in the coach on the way here, I presume you came up with a strategy for how we should proceed."

"You don't have a plan?"

He was teasing, of course. And suddenly anxious, for right then he reached up to the battle wound on his left arm and gave it a squeeze.

"I suppose I shall mingle with the crowds gathering around the track," she said. "Do you know the order of races?"

"It's my understanding that Aldrich's horse will run in the second set of racing heats. The harness races come after that."

A man flapping notepapers in his upraised hand had attracted a knot of bettors reaching for money to hand over. Mr. Greaves leveled his hat and gestured in their direction. "I think I'll go and place a bet on Validus."

"The animal should be heavily favored. You'll not win any sort of money."

"I didn't know you were a gambler, Mrs. Davies."

"I am not, but I did spend enough time around my uncle and his acquaintances, who were." Long hours in his library had been spent debating the racing form as well as politics and other topics, her aunt pacing unhappily in the passageway outside the room. A time and place so distant that it seemed a lifetime had passed, even though she'd been gone from England for only six years. "As for me, I believe I shall wander over to the side of the track and strike up a conversation with some ladies. Good luck, Mr. Greaves."

"I'd wish you good luck too, Mrs. Davies, but I have a feeling you'll be perfectly fine."

"I do not know what to do with all of your compliments lately, Mr. Greaves. Whatever has happened to you?"

His eyes lingered on her face for a long time, heating her cheeks. *I should not be so coy and flirtatious with him. What am I doing?*

"I must've forgotten myself. Don't get too close to the edge of the track, ma'am. It looks a bit muddy from all the rain. Wouldn't want you to get dirty." He tapped his fingertips to the brim of his hat and strode off to join the gaggle of bettors.

Now, where do I start?

She located a likely set of individuals who were more expensively dressed than the rest of the crowd in their sturdy everyday clothes. Not that Celia was in her finery. Not that she actually possessed much finery. They, however, might be the sort who'd gossip with her about a man like J. Lyman Aldrich or Matthew Hollis.

"This is quite exciting," she announced to a woman—close to her own age, Celia judged—and swathed in a gown with a dark bodice and a sweeping skirt of dove gray. Which were uncrushed, unlike Celia's outfit. She cast a glance at her own skirt, wrinkled from the journey in the coach. Perhaps the woman had simply walked over from her rooms at the Ocean House, where she was enjoying a brief holiday near the beach. "Do you not agree?" Celia added when the woman ignored her initial comment.

Her gaze scanned Celia, checking for acceptableness. "Have you never come to see the horses before?" she asked, offering a tight smile. She must have decided that Celia met her standards.

She had a faint accent which Celia believed indicated she came from the northernmost states. She did have difficulty pinpointing the origin of American accents.

"No, I've not ever been." Celia returned the woman's taut smile with a broad one of her own. "My housekeeper enjoys visiting the Willows near the Mission, and it was she who encouraged me to enjoy an afternoon of leisure at the Ocean House racecourse."

The mention of a housekeeper improved the woman's attitude, and she turned to face Celia. "Validus is due to run today." Her eyes—they were the color of roasted chestnuts and were all that was warm about her—sparkled at the idea. The horse truly must be exceptional.

"That is why I chose today in particular to attend. I have heard so much about the creature."

"At least none of those dark-skinned jockeys like they use back East will be riding today."

Celia suppressed the response she'd like to make to that statement. "It is my understanding that Mr. Aldrich obtained the animal from a Mr. Matthew Hollis," she said. "It surprises me that Mr. Hollis would have let the horse go, if Validus is indeed so remarkable."

"I don't know Mr. Hollis, but Mr. Aldrich was very pleased with himself for obtaining the horse. And that a large amount of money was involved."

"Five hundred dollars, perhaps?" Celia asked.

The other woman's previously smooth forehead creased. "No, that wasn't it, although I did hear something about five hundred dollars. But what . . ." She shook her head and giggled. "I do wish I'd been paying more attention at that soirée when the topic came up, but the sparkling wine served had been so delicious."

Blast it. I also wish you had been paying more attention. "I completely understand. I myself have a terrible weakness for champagne."

The pretense appeared to have encouraged the woman to take Celia in her confidence, for she leaned in close, ready to impart her knowledge. "Frankly, I'm astounded that Mr. Aldrich dared to return with Validus."

"And why is that?"

"Because of that poor horse that died late last month. Didn't you read about it in the newspapers?"

"I did hear, but since I learned the news from a domestic, I dismissed it as merely sensational." She rolled her eyes as though domestics could not be trusted to differentiate the truth from fiction. The remark made her sound nearly as prejudiced as the woman she was speaking to. *My deepest apologies, Addie.*

"We were here when it happened. I and my husband . . ." She glanced around, as if abruptly recalling she had come with the fellow but had forgotten where she'd left him. "Oh, there he is. Anyway, we were in attendance that afternoon. Shocking."

"I can imagine!"

"And I'm saying it's very daring of Mr. Aldrich to *ever* return with one of his horses because it was . . ." She paused again, this time to inspect their surroundings for eavesdroppers. No one was paying any attention, least of all her bewhiskered husband. "Because it was Mr. Aldrich's trainer who was accused of the crime, you know. Getting rid of the competition for his boss."

"I cannot comprehend . . . Mr. Aldrich?" Celia said, hoping she sounded stunned by the news. "I recently purchased a policy at the insurance company that he presides over. Should I cancel?"

"You might want to, if you can. Lots of suspicious doings at his agency, you know."

Like profiting off of arson, perchance? "Was Mr. Aldrich's trainer convicted?"

Her companion screwed up her face. "Not that I remember. A travesty, if you ask me. The poor animal. Foaming at the mouth and writhing about . . . Oh, do forgive me. That was tasteless."

Celia indicated with a wave that she was not offended. "It is quite terrible, though."

A loud murmur overtook the crowd, which surged forward, a man behind Celia bumping her aside. The jockeys—kitted out in pale trousers, short silk jackets in bright colors, and black caps—were given a knee up, their horses then led onto the track. Mr. Aldrich, who'd been standing near the gate in the track fence, strode away. Probably to ensure Validus was ready for his set of races when the animal's turn came.

"How the rumors swirled. Oh, yes! Now I recall. The five hundred dollars didn't have anything to do with Mr. Aldrich purchasing Validus." The woman brightened. "It's rumored to have been a bounty on the poor creature!"

A bounty? "On Validus or on the one that was poisoned?"

"On Validus!"

• • •

"You're telling me Matthew Hollis lost Validus to Aldrich in a bet." Nick leaned against a railing behind the largest of the outbuildings, a stable where the racehorses could be tended to before being called to the post, and eyed the kid who'd been willing to talk. "Right?"

"Yep. He and Mr. Aldrich had been going at it for weeks." The kid had an unfortunate number of smallpox scars on his face and neck, but a broad, bright smile and keen eyes. "Money bets mostly. Things like which of them could toss their hats furthest or guess the vote count of an election. Eventually, Mr. Hollis challenged Mr. Aldrich to a footrace."

"Hollis gambled Validus on the outcome of a footrace."

"He shouldn't have lost, you know?"

"I've seen the guy box, so I'm surprised he did."

"Shoot, everybody was. Some folks made some big money on that footrace, betting on Mr. Aldrich. His friends, mostly." The kid turned to spit on the ground. "The ponies is expensive business, especially if you've had a string of dead busts like Mr. Hollis had before Validus came along and proved to be worth all that money he'd spent on him."

"Bad blood between the two men after that?"

He waited until a pair of riders trotted their horses past to answer. "Not as far as I could tell. Mr. Hollis was a good sport about the outcome. Heard he's bought another horse since," he said. "Wish everybody was as good a sport. None of 'em like losing to Mr. Aldrich. He has a habit of rubbing his opponents' noses in it when he wins."

What a great guy. "Has a fellow named Caleb Griffin ever worked here?"

The kid's eyebrows shot up his scarred forehead. "Heard he got killed the other day."

"You knew him."

"Lots of folks knew Caleb Griffin, Detective," he replied. "I wouldn't say he ever worked here, though. Not officially, at least."

"Was he unofficially employed by Mr. Aldrich when that horse tragically died a few weeks ago?"

The kid shrugged. "Ooh, that was a mess, though," he said. "Felt sorta sorry for Mr. Pierson. His first and only thoroughbred, far as I know. Rotten way to go."

Well, well. Wish you'd been a little more forthcoming last night when I questioned you, Mr. Pierson. "You're positive that Edward Pierson owned the horse."

"I am. But to accuse Mr. Aldrich's trainer of killing the animal?" He laughed. "Like Mr. Aldrich would bother to get rid of the competition. Although Apollo was solid. Might've even whipped Validus that day."

"You didn't believe the accusation."

"No way. Which is what I told the cops when they came here to investigate." He peered at Nick. "Didn't you hear about it from them?"

"We don't sit around and swap tales every day." Besides, Nick never would've heard about an event that had occurred well outside of his jurisdiction.

"Well, Mr. Aldrich's trainer showed up late that day and hadn't been anywhere near the stable." He pointed a thumb toward the building right behind them. "I saw the man who did it, though, and he sure wasn't Mr. Aldrich's trainer, who was a dark-skinned fellow at the time. Mr. Aldrich has a different man working with his racehorses now."

The trainer's race made it pretty understandable why the blame had been cast on him. Unless somebody simply had it in for Aldrich and didn't mind seeing his name tarnished. "You think you saw the person who might've poisoned the horse?"

"I did. Some guy I'd never seen around before, which is what made me suspicious when I saw him sneaking out of the stable."

"How would you describe the suspicious fellow?"

"Lean, not quite your height. I chased after him, but he got away." The kid frowned, regretful. "I checked on the horses and didn't notice anything wrong, and since it was getting close to the first race, I had to go help out with that. It was after the second heat that we heard the almighty commotion over here and some fellow screaming bloody murder. Turned out to be Mr. Pierson. It was too late to do anything about his poor horse. Too late."

* * *

A pistol shot sounded, sending the horses charging down the track, the first of multiple heats a mile in length to be run. The crowd surged forward, crushing Celia against the back of a fellow brandishing his hat in the air. His female companion cheered so loudly that she went red-faced, causing Celia to worry for the woman's heart. The racehorses, kicking up clumps of mud, rounded the far bend. Celia's gaze moved over the throng, greatly enjoying itself. And spotted a man in an ill-fitting, faded army overcoat.

"Excuse me." Celia elbowed her way back through the people pressed in all around her, who exclaimed at her rudeness before rushing forward to take the spot she'd vacated.

"Mr. Greaves! That man. Stop him!" Celia waved her arms, catching the attention of Mr. Greaves, strolling out from behind the stables. She motioned toward the fellow, who noticed her in turn and stopped, debating whether to approach. When he noticed Mr. Greaves running his direction, he changed his mind and sprinted for the horses tied up alongside the nearest shed. "Stop him!"

Mr. Greaves turned so that he'd intercept the man before he reached the horses and a chance at an escape. Celia gathered up her skirts, hurrying to join him when suddenly her ankle met an obstruction. She stumbled and fell to the ground, her hands skidding across the sandy dirt.

"My goodness! What is going on here?" a woman exclaimed.

"Are you all right, ma'am? That was a nasty fall." A severely handsome face, bracketed by silver-gray hair at the temples, looked down at her. He extended his hand, which she took, and yanked her to her feet. She'd twisted her right ankle, and the sudden pressure of her weight on it caused her to wince. "Mrs. Davies, if I recall."

She swiped her grit-crusted hands across her skirt. Her gloves were torn to shreds and her palms were bleeding. Fortunately for her outfit, she'd fallen onto a dry spot and not tumbled into a muddy puddle. "You remember correctly, Mr. Aldrich. Now, please excuse me."

Her ankle rebelled as she half ran, half limped toward the outbuildings. She'd lost track of Mr. Greaves. Had he caught the fellow? Or had the man gotten away? Most people were too preoccupied with the race to notice her graceless dash toward the area behind the stables. A boy holding a pail of feed walked out of a shed and eyed her as she rushed past. She frightened a horse tied to a post and it skittered sideways.

Bloody . . . where are they?

She rounded the building to find Mr. Greaves sprawled atop the fellow in the army overcoat, who was struggling to break free. Several men and a smattering of boys had come to assist. Or at least to watch.

"It appears you have matters well in hand, Mr. Greaves," Celia called out.

He looked over. "Very amusing, Mrs. Davies. Perhaps you can explain why I was supposed to stop this guy."

"Because he has been following me. Ever since I engaged—" She studied the fellow, squirming and yelping as Mr. Greaves leaned harder into his back. "Ever since I engaged a certain individual to search for our friend." The less said in front of the man, the better.

Mr. Greaves looked daggers at her. "If I find out you're keeping anything else from me, ma'am . . ."

"I am not, Mr. Greaves. Trust me."

A response he answered with a lengthy string of curse words.

"Why have you been following me?" Celia Davies leaned over the fellow slouched in the chair in front of Nick's desk.

Johnny Doherty clamped his mouth shut.

He'd been cooperative about returning to the station with Nick. More so than some folks he'd brought in for questioning. It probably had helped that Nick had recruited the brawniest fellow in the crowd to accompany them back to the city. As scrawny and undernourished as Doherty looked, though, Nick probably hadn't required the assistance.

"And where is Owen?" Mrs. Davies continued. "You are the Johnny he told me about. Admit that you are."

"Mrs. Davies, can you please step outside?" Nick asked. She'd refused to go home until after Doherty had been questioned. And now it looked like he wouldn't even be able to pry her loose from the detectives' office with a crowbar. "Besides, I thought you hurt your ankle at the track. Don't you need to give it a rest? There are plenty of chairs in the main office. I can handle the questioning in here."

"I shall not interfere, Mr. Greaves," she stated.

Except she already had been interfering. "Mr. Doherty, please answer the lady. Why have you been following her?"

Doherty slumped lower in the chair, as if he wanted to slide right off it and onto the ground. "Ain't been me," he said, exposing a mouthful of gaps where teeth used to be.

"It has been you," Mrs. Davies countered. "It was you who was at the saloon on Wednesday and followed me out of there and down the street. You who were near a secondhand shop yesterday when I left it. If you are not actually following me, then can you possibly explain the coincidence of you appearing at such disparate places at the precise time that I was there?"

"Dunno what you're talking about. Mighty strange-sounding, though."

Celia Davies readied a retort, which Nick cut off. "Please, ma'am, you need to leave the office so I can carry out police business in peace." If she didn't, Nick expected that the news would reach Captain Eagan and he'd be hauled into his boss's office again to discuss his abilities—or lack of abilities—as a detective.

"I deserve to hear this man's answers, Mr. Greaves."

"Which I'll be sure to relay to you later," Nick said just as Taylor slipped in through the partly open door.

Sighing loudly, she marched out. Taylor closed the office door behind her. Doherty snorted a chuckle.

"Enjoying a laugh, Mr. Doherty? There are two men dead, murdered by an unknown person, and another fellow missing. We have our suspicions that you're involved in some way. Very strong suspicions. So you might want to stop chuckling and start talking instead." Nick opened the top drawer in his desk and took out the note that Griffin had given Cassidy. He slid it across the desk toward Doherty. "First, maybe you can tell me if this is what you've been looking for."

"Don't know what you mean."

Those were the man's words, but he stared at the piece of paper with the keen interest of a hunter who'd just discovered his long-searched-for prey dumped in front of him.

"You sure about that?" he asked. "As Mrs. Davies mentioned, we know you visited Owen Cassidy in order to locate this very note."

"I don't know some kid named Owen Cassidy." His gaze had shifted from the piece of paper to a spot on the floor. Anyplace but Nick's face, where his lies might be clearly seen in his beady eyes.

"We can bring the landlady from his boardinghouse in here and ask if she's ever seen you before," said Nick. "I'm sure she'd remember a fellow like you. So why not admit that you know Cassidy and that you're the Johnny he meant?"

"Haven't got a clue, Detective, what you mean."

Nick leaned across the desk. "Yes, you do. And don't decide to pretend that your name isn't Johnny Doherty, because you were recognized by one of the boys who help at the Ocean House Course. You've worked there in the past, according to him."

"What's some kid know?"

"A lot, based on how uncomfortable you look."

Doherty scowled and resumed looking more interested in finding a way out of his chair than in talking to any policeman. He hadn't said a word on the way to the station, either. Other than to protest his innocence and that he'd been at the track to admire the ponies, that was all. He'd sweated and shook all the way into town, and Nick hadn't even told him what he was accused of. Hell, he didn't even know what accusation to level. Following Celia Davies wasn't exactly a crime. Questioning Cassidy about this note wasn't one, either.

"Come on now, Mr. Doherty. You don't want to enjoy a stay in one of our nice holdings cells, do you? They're a bit cold and damp and the rats . . ." Nick did a theatrical shiver. "They do keep our inhabitants up at night, I admit. Have a habit of nibbling that's downright uncomfortable."

Doherty bolted upright in the chair. "You can't throw me in the hoosegow."

"Yes, I can. Two murders, Mr. Doherty, and you acting mighty suspicious . . ." Nick let the fellow draw his own conclusions. "What's so important about this note?"

"I was paid by a fella to get it back. Pa Frank. He hired me 'cause I'm pretty well known for my ability to get jobs done." He puffed out his chest. Nick supposed a person could be proud about all sorts of things.

"Pa Frank?" They hadn't had any crooks in the station with that name before. Not since Nick had been there. He glanced over at Taylor, who shook his head. "That's his full name?"

"That's what we call him," Doherty answered.

"Did Pa Frank explain what's so important about that note?" Nick asked. Taylor hastily flipped to a fresh page of his notebook. "I mean, if you're out there risking your health to snatch some scrap of paper, you deserve an explanation, right?"

Doherty resumed slouching. "He said it was proof of a debt and promised me ten dollars if I got it back. I agreed, because I need the money."

"We've learned the note could be a reward offered for the killing of a racehorse named Validus." Mrs. Davies *had* been lucky at the racecourse to learn that tidbit.

"Well, I'll be," said Doherty.

"Pa Frank didn't tell you that detail."

"All I reckoned was that it had to do with a horse. That Validus horse. But when Pa Frank told me to get the scrap of paper off Griffin . . ."

"You asked for more money?" Nick asked.

Doherty reached up and scratched at his neck. His fingernails were dirty and chewed to nubs. "I tried."

And failed. "There isn't a signature. This note doesn't prove anything. Anybody could have written it."

"Pa Frank has the half with the signature. See how it's torn?" He grabbed the piece of paper, springing Taylor out of his chair to stop him from fleeing with it.

"It's okay, Taylor. Mr. Doherty isn't going anywhere."

Taylor retook his chair.

"You see here." Doherty ran a grimy fingertip along the torn edge.

"I do." Nick stretched out his hand and Doherty reluctantly returned the note. "What was the name on that other half?"

"I ain't seen the signature, Detective. Pa Frank just told me he had it, that's all," he said. "Pretty smart of Griffin to tear the note in half. Ain't got a clue how Pa Frank got ahold of part of it, though."

"Is that why you were at the Ocean House Course, Mr. Doherty?" Nick asked. "You were poking around, attempting to discover who might've signed the note and if this half might be worth more than ten bucks to them?"

"Mighta been. But that ain't a crime, Detective."

Knuckles rapped on the door and Mullahey poked his head inside the office. "Thought you'd like to know that we haven't found much of anything yet at Fulton's lodgings, Mr. Greaves. We'll keep searching, though. Oh, and Mrs. Davies is pacing out in the station looking mad as a wet hen."

Great. "Do you have those papers I asked you to locate, Mullahey?"

"I do."

Taylor hopped up to take them off Mullahey and set them on Nick's desk. Mullahey slipped back out, reclosing the door.

"Where were we? Ah, yes. How did you learn that Griffin had given this half of the note to Owen Cassidy for safekeeping?"

"Heard from some mates. Won't be telling you my sources, though, Detective," he replied. "Boy, was I relieved to learn I wasn't going to have to deal with Griffin! Especially if Pa Frank wasn't gonna pay me more to take the risk." He sliced his thumbnail across his neck. "Of course, now Griffin's dead. Coulda knocked me over with a feather when I heard that."

Nick folded the note, creasing the paper between his forefinger and thumb. "Who do you think murdered him?"

"Somebody who wanted that note, I suppose," Doherty said and scratched his neck some more. Nick hoped the fellow hadn't brought any fleas with him into the station.

"Somebody like Pa Frank, you mean."

Realization dawned that he might've been dealing with a killer. "Dang it."

"Did you ever get a lead on where Cassidy is?" Nick asked.

Doherty eyed Nick as if hoping he might cough up some money in return for any information he had. Which he didn't do.

Doherty sighed. "Cassidy went underground. Lots of places to hide where a fellow won't be found for a long time if he wants not to be found. I'd heard the lady . . ." He gestured in the direction of the station. "I'd heard she was a friend of his, though. Thought she might know."

"Which is why you were following her."

"I just wanted to talk to her, Detective, that's all. But she kept running off."

"Can you blame her?" Nick returned the note to the drawer in his desk, locking it. "How were you to contact Pa Frank, Mr. Doherty? When the time came to collect your reward for getting ahold of the rest of the note."

"I was to leave a message at McNair's saloon for him saying Mr. Doherty had a pony to sell. You know, because of the horse named on that there piece of paper you locked away. That was my idea." He grinned, glancing around to see if Nick or Taylor appreciated how clever he'd been.

"After you left your message about a pony for sale, what then?"

"I was to wait for Pa Frank to turn up."

"I could watch the place, sir. Grab the fellow who responds to the message," Taylor offered.

Doherty waggled his head. "Nope. If anybody spots a cop keeping an eye on the place while I'm in there waiting for Pa Frank . . . I'll end up dead for sure. Marked out as a pigeon working for the police."

"We can make it worth your while. Might even forget about these prior cases you were a suspect in." Nick laid his hand atop the stack of papers Mullahey had delivered. The cases they covered didn't have anything to do with Doherty. Nick didn't feel all that proud of the deception, but he figured it might do the trick.

"I . . ." Doherty took to sweating. "I'm innocent."

"Help us out, Mr. Doherty."

"I can't have your men hanging around outside McNair's while I'm waiting for Pa Frank, Detective. I can't. You can't do that to me."

"What if I went there and pretended *I* had a pony to sell?" Nick asked.

"Pa Frank would know you got the secret message from me, Detective. Wouldn't look good, me sharing the information with a cop."

"Where is McNair's located?"

Doherty gave an address close to Market Street.

"I'll tell McNair to tell Pa Frank that I'm a friend and that you sent me," Nick said. "I'm not known in that part of town. It's not my jurisdiction."

Taylor had looked up from his note-taking, his expression implying that he thought the idea was a sure way for Nick to end up dead.

Doherty frowned. "Might work."

Or it might not.

• • •

The moment the detectives' office door opened to Mr. Taylor showing out Mr. Doherty, Celia bolted inside.

"Well?" she asked.

Mr. Greaves stood staring out the room's window, set at a level with the pavement outside, massaging his old wound. The interview with Mr. Doherty must not have gone as well as he had hoped.

"Mr. Doherty was following you because he hoped you'd lead him to Owen and the half of the note Griffin had given to him," he replied. "He'd been paid by the fellow who has the portion with the signature to recover the rest of the note."

"Is it a bounty to kill Validus?"

"Doherty couldn't say, but I'm guessing it is."

"Do you think this fellow became impatient and decided to confront Mr. Griffin himself?" Unaware Mr. Griffin no longer possessed the half he was seeking.

"It's very possible, ma'am," he replied, his head turning as he tracked a passing pedestrian.

"Did Mr. Doherty inform you where to find the man who hired him?"

"He was supposed to meet with the fellow at a saloon to make the exchange."

"I trust Mr. Doherty has agreed to lay in wait for this fellow at the saloon so that you can then arrest him."

Mr. Greaves gave his arm a lengthy massage rather than reply.

"*You* mean to be the bait in the trap, do you not, Mr. Greaves?" she asked. He could be so infuriating. "You cannot be thinking of going to that saloon and pretending to be Mr. Doherty, Mr. Greaves."

He glanced over his shoulder at her. "Doherty won't do the job for us. It's too dangerous for him and he's refused."

"It is far too dangerous for you."

"Taylor would probably agree, ma'am," he said. "I'm simply planning on waiting for the fellow to show up then follow him. Arrest him when it's clear. It'll be fine."

Was he truly as calm about his plan as he sounded? Celia certainly was not calm about the idea. "It will likely not be fine."

"We can at least exclude Doherty as a suspect in Griffin's death," he said. "Once he learned Cassidy had been given the note he didn't have to bother with Griffin."

"Owen remains in danger, however, even though *you* now have possession of his portion of the note."

He turned and rested his back against the windowsill. "I can't advertise that we've got it in order to protect Owen, ma'am. We'd never be able to snag the fellow who hired Doherty if I did. I'm sorry."

She started to protest but realized he was right. She would hold on to hope that Owen remained safe. It was all she could do.

"There's more, ma'am," Mr. Greaves said. "The horse that was poisoned—Apollo—belonged to Pierson."

Bloody . . . "Neither of the Piersons mentioned this."

"Maybe they thought the animal's death was irrelevant to the murders."

"You are being awfully generous, Mr. Greaves, but I now comprehend why Georgiana despises Mr. Aldrich, since his trainer was accused of the crime." Why she hated him enough to blame him for stealing her locket. "Yet Mr. Pierson continued his employment at the insurance agency. Why?"

"Remember that Pierson said he didn't believe the allegation."

"Possibly because he knew better?" Celia asked. "I wonder how large of an insurance policy Mr. Pierson took out on Apollo, Mr. Greaves. Enough of a sum to be behind the poisoning himself?"

"Now there's a thought, Mrs. Davies."

"Here is another," she said. "I suspect that Mr. Aldrich tripped me."

"Tripped you?"

"When I attempted to chase after Mr. Doherty, an object struck my leg. I believe it was Mr. Aldrich's umbrella, which he was carrying," she explained. "He was at my side to help me stand far too quickly to have not been in close proximity."

"Why would he have tripped you?"

"Because he did not wish me to catch up with Mr. Doherty, Mr. Greaves." He had to comprehend the likely reason, as well. Sometimes she believed he asked questions with obvious answers simply to ascertain if his thoughts made sense.

"But Aldrich is not the fellow who paid Doherty to retrieve the note." He tapped his desk where the piece of paper had been locked away.

"Are you positive?"

He scowled. "We'll nab the fellow and get some answers, ma'am. And you may not accompany me to the saloon, if you were considering asking."

"I was not."

"Somehow I don't believe you, Mrs. Davies."

• • •

"There truly was no need for you to accompany me home, Mr. Taylor." Celia took the hand he offered, helping her climb down from the hackney he'd hired.

"Mr. Greaves wouldn't like me to just send you off on foot, ma'am. Not with your bum ankle and all." He paid the driver, who wheeled off toward town. "Besides, I haven't seen you all the way home. Still have to walk up Vallejo to get to your house."

Which was not where she intended to end up; she had urgent business with Georgiana Pierson. The niggling matter of a poisoned horse that had belonged to her husband.

Mr. Taylor started up the incline, halting when he realized she was not following. "Ma'am?"

"Did you disembark from the hackney with me, Mr. Taylor, because you wish to visit with Addie?"

"Well . . . I might," he stammered. "But she's probably busy making dinner."

"She will happily take time to see you, Mr. Taylor." Addie would drop any task in order to visit with her beau.

He grinned. "Then I'll stop in, if you and Miss Barbara don't mind."

"Go on ahead and knock. I have a patient across the road whom I need to check on."

He glanced at her foot. "Are you going to be all right, ma'am?"

"My ankle feels much better." Actually, it had taken to throbbing again, but she could not delay speaking with Georgiana. "So go on ahead."

He tipped his policeman's hat and rushed up the road.

Celia slowly crossed the street, watching for him to climb the steps of her house and go inside before she turned around and headed for the Piersons'.

Celia's firm twist of the doorbell was answered by Georgiana herself. Again.

"Mrs. Davies, I wasn't expecting you. I thought we'd concluded our business," she said. "Or are you here to ask questions about the local policeman's death, too?"

"I was in the neighborhood visiting a patient and thought I would see how you were doing. The trauma of the past few days . . ." *Please invite me in. Please invite me in.*

Georgiana Pierson stood for so long with her hand upon the door handle that Celia expected to be turned away.

"Come inside, then," she said at last.

"I do not wish to intrude, Mrs. Pierson." Celia stepped over the threshold before Georgiana could process her comment and shut the door. "Is your husband at home?"

"No, he isn't."

"Ah, good. I can speak with you in confidence then."

Celia's comment intrigued Georgiana, and she shepherded Celia toward the parlor.

"Well?" Georgiana asked, sliding the doors closed behind her.

"I've learned of a very alarming incident, Mrs. Pierson, that occurred involving a racehorse your husband owned," she said. "You never mentioned to me that Apollo had died and that Mr. Aldrich's trainer was accused in its death. Why not?"

"It was a shameful and embarrassing situation I wanted to forget all about," she said. "The police were aware. It wasn't a secret. Besides, the tragic death of that animal has nothing to do with the murder of that Mr. Griffin fellow or the loss of my locket. Or the death of the local policeman. Just like Edward told Detective Greaves."

Without clarifying that the horse involved had been his.

"Your husband had to have been upset, however."

"He was. He loved that animal." Georgiana sounded jealous.

"Did he confront Mr. Aldrich about the accusation?"

She slitted her eyes. "You mean, was Apollo's death the reason they'd argued?" she asked. "Mr. Greaves has already questioned Edward about their disagreement, Mrs. Davies. You're a tad late."

Late and not uncovering any fresh information. "I hope, at least, that Mr. Pierson had adequately insured Apollo."

"If he had, he might not have needed to beg Mr. Aldrich and Mr. Hollis to invest in his business."

"Are you telling me he did not sufficiently insure the animal?"

"Edward does not consult me, Mrs. Davies, or else he would've."

Celia regarded the woman across from her, observed the way the light from the window fell upon her smooth-skinned, lovely face. How had she come to marry a man she clearly disrespected? *And need I ask?* When she herself well understood how such mistakes occurred.

"Your husband must greatly admire Mr. Aldrich, Mrs. Pierson, if he asked him to join his business venture after the scandal surrounding Apollo," she said. "And to stay on at Western States."

"He's not there any longer, Mrs. Davies."

"He left weeks after the death of his prized racehorse."

"My husband is willing to believe the best of people." Georgiana made the trait sound both foolish and unfathomable. "And was keen to keep his position."

"Because your husband is in debt, Mrs. Pierson? This house, the furnishings . . ." Celia asked, closely watching Georgiana. Her nursing training had taught her how to be observant, a skill that had often proven useful.

Georgiana paused. Concocting another tale perhaps. Or finally deciding to settle upon honesty.

"Edward might be in debt, Mrs. Davies. I don't know for sure."

"Did he owe Mr. Griffin money?" Celia asked.

"I don't think so, not when he has so many friends willing to lend." She surveyed the parlor, all the beautiful furnishings, the curtains draped gracefully at the window, the lamps and candlesticks polished to a high gleam. "All Edward has wanted is to please me. Give me all that he'd promised. The house is lovely, isn't it? Perfect."

Unnaturally perfect. "Who sold your locket, Georgiana?" she asked softly.

She sighed. "It might've been Edward. Hardly enough to pay off the debts I fear he owes, though."

"Why tell me that Mr. Aldrich had stolen it? Because you blamed him for Apollo's death?"

"Maybe I wanted to believe he had taken it. He's caused so many people so much heartache." She squeezed her eyes shut for a moment. "Edward's never admitted to the debts, Mrs. Davies. Never mentioned Mr. Griffin's name. You have to believe me."

"It is not easy, when you've misled me about so much."

"Edward did not murder Mr. Griffin, if that's what you're trying to get me to say, Mrs. Davies. He gets sick at the sight of blood," she said. "Mr. Aldrich has to be the killer. He murdered that fellow outside our house, hoping to pin the crime on Edward. First he exacts some sort of petty revenge on Edward by having Apollo poisoned and then he murders that man in our yard."

"Revenge for what, Mrs. Pierson? Implicating the agency in insurance fraud, perhaps?"

Georgiana scowled. "Edward did not commit any fraud, Mrs. Davies."

"In order for Mr. Aldrich to be the murderer, Mrs. Pierson, he would have had to be aware that Mr. Griffin would be outside your house Monday evening," Celia pointed out.

"He must have summoned him here."

"However, the carriage driver Mr. Aldrich had hired was waiting for him. The fellow testified that he did not observe Mr. Griffin getting murdered."

"The carriage wouldn't have been waiting right outside our house, Mrs. Davies," she replied. "You've got to remember where the hackney left us that evening. A good hundred feet away."

"Yes, I do remember."

"Mr. Aldrich's carriage driver wouldn't have gotten any nearer. He was likely waiting on the corner, faced downhill and away from the house." Her voice rose on the certainty of her statement. "Waiting in a driving rainstorm, hunched beneath his waterproof coat, and unable to witness anything!"

℘ Chapter 16 ☙

The next morning, the doorbell interrupted Celia at her breakfast, Addie rushing out of the kitchen to answer. "If that is Mrs. Duncan for her appointment, Addie, tell her I will be with her as soon as I have another bite or two."

"It's me, Celia," called Jane. She paused in the parlor to hand Addie her bonnet and gloves.

"Good morning, Jane. Come and have some tea."

"I'll fetch you a cup, Mrs. Hutchinson," Addie said, returning to the kitchen.

"You have news from your friend?" Celia rather wished she had a notebook like the one belonging to Mr. Taylor. She should . . . no, she could *not* purchase one at Mr. Everett's shop any longer.

"I do." Jane smiled and took the seat catercorner from Celia's. "Alice was pretty willing to gossip. Most interestingly, she hadn't heard a peep about Georgiana's missing locket."

"She tells me now that Edward might have sold it." But which—if any—of Georgiana Pierson's tales should be believed?

"Maybe he did," Jane said, spreading her napkin across her lap. "Apparently, it's well known that Edward has been having financial problems. Off and on for some time. Bad investments, including in a racehorse that unexpectedly died a few weeks ago."

"Which Edward Pierson had inadequately insured, according to Georgiana," Celia said. "Mr. Aldrich's trainer was suspected of poisoning the animal, Jane. Did Alice tell you that?"

"She had heard, but everybody's dismissed it as idle tittle-tattle, because why would J. Lyman Aldrich want to poison Edward Pierson's horse?"

"Possibly because Mr. Pierson had embroiled Western States in insurance fraud?"

"Oh, my. I'm amazed Alice didn't know about that," Jane said.

She paused while Addie served her tea, along with some toast and sausage. Celia's housekeeper could never resist feeding people.

"Alice did hear that Edward had come into a sum of money earlier this year and was splashing it around town," Jane continued. "Outfitting their house on Russian Hill, for instance. Spending lavishly at the opera and at the best restaurants. Renting out office space on Montgomery for his new business concern. Alice didn't know where the cash had come from, which bothered her."

"Profits from dubious insurance claims?" Celia suggested. "Gambling? Loans from disreputable individuals such as Mr. Griffin?"

"Edward was rather reluctant to tell anybody the source."

Addie refreshed Celia's cup of tea before returning to the kitchen. "Yesterday, Georgiana did finally admit that he's gone into debt."

"Better late than never to tell the truth, I suppose."

Celia would have preferred rather sooner than later. "Edward Pierson's lavish spending must have exhausted the money, though, if he'd been forced to invite Mr. Hollis and Mr. Aldrich to his house to entreat them to back his new venture."

"By the way, Alice had no more news about Mr. Hollis than any of my other friends," Jane said, tucking into her food at a leisurely and ladylike pace, even though she'd likely already eaten. "Which means he hasn't been involved in any scandals or else she would."

"Does the absence of scandal make him less likely to be guilty of murder?" Celia asked. "You know as well as I that people lead secret lives, Jane. They can appear to be one person on the outside—affable, perhaps, upright and respectable—and be quite another on the inside."

"Good morning, Mrs. Hutchinson." Barbara swept into the dining room and planted a kiss on Jane's upraised cheek. "How is Grace?"

Jane smiled at Celia's cousin. "She is well and missing you terribly. She'll be home over the Christmas holidays."

"That's wonderful. I can't wait to see her." Barbara's gaze took them both in and her happiness over the prospect of soon seeing her dearest friend faded. "You were talking about Mr. Griffin's murder, weren't you?"

"I believe your tutor should be here at any time, Barbara," Celia said before her cousin could embark on a criticism that Celia would deserve. "You should prepare for her arrival."

"It's Saturday, Cousin."

Gad. She *had* been consumed by this case. "Indeed, Barbara."

"Nonetheless, I will happily take a breakfast tray up to my room." She bid Jane a good day and stomped off.

Celia sighed and pushed away her plate; she'd lost her appetite. "I did promise Barbara I'd no longer get involved in Mr. Greaves's cases."

"You and Georgie found the man's deceased body, Celia. It would be impossible for you to not get involved. Plus, Owen . . ."

"Is in the middle of this," Celia said. "Was that all your friend had to say?"

"Not at all," she replied. "Alice had news about a quarrel at the City Temperance Society involving Mr. Aldrich."

"He is a member there? I thought he was at the Dashaway Association."

"He's with both organizations, apparently," Jane said. "The quarrel involved a fellow who reportedly had resumed drinking. Rumors were flying and Mr. Aldrich got drawn into the middle of the situation. The member was so vilified, though, that he was drummed out of the group."

"Did Mr. Aldrich start the rumors?"

"Alice wasn't certain who was behind them, but the member forced out was the fellow who owns the stationery store you shop at. Mr. Everett."

Celia's hand, which held her teacup, paused on its ascent to her mouth. "You mean where I used to shop before an arson destroyed the building," she said. "Are you absolutely certain?"

"Oh, yes, Celia. That was the name."

• • •

"What's it say, sir?" Taylor tried to peer over the edge of the paper Nick held. Which wasn't easy, since Nick was striding down the sidewalk at a good clip.

"It's from Mrs. Davies, informing us she went to visit Mrs. Pierson after leaving the station yesterday." Nick looked up from the message. Just in time to avoid colliding with a telegraph pole. "I thought you took her to her house last night, Taylor."

Taylor flushed a pink the same shade as the peonies that grew in Mrs. Jewett's garden. "She told me she wanted to stop in on a patient, sir. I wasn't going to follow her to see if she was telling the truth," he said. "Besides, I had a talk with Miss Ferguson about Mrs. Davies pawning her mother's jewelry to pay . . . certain folks to help search for Owen."

"I know she's hired her husband, Taylor."

"Didn't think you'd want to hear about him."

I don't. "Her message says that Mrs. Pierson does believe that Aldrich was responsible for poisoning her husband's racehorse."

"Even though the investigating police had concluded it was an accident, sir?" Taylor asked. He'd had time to look into the report that had been filed.

"Guess so," Nick said. "Mrs. Davies also says Aldrich's and Hollis's hired carriages couldn't have parked close to the house because of the condition of the steep road." She'd neglected to add how she'd come to that conclusion.

"So anybody could've killed Mr. Griffin without being noticed by the cab drivers."

"There's also something here about Zacharias Everett. That he was ousted from the City Temperance Society and Aldrich was somehow involved. There's more, but the ink is smeared and I can't read it." Whichever of the cops she'd given the note to had been careless while handling it.

"Mr. Everett couldn't have liked getting kicked out, sir."

"Which makes two people—Everett and Pierson—who might want revenge against Aldrich, Taylor. What better way to get back at the fellow than plotting to kill his precious thoroughbred?" Nick folded Mrs. Davies's message and tucked it away. "We need to get Everett's alibis, Taylor."

"Will do. Oh, I followed up on Mr. Aldrich's and Mr. Hollis's alibis for Thursday evening. They both were at the Dashaway Association committee meeting that night like Mr. Hollis told you, and it did end early. Around six thirty, or so," Taylor said, stepping off the curb. "He got home when he said, but get this. Mrs. Aldrich told me her husband didn't make it to their house until eight. No way the trip should take that long."

"Meaning he had time to hotfoot it to Russian Hill and shoot Fulton?"

Taylor whistled. Enough of a reply.

• • •

"Sorry I couldn't come to the clinic like we'd arranged, ma'am." Essie Duncan opened the door to her tiny wood-frame house, which cowered in the shadows of the larger and more substantial homes climbing the hillside behind and above it. One day, the owners of those homes might seek to sweep away the squat houses at their feet rather than endure gazing upon them.

"It is perfectly fine to send for me, Mrs. Duncan," said Celia.

"I wouldn't have, but my boy–" The child let out a wail from somewhere inside the house. "He's always going on. Annie wasn't like that. Such a sweet child she was . . ." Her voice trailed off as her mind wandered into mournful recollections.

"Is your boy unwell? Would you like me to have a look at him?"

"If you would, ma'am." Essie gestured at the room to Celia's left, the only one on the ground floor that faced the street. "He's in here. I was trying to get some mending done, but I can hardly think for all his crying. My husband can't stand to be here when the boy is going on like he is."

A sad excuse to leave his wife to tend to everything on her own, like so many women in her situation.

The boy, six or seven months old, was sitting up next to the cold hearth, his face red from crying, his lips wet from drool. "Is he teething, Mrs. Duncan?"

"Yes, but Annie never fussed over some teeth like this one. He's had the colic too."

Celia skirted Essie's mending, piled next to a stool, and the other, few pieces of furniture in the room, which included a secondhand—or thirdhand—cradle. "What have you given him for the colic?"

"The same as for his teething pains. Mrs. Winslow's Soothing Syrup. Which does help him sleep, but then he's near impossible to wake up in the morning."

Because the patent medicine contained morphine, thought Celia. She bent over Essie's young son, whose blue eyes were as clear as a fresh stream. He had long lashes that swept his cheeks when he blinked. "Are you feeling unwell, young man?"

Essie produced a not very clean cloth and wiped the drool off his chin. Celia lifted the child. The feel of him, vulnerable yet solid and strong, made her heart contract around an emotion she rarely permitted herself to experience. She'd never been able to carry a child to term and she suffered the loss more than she cared to admit.

He squirmed in her grip and let out a healthy yowl.

"I'm sorry, ma'am."

"No need to apologize, Mrs. Duncan." Settling the child on her hip, Celia slipped a finger inside his mouth. Two bumps, one quite sharp, announced the arrival of a pair of teeth. "You may wish to try castor oil for his colic. And allow him to chew on something cold and hard to help his teething pains. Along with a preparation of chamomile. But no more Mrs. Winslow's Soothing Syrup."

"If you're sure . . ."

Celia smiled at the child, his face scrunching in preparation of another cry. *Poor thing.* Reluctantly, she handed him over to Essie.

"Beyond that, he looks perfectly healthy."

Essie returned him to his place by the empty hearth, which hadn't seen a fire in ages, given the absence of ashes. "He looks like his father, you know?" she said, handing the boy a tin rattle.

"He is a handsome child," said Celia. "Now, Mrs. Duncan, let me examine your wound. Over here by the window."

Brushing back the fringe of hair that covered Essie's forehead, Celia examined the cut. The sticking plasters had become soiled; the woman would not have the funds to spare to purchase fresh ones. Nonetheless, between the strips, the angry redness of the wound had lessened and the wound had begun to heal. Essie Duncan was strong.

"You are healing well, Mrs. Duncan. Come by my clinic on Monday so that I can remove those stitches," she said. "I would like to clean around the plasters, however. Do you have fresh water I might use? And a clean cloth of any material."

"I have a kettle on the hob. Would that work?"

"Bring some of that, if you will."

Essie hurried over to a door at the back of the room, its latch secured with the handle of a rusty iron ladle. To keep her son from venturing through it, Celia assumed, and into the kitchen beyond. The boy, who'd been chewing on the rattle, watched her depart and return with a mug of hot water and a scrap of cotton, stained but recently washed.

"I got to thinking about our conversation the other day, ma'am. When we were talking about that horse track," she said as Celia wet the cloth and proceeded to wipe the area around the plasters. "I spoke to my husband about it. I hope you don't mind."

"Not at all."

"Anyway, he told me he'd kept an article about that horse getting poisoned and dying. It happened at the same course that was looking for workers," Essie said. "Likely needing hands because the place has troubles, if horses are falling sick and all. Probably can't keep help for love nor money. He kept the article because the story was so queer."

"I would like to read the cutting, if possible."

"I'll fetch it for you." She hurried off again. This time, her child tossed his rattle and bawled. Celia gathered him into her arms and jiggled him on her hip, cooing whatever comforting words she could think of. Amazingly, her efforts worked.

Essie returned with a scrap of paper. "Here, Mrs. Davies," she said and took back her son. "I can only read a couple of words—I've been meaning to learn more—but I think this is it."

Celia smiled to ease the woman's embarrassment over her illiteracy. The article describing the scandal around the horse's death had been ripped from a newspaper. An advertisement for a superior brand of lemonade had been included in the hasty tear.

Essie peered around Celia's shoulder. "What's it say?"

"It does describe what happened with the racehorse and that the police concluded the animal's death was accidental," she said. They'd spoken to Mr. Pierson and Mr. Aldrich, along with a variety of others at the Ocean House Course that day.

"It was killed, I'm telling you, Mrs. Davies. At least, that's what my husband says."

"It is possible—" A name in a line of the article stopped her cold. P. Frank and C. Griffin were questioned about the incident but released.

Caleb Griffin. What were you doing there?

Celia handed back the scrap of paper. "Thank you, Mrs. Duncan. That was most informative."

• • •

"Mr. Greaves. Back again?" J. Lyman Aldrich's gaze shifted to Taylor, standing at Nick's side in the Western States office.

"My assistant, Officer Taylor," said Nick by way of introduction. "Hope we're not intruding."

Aldrich smiled. The expression wasn't genuine, but at least he'd put in the effort. Nick hadn't been sincere about hoping he and Taylor weren't intruding, either.

Aldrich had carved out an office at the rear of the insurance agency, a chest-high partition separating him from the rest of the space. A spot that was closest to the cast-iron Franklin stove. Wouldn't want the head of the agency's board to suffer on a cold San Francisco day. The fellow Nick had encountered the first day he'd been in the agency sat at his desk by the front door, on the watch for possible clients, but the other desks were empty. Not much business on a Saturday, maybe.

"Not at all, Detective. Please, have a seat." Aldrich gestured toward the chairs set across from his desk. "Did the fellow you hauled off yesterday provide any information on the spate of recent murders? I presume that's why you arrested him."

He made it sound as though San Francisco was suffering from a plague of killings.

"We're following up." Nick removed his hat and took one of the chairs. Taylor declined; he was good at taking notes while standing.

"How is Mrs. Davies, by the way?" Aldrich asked. "Terrible fall."

"She got this idea that you'd tripped her."

He chuckled. "Ladies and their whims."

"I know Mrs. Davies fairly well, and she's not prone to whims."

Aldrich inclined his head. "My apologies, Detective. It's clear you regard her highly."

My feelings are that obvious? "She believes you were trying to stop her from chasing after that fellow we detained yesterday."

"Why might I do that?" he asked.

"I don't know. Maybe you can tell me about Mr. Doherty so I can fill in the blanks."

"If he's the man you arrested, I've never heard of him nor laid eyes on him before."

"He'd been paid to locate and retrieve a note with your horse's name and a substantial sum of money written on it, Mr. Aldrich. We believe it's a reward to harm or kill Validus," Nick said.

Aldrich narrowed his gaze. "Why on earth would I want to stop anyone from apprehending a man involved in a plot to kill Validus, Detective?"

"Because you were afraid Mr. Doherty also had information about the poisoning of Apollo?" Nick suggested. "You tell me why."

Aldrich glanced at Taylor before turning back to Nick. "What are you accusing me of?"

"I think you know, Mr. Aldrich."

"My trainer was cleared of suspicion, Detective. Pierson's horse died from a case of botulism caused by bad feed. Tragic but an accident," he said stiffly. "Pierson never blamed me or my trainer. I lost a good boy as a result of the allegations, though."

"Has anybody ever threatened Validus?"

"Yes, and I've ensured that he is always attended by someone I trust."

Aldrich folded his arms and blandly returned Nick's stare. He'd hate to play poker against the guy.

"We've looked into your whereabouts on the night that Fulton was killed, Mr. Aldrich," he said. "The Dashaway Association meeting you attended ended earlier than scheduled, we're told. Is that right?"

"Yes, because the weather was terrible. Members were afraid they'd have trouble getting home if the roads got too bad."

The roads he liked to criticize, which always got bad during heavy storms. Half the time they were bad when it was sunny. "When did you leave?"

"Not long after. I stayed to speak with a couple of the members, then departed."

"Your wife tells us you got in around eight," Nick said. "What took so long?"

"I did not go and kill a local policeman, Detective. I have even less reason to do that than to trip Mrs. Davies."

"Maybe you didn't like that he'd witnessed you stabbing Mr. Griffin to death."

"And maybe the police should be attempting to locate the fellow in the plaid coat, instead of questioning me," he snapped. "Your officers searched my house and did not find one, correct? And the papers have reported that the fellow was again spotted when Mr. Fulton was murdered."

"How do I know the fellow wasn't you and you've found somewhere other than your house to hide the coat?"

Aldrich rolled his eyes and leaned back in his chair. Which didn't squeak like Nick's tended to do. "I did not kill Mr. Fulton and I did not kill Mr. Griffin. I don't know how many times I need to repeat myself," he said. "Besides, the driver who picked me up at the Piersons' house stated that he did not witness a murder Monday evening. How isn't that sufficient proof that I'm not responsible for Mr. Griffin's death?"

"We've learned that the hack was waiting down near the corner, Mr. Aldrich." They hadn't confirmed Mrs. Davies's assertion, but Aldrich didn't need to know that. "Too far for the fellow to have seen what was going on at the house in a heavy rainstorm."

Aldrich glared at Taylor, busy scratching away in his notebook. His assistant's noisy writing sometimes unnerved people they were interviewing; Nick needed to thank Taylor one of these days.

"All right," he said. "The cab *was* waiting a few doors down and my shoes were ruined by the time I reached it. What does it matter if I wasn't precise in stating exactly where that carriage was located on the road?"

"I have a thing for honesty, Mr. Aldrich," Nick replied. "I'd still like to know what took you so long to get home Thursday night."

"The carriage I'd engaged became mired in the street. It took awhile to free the wheels," he said. "That's all."

"Of course," Nick replied. "Funny that you and Mr. Hollis were at the Dashaway Association that night. Was Mr. Everett also at the meeting?"

A shadow crossed Aldrich's eyes. There was no mistaking it. "He is not a member of the Dashaway Association."

"Or at the City Temperance Society either, I gather," Nick said. "You and he had an argument or something. What was that about?"

Aldrich exhaled. "Men have disagreements, Detective. And I was not the source of the disagreement."

"Was it the sort of disagreement that might've led to his store getting burned down, though?" Nick asked. "Or maybe encourage him to put out a reward in exchange for killing Validus?"

Aldrich glanced over at Taylor again, whose pencil sounded louder than normal in the unnatural silence that had fallen over the office. The fellow near the front door must have been holding his breath in order to hear every word.

"The members of the society are not vile schoolboys who engage in tit for tat, Detective Greaves," Aldrich answered. "Like the Dashaway Association, the City Temperance Society is an organization supporting men who have struggled with alcohol use. There are many men in San Francisco who need our help, and we are there to provide it. However, we're not always successful and men relapse. They get upset when they fail."

"Is that what happened to Mr. Everett? He failed?"

"He'd heard that stories were spreading that he'd returned to the bottle. He was understandably angered."

"Did *you* spread those stories?"

"I did not," Aldrich said firmly. "Nonetheless, for the sake of the society I apologized profusely, not wanting a misunderstanding to spring up. I was concerned about the fellow. I'm concerned about all of the members."

"But Mr. Everett didn't accept the apology, I take it."

"He felt under attack and believed that the very organization created to support men like him had betrayed him. It was unfortunate, but he left."

"Wait, I remember," Taylor said, looking up from his note-taking. "There was an article in the newspaper written by some fellow complaining about being forced out of his temperance association."

"Mr. Everett decided to air his complaint in the public arena rather than handle matters in a private and confidential fashion," Aldrich said. "Months have passed and I've tried to forget the entire dispute, Detective. Let bygones be bygones, as they say. I presumed that Mr.

Everett felt the same."

"'Presumed'? You have reason to suspect that he hadn't let bygones be bygones?"

"Aside from tersely informing me that he did not intend to renew the policy he had with us?" he asked. "Mr. Everett was at the Ocean House Course the day Edward Pierson's horse was poisoned."

This was a turn Nick hadn't anticipated. "Are you telling me you actually *do* suspect the horse didn't die from bad feed and that Everett was involved?"

"All I can say is that Zacharias Everett is not, so far as I'm aware, a gambler."

"He hadn't had an argument with Mr. Pierson, though."

J. Lyman Aldrich tilted his head and peered at Nick down the length of his nose. "It wasn't me who'd been circulating the rumor that Zacharias Everett had taken up drinking heavily again, Mr. Greaves, though everyone was inclined to believe that it had been. It was Edward Pierson."

● ● ●

"Mr. Everett has to hate Mr. Pierson," Taylor said, struggling to keep up with Nick's long strides while lighting a cigar at the same time. "Could he have killed the fellow's horse, then, like Mr. Aldrich said?"

"Like Aldrich hinted, Taylor. He was awfully clever to not directly accuse him."

The cigar finally lit, and Taylor tossed aside his match. "I suppose Mr. Everett wasn't behind the reward on Validus, though."

"Maybe he resented both Pierson and Aldrich, Taylor." *I know I would.* "We need to talk to him after we stop in at McNair's saloon."

Mullahey came running along the road, waving at them to halt.

"Glad I found you, Mr. Greaves. Taylor. I've got news." The officer looked grim. "About the Cassidy lad. Thought you'd want to know straightaway. It's not good."

A pit opened in Nick's stomach and dread like he hadn't felt since the war—since he'd returned to San Francisco to learn that Meg had killed herself—spread cold through his body.

Taylor groaned. "Sir, it can't . . . Mrs. Davies, she'll be—"

"Let Mullahey tell us what's happened before we decide how and what to inform her." He wanted to be optimistic, but optimism was a commodity he'd lost possession of when he'd gained all that dread. "Go on."

"Sorry to say, but a body's washed up on the shore near Black Point. The body of a teenaged lad."

CHAPTER 17

A cold breeze whipped through the Golden Gate and dashed spray onto Nick's face, chilling him. Taylor had stayed on the bluff above, where the San Francisco City Water Works aqueduct snaked along the outline of the shore, bound for the reservoirs nearer to town. Tufts of smoke drifted from the stacks looming above the sprawling bulk of the Pioneer Woolen Mill, and out on the water, steamships chugged along under the watchful eyes of the cannons perched at the tip of Black Point. The boy, facedown in the gravelly sand at Nick's feet, couldn't see the ships or the cannons or the manufactory. Or the houses clinging to the hills that rose up from the strait. Couldn't see anything at all anymore. His dark hair was crusted with grit, his thin body half in, half out of the water, one arm outflung as if he'd been trying to reach for safety, grab hold, but it had eluded him just out of reach.

Bile rose in Nick's throat. "Turn him over, Mullahey."

"Aye, Mr. Greaves." The policeman, who hadn't known Cassidy beyond having seen him at the station, bent to the task.

The men who'd found the body stood to one side, arms crossed over their dark pea jackets, faces impassive. Maybe they'd found other bodies on this beach, victims of boating accidents or sailors swept off their ships by rough waters and errant booms, and had passed the point of being shocked to find another.

"Is it him, Mr. Greaves?" Mullahey asked, drawing Nick's attention back to where it should be instead of looking anywhere else except at a dead boy.

"Is it him?" shouted Taylor. He must've stepped closer, his feet showering rocks and dirt down the side of the incline. "Is it Owen?"

Nick pulled in a breath. "No." *God. Thank god.* "No, it's not, Taylor." He looked up at Mullahey. "It's not Cassidy. I'm sure we'll get a report of a missing seaman soon. Have the boy's body collected and sent to the morgue."

"Will do." Mullahey, a stout Catholic, mouthed a prayer, crossed himself, and turned to shout instructions to the men who'd found the poor kid.

Taylor hurried down the side of the hill, slipping and sliding in his rush to join Nick, who was walking away from the beach as quickly as he could. "That's a relief, sir."

"Not for that boy's mother." A woman who wouldn't be hearing from her son any longer.

"Didn't mean to suggest . . . I mean . . ."

"It's okay to be relieved it's not Owen, Taylor. I am." Nick lengthened his strides, impatient to get away from the shoreline. He was tired of being called to examine bodies that might belong to friends. Or family members. "But we're not any closer to discovering where Cassidy is."

"I went to the bowling alley to talk to that kid again, the one you interviewed. Tommy O'Brien."

"Don't expect he had much left to say." Although maybe Taylor's ability to get women to talk worked with kids, too.

"He didn't, because he's not at the bowling alley anymore." Taylor scrambled up the steep incline of the beach access road alongside Nick. "His boss told me he's had enough trouble with the boys he's hired to set pins and didn't need to employ one who gets visited by the cops."

"I suppose we have no idea where Tommy O'Brien is now."

"I couldn't find him in the city directory, sir. Plenty of O'Briens, though. I could start asking—"

Nick cut Taylor off. "That'll take too long and probably prove pointless. They won't talk to you even if they know where Tommy is. They'd presume that we want him for a crime, and who'd want to inform a police officer where they could locate a loved one who's hiding?"

"Owen's done a good job of lying low, hasn't he, sir? Mr. Greaves, sir."

"Too good." The wind snatched at Nick's hat and he reseated it, his gaze taking in the hills rising ahead of them. Ever southward and westward. To the ocean. To the racetrack he and Celia Davies had visited yesterday. To wherever it was that Owen Cassidy had hidden away.

"Still want me to come with you to McNair's, sir? Or do you want me to head over to Mr. Everett's?"

"McNair's first, Taylor. We'll get to Everett once I'm finished pretending to be Johnny Doherty's trusted friend."

• • •

Celia stopped at home to deposit her medical bag, rushing out again before Addie could even realize she'd been in the house. She needed to inform Mr. Greaves that Caleb Griffin had definitely been at the Ocean House Course the day that Apollo had been poisoned. But first, a visit to Mr. Everett, whose reaction to being forced out of the City Temperance Society may have led him to commit a crime. Or numerous crimes.

Hastily constructed barricades cluttered the pavement in front of Mr. Everett's stationery shop. Or rather what used to be Mr. Everett's shop, thought Celia. Men had been employed to tear down the charred timbers, and the crash of falling debris was cacophonous. Each thunderous boom was followed by a cloud of dust billowing out into the street, coating anyone unfortunate enough to pass too near in a gritty powder.

Celia stood on her toes to see past the piles of rubble. Mr. Everett was not around to supervise the proceedings. She'd wasted her time in coming to his shop rather than going directly to his house.

"It's a mess, ain't it," observed a young man—no, strike that, a lad—standing alongside Celia. "I heard it was arson."

"I also heard it was arson," replied Celia. "Which is utterly dreadful."

The boy screwed up his face and eyed her. "You ever shop at Mr. Everett's place?"

"Oh, yes, most definitely. He had the loveliest of notebooks to write in and countless other items to admire."

"Well, they're all gone for sure. The flames when the place went up were tall as buildings, sparks flyin' everywhere." He flung his hands into the air to illustrate. "Almost as much fun as watchin' the fireworks at the Fourth of July."

Mr. Everett would not appreciate hearing the demise of his shop described in such terms. "Did you or a friend happen to notice anyone suspicious in the area who might have been responsible?"

"There's lots of suspicious folks 'round here, ma'am. Wouldn't remark on one or the other, frankly. And wouldn't care to, neither." He shook his head, covered in a tattered cap, strands of dark hair poking through a hole in the wool. "It's just not smart to mess around with folks who might cause a person a whole heap of trouble."

The sort of pronouncement Owen was fond of making.

"I am very worried for Mr. Everett. I heard he'd had a falling-out with some powerful men, and I wonder if the argument explains this damage." She nodded in the direction of the shop. Another crash sounded and more ashen dust swirled into the road.

"He don't seem the sort of fellow who might fight with anybody. But you never can tell, can you?"

People leading secret lives. "A wise observation, young man."

He grinned, pleased by the compliment. "Ain't got to worry about some suspicious fellow burnin' down the place, though, when the story goes that Everett done it himself."

"Oh?"

"Yep. One of my pals was headin' out before sunrise to pick up the papers he sells and saw Everett runnin' down the alley like a pack of wolves was chasin' him," he said. "And then the flames started dancing . . ."

• • •

"Ready, Taylor?" Nick eyed the entrance to McNair's as a laborer slipped inside its shadowed depths. The Market Street wharves were close by, and the place would profit off the men who worked and bunked in the area—sailors, carpenters, boat builders, the coopers right now rolling new casks and barrels onto the street and into waiting wagons. Men looking to chase their thirst with beer from the Hibernia Brewery, which black-and-gold signs on either side of the doorway proudly advertised.

Taylor nodded rather than attempt to be heard over the shriek of ferry whistles piercing the air.

A gaggle of recently arrived passengers hurried by, ignoring the saloon as well as Nick and Taylor. Maybe, after the passengers had settled into their lodgings, they'd venture back. Their eyes wide at the wonders San Francisco could provide. Wonders and troubles.

"You did remember to bring your gun, right?" Nick asked his assistant.

At Nick's request, Taylor had changed out of his policeman's uniform and into ordinary street clothes. The change in outfit hadn't done a whole lot to conceal his identity. Taylor would always look like a cop and the passing dockworkers were noticing.

"Right here, sir." Taylor patted the pocket of his coat.

"Hopefully you won't need to use it," Nick said. "Keep a watch out for anybody running out of that saloon like the devil's after them. In case they're acquainted with Doherty, know I'm not a friend of his, and mean to warn Pa Frank."

Taylor's face twisted with a worried frown. "Be careful, sir."

"I don't expect too much trouble. After all, when was the last time somebody assaulted a police officer in the middle of the day?" Nick adjusted his coat to straighten it, the bulge of his Colt bumping reassuringly against his forearm. "Don't answer that question, Taylor."

Nick dashed across the street, evading a heavily laden wagon bound for the wharf, crates rattling against each other on the bed. He stepped inside McNair's, the sour smell of spilled beer and men and tobacco all mixed together like a fetid stew. Most of the chairs scattered about were empty—the place didn't serve lunch; however, one could be had for thirty-five cents at the coffee saloon three doors down, according to its placard out front—but the footrail that spanned the length of the long bar had plenty of boots and shoes propped on it, their owners not even pausing their lager drinking to mark the arrival of a new customer. In the corner, some fellow listlessly plucked at a guitar. His tune wasn't easy to hear above the other occupants' chatter.

The saloon owner looked over. "What can I get you?" He swiped his towel across an open spot on the bar, inviting Nick to stand there.

"I'm not here for a drink today."

"They serve lunch down the street," he said, starting to turn aside.

"I'm here because I have a message about a pony that's up for sale," he said. "I was told I could leave that message with you. For Pa Frank."

The name prompted one of two reactions in the men hearing it—slack-jawed silence or furious whispering.

The saloon owner eyed Nick. "And who are you?"

"A man who knows about a pony for sale. Like I said. He'll understand." Nick scanned the interior of the saloon. "Is he here?"

"You don't know him?" The saloonkeeper sounded suspicious.

Nick shot a glance over his shoulder at the fellow. "I'm delivering the message for a friend. The man who actually has the pony. He thinks he's being followed by cops. Wants to keep out of sight."

"Pa Frank doesn't come in here," the saloonkeeper replied. "Not any longer. When anybody has a message for him, he gets it and sets the time and place of the meeting, if he wants one. Your friend should've told you that. Didn't he?"

Nick turned back to face him. The moment he did, chair legs scraped against the grit-covered wood floor and the fellow playing the guitar sprinted from the room. Nick did likewise.

Wherever the guitar player had gone, Taylor must have too.

"That way, mister." A dirty-faced kid, his black cap sagging over his ears, pointed up the busy road. "They went that way. The corner where the bank is."

"If you're lying, I'll come back and find you."

"I ain't lying," the kid yelled after him.

Nick shoved through the parade of folks clogging the sidewalk. "Police!" he shouted, startling enough people that a path cleared.

He rounded the corner and ran down the center of the road, splashing through puddles and muck, searching open doorways and tight paths between buildings. People called out, some pointing one direction, others pointing the opposite. Nick dodged carts and horses, workers running across the road, and skidded to a halt at the end of the street.

"Sir!" Taylor jogged out from an alley. "I lost him. Sorry, sir." He reholstered the gun he'd drawn.

"It's okay, Taylor. I expect he ducked into some building and we'll never find him." Nick scanned the rows of windows staring down on the street. "He's probably watching us right now and laughing."

Taylor looked up at the buildings surrounding them. "Gives you the creeps, doesn't it, sir? Thinking about it like that," he said. "Want me to go back to McNair's and ask about the fellow?"

"Don't bother. The saloonkeeper wouldn't want to get on the wrong side of Pa Frank by answering." Nick started up the road and back toward the station. Taylor fell into step alongside.

"You think that fellow who ran out will inform Pa Frank that cops are looking for him?"

"I do. Even worse, he'll probably tell Pa Frank that the cops know about the note and might even have it," Nick said. "Which means, Taylor, we've likely lost our chance to collar the guy."

• • •

When Celia arrived at Mr. Everett's, she found an auction of the contents of his house in full swing. She made her way past the wagons parked along the curb, nearly colliding with a fellow wrestling an elegant mahogany commode onto the back of a buckboard.

"Is Mr. Everett here?" she asked the fellow standing just outside the front door and who appeared to be directing the proceedings.

The man gave her a harried look. "If you're here for the sale of the parlor set, it's in progress in the first room to your right." He handed her a sheet of paper listing all of the items that were available. Walnut hall furniture. A rosewood library set, though the house did not appear large enough to contain a room that might function as a library. Curtains of damask and silk brocatelle and lace. Paintings and porcelain figurines and even an aquarium. "If you're not here for the sale of the parlor set, you're free to go inside and inspect the contents of the other rooms. But don't dawdle if you're not here to buy, because we don't have time for window shoppers."

He turned away, indicating their conversation was concluded.

Celia squeezed past a woman dragging a marble-top bouquet stand down the front steps and ventured into the entry area. In the parlor to her right, as promised by the fellow outside, a man stood before a collection of bidders.

His hand rested on one of a pair of easy chairs, upholstered in maroon silk damask. "That will be two dollars for the pair. Do I have three? These are fine chairs. Like new. Barely worn. Three? Three dollars to you, sir." He pointed at the gentleman who'd raised his hand. "Now how about four?"

In the room across the entryway, people mingled among an array of armchairs, side tables, and piles of rugs—medallion, Brussels, a sheepskin among the collection.

She stopped a man carrying a ledger book, who paused every few seconds to scribble entries in it. "Pardon me, do you know if Mr. Everett is in the house? It is most important that I speak with him."

"No, he's not."

"Do you know when he might return?"

"No idea." He continued on into the parlor.

Perhaps someone else would. Celia climbed the stairs, encountering another group of people descending from the upstairs bedchambers. One grumbled over the poor quality of linens left, complaining that she'd been expecting white Witney blankets and Marseille counterpanes and not some cheap patchwork quilts. Celia peered into each room, finding bedsteads broken down to their components and mattresses stacked on the floor alongside the supposedly inferior patchwork quilts. Dressing bureaus and wardrobes were pushed to one side.

In the final room, the largest of the lot and one that looked out over the quieter rear of the house, a woman, her shirtsleeves rolled up, removed garments from a clothes cupboard. A large trunk stood in the center of the bedchamber.

Celia tapped on the doorframe. "Pardon me, do you happen to know if Mr. Everett is in the house?" She glanced around with an air of hopefulness, as though he might be hiding behind the oak chest of drawers and step out at the sound of his name. "Or when he might return?"

"Mr. Everett? He's gone," she said, depositing a bundle of linen shirts inside the case.

"Gone?"

"Yep. Leaving me to crate what he didn't want." Woolen socks followed the linen shirts. "Or didn't have the time to pack and take with him when he ran out of here this morning, quick as a streak."

"I did not realize he meant to depart today."

"He's headed to San Diego."

"Not Sacramento?"

The woman cast Celia a quick glance. "What gave you that idea?"

The fact that Mr. Everett told me that was where he planned to go? But which of them had he misled about his intended destination? Celia, or the servant shoving more clothes into an already brimful trunk?

"Are you to send those items on to him?" Celia asked her, hoping the woman might have been given a forwarding address.

"They're to be sold, but I expect they won't fetch as much as he's hoping. Mr. Everett might've spent a pretty penny on the furniture downstairs, where folks could ooh and ahh over his possessions, but look at this stuff." She gestured in the direction of the clothes cupboard, its doors flung wide. "He could dress well when he wanted to, but a lot of it . . ."

She'd emptied most of the shelves and hooks, but an odd collection of clothing in vivid patterns and colors remained. One item in particular stood out.

"Is that a plaid waistcoat, by any chance?" Celia asked.

"Waistcoat?"

"A vest. Excuse me."

"That ugly thing?" The woman yanked the waistcoat off its hook and held it out. "Don't get why Mr. Everett ever bought it. Used to have a matching coat and pants, but I don't know where they've gone."

Was Mr. Everett the fellow in the plaid coat? The man whose shop Celia had lovingly perused on many a Saturday afternoon? Whose soft leather-bound notebooks lined the bookshelves of her clinic office? A man who was one person on the outside yet quite another on the inside?

"The girl who comes to do the laundry read that the police were hunting for a killer wearing a plaid coat," the servant was saying. "We had a good laugh over the idea that Mr. Everett might be a murderer, but I haven't seen him in that coat and pants in ages."

"I would like to purchase that vest." Celia rifled through her reticule, retrieving her coin purse. "I can offer you a dollar for it right now."

The woman hugged it close. "It's likely worth more."

"Money the auction house and not *you* shall see." Celia jingled the coins. "I highly doubt that the auctioneer will miss this particular item of clothing. Furthermore, I really and truly want that vest."

The woman pondered her choices for no more than a second before snatching the money. "Here." She tossed the waistcoat at Celia then turned back to her task.

"Thank you." Celia bundled it into a ball and hurried out of the house before anyone could stop her.

• • •

Nick slammed open the alley-side door to the police station. The loud clank startled the booking sergeant, standing at his desk by the door to the holding cells. Celia Davies hopped up from the chair she'd been seated on, looking paler than normal.

"Mr. Greaves. Mr. Taylor."

Nick bounded down the three stairs into the main room, Taylor not far behind. "Ah, Mrs. Davies, our trap failed." He strode across the room toward her. "We didn't corner the fellow who was going to pay Doherty for that note. Instead, we tipped him off that the cops are on his trail." Nick strode past her and into the empty detectives' office, yanking off his hat and tossing it onto his desk. "But at least I'm still in one piece."

Taylor stopped at his desk in the main station.

Mrs. Davies tucked under her arm a bundle she was carrying and followed Nick into the office. "Unfortunate that your attempt failed, Mr. Greaves."

"Thank you for the information on Aldrich and Everett, by the way. Aldrich admitted that the driver might've been too far away to witness Griffin's murder." He indicated she should take a chair and dropped onto his. He got back up when she didn't sit. "He also claimed that Edward Pierson was behind the gossiping that forced Everett out of the City Temperance Society. Though I wouldn't be surprised if both Pierson and Aldrich helped show him the door."

"Edward Pierson? Is that so?"

"I've learned to never fully trust folks I'm questioning about crimes, ma'am, so maybe it's not the truth," he replied, leaning against the wall behind him. "Aldrich went on to also imply that Everett could've been behind the poisoning of Pierson's horse."

"Not Mr. Griffin?" she asked. "He was at the track that day, Mr. Greaves. I have seen a news clipping about the incident naming him."

"Everett could've paid Griffin." A fellow who sometimes worked unofficially at the Ocean House Course. "Taylor's off to interview Everett now."

"Mr. Taylor may not find him, Mr. Greaves." She unrolled the bundle under her arm, revealing a plaid vest. "This belonged to Mr. Everett."

Nick pushed away from the wall. "Is there a matching coat?"

"There once was. And a pair of trousers." She set the vest atop his desk. "The contents of Mr. Everett's house are being auctioned as we speak, Mr. Greaves. This was among his belongings. It seems he has upped sticks."

He cursed and grabbed his hat. "When did he leave?"

"This morning. He is on his way to San Diego, if he was honest with the woman packing his clothing," she said. "Furthermore, a lad who lives near his shop told me Mr. Everett was witnessed running from it moments after the fire started. Sadly, the boy did not share that news with the police when it might have helped."

Everett. An arsonist and a murderer.

"Taylor! Don't leave yet!" Nick shouted, skirting his desk. "We need to get to the Pacific Street Wharf. Now!"

CHAPTER 18

Celia returned home, limping through the front door to find Addie waiting. She glanced at the door to her examination room, which was closed. "Was I expecting a patient?"

"It's that man again." Addie gave the examination room door a hasty, irritated look. An expression she reserved for only one particular man.

Celia tore off her bonnet and tossed aside her cloak. "He's located Owen."

"He's going to tell you that's what he's done, ma'am," Addie whispered furiously. "Isna possible he actually has."

Celia squeezed Addie's upper arm. "As I said before, we must have faith."

"Faith in that man?" Addie asked. "You shouldna have pawned your mother's jewelry in order to give him money, ma'am. You will see neither again."

"I cannot know the outcome if I do not go in there and speak with him."

"Hmph." She frowned. "And you should rest your ankle."

"Later." Celia squared her shoulders and opened the door to her clinic. Patrick was poking around in her medical supply cabinet, examining a small paper box labeled *alum powder*.

"Dissolved in water, it makes an excellent gargle for sore throat," she said. "However, I would appreciate it if you would put it back, Patrick."

"Ah, Celia, there you are at last." He peered at the box. "Never could understand you wantin' to be a nurse." He returned the powdered alum to the cabinet, shutting the glass-paned door with a click. "Do you make money at it?"

"My clinic is a free clinic, thanks to Uncle Walford's generosity."

Patrick's eyebrows perked with interest. She should not have mentioned Uncle Walford's generosity. Her husband would be upping the price for the information he possessed.

She folded her arms and stared at him. "Have you located Owen Cassidy?"

"I have, Celia, my dear. And I can see that you're frettin' that I'll be askin' for more money than we agreed upon."

He could read her; he'd always been able to. "Please, just give me the information, Patrick."

He dug a dirty scrap of paper out of his pocket. "I've written the address of the rooming house where he's hidin' on here."

"Does that mean Owen is still alive?"

"I can't be vouchin' for somethin' I don't know. But he could be."

"I committed to paying you the rest of the money, Patrick, when you located Owen. Alive."

"Let me remind you that you paid me to locate him. That was all. I won't be held to account if he's gone and gotten himself killed." He held out the paper, pinched between forefinger and thumb. "Do you want it or not?"

"How do I know you've not simply written down a false address?"

He lowered his hand. "You don't want it, then."

"Of course I do." *Have faith.* Celia snatched the paper from his fingers and went over to her desk. "Five dollars is what we agreed upon, I believe."

"That would be the amount. I'll be able to buy myself a new pair of boots now." He winked.

She retrieved the amount from a money box stored inside her desk. "Tell me you are being honest with me, Patrick. For once."

"I am sorry I am for ever hurtin' you." He reached out and she didn't wince, permitting him to briefly stroke his fingertip down her cheek. The contact of his skin left her feeling nothing but regret over the years of shared suffering.

"We've already apologized to each other, Patrick. When we spoke at the saloon," she said. "There no longer remains a need to repeat our regrets."

"Cold as ever, eh, Celia darlin'?"

His words stung. She might no longer respond to his touch, but his opinions . . . they could still hurt.

"What *did* happen in Mexico, Patrick? The death certificate I saw had your name on it. And the handkerchief returned to me was one I'd gifted to you, stained with your blood."

She'd believed herself to be a widow when she'd been handed those items. Felt a guilty relief that she and Patrick were finally free of each other and the hurt. But here he was, far from dead, and her far from being a widow.

"Well, that was my handkerchief but not my blood. I escaped the long hand of death more than once in Mexico, my dear. Cheated the grave from takin' me." His blue eyes sparkled. "Didn't drown when my ship sank off Monterrey. And the fellow who'd won that handkerchief off of me died in a terrible knife fight in a cantina. I didn't mind havin' people think it was me, though. I was escapin' more than just the grave."

All his life he'd been needing to escape the consequences of his actions. "Now what, Patrick?"

"This will be the last you'll be seeing of me, Celia. I'm makin' good on my plans to leave this town forever." Patrick folded the dollar bills and tucked them inside his coat. "I'll be headin' out soon to join my brother. You remember him?"

"Of course I remember your brother."

He chuckled. "Most certainly, you do. Thanks to you, he escaped the noose. Along with your wantin' to be a nurse, I've never fathomed why you saved him from hangin'."

"I'm not vengeful, Patrick. He'd done me no harm and I wished to see the person who'd actually murdered my friend punished." Which they had been. Her first encounter with Mr. Greaves. Their first investigation together. And this would be their last. It had to be.

"Well, he does appreciate it," he said. "He means to strike it rich in Silver City. I'll be joinin' him there."

"It sounds perfect." The sort of place where people like Patrick and his brother went to make their mark. Start over. Possibly fail, but Patrick would land on his feet again. Somehow. He was catlike, in that regard.

Patrick studied her face. "You're not goin' to miss me, are you?"

He sounded sad, and for a moment, the briefest of moments, she pitied him. Them. "I stopped missing you three years ago, Patrick. When you climbed aboard that merchant ship without saying goodbye. Our marriage failed and I did mourn it. But I moved on, and you must too."

His sadness passed and he grinned, pinching her cheek. "You be careful, Mrs. Davies. I'd not be wantin' you to come to harm." He shot a glance at the paper gripped in her hand. "Especially when you head to the Tar Flats to search for that lad. Cassidy was smart to hide down there, but if I found him, others will too."

"The police have the note he'd been given by Caleb Griffin. There is no need for him to hide now."

Patrick's gaze sharpened like that of a hawk spying a mouse in a field. "What are you meanin', Celia?"

She tensed. "Nothing, Patrick. Thank you for the information. I greatly appreciate it."

The acuteness of his gaze softened, faded as though the mouse had disappeared into a covering of thatch. Perhaps she'd misread his expression.

"Be careful," he repeated.

"I'll not go to the Tar Flats alone, Patrick," she said. "And goodbye."

"Bring a weapon, too." He doffed his cap and strode out of the room, calling a farewell to Addie, who'd been eavesdropping out in the entryway.

The front door closed. Celia took in breath, painfully aware of the slamming of her heart against her ribs. Willing it to calm.

Addie marched into the room. "I'll go with you, ma'am. To the Tar Flats to find Owen."

"No. I will take Joaquin."

"He's just a wee boy. I'll send a message for Mr. Taylor to go with you, if I'm no use to you," she said, hurt.

"You *are* a great use to me, Addie, which is why I need you to stay here with Barbara. And Mr. Taylor is with Mr. Greaves, hunting down Mr. Everett, who may be our murderer."

Everything was tantalizingly close to a resolution. Why, though, did she not feel reassured?

"Mr. Everett." Addie tutted. "I canna believe it."

"Neither can I." Celia locked her money box inside her desk. "So do not fret, Addie, and I will return with Owen as soon as possible. Have biscuits ready for him."

"And warm chocolate?"

"Yes."

Yes.

• • •

The harbor police officer who'd apprehended Everett hauled him down the stairs into the police station, smirking like he enjoyed manhandling a murder suspect. A change of pace from policing for shipboard stowaways or helping the customs officers inspect crates for contraband, Nick supposed.

"Thank you, Officer," said Nick, trailing them into the main room. "Officer Taylor and I will take it from here."

The officer pushed Everett into the nearest unoccupied chair. He'd tackled Everett at the dock, throwing him to the ground, and the right knee of the man's pants was torn. "Let me know if you'll be needing me to testify against this here fellow, Detective. Explain how he fought me and tried to evade rightful arrest."

Actually, Everett had done very little fighting. "I'll do that. Thanks again."

The man nodded and darted off.

"Taylor, bring Mr. Everett into my office, will you."

Nick hooked his hat on the peg by the door. He'd raced to intercept

Everett before the fellow stepped onto the clipper ship's gangway, his hat flying off and landing in a pile of manure. A gift left by one of the downtown hotel carriage horses. Hopefully, Mrs. Jewett could get the hat clean. Until then, he wasn't setting it on his desk.

Taylor encouraged Everett to accompany him into the detectives' office.

"I don't understand what you want with me, Officers," Everett protested, collapsing onto the chair in front of the desk. He'd been wearing wire-rimmed spectacles when Nick had first spotted him, but somewhere along the way they'd been lost. Probably stuck in a pile of manure at the dock. "And you've made me miss my ship to San Diego."

Nick grabbed the plaid vest from where he'd draped it over the back of his chair. "This is yours, I believe. I know it is, so you don't have to deny it."

"Yes, it is mine." He blinked. "Yes."

"What happened to its matching coat and pants?"

"I don't have them any longer. I . . . I gave them to a men's charity weeks ago."

Nick eyed the vest as though hoping it might reveal whether Everett was being honest. "Is that so?"

"I didn't kill that fellow outside Edward's house Monday evening, Detective," Everett replied. "I saw the notice in the newspaper about the man in the plaid coat. That wasn't me, and it was not me fleeing from the killing of the local policeman on Thursday, either. I was nowhere near Russian Hill that night."

Nick dropped the vest onto his desk. "You have somebody who can verify that?"

Everett reached for his glasses to adjust them but realized they weren't perched on his nose. "My wife died, Detective. I have no one. That is why I was leaving San Francisco. What else do I have here? Nothing."

"Because you lost your business. In a fire you set."

"I . . . I . . ." he sputtered before lapsing into silence.

Nick lazily took his chair, leaving Everett to fidget.

"Tell me about Edward Pierson and J. Lyman Aldrich, Mr. Everett," he said. "About the argument at the City Temperance Society that ended with you leaving the organization and later posting an angry letter in the newspapers about your treatment."

"I didn't name Edward in that letter."

It *had* been Pierson behind the rumors. "You left the society afterward."

"I was forced out. It was humiliating, Detective. I lost customers." Everett exhaled a long, shuddering breath. "I'd discovered that Lyman and Edward were hiring men to burn down clients' properties in exchange for a take on the insurance money. Or, I should say, I'd discovered that reasonable evidence existed."

"Both Aldrich and Pierson." *I knew I didn't like you, Aldrich.*

"Yes. Both," he said. "I wanted to warn them, get their version of what I'd heard. Surely they couldn't be profiting off of false insurance claims. Not men I'd known for years. They misunderstood me, though. Thought I was threatening them."

"Were you?"

"Certainly not, but they were both furious. Especially Edward. He told people that I'd started drinking again. Maybe I had, but it wasn't as bad as he was claiming. We were meant to be brothers on a shared mission of betterment, Detective. Loyal to each other," he said, dismayed to discover that brotherhood and loyalty only went so far sometimes. "I was angry. I got an idea to damage my store. You're right that I set the fire. Just a little one, was what I'd planned. I wanted to accuse one of Aldrich's arsonists of starting it. I purchased some black powder from a nearby dry goods store—it was easier to buy than I'd imagined it would be—and set it ablaze."

Well, well. He'd confessed to the arson. "But it wasn't a little fire."

"It got out of control. A complete blunder on my part."

"Did you attempt to collect on your insurance money?"

He frowned. "I went to the agency as soon as it opened on Monday to explain that there'd been an accident, but Lyman wasn't willing to help. After all, my policy was about to expire and I'd told him I planned to take my business elsewhere. I was hoping, though, that he might want to make amends for what had occurred at the City Temperance Society. He didn't."

Awfully optimistic, thought Nick, when J. Lyman Aldrich didn't exactly seem the sympathetic, forgiving type. "Pierson stopped by your store that morning. Why?"

"He wanted me to believe he was concerned about me," Everett said. "But I think he'd come to gloat."

Movement out in the station was one of the policemen striding toward the detectives' office. He stopped just outside. "The men have searched all of Mr. Everett's baggage, Mr. Greaves. Just clothing—no plaid coat—and personal items. Some money."

Meaning no small-caliber gun, either. "What about his house?"

"Nothing there, either. It's been picked clean by the folks attending the auction."

Nick thanked the officer and sent him on his way. "Tell me about Pierson's horse, Mr. Everett. You know. The one that took ill and died at the Ocean House Course a few weeks back."

He swallowed, his Adam's apple bobbing above his black necktie, which had come undone in the tussle with the harbor police officer.

"My understanding is that it was an unfortunate accident. Bad hay, or something," he said. "Edward had spent a small fortune on the animal. I told him when he purchased the horse—we were still friends back then—that it was a foolish waste of money, but he wasn't about to listen to me. He wanted to emulate Lyman and there was no talking him out of it. Stubborn as a mule when he gets an idea in his head. Even his wife tried and failed."

"Curious, though, that you were at the track that day. The day the animal died." Nick propped his elbows on the arms of his chair and tented his fingers. "You're not a regular there, are you? Seems mighty coincidental and I hate coincidences, Mr. Everett."

Sweat beaded on Everett's broad forehead. It wasn't hot in the detectives' office. Stuffy, smelly like usual, but not hot.

"I wanted to see the race between Apollo and Validus," he said. "I admit I went hoping to see Apollo lose, after having to slink out of the City Temperance Society in disgrace because of Edward's lies. Not a proud moment but that was my motive."

"Not to make sure that the person you'd hired to poison Apollo did their job? Mr. Griffin, was it?" Or maybe Pa Frank.

"No. What? It was a tragic accident," he said, his voice trembling.

"And you don't know anything about this note. It had been in Mr. Griffin's possession at one time." Nick pulled out the piece of paper and slid it across the desk toward the fellow. "We believe it's half of a contract, let's call it, detailing the sum of money to be paid in exchange for the killing of Validus. Maybe you weren't content to see only Pierson punished for your disgrace."

Everett stared at the note. "What?"

"We're missing the bottom half with the signature of the person offering the bounty. Was it your signature, Mr. Everett?"

"No. No."

"Did you arrange to meet with Griffin, wanting to get the note back? Because you'd changed your mind about hiring him to kill Validus," Nick said. "Maybe you got chicken-hearted after Apollo died. Had to have been satisfying to get even with Pierson, though. He likely bragged and bragged about that animal. Hearing him go on about the horse must've been as irritating as a heat rash on a sweltering day, I imagine."

Everett's forehead wasn't just beading sweat now; his pores were threatening to release a gusher. Nick opened the window behind his desk, letting in fresher and cooler air. He wasn't trying to go easy on Everett, but the man's sweating was making him start to sweat, too.

"I did *not* put out a bounty on Validus, Detective. I swear," he said. "And I'm not responsible for Apollo's death."

Keep probing, Nick, when you've got the fellow in front of you. Keep probing until it comes clear. Uncle Asa, his voice in Nick's head as clear as when he'd spoken those words to him six, seven years ago.

"Or maybe Griffin wasn't the man you'd hired, but he'd gotten ahold of the note somehow. Threatened to take it to Mr. Aldrich as proof of your plot," Nick continued. "Except you didn't know that he'd taken care to tear the message in half and given the pieces to two fellows he trusted." One being Owen. "Didn't know that he didn't have it on him Monday night when he met you in front of Edward Pierson's house."

"None of this is true."

Taylor licked the tip of his finger and used it to flip the page in his notebook.

Nick leaned back and studied Everett, who'd dug out a handkerchief from his vest pocket and was using it to mop his forehead. "You must've been scared. I get it. You'd just lost your store and now some common criminal was going to snitch about your plot to poison Validus. Maybe snitch about Apollo, too."

"This is not true!"

"Maybe your meeting with Griffin Monday night didn't go as planned. Just like the fire at your store. Botched," Nick said. "And then you had to kill Mr. Fulton, the local policeman, because he'd witnessed the crime."

"I'm not responsible for any of this!" He twisted his handkerchief with both hands. "The officer said they didn't find a gun among my things. I didn't shoot that policeman."

Taylor uttered a skeptical grunt, not looking up from his note-taking to make the noise. Everett, his forehead puckering, glanced over at him.

"I remind you about the man wearing a plaid coat seen near the Piersons' house not long before Griffin was murdered," Nick said. "And on the night Mr. Fulton was shot dead."

"I did not murder Mr. Griffin, Detective. And I didn't write that note. No matter what he—" Everett clamped his mouth shut around the rest of the sentence.

Nick sat up so fast he almost pitched himself forward off his chair.

"You did meet with Griffin, didn't you, Mr. Everett? Damn it, didn't you?"

Taylor, startled by Nick's outburst, looked up from his notes. *Calm down, Greaves. Calm down.*

Everett paled. Was he considering how he could walk back his words, retreat to the point in the conversation before he'd blurted out a comment that might hang him, choose a different and safer path?

"He came to my store last week," Everett said, his voice tight, barely above a whisper.

Taylor whistled through his teeth.

"He said he had a piece of paper with my name on it that I might not like certain people to learn about. That piece of paper, Detective Greaves. Before it was torn in half." He nodded at the scrap atop Nick's desk. "But I didn't write that note. Someone else put my name to it."

"Who?"

He blinked a few times. "I won't give you a name just to save my skin, Detective. I'm not that sort of man."

Aren't you? "How much did Griffin want in return for it?"

"Seventy dollars. Far more than I had to spare."

Nick refolded the note and tucked it away. "Was it *then* that you had the bright idea to burn down your store and collect the insurance money?"

Everett did not respond. He didn't deny Nick's claim, either.

"Things moved quickly, though, didn't they, Mr. Everett? Mr. Aldrich refused to pay the claim and now you didn't have the money to pay Mr. Griffin," he said. "But you'd already arranged to meet Griffin Monday night at Pierson's house. Why there?"

"It was Mr. Griffin's suggestion and I agreed," he said.

Was that the only reason to head to Pierson's? Griffin's recommendation? "Who put your name to that note, Mr. Everett, if you didn't?"

His chin sunk to his chest, crushing the disheveled knot of his tie. "I'm convinced it was Edward," he said, proving he was the sort of fellow who would squeal to save his own skin. Hell, most folks were. "I wanted to confront him in front of Lyman. Have Mr. Griffin show them both the note, then I'd demand an explanation. I don't know what happened with Edward's horse, Detective. Maybe when it died Edward got the idea to kill off Validus."

"Because he believed Aldrich was responsible for Apollo's death?"

"All I know is he hates Lyman, Detective."

Just like you hate Pierson? "Did you argue with Griffin when you met him that night, Mr. Everett?"

"I did head to Edward's house, but I couldn't go through with it," he said. "I turned around and went home."

"It *was* you in your plaid coat."

"No, it wasn't," he insisted. "I don't know who Lyman saw, or who it was the night the local policeman was killed. Someone else who happens to own a plaid coat. They're not completely uncommon."

Nick's arm took to aching and he rubbed it.

"You know, Mr. Everett, I like this version of the story better. You arranged to meet Griffin outside Edward Pierson's house, even though you didn't have the money he'd asked for. Killed him with a gimlet—why, I keep asking myself, when you used a gun to kill the local—and hunted for the note. Didn't find it, unfortunately," Nick said, confidence growing in the sequence of events. "Left the body in Pierson's yard hoping to incriminate him in the crime, which is what you'd intended all along. A bit of revenge for getting kicked out of the society. And when you realized there'd been a witness, you had to get rid of him, too."

If Fulton had seen the crime, though, why hadn't he said so? *Damn, Nick, this isn't as tidy a story as you think it is.*

"I didn't kill either of those men, Detective. You have to believe me." Everett's gaze was pleading. "You simply have to."

Nick scowled. "Taylor, have Mr. Everett booked on suspicion of murder."

Taylor scrambled to his feet, stuffing his notebook into his coat pocket. Everett, white-faced, sputtered his innocence. Nick stood and turned away as his assistant tugged the fellow toward the holding cells. The afternoon was drawing to a close, bringing the daylight with it, shadows settling heavily out on the plaza. Another bout of rain looked to be rolling in, as well.

"Is that it then, Mr. Greaves?" Mullahey was at the doorway to the detectives' office. "Mr. Everett is the killer?"

"Looks like it, Mullahey. Though there are a few threads to join up." He locked the note and Mr. Everett's vest inside his desk. "He has motive and no alibi for either murder. Plus, he's admitted to setting fire to his own store."

Out in the station, the door to the holding cells clanked shut, the noise reverberating.

"Well then, what we found beneath a loose floorboard in Fulton's lodgings might not be so important, after all." Mullahey held a tightly rolled wad of greenbacks and grinned, the expression twisting his crooked nose out of shape even more. "There'd be forty of them, Mr. Greaves. Apparently, there used to be fifty. But Mr. Fulton did a wee bit of celebratin' not long before someone killed him. Accordin' to this here fellow I've brought with me."

Mullahey reached over and grabbed the coat sleeve of a scrawny fellow who'd been standing out of view, dragging him to where Nick could see him. "Found him cowerin' at Fulton's lodging house when I and one of the lads went back to scour Fulton's room again. After finishin' up with Mr. Everett's place."

The fellow gulped. "Am I in trouble, Officer?"

"I'll let you know," Nick said. Taylor had finished with Everett and stood behind Mullahey and the scrawny fellow. He motioned for his assistant to come into the office. "Do we know where the money came from, Mullahey?"

Mullahey nudged the man. "Tell the detective what Fulton said at the saloon, Mr. Quinn."

"Fulton said he'd just been paid for killing a man he didn't even kill." Quinn glanced around to check everybody's reaction. Deciding he wasn't in trouble, he continued. "Got a big laugh out of it. We all did. Said he thought he'd share his good fortune with us."

"Did he explain who'd given him all that cash?"

The fellow gulped again. "A lady, Officer. A fine, pretty lady with hazel eyes and a gap between her front teeth. That's what he said."

"Mrs. Pierson, sir," Taylor said. "It's got to be her."

"Thank you, Mr. Quinn. Mullahey, good work." Nick rounded his desk and grabbed his hat, shaking off the manure that had dried on the brim. "Taylor, bring that roll of money and come with me."

"We find Owen in the Tar Flats, Señora Davies?" Joaquin's voice trembled. "Is dangerous there for you. And me."

Perhaps she should have waited until Mr. Taylor or Mr. Greaves was available. A Chilean boy might not be welcome in the Tar Flats, where a large population of Irish lived.

"I have a weapon with me, Joaquin."

Celia sneaked a look around them. They had left the clamor of Market Street behind, but even Fourth Street, in the impressive shadow of St. Ignatius College, was still crowded with wagons and foot traffic. Enough commotion for folks to ignore two more individuals among the throng. She loosened the strings of her reticule enough for Joaquin to examine the contents.

He slapped a hand over his mouth. Not because he was impressed by the folding pocketknife—it had once belonged to Patrick, which he had left behind for some unfathomable reason—but to keep his peal of laughter from bursting free.

"I am sorry, Señora."

She secured her reticule and wound its straps around her wrist. "I neglected to ask Mr. Greaves for his Colt, which would have been a far better weapon."

Joaquin looked at her, wide-eyed.

"I am teasing. Now, where are we?"

She scanned their surroundings. Homes of brick and stone rose between squat shacks constructed of hastily nailed-together wood. The individuals on the street did not appear quite as comfortable and established as the residents living alongside her on Telegraph Hill. More recent arrivals in San Francisco, perhaps. People who'd yet to find a toehold in the city and become settled. Or perhaps those whose toehold had proven precarious, plummeting them into an abyss of uncertainty. And then there was the smell. The noxious stench of the gasworks reached them where they stood, three blocks distant from the manufactory. She'd heard that mothers would bring their ill children to the place, believing the fumes would cure their young ones' lung diseases, when in truth it would only sicken them more. It was not always easy to explain facts to people desperate for answers, for healing. People who trusted their neighbors' opinions more than some medical person who was a stranger to them.

"You see, Joaquin? It is not so dangerous around here and no one is paying you or me any mind."

"That man there. He does not like me."

The fellow he indicated was eyeing them from across the street. One of his feet dangled over the edge of the curb, as if he was debating whether to step off the pavement and confront a woman dressed better than most of the women walking these streets. Someone who clearly did not belong and whose only protector, should she develop a need for one, was a spindly boy.

"We shall move on." With haste.

Joaquin did not need encouragement to walk quickly. "Where do we find Owen?"

"I believe the rooming house is not far. Down the next alley, if I understand the directions I was given."

The place was as grim as Celia had feared, paint peeling off the wood, roof shingles missing. A tall man, his shirtsleeves rolled up to expose thick-muscled arms, answered her brisk knock. The doors leading off the entryway at his back were closed, shadows darkening the hall. Only the staircase, missing a number of balusters, and its tattered carpet were visible.

"Only fellows board here, ma'am." Irish. Which was no surprise. Who else would Patrick be acquainted with? The man's dark eyes scanned her from tip to toe before doing the same to Joaquin, who took a step behind her broad skirts. "We can find space for the lad with one of the other fellows, but you'll be havin' to look elsewhere."

"We do not require accommodations, sir." She reached behind her to move Joaquin out from the cover of her dress. This man would not hurt either of them, she was positive. And if she was wrong, she had a compact, likely useless, knife in her reticule. "I am looking for Owen Cassidy, and I was told I could find him here."

"He is not here."

Blast, Patrick. "I was assured by a . . . friend that he was. I am very worried about him and would like him to know it is safe now."

"Safe? Has he got himself some trouble with someone?"

"So you do know who I mean," she said. "Please tell me where he is. I have to speak with him. I have to."

"He's gone, ma'am." The urgent tone of her voice had persuaded him to part with some details.

"Then he *is* alive."

"He was yesterday. Today." He shrugged. "I've not seen hide nor hair. Maybe 'tis a glad thing too, if he's in trouble."

"He left?" Had Patrick been aware that Owen had fled again? *And let me pay him for useless information.*

"His friend might be able . . ." Just then, one of the treads of the staircase creaked and the lower limbs of a teenaged boy came into view as he descended the steps. "You. Where is your friend Owen? This lady wants to know."

The boy crouched to peer at her through the opening in the front door, realized he didn't know her, and turned to scuttle back up the stairs. Joaquin, quick on his feet, shot past Celia and scrambled up the steps after the boy. Celia hurried inside.

"Hey!" the rooming house keeper shouted. "Blessed Mary, what is this now?"

The boy stumbled on the stairs and Joaquin lunged for him, grabbing his ankles.

"Let go!" The boy kicked out, trying to rid himself of Joaquin, attached to his legs like a pair of fetters.

"I'll be havin' none of this in my place." The man climbed the stairs and tried to pull Joaquin off.

"Please, there is no need for any of this," said Celia. "I only want to find Owen Cassidy. Not cause any trouble."

One of the other roomers, a lad with orange hair and freckles to match, stood at the top of the stairs, effectively blocking the boy's escape. "What sort of a ruckus you causin' now, Tommy?"

"Dang it, these people are after Owen!" he shouted.

"Please, can we exhibit some composure?" Celia pleaded. "I merely want your help, Tommy."

The rooming house owner released Joaquin, still latched on to Tommy's legs, and retreated down the stairs. "Come down here, O'Brien, and speak to the fine lady. She'll not be bitin' your head off. A wee harmless thing, she looks to be."

She did? "Joaquin, you may let go," she said. "I trust that Tommy will not run off."

Tommy looked up at the redheaded fellow who blocked his exit and exhaled. "You can let go, all right, kid?"

After a quick check with Celia, Joaquin reluctantly released the boy's legs. Tommy kicked out again, barely missing Joaquin, stood, and came down the stairs. "Well, what is it you want?" he asked Celia.

"Where is Owen?"

"You tell her," Joaquin demanded.

The boy plopped onto the bottom step and glared in response.

"You are Owen's friend, correct?" she asked. "I was told he has been hiding with a friend, although your landlord informs me that he is no longer here. Can you help me find him?"

"I won't and you can't make me. You wouldn't hurt me to get it outta me, either. Not a lady like you."

He made the word sound insulting. Which was a first in Celia's experience. She could hardly threaten him with her knife, however. Certainly not in front of the rooming-house keeper, who was watching them with a definite look of amusement.

"If you'll not tell me where I can find Owen, can you at least give him a message?"

"How much is it worth?"

Did everyone in San Francisco have a price for their cooperation? Sighing, she foraged inside her reticule and produced a few coins.

"Here," she said, handing them over. "Please tell Owen this. Tell him he can come to the clinic. That the item he was protecting is safely in police hands and they are near to resolving Mr. Griffin's murder." *I hope.*

"All right, all right. I'll do what I can. Ain't making any promises, though." He pocketed the coins and gave Joaquin a black look. "And you can stop staring at me, kid."

Celia thanked Tommy and the rooming-house keeper and departed, Joaquin hurrying along at her side.

"Will he tell Owen what you say, Señora?" he asked.

"We shall see, I suppose."

Joaquin considered that. "I will pray, Señora."

Celia took his hand, thin and sinewy. Holding on seemed the right thing, the necessary thing to do. "So shall I, Joaquin."

• • •

"They're at dinner, Officers."

"Not any longer," said Nick.

The servant who'd answered his pounding shuffled ahead of them, looking back over her shoulder as frequently as she could without bumping into the furniture cluttering the parlor or tripping over the carpets. A grin flitted across her face, looking tickled that policemen were crawling through the Piersons' house again. It flitted off when she remembered she wasn't supposed to look tickled.

She slid open the door between the parlor and the dining room.

"We're eating," Pierson snapped, his back to them. "You're supposed to tell visitors at this hour to go away."

Georgiana Pierson, seated across from her husband, went sheet white. "Detective Greaves," she intoned in a voice as cold as well water. "Officer."

Pierson spun about in his chair, his elbow knocking against his glass of red wine, spilling it across the linen tablecloth like a stream of blood. The servant rushed to mop up the mess. "What in . . . Mr. Greaves."

"Sorry to disturb you both, but we've just been provided some information that we're hoping you can clear up."

"What else could I possibly have to tell you?" Pierson asked, swiping away the maid's busy hands. "Leave that alone, will you?"

She scuttled aside to linger just outside the doorway.

"Not you, Mr. Pierson." Nick nodded toward the hazel-eyed woman at the far end of the table, the fire set in the fireplace casting a warm glow over her skin. Her lips were pressed together, concealing the gap between her top front teeth. "I'm here to talk to Mrs. Pierson."

She sedately folded her napkin and laid it alongside her dinner plate. "You haven't been able to prove who killed those two men, Detective, so you've resumed suspecting us?"

"Just you." Nick extended his open palm toward Taylor, who fumbled through his coat pockets and produced the roll of dollar bills. He set them in Nick's hand. Georgiana Pierson, her eyes narrowing, clutched the pendant suspended from her throat.

"Recognize these bills, Mrs. Pierson? I think you do," Nick said. "There are only forty in here, I'm told by the officer who counted them. Guess there used to be at least fifty, but Mr. Fulton got carried away and spent a good amount buying drinks for his friends. Celebrating being paid to kill a fellow he didn't actually kill."

"What?" Pierson's gaze darted from his wife's face to Nick's. "What are you accusing my wife of, Detective Greaves? That she gave that money to Mr. Fulton?"

"Pretty much, Mr. Pierson." Nick ran a thumb over the edge of the bills, riffling them. "Nice fresh greenbacks."

"Whoever told you that I paid Mr. Fulton is lying, Mr. Greaves."

"The fellow remembered Fulton's description of the woman who'd given him the money. You made quite an impression, ma'am. Described her hazel eyes and gap teeth." Nick returned the wad of bills to Taylor.

"You were seen with Fulton a few hours before he was shot, Mrs. Pierson. It wasn't some fellow you were having an affair with, like you wanted me to believe, but Fulton."

"Georgiana, what does he mean?" Pierson asked. "Mr. Greaves, you've got everything wrong."

The doorbell jangled. The Piersons' servant looked around, waiting to see if anybody else meant to answer it. Maybe she didn't want to miss a second of the excitement unfolding in the dining room.

"Mr. Greaves? Mr. Taylor?" a woman's voice called from the entry hall. Of course she hadn't bothered to wait for somebody to come to the door. Celia Davies strode into the parlor. Her blue mantle was dotted with water droplets, which sparkled when she moved. It was raining again, the wind picking up, as well. "Ah, there you are. Officer Mullahey was still at the station and informed me that I would find you both here. A payment Mrs. Pierson made to Mr. Fulton, I believe."

"Mrs. Davies, it'd be best if you turned around and went home."

"To wait for you to visit so I might learn what you've uncovered, Mr. Greaves?" she asked. "As you have a tendency to never show up, I believe I shall stay right here."

Blasted woman.

"So, Mrs. Pierson, it *was* Mr. Fulton I saw you with that afternoon, wasn't it?" she asked, cutting in on Nick's interrogation.

"This is nonsense," the woman replied. "Detective Greaves just said that the fellow told everyone in some saloon that he hadn't killed anybody. It would've been a stupid waste of my money to give him fifty dollars for doing nothing."

"Perhaps you were unaware that someone else had actually killed Mr. Griffin," Mrs. Davies suggested. "Mr. Fulton was not so virtuous, though, as to decline the money you'd promised."

"Georgiana, what on earth does she mean?" Pierson asked.

"Nothing, Edward. Nothing at all," she replied. "Mrs. Davies and Detective Greaves are simply attempting to make me look guilty."

Nick debated pointing out that the fifty dollars she'd paid to Fulton was what made her look guilty.

"I have always thought it serendipitous that our abruptly arranged meeting Monday evening took you away from this house on the night of a murder, Mrs. Pierson. Your sudden request to have me recover a locket that had not been stolen, after all," Mrs. Davies said. "How could you have known to be away, though, unless you'd arranged for Mr. Fulton to kill Mr. Griffin at that very hour?"

"Utter nonsense."

"Why, though, might you wish to see Mr. Griffin murdered?" Mrs. Davies continued. "Because your husband owed him a debt he found he could not repay. Is that not so? Were you afraid of what Mr. Griffin might do if the money was not produced?"

Nick folded his arms. *Maybe I should just let Mrs. Davies ask all the questions.* It seemed to be working pretty well so far.

"My wife would *never* do what she's being accused of, Detective," Pierson said to Nick, even though Mrs. Davies had been the one doing the interrogating. "Georgiana had no reason to want Mr. Griffin dead, because I didn't ask him for a loan."

"No, Mr. Pierson? With all the bills coming due for this fine house and its furnishings? Those visits to the opera and the best restaurants? The business you wished to start?" Mrs. Davies's voice was gentle, as if she understood how dire necessity could drive a person to do things they normally wouldn't. "You were one of the debts Mr. Griffin meant to collect on that evening. Were you not?"

"It's true that I've had a run of bad luck, but I did *not* approach that man for a loan. How undignified."

Lots of "dignified" men stooped to consorting with criminals if it served their needs, thought Nick. Edward Pierson wouldn't be the first or the last.

Mrs. Davies regarded the fellow. "I expect you told your wife about the meeting with Mr. Griffin, which is how she knew when he was to make an appearance and when she needed to absent herself," she said. "Your ruse of a stolen locket was clever, Mrs. Pierson. Who, though, did you employ to sell it to that secondhand shop? Your husband? Or Mr. Fulton?"

Excellent, Mrs. Davies.

Georgiana Pierson chose to not answer. The woman's servant, standing by the oak sideboard, mumbled *oh my* over and over. Taylor, as usual, scribbled in his notebook.

"It is sad about your run of bad luck, Mr. Pierson," Nick said. "Beginning with Zacharias Everett learning about what was going on at Western States Fire and Life. He tried to warn you and Mr. Aldrich that word had leaked about suspicious insurance claims, didn't he? But you thought he was threatening to go to the authorities himself, and you drummed him out of the City Temperance Society. Ruining his reputation."

Pierson frowned. "Zacharias *did* threaten to tell the authorities, Mr. Greaves."

Lies, Mr. Everett? "Then J. Lyman Aldrich had the nerve to ask you to leave Western States," he said. "Followed by the unfortunate death of your racehorse, Mr. Pierson. More bad luck."

"An animal you had underinsured," added Mrs. Davies.

"More money needed to pay your debts. More money owed to Caleb Griffin." Nick tutted. "We found a fascinating book at Griffin's lodgings, by the way." He indicated Taylor with a wave of his hand. "A book that kept track of the money he'd lent. Your name was in it."

Georgiana Pierson released a hiss of breath. "Edward, this *is* all your fault. Go ahead and admit that you'd borrowed money from that criminal. I'm tired of shielding you."

"No!" Pierson cried.

Just then, a gust of wind rattled the window panes, swung open a door at the back of the room.

"That pantry door never stays shut anymore," the servant grumbled.

"Wait." Celia Davies took a step forward. "Are you missing the tool that used to secure the latch?" She looked over at the dining room table, at the Piersons arranged like clothed statues on either end of the expanse of white tablecloth, food going cold on plates, fire and gaslight flickering in the glassware, then back at the girl. "A gimlet, perhaps?"

"Is that what that nasty, pointy thing was called? The thing that held that door shut?" The servant blinked a few times and pointed at the Piersons. "Merciful Jesus! They done it!"

• • •

A great commotion followed the maid's declaration. Edward Pierson jumped to his feet, Mr. Taylor running over to keep him from fleeing the house. Georgiana knocked over her chair as she stood. Mr. Greaves scowled in the fierce way that he could. The maid sobbed about working in the household of a murderer and that she was lucky to be alive. If the Piersons had owned a dog, thought Celia, no doubt it would be dissolved in a frenzy of barking. Fortunately, they did not.

"Everybody, shut up!" Mr. Greaves shouted, which succeeded in stunning everyone into silence. "Mr. Pierson, sit down. You too, Mrs. Pierson. And you . . ." He glared at the maid. "Taylor, make her stop bawling."

Mr. Taylor hurried to the young woman's side.

"Well, Mr. Pierson?" Mr. Greaves asked. "Tell me about the gimlet. The one that's not jammed into the pantry door latch any longer."

His shoulders drooped. "It belonged to a carpenter who was going to repair the door."

"Merciful Jesus," the maid whispered.

Indeed. Edward Pierson must have been very quick with tidying up the mud he'd tracked into the house that night, after all.

"Does the carpenter know you used it to stab Mr. Griffin to death?" Mr. Greaves asked.

"I did not stab Mr. Griffin," Edward Pierson insisted.

"Then what did happen, Mr. Pierson?" Celia asked.

He turned to stare at a wine stain splashed across the tablecloth. "The weather was wretched. The wind, the rain," he said, although none of them would have forgotten. "I heard banging outside. It was the gate slamming, except why was it unlatched? Alarmed, I grabbed up the first thing I could lay hands on, which happened to be the gimlet securing the pantry door."

"You ran outside and found Griffin there, waiting for you," Mr. Greaves prompted.

"I went outside, but Mr. Griffin wasn't there. The gate was swinging in the storm but it was raining too hard to run out and secure it," he said. "A huge gust of wind came along, sending something nearby crashing. I startled and dropped the gimlet on the porch. Ran back inside."

Mr. Greaves reached up to massage the spot in his arm that so often ached and considered Edward Pierson. "Are you sure that's what took place?"

"Yes, of course I'm sure."

"He killed him," the maid screeched. "He killed him!"

"Please, miss, that's quite enough," Mr. Greaves said. "Why not clear away the dishes in here?"

She did not budge.

"The meeting on Monday with Mr. Aldrich and Mr. Hollis was not to solicit funds for your business proposition, was it?" Celia asked. Of course, it had not been. "You'd sent for your friends to beg them to lend you money to pay off Mr. Griffin, who was due to arrive at any minute."

"Your brothers." Nicholas Greaves looked over at her. "Everett called them brothers. Loyal friends."

"Except they weren't so loyal," Mr. Pierson said. "I lost a lot of money on Apollo. I couldn't afford to adequately insure him. Never thought I'd need to make a claim. Oh, Matthew gave me a few dollars on Monday and promised more. Lyman, though . . . he refused. Laughed at me." He drew in a long breath. "I was angered enough to punch him. I'd taken lessons with Matthew."

"The mark on his chin," Mr. Greaves said. "On the right side. You're left-handed, Mr. Pierson."

"I'm rusty, though. Barely fazed him. He'd trained at the Olympic

Club too, though. We all had. Even Zacharias." He chuckled to himself, a scornful noise. "Matthew was going to make men of us."

Georgiana mumbled something unkind under her breath.

"So who used that gimlet to kill Griffin if you didn't, Mr. Pierson? Not Fulton, because the fellow owned a gun and would've used that, not some tool he'd found on your front porch," Mr. Greaves said. "He could've easily explained the need to fire the weapon by claiming he'd stopped a crime from happening. It was his job. Except he didn't make that claim, because he hadn't killed Griffin, even though he'd been paid for the job. Right, Mrs. Pierson?"

"I'd hired him to threaten the fellow, Detective, not kill him," Georgiana replied. "I don't care what Mr. Fulton told a bunch of drunks at a saloon."

"I think I could convince a jury otherwise." Mr. Greaves turned back to Mr. Pierson, who slumped on the dining room chair. "I repeat . . . who used the gimlet to kill Griffin if you didn't, Mr. Pierson?"

"If not Fulton, then I have no idea. A stranger. The crime is terrible around here."

Not *that* terrible, thought Celia.

"J. Lyman Aldrich, Detective," Georgiana said. "He paid Mr. Griffin to poison Apollo and wanted his crime concealed. I can only imagine his surprise when his carriage was driving away from here and he spotted the fellow walking along the road. He must've jumped out, run back, confronted Mr. Griffin, grabbed up the first thing he saw—"

"Georgiana, honestly," Mr. Pierson interrupted her. "She's always believed Lyman was behind Apollo's death. She told everybody his trainer was responsible."

"You know he was, Edward."

"It was an accident, Georgiana. A terrible accident," he said.

"Lyman would like you to believe that," she shot back.

"Mr. Pierson, you know, I'm surprised you haven't accused Zacharias Everett of killing Mr. Griffin," Mr. Greaves said. "Or of poisoning your horse."

"Zacharias? Why Zacharias?"

"Because he hated you for getting him tossed out of the City Temperance Society," he said. "You knew he'd owned a plaid coat and that we were looking for a man wearing one in connection with both murders. Why not name him? Would've been easy."

Was Edward Pierson trembling? Celia was standing too far away to tell.

"Maybe you didn't accuse him, Mr. Pierson, because it was *you* who'd forged Everett's signature on a note promising to pay five hundred dollars in exchange for killing Validus," he said. "Revenge against Aldrich? A plot to retaliate for Apollo's death by killing his precious racehorse. And while you were at it, you signed Everett's name to that note instead of your own. Payback against him, too, for his role in you losing your position at Western States."

Edward Pierson's shaking became pronounced. "I didn't. I didn't."

"That note ended up in Griffin's hands," Mr. Greaves continued. "He recognized how incriminating it was and, as a result, how valuable it could be to the right buyer. He tried to sell it to Everett for seventy bucks."

"Edward, you are a fool."

"Don't believe him, Georgiana."

"Unfortunately, you couldn't be sure Hollis and Aldrich would give you enough money to cover what you owed Griffin. And you had to get back that note, too," Mr. Greaves said, staring hard at Mr. Pierson. Hoping, perhaps, that the force of his gaze would elicit a confession. "But you weren't positive Griffin would cooperate. So you plotted murder, just in case, complete with a disguise."

"No. No, Detective!"

Mr. Greaves went on as though he'd not heard. "You'd somehow laid hands on Everett's plaid coat. Did you change into it once Hollis and Aldrich left? Then change back out after the crime was committed and before your wife got home?"

Could that be what had unfolded that night?

"Has Zacharias accused me of killing that man?" Mr. Pierson asked. "Is that what this is all about? He's accused *me* of killing Griffin?"

"Should he have?" Mr. Greaves crossed to where the man sat and leaned over him, his face inches from Mr. Pierson's. "Should he have?"

The other man recoiled, his body pressing into the seat of his chair, but he could not get away. "Damn him."

"For protecting you, of all people, these past few days?" he asked.

"Protecting me? He hasn't been protecting me. He's protecting Matthew," he snarled. "Because it was Matthew that night. Matthew who stabbed that man. There was blood everywhere . . . Matthew."

CHAPTER 20

"What do you mean, Edward?" Georgiana cried. "Lyman must have killed Mr. Griffin, not Matthew Hollis. J. Lyman Aldrich!"

"I know what I'm saying, Georgiana," her husband replied, sounding flat, defeated. "I know what I saw that night."

Celia glanced over at Mr. Greaves, stern-faced but also appearing relieved. Imagining, perhaps, that the end of the case was approaching.

"This is all ludicrous." Georgiana's gaze connected with Celia's before she turned aside to avoid having to look at her husband any longer.

Celia limped over to the chairs arranged before the bay window, the throbbing of her ankle having resumed, and sat. Outside, the night was velvety dark, the light from the room's gas jets flickering off the window glass. The maid, whimpering, allowed Mr. Taylor to escort her into the kitchen.

Mr. Greaves waited for his assistant to return before proceeding with his questioning. "Whenever you're ready to tell the truth, Mr. Pierson, I'm ready to listen."

"What I've explained is the truth, Mr. Greaves. To a point," Edward Pierson said. "The meeting with Matthew and Lyman occurred as I've told you. My argument with Lyman was just as I stated. The fact that I dropped the gimlet out on the porch. That I was expecting Mr. Griffin to arrive to demand payment on that idiotic loan."

"And also wanting money to hand over that note."

"Not from me, Mr. Greaves, because I did *not* offer a bounty on Validus. That is the truth." He looked over at Georgiana, who remained obstinately facing the fireplace. "Not long after Lyman left, I heard raised voices outside. After I'd gone to use the . . . umm . . ."

"Privy," Mr. Greaves supplied.

"Oh, Edward," Georgiana grumbled.

"I heard arguing and looked out the front window," her husband continued. "Mr. Griffin had shown up unexpectedly early and was arguing with Zacharias. I didn't know when Zacharias had arrived or even why he was outside my house."

"According to Mr. Everett, Griffin had arranged to meet him there to sell him that note. Except Everett hadn't gotten ahold of that seventy dollars," Mr. Greaves said. "Everett still wanted to confront you, though, and in front of Aldrich. Because he's convinced you forged his signature."

"That's why he was so angry when I went to his store Monday morning after the fire. He didn't explain."

Mr. Greaves looked over at Celia before carrying on with his questioning. "So, you saw Zacharias arguing with Griffin . . ."

"Zacharias had spotted the gimlet and was waving it at Mr. Griffin—he's never carried a weapon—but the fellow knocked it from his hand. And out of the blue Matthew showed up, wearing Zacharias's old plaid coat. I couldn't comprehend what I was seeing. He picked up the gimlet and stabbed Mr. Griffin with it in the back. He was defending Zacharias, that's what it looked like, but then . . ." He paused, his face contorting. "Mr. Griffin fell to the ground and Matthew stabbed him again. And again. There was blood everywhere. I was transfixed, unable to move. Appalled by what he'd done."

"You didn't try to stop him."

"I know I should have, Detective, but I was in a stupor, frozen," he said. "It was over so quickly. Zacharias ran off, and Matthew hunted through Mr. Griffin's pockets. But he must've heard someone coming—I'm pretty sure it was Fulton—because Matthew glanced down the street and hurriedly dragged Mr. Griffin's body out of sight. And then he fled."

"Leaving you with a dead body in your front yard," Mr. Greaves said. "Did you hope your wife would help you get rid of Griffin's body when she returned home?"

"I . . . I . . ." he sputtered.

"He may have done, Mr. Greaves, except I was in tow," said Celia. "My presence spoiled those plans."

Georgiana began to cry. Her life of privilege in this lovely house, with her lovely jewels and lovely clothes, would soon be over.

"Was it loyalty to your friend, your brother, that kept you from telling us this earlier, Mr. Pierson?" Mr. Greaves asked. "Before Matthew Hollis ended up killing another man."

"Those loyal, loyal friends," Georgiana sneered, her eyes glittering with tears. "I warned you about them, Edward, and look what they've done to you."

"Mr. Griffin's death did conveniently free you from having to pay that debt, didn't it?" Mr. Greaves said. "Another reason to conceal what had happened. You wanted Griffin dead and you felt guilty."

Edward Pierson hung his head.

"Taylor, take him to the station." He gestured for Georgiana, who'd risen from her chair, to remain seated. "You can stay here for now, Mrs. Pierson. One of the officers will be collecting you in the morning. Mrs. Davies."

He lifted his brows, indicating he wanted Celia to join him. She got to her feet, wishing she could think of parting words to share with Georgiana. But sympathy for the woman who'd paid Mr. Fulton to threaten Mr. Griffin—if that truly was all Georgiana had intended—and who'd concocted a story in order to be absent from the house the night the threat was to occur was misplaced. So Celia merely nodded at her and followed Mr. Greaves out of the house.

He was holding the gate for her. Thankfully, the rain was easing.

"A good guess about the gimlet, Mrs. Davies," he said, letting the gate swing shut before marching up the pavement, his long strides impossible for her to match.

"Mr. Greaves, do slow down," she scolded, clawing her skirts out of the way as they dashed up Vallejo. "If Mr. Hollis has not already left town, he shall not be going anywhere soon."

If he slowed, it was not particularly noticeable. "Pierson might warn him, though."

"He'd not get a message to his friend so quickly that you need to run up the street to prevent it," she said. "Moreover, my ankle is not fully recovered from Mr. Aldrich tripping me at the racecourse."

The appeal finally slackened his pace. "Speaking of Aldrich, I wonder how much he knows about Monday's events."

"More than he has admitted, I would presume."

"All of them loyal to each other," Mr. Greaves said. "Hollis, Pierson, Everett. Aldrich, even. They dared to lie to the police."

She glanced up at him. It was dark on the street, the only light provided by the infrequent lanterns hung at doorways or shining through windows, and his expression was difficult to make out. "'Nothing is more noble, nothing more venerable, than loyalty.'"

"Shakespeare again, ma'am?"

"In this case, Cicero. A Roman philosopher and academic," she added. "My uncle was fond of the quote."

A judgment against acquaintances who proved less than loyal in his estimation. She herself had occasioned its usage when she'd followed her soldier brother to the Crimea. Both she and Harry disloyal to have left the family and caused such fear, such heartbreak.

"Ah."

"As for the gimlet, I visited a patient this morning who uses a metal ladle handle as a temporary lock on her kitchen door latch. To keep her young son from wandering into the room." Only just this morning? What a long, eventful day it had been. "So you see, Mr. Greaves, not so astonishing a guess. Merely a timely observation."

"Thank you for being observant, Mrs. Davies."

She smiled into the darkness. "I came looking for you at the station earlier this evening to inform you that my attempts to locate Owen have failed, Mr. Greaves."

"He'll turn up, ma'am."

"I pray you are right."

A rider, singing "Oh! Susanna" at the top of his lungs, trotted his horse up the road. The corner grocer, sweeping puddled water away from his shop's front door, shouted at him to keep it down.

"I guess we can conclude that Hollis put out that bounty on Validus, the horse he'd lost to Aldrich, and forged Everett's signature," Mr. Greaves said once it grew quiet again. "I wonder how he'd discovered that Griffin had that note. And that Griffin was going to be at Pierson's on Monday night."

"Mr. Griffin told Owen he had a *few* debts to close that evening, Mr. Greaves," she reminded him. "Perhaps one of them was with Mr. Hollis. An exchange of money for a note Mr. Hollis no longer wanted in circulation. Perhaps Mr. Hollis had bruited about that he needed it back."

"Aldrich heard about the threats to Validus and hired guards. Would've made killing the horse a lot harder."

"Do you think Mr. Hollis was also responsible for the death of Mr. Pierson's horse?" Celia asked. "I cannot fathom a possible motive there, though."

"Hopefully he'll explain, ma'am."

Would he? "How very reckless of Mr. Griffin to arrange to meet all three men at the same time and place, though. Efficient, but reckless."

"Griffin mustn't have viewed three businessmen to be much of a threat, ma'am."

"A fatal error," she replied. "I remain perplexed about why Mr. Hollis did not draw his weapon when he came upon Mr. Everett and Mr. Griffin arguing. He must own one, because he shot Mr. Fulton."

"Folks can behave unpredictably, ma'am."

"As my time with you has taught me, Mr. Greaves."

They arrived at her house. Every lamp and gas jet on the ground floor appeared to be lit. Addie must have set them all ablaze, as if doing so could ward off the darkness, the harm that Celia was likely finding herself in.

"How long have you been aware that Edward Pierson owed Mr. Griffin money?" she asked.

"A few minutes," he replied, a smile in his voice. "We found that book I mentioned, but Taylor could never make sense of the code

Griffin had used."

"A white lie, Mr. Greaves?"

"They do come in handy sometimes."

"What happened to that plaid coat, though?" Celia asked, glancing up at the house. Addie had heard them talking and was peeping around the edge of the parlor curtains.

"Hollis probably tossed it onto a trash pile someplace."

"Mr. Everett must have been shocked to see his coat on his friend's back." More shocked to comprehend what Matthew Hollis had intended by wearing it. "Although, where *did* he store the coat between Mr. Griffin's killing and Mr. Fulton's? Your officers searched his house for the item, correct?"

"Yes, but . . . they'd all trained at the Olympic Club . . ." Mr. Greaves tapped his fingertips to the brim of his hat. "I'll speak with you later, Mrs. Davies. Looks like Miss Ferguson is getting anxious about what you're doing out here."

He turned and took off at a run.

Celia watched him go before climbing the stairs to the house. She unclasped her mantle and shook off the rainwater.

"The killer doesn't appear to be Mr. Everett after all, Addie, although he is not fully innocent," she announced to the empty entrance hall and hung her mantle by the door. A sealed letter with her name on it had been pushed under the door. She picked it up and stuffed it into her skirt pocket to read later. "Addie?"

"In here, ma'am!"

Celia turned into the parlor. A boy in a tattered cap and stained pants jumped up from the settee, his green eyes bright, a grin on his face. At his side, Addie beamed, her arm draped around his waist, holding him close.

"Here I am, Mrs. Davies!" he declared.

Celia rushed across the room and gathered him into her arms, heedless of the dirt crusting his clothes or that he smelled of staleness and sweat. "Owen, thank God you're alive. Thank God!"

• • •

By the time Nick arrived at the Olympic Club, the rain had stopped but not the wind, which gusted and made the flames of the gas lamps hissing outside the main door dance. Lanterns blazed inside a large second-floor room, packed with people. Every so often, the sound of laughter echoed out onto the street. A Saturday night soiree among the loyal, brotherly friends.

Nick strode through the front door. A different fellow stopped him this time, just as imperiously as the prior fellow.

He leaped in front of Nick, arms outstretched. "This evening's party is not open to the public, sir."

"I'm not the public." Out came his badge, which caused the fellow to gawk. "I've got a warrant to search the lockers here for evidence crucial to a murder case."

Another white lie, Mrs. Davies.

Nick walked toward the main exercise room, the equipment stashed to one side and empty of gymnasts at this hour. All upstairs enjoying the private party, maybe.

The doorman scuttled after him. "Wait, sir. Wait."

"I know where the lockers are, so you don't have to follow me."

"But how do you intend to get them open to search them?" he asked.

Nick stopped. "You could give me the keys or I could use my gun." He patted his hip where his Colt was holstered. "Mighty noisy, though. Might disturb the partygoers upstairs."

"Let me get the keys." He rushed off and took so long to come back that Nick figured he'd run upstairs to warn whoever was in charge that the police were nosing around again. Just when Nick decided to track him down, he rushed back, a ring jangling with keys in his grip. "Here. Here we are. Now, whose locker do you want to look at?"

"All of them, if need be," Nick replied. "But let's start with Mr. Hollis's and move on from there."

Nick let the doorman lead the way through the second gymnasium, equally empty as the first, and into the cramped room at the back. The fellow struggled with the gas lamp, his fingers shaking as he held a match to the underside of the mantle before the flame took hold and flooded the space with light.

"Let's see." The fellow thumbed through the keys, peering at the numbers inscribed on them. "Yes, this is Mr. Hollis's."

The one on the end. There hadn't been a plaid coat inside when Nick had questioned Hollis the other day, but maybe there was now.

And maybe he disposed of it after killing Fulton, Greaves, and you won't find so much as a thread.

The doorman rattled the key in the lock and swung open the door. There was even less inside than last time. No spare clothes or pairs of shoes. No bloodstained plaid coat. Just a stack of clean towels and a comb.

Nick slammed shut the door. "I want to see the rest."

The doorman moved on to the others, opening one after the other. The contents became a parade of the typical items men who sweated away mornings or afternoons might need—towels and undershirts and socks. Hair tonic and combs. An old bottle of Burnett's Kalliston for treating rough skin and calluses. A half-used bar of castile soap.

"Do the members have their own keys or do they have to come to you?" Nick asked the doorman.

"They have their own keys in addition to what we keep," he replied, shutting the door on the latest locker. Its owner had left behind an oily paper wrapper from his lunch. The doorman flipped through his keys. "Here's one that hasn't been used for a while, Officer. The fellow quit the Olympic Club, if you can imagine."

He made it sound a heresy, like ceasing to believe in God. "Hm."

"He never returned his copy of the key, though," the doorman said. The locker squealed on its hinges as it swung open. "He must've given it to the member who recommended him. I do wish he'd followed protocol."

Feet pounded out in the gymnasium. Hollis, dressed in a black frock coat, a heavy gold watch chain draped across his vest, burst through the doorway. "What are you up to now, Detective?"

The doorman *had* gone up to the party to alert somebody likely to care about what Nick was "up to."

"Just looking for a plaid coat, Mr. Hollis," Nick said, pulling out a jacket tossed inside the locker. He held it up to the gas lamp. Not that he needed more light to illuminate the small-caliber Remington weighing down one of the pockets. Or to show the streaks of dried blood marring the pattern of the garish plaid. "And finding one."

The doorman choked on his breath. "What in tarnation?"

Hollis blanched. "What is that doing in there?"

"Which member recommended the fellow who'd used this locker?" Nick asked the doorman, all the while not taking his eyes off Hollis.

"Didn't I say? Mr. Hollis did, Officer," the man replied. "Right, Mr. Hollis?"

• • •

Barbara had heard Celia and Addie's shouts and stumbled down the stairs in her robe to hug Owen as if she never would let go. He had basked in the attention, Celia forced to finally insist that they let him clean up before he fainted from all the excitement. Or from an obvious lack of food. After a quick wash, Owen changed into an old shirt and trousers that had belonged to Barbara's father and never been sold. The clothing was too large for Owen, who was far leaner and shorter than Uncle Walford, but at least the items were warm and clean, if musty from hanging in an old clothes press for years.

"I meant to take the note to Mr. Greaves, Mrs. Davies," he said between mouthfuls of soup that Addie had quickly warmed. "But I panicked when I saw that fellow on the street, watching my place. So I stuck it under Mr. Roesler's door instead."

"Did you ever discover who that man was?"

"Nope. I didn't let him get close enough to find out," he said, reaching for a slice of bread. "It had to be the fellow who paid Johnny Doherty to get Mr. Griffin's note from me. Maybe he'd gotten tired of waiting for Johnny to come through and found me somehow."

He stuffed half of the bread into his mouth and chewed vigorously.

"At least you're safe," Barbara said, squeezing his hand, which made him blush.

"I bolted out of my place as quick as I could, knocking over some fellow standing in the hallway who I thought was gonna shoot me for bumping into him. Snuck out the back way," he said and finished off the rest of the slice.

Addie produced more bread and set the plate in front of him. If they had precious Devonshire cream and honey to spread, Addie would have handed those over, too.

He grinned at her before continuing his story. "I went to Tommy's. I knew he'd take me in. The confectionery is on the way, so I slipped the note under the door with my name on the outside, hoping that Mr. Roesler wouldn't throw it away."

"He nearly did," Celia said. "I arrived just in the nick of time."

"Wish I'd known earlier that you'd given Mr. Greaves the note," he said. "But I suppose that fellow might've killed me out of spite for letting the police get their hands on it."

"Please stop getting into trouble, Owen," said Barbara. "You're nearly as bad as Cousin Celia."

Her tone was teasing, so Celia did not take offense.

"I don't try to get into trouble, Miss Barbara," Owen said. "I just can't seem to help myself, though."

Barbara slid Celia a look. "That is what she says all the time, too."

"Shoot, she doesn't mean any harm, Miss Barbara."

"Thank you for defending me, Owen. Addie, I believe I will have a bite to eat after all. My appetite has returned."

Celia unfolded a napkin and spread it across her lap, her hand brushing across the letter crumpled in her skirt pocket. She took it out and set it on the table.

"*Och*, another message from that man?" Addie eyed Celia's name scrawled across the front. "I thought he'd gone and left the city, ma'am."

"What do you mean? Oh, I see." The handwriting on the outside was unmistakably Patrick's.

She broke the wafer sealing the folded outer envelope. Inside, a piece of paper was wrapped around a smaller scrap.

"What's it say?" Barbara asked, craning her neck to see across the table.

"'I believe you're wanting this,' is Patrick's message." She did not add that he'd sent his affection to her. Those gathered around the table did not need to hear her husband's dubious proclamations. "As for what he is referring to . . ."

She held the scrap aloft, half of a torn note that had led to Mr. Griffin's murder.

"It's the note!" Owen exclaimed. "And it says 'paid in full on completion of task,' signed Z. Everett. Mr. Davies must be the fellow who paid Johnny Doherty, ma'am. The fellow who was outside on the street, watching for me."

A shiver danced along her spine. "He told me where to find you, Owen. Perhaps he'd been unsuccessful in accosting you and hoped my visit would flush you out of hiding." Like a grouse flushed from cover by a hunting dog.

"Some fellow did turn up at Tommy's, Mrs. Davies. Looking for me. Yesterday," he said. "A blue-eyed Irish fellow called Pa Frank. But I got away without him spotting me."

Patrick Francis Davies. Was Patrick Pa Frank? And was he the P. Frank who had been interviewed along with Caleb Griffin about Apollo's death? Oh, Patrick. What did you do?

Celia, her fingers trembling, refolded the note. "However, right after he told me where you were staying, he learned—from me—that the police are in possession of the other half, Owen."

"So he gave up trying to get ahold of the entire note?" Barbara asked.

Celia stared at the envelope, the looping letters of her name written by a man she'd wed but had never truly known. "It appears so."

Owen was watching Celia with wide eyes. "Did he kill Caleb, ma'am?"

"No, he did not, Owen," she replied, certain at least that much was true. "Patrick was aware that Mr. Griffin had handed part of the note off to you, which was why Mr. Doherty had been paid to retrieve it. But what Patrick meant to do once he possessed both halves, I cannot positively say."

"Cousin Patrick meant to cash in on the bounty," Barbara said. "He was going to kill that horse."

"I am afraid you are right, Barbara."

"The devil," Addie muttered. "And I willna apologize for wishing he comes to a bad end, ma'am. No, I willna."

• • •

Patrick weighed the coins in his pocket, sifting them through his fingers like they might turn to gold dust if he rubbed them often enough. There'd been more of them before he'd departed San Francisco. Would've been many, many more if he'd been able to go through with collecting on the reward to kill that horse. But he'd been slipshod in tracking down that kid and had let the police get ahold of half of that note. All his plans going for nothing. He wondered what Celia had thought about his little gift. A lovely final touch. He grinned to himself, imagining the expression on her face when she'd opened that envelope.

The stagecoach bounced over a rough patch and the coins jingled together. A ringing noise loud enough for the fellow with tobacco-stained teeth seated across from him to prop open a rheumy eye and glance at Patrick's coat pocket like he might want to count for himself just how many coins were in there.

"What might you be lookin' at?" Patrick asked the man, his voice pitched low so that the question didn't sound a bit friendly. Because it wasn't meant to be friendly.

"Nothin', mister. Nothin'." He obliged Patrick by closing his eyes again.

A Mexican fellow bundled in a serape and squashed in the corner of the coach pretended not to hear the exchange. But since he flinched, Patrick knew he wasn't as deaf as he'd been pretending.

Patrick squinted around the shade drawn down over the window. They'd been climbing the side of this mountain for what seemed hours, bumping and rattling, the driver pushing the horses because they'd set out from Nevada City an hour late and he was trying to make up the time. Stones clattered down the side of the ravine they were skirting, thrown from the wheels. The small woman seated next to Patrick—she did smell fair, better than his fellow male passengers—had been praying on a rosary the entire trip, her gnarled fingers working the beads. He hadn't seen a rosary since he'd left Ireland, so many years ago. It reminded him of his mother, to see the woman's fingers rubbing the loop of beads, the silver cross dangling at the end. He used to know the prayers to say on each one, but he'd forgotten. He'd almost forgotten Ireland itself. Maybe he'd go back and see his mother someday. He and his brother could both go. Wouldn't she be surprised. Or maybe she'd rather not see him ever again. His mother just as disappointed in him as Celia.

'Tis sorry I am, colleen. I did mean to be better. But somehow . . .

The stagecoach rounded a turn, the wheels skidding close to the edge, sending more stones over the brink. Outside, the man riding with the driver cursed and shouted. The rheumy-eyed fellow bolted wide awake and grabbed for the strap slung across the window. It broke in his thick fist, the leather rotted.

The woman stiffened and clutched her rosary. "Dearest God."

"We'll be fine, ma'am. Don't you be worryin', now," Patrick said as soothingly as he knew how. Which could be rather soothing.

She glanced at him from beneath the brim of her dark bonnet. Her eyes were almost as clear and pale as Celia's. He was going to miss his wife's eyes, come to think of it. Just not the unhappiness that was always inside them.

"What do you know?" the woman asked accusingly.

He smiled. "Never you worry, ma'am." He'd always scraped through. Always. He'd survived the sinking of a ship, hadn't he? Many a brawl in far-off saloons? Smiled and added a wink.

She frowned and took to praying aloud.

Another bend in the track came, a sharper one this time. The coach bumped hard, skittered sideways. Jerked as the right rear wheel slid and slid, until they hit the very edge and went over. The carriage tilted, tossing him onto the woman with the rosary. She screamed as they tumbled, her luggage flying to knock him in the shins. The Mexican fell to the floorboards in a great flapping of colorful serape. Patrick grabbed for the edge of his seat as he pitched forward into the rheumy-eyed fellow's lap. The coins in his pocket jingled and spilled.

He gritted his teeth as the side of the coach caved in. *Holy Mary, this is a turn.*

Maybe he wouldn't be seein' Ireland again, after all.

CHAPTER 21

"I've a telegram from Vi, Mr. Greaves." Mrs. Jewett bustled into the dining room waving the evidence. "She sends her regards."

Nick looked up from his breakfast of toast and eggs. "She spent money on extra words to send me her regards?"

The sun streaming through the window highlighted his landlady's frown. "It's a beautiful morning, Mr. Greaves. There's no need for sarcasm to ruin it."

Which sounded like something Celia Davies might say. A week had passed since she'd sent Nick the torn scrap of paper with Everett's forged signature and informed him that Patrick Davies was Pa Frank. Since then, there hadn't been another word from her. Maybe, after hearing from Taylor that her husband had left the city for good, Nick had been expecting too much to think she'd contact him.

"What else does Miss Westerfield have to say? Anything about fortune smiling on me, perhaps?" he asked.

Mrs. Jewett eyed him. "You all right this morning, Mrs. Greaves?"

"You know how I get after I've successfully closed a case, Mrs. Jewett. I get jittery from all the peace and quiet."

"Yes. I do know how you get," she responded and bent over the telegram. "She wants me to know she's safely settled back at home and that there was good news while she was here with us. Her brother received a scholarship to attend college, it seems."

Fortune smiling on you and yours, Miss Westerfield. "That's good."

"She added some news about my sister's husband and their financial situation. Reckless man. Never has been able to handle money properly. And a final message for you to let her know how things go." She looked up from the telegram. "What 'things,' Mr. Greaves?"

"Haven't a clue, Mrs. Jewett."

A knock sounded on the front door and she rushed off to answer it. "Good morning, Mr. Taylor."

Nick's assistant strode into the dining room. "Morning, sir. Mr. Greaves, sir."

Nick tossed his napkin onto the table and stood. "Am I needed at the station?" Peace never lasted long.

"No, that's not it," he said, a dour expression on his face. "It's news about Mr. Davies, sir. News I thought you'd want to know."

• • •

The account of the accident arrived several days after Patrick had departed San Francisco, a brief telegram addressed to Celia informing her of her husband's death. The stagecoach he'd been riding in had plunged off the side of a cliff while traversing the Sierra Nevada mountains, killing all of the occupants save for the driver. There had been no doubt in this instance if the account of Patrick's death was accurate. His body had been returned to the city morgue, where Dr. Harris had shown her Patrick's corpse, cold and stiff upon the table in the basement of the undertaker's, her husband's once handsome face blue and heavily bruised. In her shock, Celia had grown light-headed, nearly fainting, and would have collapsed if Addie had not held her up. Patrick had not escaped the grave, after all.

"More tea, ma'am?" Addie softly asked.

Celia looked over. She'd been staring out the parlor window, not really noticing what was going on outside, unable to comprehend why Patrick's death had rendered her so numb. She'd believed him deceased once before, mourned him then, in her way. And recovered. She'd presumed she would recover far more quickly the second time, especially considering what she'd learned about him. Presumed that she would not mind that their story, finally, had reached its ill-fated conclusion.

"No, thank you, Addie." She smiled at her housekeeper. When that telegram had arrived, Addie had been stricken with remorse over wishing Patrick would come to a bad end. Until Celia had convinced her that she was not responsible for his demise and the best thing for the both of them was to move forward with their lives. *Advice you should be heeding right now, Celia.* "But take some tea up to Barbara, if you will."

"Aye, ma'am."

The front bell rang, summoning Addie. From the entry hall came the voice of a man. Not just any man, though.

Celia stood, hastily checking for loose strands of hair and repinning them.

Mr. Greaves ducked into the parlor and swept his hat from his head. "Hope I'm not disturbing you, ma'am."

"Of course not, Mr. Greaves." Not when he was the one person she'd so wished to see. Yet had resisted visiting. *Coward.* "I read that Mr. Hollis confessed."

"Once his maid admitted that she'd given him a false alibi. Two false alibis," he said, oblivious—she hoped—to her thoughts.

"I suspected she might lie for him to protect her position."

"Yes, you did." He turned his hat through his hands, his gaze on her face.

Celia's cheeks heated, and she stumbled on with the banalities of discussing the case. A safer conversation than the one she wished they'd have. "However, I still do not comprehend why Matthew Hollis killed Mr. Griffin with a gimlet. The unpredictability of humans aside."

"He'd gone to that meeting believing he wouldn't need a weapon, ma'am. That's all I can think," he said. "Got carried away defending Everett."

"But he'd worn a disguise?"

"Our Mr. Hollis is a bit of a stage actor, Mrs. Davies," he replied. "I think he enjoyed playing the part of Zacharias Everett. Complete with the coat the fellow had left behind at the Olympic Club, as it turns out, and where Hollis found it."

"If only Edward Pierson had admitted what he'd witnessed." *If only we were not dancing around the issue uppermost in both our minds.* Or in her mind, at least. "And Georgiana had never schemed to pay Mr. Fulton to threaten Mr. Griffin, which kept Mr. Fulton from also coming forward because he was afraid he'd be accused of murder."

"He paid with his life for his reluctance to admit he'd spotted Hollis running away from the scene of the crime."

She heard Addie coming down the stairs, returning from Barbara's bedchamber. Her footsteps did not continue into the clinic and on to the kitchen, however. Eavesdropping nearby?

"What will happen with Mr. Everett?" Celia asked.

"He won't be leaving town any time soon. He's been charged with arson and, like Edward Pierson, as an accomplice to Griffin's murder for withholding evidence," he said. "He's admitted that he met Griffin Monday night and they got into an argument. Griffin insisted he didn't have the note with him. Everett didn't believe him."

To think of Mr. Everett, who'd sold Celia a gorgeous engraved silver pen, his slim fingers lovingly cradling it as he'd rested the pen in a padded box for her, as a criminal . . . how badly she'd misjudged him. "A sad end for so many, Mr. Greaves."

"Justice, ma'am. Justice."

"And all because Mr. Hollis lost Validus in a foolish bet. An animal he would rather have destroyed than permit Mr. Aldrich to continue to possess." Like a jealous lover. "Did you find any evidence that my husband poisoned Apollo, Mr. Greaves?"

"We didn't, ma'am," he replied. "The horse's death could've been an accident, after all. I'd wager Mr. Davies was simply at the track that day working out his plan to finish off Validus."

"A coincidence, Mr. Greaves?"

"Maybe they do happen every once in a while." His gaze traveled over the gown she wore, appearing to finally notice its black color. "I *am* disturbing you."

"Patrick's role in this case and his subsequent death have stunned me, Mr. Greaves," she replied. "But you are not disturbing me. In fact, I am happy to see you. Very happy."

He paused the turning of his hat, and her breath caught in her throat. Was it wrong to have admitted her feelings? She wished she could read his face, understand him.

"Then maybe it's all right for me to give you this right now." He set down his hat and reached inside his coat, pulling out a small box and handing it to her.

"A gift, Mr. Greaves?"

"Just returning some items to their rightful owner, ma'am."

She lifted the lid. Inside, arrayed on a soft bed of sapphire-colored velvet, were her mother's earrings and matching pin. "Oh, Mr. Greaves," she cried out. "How did you—"

"Taylor told me you'd pawned them to pay Mr. Davies to find Cassidy," he said. "I hope you don't mind."

"Mind? Why would I mind?" she asked. "I cannot thank you enough. You do not know how much your generosity means to me."

His eyes searched hers. "Mrs. Davies, what do—"

Celia stopped him with a shake of her head. "Please call me Celia."

He smiled and took her hand in his, tucking it tight against his chest, where she could feel the pounding of his heart. "Celia, what do you say about starting over? I mean, once you're—"

"Out of mourning?"

"Once you're out of mourning." He stepped closer. "But only if you're sure."

She looked up into his face, into his warm brown eyes. Would she be able to heal the pain that lingered in their depths? Within her own heart? She was certain, though, that she was willing to try.

"I am certain, Nicholas." *This time, I am not wrong.* She had learned from her mistakes with Patrick. "I am."

"In that case, Celia, it looks like I have a message to send to Violet Westerfield."

"Who?" she asked, annoyed by her flare of jealousy.

He chuckled. "No one important, Celia. Not to us. Celia," he repeated, his breath stirring her hair.

November and December of 1867 were particularly wet, stormy months in San Francisco, which is not unusual for that time of year in northern California. Blasting to level the city's hills regularly wreaked havoc when the heavy rains came, though, leading to landslides. By the time the winter gales of 1867 subsided in January, several people had died and many were injured due to avalanches, ships sinking, and buildings collapsing. The amazing meteor shower that Addie claims presaged it all had been reported in numerous parts of the country and in Sacramento on November 14, much to the wonderment of the residents. San Francisco's view of the show was hampered by all the clouds.

Fire was an almost daily problem in a city built as much of timber as brick and stone. In the year ending June 30, 1867, there were over two hundred forty fires in San Francisco, seventy-seven of which were connected to arson. With businesses failing on a regular basis, their owners, knowing that insurance companies were historically quick to make payments on claims, sometimes sought illegal means to recover their losses. In mid-1868, the Board of Underwriters resolved to hire arson detective in hopes of cracking down on the rampant problem.

Many of the organizations and locations mentioned in *No Refuge from the Grave* actually existed. The Dashaway Association, for instance, was founded in 1859 by a group of volunteer firemen as a temperance fraternity. Attracting the attention of charitable San Francisco society, the association grew rapidly, becoming the largest charity organization in California by the mid-1860s. As the temperance movement shifted from male-only groups to ones run by women, membership in the Dashaway Association dwindled. In 1882, it folded and sold its hall to Levi Strauss.

As for the Ocean House Course, it was one of two racetracks in the area at the time. Situated near Lake Merced and near to the beach, it operated from 1865 to 1873. The Olympic Club, where the character Mr. Hollis boxes, still exists today and is the oldest athletic club in the

United States. As mentioned in the book, it has enjoyed many famous members since its founding in 1860. The present city clubhouse on Post Street dates to 1912, after the prior clubhouse was destroyed in the 1906 earthquake and fire.

ABOUT THE AUTHOR

Nancy Herriman left an engineering career to take up the pen and has never looked back. She is the author of the Mysteries of Old San Francisco, the Bess Ellyott Mysteries, and several stand-alone novels. A winner of the Daphne du Maurier Award, when she's not writing, she enjoys singing, gabbing about writing, and eating dark chocolate. After two decades in Arizona, she now lives in her home state of Ohio with her family.